D0275517

DEATH ON A
SHETLAND ISLE

By Marsali Taylor

Death in Shetland Waters
Death on a Shetland Isle

DEATH ON A SHETLAND ISLE

Marsali Taylor

Allison & Busby Limited
11 Wardour Mews
London W1F 8AN
allisonandbusby.com

First published in Great Britain by Allison & Busby in 2018.

Copyright © 2018 by Marsali Taylor

The moral right of the author is hereby asserted in accordance with
the Copyright, Designs and Patents Act 1988.

All characters and events in this publication,
other than those clearly in the public domain,
are fictitious and any resemblance to actual persons,
living or dead, is purely coincidental.

All rights reserved. No part of this publication may be reproduced,
stored in a retrieval system, or transmitted, in any form or by
any means without the prior written permission of the publisher,
nor be otherwise circulated in any form of binding or cover
other than that in which it is published and without a similar
condition being imposed on the subsequent buyer.

A CIP catalogue record for this book is available from
the British Library.

First Edition

ISBN 978-0-7490-2384-3

Typeset in 11/16 pt Adobe Garamond Pro by
Allison & Busby Ltd.

The paper used for this Allison & Busby publication
has been produced from trees that have been legally sourced
from well-managed and credibly certified forests.

Printed and bound by
CPI Group (UK) Ltd, Croydon, CR0 4YY

To the members of the Shetland Coastguard, and to the crews of the Aith and Lerwick lifeboats: dedicated volunteers who spend a good deal of their own time practising their skills on land and sea so that those of us who walk the hills or mess about in boats can be saved if the worst happens. We hope never to need you, but it's hugely reassuring to know you're there.

RENFREWSHIRE COUNCIL	
245880121	
Bertrams	28/11/2018
	£19.99
JOH	

THE CREW OF SØRLANDET

Captain Sigurd

Henrik	Agnetha	Johanna
Chief Steward	First Officer	Chief Engineer

Nils, First Mate	Cass, Second Mate	Rafael, Third Mate
Red watch (0–4)	White watch (4–8)	Blue watch (8–12)

Each watch has a watch leader and two able seamen (ABs)
For Cass's watch, these are: Petter, Watch Leader
Mona and Johan, ABs

Each watch has between fifteen and twenty-five trainees.
In Cass's watch these are:
The Swedish couple, Valter Bengtsson and Axel Lindberg
The firefighter, Frederik Berg
The Danish couple, Carl and Signe Frandsen

The Norwegian family, Egil, Berit, Erling (17), Geir (15), and Kirsten (12) Hansen

The ship's sirens, Janne Jensen and Grethe Kristiansen

The older sailors, Finn Nilsen and Ivar Olsen

The teacher, Unni Pedersen

The golden boy, Oliver Eastley, and his sister, Laura

and joining in Shetland

The policeman, DI Gavin Macrae

Other officers:

Sadie, Medical Officer

Rolf Mathisen, Bosun

Jenn, Liaison Officer

Lars, 2nd Engineer

James, Steward

Elmer, Cook

Laila and Ruth, Galley Girls

PART ONE

The Board Set Up

CHAPTER ONE

Wednesday 28th July, Kristiansand

Low water 05.12, BST + 1 (0.02m)
High water 11.31 (0.26m)
Low water 17.58 (0.01m)
High water 00.19 (0.026m)

Moonrise 00.51; sunrise 05.14; moonset 16.38; sunset 22.08
Crescent moon

Cat's pre-leaving vet visit went as I expected. He lashed his tail from the moment of setting paw in the surgery, crouched sulkily on the table with me holding his harness in a vice-like grip, and greeted the thermometer with an indignant hiss. After it, I took him to our favourite cafe, where we shared the swirled cream on a cup of drinking chocolate, and he smoothed his rumpled fur, tail still twitching from time to time. Then we strolled down to the grass by the marina, where I could let him off his lead to scamper around the Shetland pony statues.

It was a bonny morning, with fluffy cumulus on the horizon promising a sea breeze to set us on our way later. The promenade was quiet, with only a couple of tourists strolling along the marina path: a fair woman in one of those puffed jackets, powder blue, her hand through the arm of the man beside her. Her head blocked my view of his face, but there was something urgent about the tension of her shoulders, the way her face turned to his.

As I watched, she shook her head violently and shoved him away from her onto the path leading to the old fish market, then headed for the street at an easy jog. I watched her go, intrigued. Maybe they hadn't been tourists; maybe she was making sure he went for a job interview, or a dentist appointment. Maybe she was his mistress, and he was off to confront his wife . . . I shut off the speculation, and clipped on Cat's lead to saunter back to our ship.

Kristiansand was *Sørlandet*'s home port. She had her own berth before the ochre-coloured Customs House, where her three masts reached up into the summer sky, and her bowsprit with the gold scrolling stretched towards the elegant tenements of downtown Kristiansand. The sight of her filled my heart with pride. I still couldn't believe my luck: Cass Lynch, teenage runaway, sailing vagabond, with two stripes on the shoulder of her navy jersey, second mate of the world's oldest square-rigged ship.

I paused at the foot of the gangplank to unclip Cat, and ran straight into Captain Sigurd. There was always something to take the gilt off the gingerbread. Captain Sigurd was an excellent seaman, and I'd trust him with my life in maritime matters, but he was a stickler of the deepest dye. Officers wore their caps at all times outside and carried them under their arm to the captain's dining room, where we ate in a glory of red velvet and portraits of King Olav and Queen Sonja.

In the stress of taking Cat to the vet I'd forgotten my cap. I straightened up quickly and stood to attention, my hand going smartly up to my eyebrow as he passed me. He took two steps on shore, then paused to look round. 'Your cap, Ms Lynch?'

Nothing to be done. 'Sorry, sir.'

'Remember that everything you do reflects on your ship.' His blue eyes met mine, totally serious, then moved along *Sørlandet*'s swan-white hull. 'You are letting her down.'

I kept my hand up. 'Yes, sir.'

'Don't forget again.' He turned away and strode off. I let the salute drop and followed Cat aboard.

There was a little knot of my fellow-crew gathered at the far side of the deck: my friend Agnetha, recently promoted to first officer, Sadie, the medical officer, and Mona, one of my ABs. I went over to join them.

'Tut, tut,' Agnetha said. 'Consider yourself rebuked, Ms Lynch.'

'He didn't have to worry about whether Cat was going to bite the vet again,' I retorted.

'Did he?'

'A close-run thing, when the thermometer went in.'

Agnetha wrinkled her nose. 'Well, never mind our esteemed captain. We're drawing lots here.'

'What for?'

She rolled her blue eyes, laughing, and linked her arm through mine. 'You don't get to join in. You're spoken for.' Her friendly tone warmed me. There had been a distance between us since the events of our voyage to Belfast, and I still hadn't dared ask what she'd finally decided about her pregnancy, whether to keep the baby or not. I had the Catholic stance on abortion, and though I hadn't preached it, just knowing how I felt had made her defensive. I smiled back at her, and repeated my question. 'What are we drawing lots for?'

'The new third mate.'

My brain caught up at last. He was to arrive this morning. 'Rafael Martin. Spanish.'

'Too young for me,' Sadie sighed. 'Early thirties.' She brightened. 'He might like older women.'

'Or be turned on by the uniform of a superior officer,' Agnetha agreed.

'More likely he'll slum it with the galley girls,' Mona said resignedly.

'Tall, dark, cheekbones to die for.' Agnetha's chin tilted backwards over her shoulder. 'Take a look.'

I wasn't turning to stare. 'I can wait.'

'What it is to have a man of your own!' Agnetha mocked. 'Doesn't stop you window-shopping.'

'More to the point, does he look as if he knows what he's doing?' I grinned. 'Or didn't you even consider his seamanship qualities?'

Agnetha wrinkled her nose at me. 'You can stop being so lofty. He's going over to talk to Cat.'

'A point in his favour,' I conceded.

Cat had headed straight for his favourite post on the afterdeck, the raised area at the back end of the ship where the officers gathered once trainees were aboard. There was a bench by the navigation hut where he sat and surveyed the harbour, washed his white paws, and looked down on cats from lesser ships.

I turned. Rafael Martin was tall and slim, with a mop of unruly curls. He was bending down to extend a hand, which Cat sniffed warily. Then he straightened, and turned, and the familiarity of the movement made me catch my breath. His face was towards us

14

now. My heart gave a great kick and began hammering so crazily that I wondered Agnetha couldn't hear it.

I was looking at a dead man – the man I'd killed eleven years ago halfway across the Atlantic.

My first thought was a sudden rush of love. The guilt had swamped out how much I'd loved him. I looked at him and felt it flood back. I'd never thought I'd see that face again this side of heaven: those upward-tilted eyebrows above slanted sea-grey eyes, the high cheekbones, the long nose, the mobile mouth that could go from laughter to curses and back in the blink of an eye; the stubborn chin, half hidden now under a stubble beard.

He was beginning to smile at us, the charming smile he used on strange women. The breath caught in my throat. 'See?' Agnetha murmured in my ear.

'A charmer,' I muttered. *Your voice gives you away*, my policeman lover, Gavin, told me. I took a deep breath and tried to persuade myself I was wrong. Some extraordinary resemblance. It had to be. At the same time my brain was reckoning up impossible scenarios. I'd thrown out the lifebelt as soon as he'd gone over. Suppose he'd grabbed it, been swept away by the waves . . . suppose another boat had come along, and picked him up . . . suppose . . . suppose . . .

He came down the steps with that same easy stride. He was right beside me. I tried to steady my breathing. His eyes met mine as if we were strangers. 'You're Cass, right?'

It was Alain's voice, velvety-brown, like pouring Guinness, but now he spoke English with an odd Spanish-American accent. He held out his hand, and I shook it, the world whirling around me. Our hands fitted together as they always had. 'Glad to know you. That's a fine cat – a pedigree one?'

'A mog,' I said. My voice was astonishingly steady. 'He likes being the highest-ranking cat in the harbour.'

'Land cats always pretend they live in the grandest house in the street,' he agreed. His eyes just touched the bullet scar running across my right cheek, and moved back to mine. 'You're all making me feel very welcome aboard.'

'We're glad to get a full crew again,' I managed. I leant back against the rail, putting a metre between us. It was Alain, back from the dead, looking at me as if he'd never known me, as if we'd never lived aboard *Marielle*, never loved and fought and made up, never dreamt of sailing the world together. It wasn't possible he didn't know me. Why he was pretending to be Spanish I didn't yet know, but presumably he'd explain . . . unless he'd decided that explanations would only lead to recriminations, and the past was best forgotten. Rafael Martin. I had to remember to call him Rafael.

He leant beside me, and smiled round at the others. 'Now, warn me about the captain. What're his particular bugbears?'

'I'd better go and get my cap,' I said, and shoved myself from the rail so hard that I almost stumbled. *Damn.* I wanted to be as cool as he was. I strode away to the door below the aft deck and felt him watch me go. By the time I'd swung past the curtain that covered my cabin entrance I was sweating as if I'd run a marathon. I dropped onto the couch in front of my berth and pressed my hands to my breast. My fingers felt my heart thudding. I took a long, deep breath, counting four in, four hold, four out, and repeated the exercise until my heart rate had steadied.

It was Alain. I wasn't being misled by a resemblance. It truly was Alain. I hadn't killed him. The relief of it flooded through me. I hadn't left him to drown in the middle of the Atlantic. By some miracle he'd been saved. He'd caught that lifebuoy and floated with it, been found by another ship, taken to America.

I caught myself up there. It just wasn't possible. It was eleven years ago, but I could see it unrolling in my memory as if it had been yesterday. The boom had gone over just as Alain had come up with our breakfast, a plate in each hand. I could still hear the crack as it hit him, and the way he'd reacted – making light of it, but with a blank look in his eyes, and swallowing as if he tasted blood. He'd insisted he was fine, and gone below for a sleep. When he came back up, his gun was in his hand, and he ordered me off the boat. He'd thought I was pirates. 'Get off my boat, or I'll shoot you. Get off. *Get off.*' When I hadn't obeyed, he'd fired at me. My hand went up to cover the snail-trail of scar along my cheek. I'd kicked the tiller across and tacked the boat, and the jib had caught him off balance and knocked him overboard. Even if he'd grabbed the lifebuoy I'd thrown, even if he'd drifted many metres on the rolling swell before I'd got the boat turned, he'd still been injured. A dip in the Atlantic wasn't an NHS-recommended cure for a severe head injury.

I was being misled by a resemblance. No matter how this Rafael moved, no matter how his hand fitted mine, Alain had died in the Atlantic. His death would always be on my conscience. As for this Spanish lookalike, I'd just have to learn to live with him. Rafael.

I picked up my cap, squared my shoulders, and headed back on deck.

Captain Sigurd was also a stickler about crew muster. At precisely two minutes to eleven, we stood to attention in line of seniority, Agnetha at the head of the line. Nils radiated importance beside her, promoted to first mate at last. I was next, and Rafael stood beside me, back straight, head up, with just one quick gleam of his eyes downwards at me to show he was playing at being the compleat officer. I felt his presence beside me, and knew he was Alain. However much I tried to rationalise it as a chance resemblance, however crazy it should seem that he was pretending not to know me, he was Alain. Every movement of his body, every turn of his head, the shape of his hands so close to mine . . . I stood beside him and argued with myself. He was Rafael, a stranger. He was Alain, being Rafael.

Captain Sigurd cast an eye along our straight line and stepped forward to address us in Norwegian. '*God morgen.*'

'Good morning, sir,' we chorused.

'Our orders for today. The trainees will be arriving from noon. For this voyage, Mr Andersen will be on red watch, Ms Lynch on white and Mr Martin on blue.'

White watch was my favourite, on duty from four to eight. Rafael would be after me. We'd meet at handover and meals, and otherwise we could avoid each other, if that was the way he wanted it. I felt a smouldering anger stirring deep within me. I'd spent eleven years believing I'd killed him.

'There will be fifty-one trainees on board, seventeen on each watch, with one more joining the white watch in Shetland.'

That one, all being quiet in the Scottish criminal world, would be Gavin. My anger subsided at the thought of him. Alain was in the past. Gavin was my present and my future. I couldn't wait to see him again. It felt a long month since we'd been together, even though we'd spoken on the phone or computer whenever the ship had a signal. We'd have the voyage round Shetland, all the way back to Kristiansand, and end with a couple of days together in Bergen before his leave ran out.

'The whole-crew muster will be at 14.00. Each watch will be taken round each part of the ship: forrard, rig training and aft. Are there any questions about this?'

We shook our heads. It was all routine.

'These sessions will end at 15.30. Then we will prepare to set sail, leaving at 17.00.' His blue eyes swept around us. 'I wish our ship a good voyage, fair winds and free sails.'

He nodded dismissal. As we moved away, I felt a hand on my shoulder. Rafael bent his head to mine and spoke softly in my ear. 'I wasn't expecting Norwegian. I'm third watch, right? Eight to twelve?'

'Yes.' I turned to face him, and saw only the intent look of a crewman checking his instructions. I made my tone matter-of-fact. 'When the trainees come on board, Jenn checks them in.' I gestured at where Jenn, our liaison officer, was setting up her table. 'She'll send them below to the banjer, where we'll help them sort out their lockers and find the hooks for their hammocks.' He nodded. 'Then we'll gather them on deck at 14.00, and each watch will get their introduction to the ship. They get a tour of the foredeck area, afterdeck area, and rig training – just up the mainmast to the first platform and down the other side. Your watch leader and ABs will lead that.'

'OK. Routine.' He stopped being official and gave me that charming smile again. 'Thanks, Cass. I'll appoint you as my personal translator.'

I waved my hand airily and turned away, speaking over my shoulder without meeting his eyes. 'Any time, no problem.'

My fingers were trembling as I strode away.

I went as far as the Customs House, and fished my phone out of my pocket. It was Gavin's tea break in Scotland, supposing he was able to get one. Police work, as far as I could see, was either non-stop with time only to send a uniform for a sandwich, or long night hours of filling in forms in front of the History channel.

He answered on the third ring. 'Cass, *halo. Ciamar a tha thu?*

19

My Gaelic could cope with that. I answered in Norwegian '*Bra. Og med deg?*'

'Hmm,' Gavin replied. 'You sound more like *ikke sa verst.*'

Not so bad. 'Mmm,' I said, and realised at once that I was at a loss. I was Gavin's girl now. How could I raise Alain's ghost? 'It's just something odd . . . I'll tell you when we meet.'

'Saturday's still looking good. I have to appear in court tomorrow, but that should be it.'

'The people-trafficking case?'

His phone crackled as he nodded. 'It's just the first hearing. The trial won't be until autumn, but I hope this middleman and his underlings will go down for as long as the judge can give him. The top man is free and rich in the Med.' He sighed. 'I suppose it makes a change from Spain. The French police know who he is, and can't find a scrap of evidence to nail him on. Three months, six at best, and he'll have built up a new chain.'

'Mmm.' He sounded down, and cynical. I tried to think of something encouraging to say. 'They got Al Capone on tax-dodging in the end.'

That made him laugh. 'Well, if you can come up with some odd Med regulation pertaining to super-yachts in Cannes, just let me know.'

'I will. The day after tomorrow, then, Lerwick, DV.'

'Weather permitting. I know. How did Cat get on at the vet?'

'Nobody got bitten this time.'

'Because he was happier, or the vet was quicker?'

'The vet was better prepared. He remembered last time.'

'But does it let him go ashore?'

I sighed. 'You tell me. I've read the regulations till I'm square-eyed. He's got his passport, he's had his injections, he's been checked within twenty-four hours of leaving. All that should let him in. But *Sørlandet*'s not a ferry, and Lerwick's not a recognised port of entry, which I think may mean he has to stay on board throughout our visit. It doesn't exactly say so. They won't impound him or anything, just stick him in quarantine till we leave again.'

'Does Lerwick have somewhere to quarantine him?'

'Of course not. Besides, it's all very well to say he has to stay on board. They can come and explain that to him. He's been a ship's cat since he was six weeks old. He's used to coming and going as he pleases when we're in port.'

Like travelling cats on every boat, he also had an uncanny sense of what the ship was up to. He occasionally spent the night ashore, but he'd always return in time to slip into his place on the aft deck for the morning all-hands muster.

'I'm sure there'll be no problem with sticking him in your dad's car for us going to dinner there.'

'I'm sure there won't.' Cat knew he could rely on Maman for a plateful of interesting scraps.

'Have you asked your captain about Glyndebourne?'

Maman was singing there in three weeks' time. 'Luckily he considers opera one of the civilised arts. Once he's met Maman, I hope he'll let me come. I've told her to be on the pier in Lerwick as we come in, so I can introduce them.'

'Machiavellian.'

His soft Highland voice sent a wave of longing through me. 'Oh, I'm looking forward to seeing you. Two days.'

'Is your stickler captain going to condemn me to a hammock?'

'He hasn't said anything. You're not a crew member.'

I could hear he was smiling. 'Perhaps he hasn't considered anything as appalling as sleeping with the trainees.'

'Oh, there are strict rules about that. I just don't know if they apply to current partners. Anyway, I hope we'll get a night aboard *Khalida*, in peace.'

'I hope so too. What other news? Has your underling arrived?'

He meant Rafael. 'Yes.'

'Ah. That's your problem?'

'I'll explain when I see you.'

Alain would have teased it out of me, between urging and guesses, but Gavin understood privacy. 'What watch are you on?'

'White. Four till eight.'

'A better one for phoning.'

'Except that I won't have a signal until we get within sight of Shetland.' I knew that we were rambling now. 'Good luck with your court thing.'

'Thank you.' I heard a voice in the background, calling his name. 'Have to go. Day after tomorrow. *Beannachd leat.*'

'Bye,' I said softly, and held the phone at my ear a moment longer, hearing the silence; then I snicked it off. It was ridiculous to have this hollow feeling about being on my own till Shetland. I squared my shoulders and turned back towards my ship.

CHAPTER TWO

I'd just reached the gangplank when I spotted two unmistakeable trainees heading for the ship, each trundling a large bag. It was the couple I'd noticed earlier at the marina. So much for my imagination; the determined mistress I'd created had obviously been some item of last-minute shopping, like sun-tan lotion or sea-sickness pills. I put new words to the woman's hand gestures: 'No, no, you go on. I'll nip back and get it and catch you up . . .'

I stepped forward. 'Hi, can I help you?'

'We've come to sign on. Oliver and Laura Eastley.'

Practice was making me smoother at this. I held out my hand. 'Cass Lynch, second mate. Welcome aboard *Sørlandet*. Have you just arrived in Kristiansand?'

'Last night,' Oliver said. He flashed me a dazzling smile, the sort of easy charm that made me feel he was one to watch: a golden son of affluent parents who'd had life given to him on a plate, and expected it to continue that way. He was fairer than I'd expected from that glimpse at the marina, with the sun gilding his hair, and taller; his wife's head barely reached his cheekbones. 'Laura wanted a last night in a bed and a wash in hot water before coming on board.'

'We wanted a look at Kristiansand too,' Laura added. 'We had a wander round the fort yesterday evening, and watched the sun set into the sea.'

Their voices placed them: unmistakeably private-school Edinburgh, although their fair hair and sleek, broad brows looked English. They were both about my age, glossy and groomed like city people, but dressed for the country; he was wearing a shaped Barbour, she had the powder-blue padded jacket I'd noticed earlier, and they both had jeans and practical footgear. Corporate: lawyers, estate agents, accountants.

I gestured them up the gangplank. 'Come aboard.' I gave a quick look around, but there was no sign of Jenn. 'Just wait by the table here. I won't be a moment.'

I headed aft to look for Jenn. She wasn't in her office, but there was laughter sounding from the kitchen: Alain's laugh. I shoved the pang down and put my head round the door. She and Rafael were leaning together over a book on the counter. I would get used to it . . .

'Hi,' I said. 'Jenn, we've got our first trainees.' I jerked my head deckwards. 'Laura and Oliver Eastley.'

'Sure,' she said. 'I'll come and get their passports.'

The trainee introduction was a fixed routine. Red watch began at the forward part of the ship, the lookout deck and foresails area, with the heads and showers below the foredeck. Blue watch was taken up to the aft deck, and shown the wheel, ship's compass and bell. White watch did the main deck first, which included rig training, so I sent my two ABs, Mona and Johan, for the net bag of climbing harnesses, and by the time they'd hauled that on deck the first of the trainees had started to fill the dock with a sea of bags. On the dot of noon, Agnetha went forward to welcome them, and the next half hour was busy with greeting and indicating lockers.

After that, we lined them all up on deck, in their watches, and Rolf, the bosun, took a photograph of each watch, then nipped off to print them out while the captain did his welcome speech. I surveyed my seventeen and matched them to the printed list Rolf slipped into my hand. Ten male, seven female. The Eastleys were the only Brits. Otherwise, we had eleven Norwegians, a Danish husband and wife, and two Swedish men. There was a family, the Hansens, with father, mother, two teenage sons and a younger daughter, twelve perhaps. The older boy was already eyeing up the mast as if it was an adventure playground; the younger was hiding under his hoodie, phone in hand. The two older men beside them wore well-used sailing jackets, and had that seaman's tan that was more like weathering. They'd be good on the team, quick to obey orders, and familiar with boat terminology. There was a pair of women in their twenties, tall, fair, and already eyeing the crew up with interest; the ship's sirens for the voyage. Another woman, standing on her own, had that teacher air of authority. As I watched, she turned and made a comment to the man beside her, also standing on his own. He was wearing a heavy black jacket and had that forces look, an off-duty soldier, or maybe an ambulance man – no, a firefighter, as he turned to show the red and white stripes on his shoulder. Three stars: *Overbranmester*, a senior officer. The Danish couple were a reversal of the usual: her sailing jacket was well-worn, while his was obviously new for the voyage, and while she was scanning the masts with sparkling eyes, his mouth was twisted down, apprehensive. The two Swedes were at the end, both in their mid-forties, looking around as if this was all new to them. Pretty average for a watch: plenty of enthusiasm, some experience, a couple of good heavyweights for rope-hauling.

I watched from the aft deck as Petter took my trainees through the rig training. They began by checking arm strength – a quick lift from the bars of the boat deck, the raised area amidships. All five of the family passed; they had that look of people who did regular sports. Oliver Eastley flexed his muscles, then pulled himself up on his arms without any visible effort. Laura looked up, hesitated, and stepped back, but Oliver cajoled her forwards, and she raised herself and swung competently enough. One of the older men swung himself up without difficulty, and the other shook his head. One non-climber. One of the Swedes and the firefighter joined him at the side rail and there was some joking comment about fear of landing. The firefighter indicated his broad shoulders and gave the ratlines a shake – not up to his weight. The teacher stepped forward, swung herself up briskly, hung for the count of fifteen, then lowered herself down. The sirens shimmied up with the air of women who went to the gym. The Danish man gave it a try, looking up apprehensively. His wife had to clamber up the ladder to reach the rail, but then swung competently enough. Eleven definites out of seventeen was good going.

Next step was emptying pockets, then fitting the harnesses. They were proper climbing harnesses with thigh and shoulder straps and a central chest buckle. Petter gave the safety talk, then led the first four up the mainmast ratlines, a spider's web of wooden horizontals and thick wire uprights bound with gripping cord. Mona joined them, encouraging, particularly at the awkward bit before the first platform, where the web narrowed to less than foot width, and they had to hang half

26

upside-down to get around and onto the jutting-out platform.

They let them stand on the platform for five minutes, looking across at the canvas-swathed spars all around them, down to the wooden deck ten metres below, then Petter led the descent on the opposite ratlines. He spoke upwards at them: 'Remember, the most dangerous part is the last two metres. Never relax until your feet are actually on the deck.'

Johan was already on his way up with the next four, leaving the last group looking upwards: Oliver Eastley and the Danish wife impatiently, Laura and the Danish man with apprehension. Rafael lounged out of the aft companionway. 'I'll stand guard below if you want to take them up, Cass.'

My heart leapt at the thought of going aloft. He'd known it would; I saw it in the slight smile that hovered around his mouth. 'Thanks,' I said, and swung down to the aft banjer door to get my harness from the crew hooks. My hands fastened it without me needing to think about it: shoulder straps, thighs, carabiner. 'Ready?'

The Danish wife nodded, and set off upwards. Her husband followed, as though he didn't want to be shown up. I suspected that once we were at sea he'd prefer to be deck team. Laura gave Oliver an uncertain glance. He nodded. 'Oh, yes.' He laid a hand on her arm. 'Come on, Lols, give it a go.'

'Are you OK with heights?' I asked her.

She nodded. 'We did a climbing wall on one of those corporate team-bonding things, and I was fine with that.' She didn't look fine, though, with her gaze flicking to Oliver every couple of seconds. I motioned them onto the ratlines, and swung onto the spider's web beside Laura, feet secure on the wooden treads, the rope paint-smooth in my bare hands. Laura climbed steadily upwards until we were almost at the first platform, then she stopped, looking up. For a moment I thought she'd frozen. Above us, Oliver was eyeing up the rope ladder that jutted out into the air above our heads, going in a diagonal from the ratlines to the edge of the platform. Laura was watching him, face anxious. Then before I could give him instructions, he'd swung himself onto it, hands tight around the wires at the upper edge of the platform, arms taking his weight as he scrambled upwards, feet fumbling to squeeze into the narrow lines at the top. With a heave and a shove, he was over and on the platform, looking down. 'The view's good up here. Come and look.'

'That was doing it the hard way,' I said to her. 'We don't have his arm strength, so what we do is imagine that we're coming down. Keep thinking downwards, and put your weight on your legs, with your hands just there to keep you balanced.'

She looked at me, face tight with concentration, looked upwards at Oliver again, then nodded and moved upwards again. She was agile, and her feet were neat enough to fit into even the sections immediately below the platform. She pushed herself up onto the iron grid, lay for a moment, then stood up. I joined her.

The view was worth the climb. At eye level and upwards, there was the elegant precision of yards and furled sails, joined by the tracery of ropes. Outwards from the ship, Kristiansand was spread below us. Straight ahead, the broad street led up to the market square, a jumble of coloured awnings and spreads of flowers and vegetables, with the rose-pink cathedral tall behind. To our left, the waterfront ran along to the railway station; to our right, the red wood buildings of the fish market basked in the sun.

'Come on,' Oliver said impatiently, and began to climb downwards. I saw Laura safely off the platform, then stood looking out, filling my lungs with the clean air. *This is what I was made for* . . .

I couldn't stand up here all day. I followed Laura down and checked my watch. 14.45. We should be finished by 15.30, giving the trainees time to relax before casting off, and the open sea.

I took my harness off and returned to the aft deck. Alain, *Rafael*, was still there, leaning against the rail. 'Thanks,' I said.

'You looked like someone who'd rather be climbing. Me too.'

'One of the downsides of officer rank.' My trainees had disappeared forrard. I kept facing out towards the main deck, as if I was still watching them.

'I'm only doing it for the money.' I could hear he was smiling. 'I have a boat. I'm fitting her out to go round the world.'

'It all costs,' I agreed. Something inside me twisted. That was what we'd planned all those years ago: the Atlantic crossing to see if we were up to it, then start again and go down Africa, work our way around, continent-hopping. We'd been young and daft. 'What do you have?'

'A Vancouver 34. Cutter-rigged.'

'That'll take you round the world, all right.'

He shifted against the rail so that he was looking at my face. 'When I've finished the work on her. She needs the lot: new rigging, new sails, the engine stripped right down. You're a live-aboard yourself, Jenn was saying?'

I nodded.

'Your boat's in Shetland?'

'Yes.'

He paused, looking at me quizzically. 'Is this personal, or doesn't your cop boyfriend let you even talk to other guys?'

I shoved myself off the rail and glared at him. 'I'm naturally taciturn, and I don't like being gossiped about.'

He straightened up, and raised his hands in a *Hey, cool it* gesture. I remembered the way I used to stand leaning against him, with his chin just the right height to rest on the top of my head, and felt tears prick my eyes. I turned away hastily, hunching my shoulder at him as if I was in a huff.

'The information about the boat came before the information about the boyfriend,' he said. 'If that makes it any better.'

Damn him for being so cool about it! I'd spent eleven years thinking I'd killed him, and he strolled in just like this . . . 'Slightly,' I conceded. If I'd been off duty I'd have stalked off, but I couldn't do that with Captain Sigurd's eye on me.

'What is she?'

That was easier. I kept my voice offhand. A Vancouver out-ranked my *Khalida* both in length and kudos. 'A Van de Stadt production model, an Offshore 8m.'

'I know the one. Shortcuts taken on the joinery, but a good, solid hull laid up in the days before they knew just how thin they could stretch glass fibre. Where do you keep her?'

'She's in Shetland now.' He didn't react to the name. 'Brae, my home port.'

His eyes flickered, but he didn't reply. Whatever game he was playing, I wasn't joining in.

'That's my watch ready to move aft.'

I walked away, leaving him standing there, and felt his eyes on my back, thoughtful, all the way down the steps.

We were all on duty for leaving Kristiansand. Our white ship motored across the harbour, where the sunlight gleamed on the white bridge and red roofs, and cast golden ripples on the curved wooden overhang of the opera house. We came through the channel to where the shore became wave-polished rock, with twisted rowans thrusting their roots down into crevices of seaweed-rich earth. The white lighthouses blinked from under scarlet conical hats.

'We'll hoist the lower two sails,' Captain Sigurd said. 'A team to each mast.'

I nodded at Petter, and he came over. He was our crew film star, tall and blonde, with a way of leaning against the rail that turned him instantly into a promotion shot for his smart jacket, or the coffee mug he was holding. He'd done time as a navy cadet before joining us, but his whole air oozed privilege – preppy, you'd say in the States. *Aristokratisch.* I was getting on better with him since I'd suggested his promotion to watch leader. Agnetha had made sure he knew it was I who'd recommended him, and he'd managed a stammered thank you before backing off as if I might bite him. I couldn't see why I made him so nervous, but his nerves made me awkward too, so we didn't work easily together. He was a good watch leader, at ease with his team, if not with me, and he'd deserved the promotion.

'Hoist the main sail and lower topsail.'

He nodded, and headed off to round up our climbing team. Harnesses on and checked, then I watched as he and Mona led them upwards. The two older men and Oliver Eastley followed Petter, climbing steadily and sliding out along the yard with no hesitation. Laura Eastley hesitated, watching Oliver, then followed Mona, the teacher, and the Danish wife out along the opposite yard. The bodies draped over the yard, fumbling with the buntlines, then the sail fell into crumpled folds, ready to be pulled down from deck level. Below, on the main deck, Johan was already organising the non-climbers into teams at the ropes. Within fifteen minutes we had the main sail pulling in a beautiful curve, and were ready to repeat the task on the lower topsail.

Once the sails were set, the red and blue watches stood down, leaving my watch on duty. The ship set her shoulder to the swell, and each curved wave reflected a crescent of sunlight. By 18.30, the coast of Norway had receded to a cloudy mass on the horizon. I glanced upwards at the tiers of sail, then out to the horizon of blue water, and my heart sang. The land-pull to Gavin receded. This was what I was made for: this great sweep of water all around me, with the wind gentle on my skin, the ship creaking, the water curling under her forefoot and pulling away along her sides in a long V of foam.

The firefighter was on the ship's wheel – an easy task now, since all we had to do was head north-west across three hundred nautical miles of sea to Lerwick. The rest of today and all tomorrow before we saw land again.

'Steady as she goes,' I said to him. '281 degrees. Mr Berg, isn't it?'

'Frederik,' he said.

'Your first shot aboard a tall ship?'

He nodded. He was dark for a Norwegian, with brown curly hair and velvet-black eyes that were surveying me in a way I didn't quite care for, almost as if he was assessing my suitability for being his boss. I felt my chin go up, my shoulders straighten. His were twice the width of mine, made even broader by his padded black jacket. 'Surprisingly, given my husband's job. I've been meaning to come, but something's always cropped up.' He smiled, showing white teeth. 'It was worth the wait.' His eyes went back to the compass, then returned to me, still with that curious, measuring gaze.

I turned to his standby, Oliver. 'How about you? Your first time?' I felt like the Queen inspecting troops: *And what do you do?*

He nodded. 'We'd always meant to go to see Shetland, and

then Laura spotted this trip, and we thought, well, why not?' His voice was smooth and warm, like poured honey, his eyes pale blue under the fair brows. There was something unsettling about him, a memory tugging. Those pale eyes – then I remembered a polecat my friend Magnie had trapped, with a glossy brown coat and a neat face dominated by those same pale eyes, sharp and malevolent.

There was no sign of malevolence in Oliver. His eyes were friendly, his smile charming; then his face clouded over. 'We lost our parents, seven months ago. Car crash. Laura's finding it hard to get over. I thought this would help take her mind off. A complete change of scene, physical exercise, people all around her.' He paused, and looked a bit embarrassed. 'I'm not meaning to make a big thing of it. It's just I thought, as you're the boss of our team, maybe you should know.' He held up one hand, as if to forestall any questions I was about to ask. 'She's not on any medication, or anything. Just not her usual self.'

'OK,' I said. 'Thanks for letting me know. I'll keep an eye on her.'

His eyes gleamed with an odd satisfaction, and I was reminded of the polecat again. I shook the memory away. My brain caught up with my ears. Our parents, he'd said. I'd taken them for husband and wife, but now I looked, of course they were brother and sister.

He looked like a gadget man. 'Have you seen inside the nav shack?'

He shook his head. 'It looked like "officers only" to me.'

'Come and look.' I showed him the chart plotter, and, as I'd expected, he worked it straight away, and asked about other functions. I left him zooming in and out, and trying different versions of the chart. We were a little pulse just starting to head out across twenty centimetres of blue. While he did that I took my hand-held compass and did a fix on the still-visible pricks of light from the land; Captain Sigurd expected a three-point fix every half hour. Standing against the rail, balancing to the ocean swell, I took a deep breath of sea air, and smiled. *Home*.

CHAPTER THREE

At 19.00, all the officers ate together in the captain's mess, seated in order of seniority, with Captain Sigurd at the head of the table, and Henrik, the chief steward, at the foot. Agnetha was on Captain Sigurd's right, and Johanna, the chief engineer, was on his left. We three sailing officers were on Agnetha's side, Nils first, me, then Alain, *Rafael*, so close that I could feel the warmth of his thigh against mine. Jenn, Sadie and Rolf faced us. Rafael began to reach out for the bread, and I just had time to nudge him in the ribs with my elbow before Captain Sigurd said his formal grace. I caught the flicker of a wink before Rafael bowed his head.

Mealtimes were silent affairs. It wasn't done for a mere officer to introduce a topic, so we waited until Captain Sigurd made a stately comment, to which we murmured assent. I ate my pasta and pork swiftly, excused myself, and headed back to my watch. There would be an all-hands muster at 19.30, led by Jenn and

Henrik, and then it would be handover time. I checked our course with the helm, then projected a line from it across the blue screen. Bang on.

I was just entering the course in the log when a shadow darkened the nav shack doorway. I didn't need to look to know that it was Alain; every nerve-end I had tingled with his presence. 'Thanks,' he said. 'I didn't realise we were on a praying ship.'

I waved my hand dismissively, and made with the words as if he was just any new shipmate. 'When I first arrived those mealtimes terrified me. Every scrape of my knife on the china seemed to echo round the room for the next ten minutes.'

'It's a lot more formal than the States.'

'Is that where you've been?' I looked up, and felt my heart thumping at the intensity of his grey eyes, so close to mine. I turned back to the log, and was about to lift the pencil when I realised that my hand was trembling.

'The States? Yeah. I trained in San Juan.'

'Is that where your Vancouver is?'

He shook his head. 'Boston. That's where her previous owner lived, and he let me keep the berth on for another season while I did her up. He's keeping an eye on her for me, and I'll check her out when we get there.'

'But your family's in San Juan?' I kept my tone casual.

I'd touched a nerve. His face closed against me. 'I don't have any family. What's our course?'

Barriers up. '281 degrees.' I indicated the chart. 'Spot on for the south mainland of Shetland on Friday morning.'

'Swell. What about this muster thing? Do we have to go down to that?'

'It won't take long – just announcements from Jenn and

Henrik. Tidy your stuff up, that kind of thing. Oh, and moments of awesome.'

'Moments of awesome?' he repeated, rather too loudly.

'You'll see.'

We clattered down the aft steps together and took our places. Jenn welcomed the trainees, and reminded them about not leaving their stuff lying about. With every trainee owning at least one gadget needing charged, the banjer could become a nightmare of trip hazards, with every plug trailing a flex to the nearest table. 'Gone by breakfast time,' Jenn warned them. Henrik reminded them about not wasting food, and then – I braced myself for it – came the moments of awesome, Jenn's way of moulding us together as a crew. I ignored Alain's amused glance downwards at me as she announced them and then left a silence for us to contribute. 'Going up the mast,' Oliver called out. 'That was awesome.'

'Cool!' Jenn said. 'How about the red watch?'

'The engine going off,' one of them said, and another nodded.

Jenn turned her head to Alain. 'Blue watch, you haven't had your turn yet, so I'll expect two moments of awesome from you tomorrow evening.'

'I'll give you one right now,' Alain said. I should have known he'd play along. 'Being on this amazing ship with all these cool people.' He got a round of applause for that, though not from me.

'Great note to end on,' Jenn said, and dismissed us. The blue watch scurried for their jackets, and mine drittled to their places on deck. Ten minutes to go. I did a last check of our heading, and reported our position and course to Captain Sigurd. No whales, no waterspouts, no oil rigs as yet, barometer steady. I came back out on deck and yawned, trying to get myself into the mood for sleep. I was due on deck at 03.30.

Alain bounded up the steps two at a time, jacket slung over his shoulder. My heart ached at the sight. I swallowed and looked away as he spoke. '281 degrees, right?'

'Right.' I signed myself off in the log. 'You have the ship.'

'I have the ship,' he agreed, and signed on.

I left him to it, and stood for a moment by the rail, looking out at the water. It hazed under my gaze. I swore to myself, and rubbed the tears away. Agnetha came up beside me, and we were silent for a moment, then Agnetha turned her back to the gleaming sea, and spoke across her shoulder at me. 'There's a trainee on board I'm not sure about.'

I turned round, hoping nothing showed on my face, and looked an enquiry.

'Daniel Christie. He's on Nils's watch, so you may not have noticed him. Late twenties, UK passport. That's a Scottish surname, isn't it?'

I nodded, intrigued now.

'He doesn't fit.' She frowned. 'I can't put my finger on it. His jacket is best sailing quality, but it's brand new, and though he's fit enough it's the kind of gym fitness you'd get in a businessman who works out. I just don't see . . . there's no reason why an office worker shouldn't decide he wants to try a tall ship, but . . .'

I knew what she meant. 'Yes. No sailing background at all's unusual. How's he getting along on watch?'

'Oh, he joined in fine hoisting the sails, but somehow he's separate from them all.' She frowned at the grey hills on the horizon. 'He just doesn't feel right. As if the ship is a cover for something else. Well, obviously we can't search his baggage. We could have a word with the customs beforehand, when we get back to Norway.'

'Difficult,' I agreed.

'Anyway, what I wondered was, could you have a casual chat with him as you do the deck round? I just want to know how he strikes you.'

'Which is he?'

She nodded down towards the main deck. 'There. Talking to the blonde charmer from your watch.'

I followed her gaze. Oliver was standing with one hand on the ropes running down from the mainsail. A man I hadn't particularly noticed was lounging against the rail beside him. They were chatting animatedly, Daniel gesturing with his free hand, and Oliver laughing.

I saw at once what Agnetha meant. Daniel's whole air said city office: a lawyer, an accountant, an admin assistant. His mid-brown hair was fashionably cut in that sleeked-back style that tends to flop over onto the brow, except that it was gelled in place. His brows were set low, his nose long and straight, and he had a long chin in an oddly shaped jaw, angled to a point at each corner, which a manicured stubble beard didn't quite disguise. He was wearing a navy and grey Musto jacket, the newest breathable offshore design at a cool £400, along with the more expensive trainer-style Musto deck shoes; those were new as well.

I nodded to Agnetha. 'I'll check him out.'

I generally took Cat for a last stroll before settling down for the night. Even as I looked round, he appeared from the nav shack, and gave me his soundless mew. 'Come on then, boy,' I said, and he followed me down the steps, magnificent tail held high to show the silvery-ash underside. We did the round of the deck, with the trainees admiring him, and asking the usual questions about whether he got seasick, and if he had a litter tray, and ended up at Oliver and Daniel. 'Hi, Oliver,' I said. I turned to Daniel and held out my hand. 'Hi. I'm Cass. I'm in charge of the white watch.'

He gave me one of those doublehanded shakes. 'Daniel Christie, of the red watch.' His voice was conventional educated Scots, east coast, similar to Oliver's, and he was the same age. I had a prickling feeling down my spine. 'Do you two know each other? From home, I mean?'

I thought Daniel gave the beginning of a nod, before Oliver leapt in smoothly. 'That's the story, isn't it? You put two Scots from Edinburgh together in the middle of the Sahara, and before you know it they're talking about Princes Street and Hogmanay parties, or the discos they went to when they were young.' He gave Daniel a considering look. 'We'd probably have gone to all the same ones, but I don't think I know your face.'

Daniel had his cue now. He shook his head. 'Which school did you go to – Fettes?'

'Stewart's Melville.'

'I was George Watson's.' He smiled, showing perfect teeth. 'But we're both Edinburgh, so here we are on a Norwegian sailing ship, talking about Princes Street.'

Oliver bent down to stroke Cat, who was stretching up against my leg, bored of not being noticed. 'Your cat's a beauty.'

Cat jumped lightly up onto the square rail surrounding the mast, and prepared to be admired.

'Have you done much sailing?' I asked Daniel.

He shook his head. 'In dinghies on a school trip, but not since. The financial crash put everyone on longer hours. It's only now I've started to get evenings to myself. Then I saw the *Sørlandet* on its website and thought, well, why not? There were plenty of flights to Kristiansand, so I decided to join it there and do the whole trip.'

There was tension underlying his light voice, and he was

explaining too much. A lightweight, I thought, the junior partner in whatever was going on. Oliver cut in again. 'This is wonderful, being at sea.' He gestured upwards, to where Alain's watch was climbing towards the upper topsail yards. 'Will we get all the sails up now, do you think?'

'A good few of them, anyway.' We spread the sail-handling load over a couple of watches to keep our speed down to about eight knots, for ease of passage planning, and to share the work round the trainees. I turned my head back to Daniel. 'Have you been aloft?'

He nodded, and the colour came back to his face. The muscles in his neck relaxed. 'It was great. I loved looking down at the water, and seeing the waves going past below, as you're up balanced on this rope high in the air.'

I couldn't keep asking questions. I made it casual. 'You sound like someone who's into extreme sports.'

'I've done a bit of rock-climbing. It's a change to be over water, rather than looking down at tumbles of rocks, or a river gully.' He pulled a face. 'It doesn't look so hard, if you know what I mean.'

'It is though,' I said. 'Hitting water from that height would be just like hitting stone.'

'Oh, I know that intellectually. But my eyes don't believe it.' Oliver, beside him, made a movement, a turn of his wrist as if he was looking at his watch, and Daniel copied it, shaking back his sleeve to show what I suspected was a Rolex. 'Is that the time? I'm on duty at midnight. Better get some shut-eye.'

He was just turning away when Laura came over. This time, there was no sign of recognition. He looked her over with the air of a man assessing his chances for a holiday romance, and considering them good. He settled back against the rail, with as easy a grace as if it had been rehearsed, and smiled. 'Hi. Daniel Christie.'

'Laura Eastley. This is fun, isn't it?' She gave him a quick, assessing look, smiled back, then looked at me and smiled again. 'Hi, Cass.' Her attention was on Oliver. 'I'm going to turn in now, get as much sleep as I can. We need to be up at four, remember.'

'I'm remembering,' he said, and didn't move. 'You know me, I can get by on practically no sleep.'

'I know how hard it is to wake you too,' she retorted. She raised a hand at Daniel. 'See you later. See you at four, Oliver.'

Daniel watched her go, then shoved himself upright. 'Well, my hammock calls. Good to meet you, Oliver.'

'I think Laura has the right idea,' I said. She wasn't the only one; the trainees were thinning out. There was nothing like sea air for upping your sleep hours. I headed back to the aft deck and joined Agnetha by the rail.

'Well?' she said.

'Something odd,' I agreed. 'They were at pains to show me they didn't know each other, but I think they did. They're the same age, and that world of Edinburgh private schools is a small one.' I remembered that from those days with Alain, who'd been a student there. Students went to one set of clubs, comprehensive school people to another, and the elite to yet another.

Agnetha gave me an old-fashioned look. 'Could they be a gay couple who've not come out?'

I hadn't thought of that. 'Maybe.' It was a simple solution, but it didn't feel right. I remembered the admiring look Daniel had given Laura, theatrical, as if it had been rehearsed in a mirror. 'Yes, that could be it. I just feel they're plotting together.'

'Keep an eye on them,' Agnetha said. 'Nip it in the bud. We've had enough trouble on board.'

* * *

I was about to head below when I noticed the younger of the teenagers turning his head, as if he was looking for someone. His eyes found me, and he began crossing the deck. I searched my memory, and found his name. '*Hei*, Geir. Can I help you?'

He nodded. 'Can I use the ship's phone?'

That was easily answered. 'I'm afraid not. If it's an emergency, you could explain it to the captain, and he could contact shore for you.'

He looked at me blankly, as if what I'd said didn't make sense, then waved his phone at me, and spoke in English. 'I don't have a signal.'

'You'll get one again as we come close to Shetland.'

'When will that be?'

'Friday morning.'

His jaw dropped. 'Friday? Like, the day after tomorrow? You've gotta be kidding. I can't be without a signal for that long. I'm in the middle of a game.'

'You'll be able to play games, so long as you keep your phone charged,' I said.

He looked at me as if I was stupid. 'Man, I'm limbering up for the tournament. Playing online.'

I gestured him towards the nav shack bench. 'Have a cup of coffee, and explain to me. What tournament?'

'Well, tafl, of course. Hnefatafl. The tournament's on while we're on Fetlar.'

At last a bell rang. We were spending Sunday on the island of Fetlar, and one of the things they'd organised was a hnefatafl tournament. 'Hnefatafl.' I tried to imitate his pronunciation. *Na-f'-taffle*. 'That's the Viking game, isn't it?'

He nodded, and got enthusiastic. 'See, it's like the Viking equivalent of chess, only the moves are simpler. It's all about how you can out-think your opponent. Fetlar was the place that really started it up again. I play online with folk all over the world, but when Mum suggested this trip, well, I saw it was coming to Fetlar at the time of the tournament, so I entered straight away. Right now I'm in the middle of three different games online, and one of them's against someone else who'll be there, so I really need to know how he thinks, in case I draw him to play.'

My friend Anders was a gamer too. 'I do understand,' I said, 'but I'm afraid I just can't help. While we're at sea we only have emergency contact with land. But, hey, do you have a board with you? I know it's not the same, but why not get a game going?' Inspiration struck. 'We usually do a talk or activities in the mid-afternoon slot. Why don't you give us a talk on hnefatafl? Show us how it's played?'

His chin was still tripping him. 'You really can't help? With the phone?'

I shook my head. 'I really can't.'

He sighed, and stuck his hands in his pockets. 'You think people would be interested? Usually everyone just says it's geeky.'

'I think they would,' I assured him. 'Because of the tournament. You wouldn't need to speak for long. Just explain how it's played.'

'OK then.' He was silent for a moment. I could see him revolving ideas in his head. 'Can you give me time to prepare notes, like I would for a talk at school?'

'Sure.'

'Could I speak tomorrow morning, then, instead of the afternoon? So I can get a game going?'

'I don't see why not.' Jenn was leaning against the leeward rail, the wind ruffling her chestnut plait. I caught her eye, and she came over. 'Jenn, this is Geir, from my watch. You know our Fetlar visit? It coincides with the World Hnefatafl Championship, it's a Viking board game, and Geir's an enthusiast. I was suggesting he might like to tell us all about it, so folk would know how to play if they wanted to join the tournament.'

'Sounds a great idea,' Jenn said.

I left her to sort out times with Geir and headed below. Brush teeth, brush hair. Into the thermals that did duty as pyjamas on board. Door closed behind me to say that I was sleeping. I lay on my bunk with Cat purring in the crook of my neck, feeling the ship move beneath me, hearing the sloosh of waves curling along the ship's sides. The last gold rays of sun slanted through the window above my bunk and shone on the white vee-lined wall. Sunset was just after ten, but it would be light at sea for a good hour and a half after that. I reached out to draw the blue velvet curtain across, blinking the sunlight out. Alain's face swam before my eyes. It was no good me trying to think of him as Rafael. He was Alain; I knew he was. It wasn't just the way he looked. Every movement, every gesture was familiar; the way he spoke, the things he said. If anything, it was more surprising how little he'd changed.

Relief flooded through me. I hadn't killed him. However it had happened, another ship had picked him up.

Yet if Rafael was Alain, he'd have known me. There hadn't been a flicker of recognition in his eyes, not when we'd been introduced, nor since, just his teasing way with any presentable female, which had caused a good few quarrels when we'd lived together. I ran a finger along the scar on my cheek and thought of how much I'd changed from the nineteen-year-old who'd set sail to America with him.

45

I wondered if I could get a look at his file in the ship's computers, or Jenn's passport box. *San Juan . . . I don't have any family.*

Alain's family had returned to France, after his death. I wondered where they were now – if they knew he was alive.

PART TWO

Opening Moves

CHAPTER FOUR

Thursday 29th July, at sea

Low water 02.14 BST
High water 07.01
Low water 13.11
High water 20.01

Moonrise 01.11; sunrise 05.05; moonset 17.40; sunset 21.50
Crescent moon

I slept badly that night. Part of it was simply going to bed when I wasn't tired yet, but most of it was Alain. I didn't relive that awful moment when he'd come up from the cabin with the gun in his hand, nor when I'd tacked *Marielle* and the jib had knocked him overboard. My night was tangled up in a dream of knowing my ship was about to leave and searching for Cat onshore, hearing him miaow but not being able to find where he was. It was dark, the night was wet, I was soaked through and cold. I awoke at last, wringing with sweat.

It was dark outside, but the crescent moon made a white pathway on the shifting water. I reached out for my watch and pressed the luminous button. Half past three. Time I was getting up. I rolled out of my bunk, hauled my laid-ready clothes on top of the thermals, and splashed cold water on my face to wake me up. There'd be a flask of coffee on the go once I got up to the aft deck. I navigated the companionway by the faint blue of the deck lights, and leant against the midships rail to take four long breaths of the crisp air. The sails were ghostly in the sliver of moonlight, their ropes a forest of darker black against the glinting sea. The dim shapes clustered around the banjer door were the red watch, dozing away their last quarter-hour. Off to starboard, a fishing boat's lights blinked. I went up to the chart plotter to check it.

'A Norwegian,' Nils said. '*Maria Christina*, headed for Hull, a mile and a half away. I took a sighting on Polaris at midnight – it's in the log. Our course is the same as it was, 281 degrees. The sails are the same, the wind is steady. You might like to add the t'gallants once it's light enough to see. Sunrise is at 05.05.'

Anyone else would have said 'in an hour', but Nils liked to be precise.

'Once my watch is awake enough for climbing.'

'That too.' He yawned, and nodded to Jonas, his watch leader. 'You could gather them now and we'll change the physicals over.'

I got Petter to round them up, and we sent the physicals off to their stations: lookout, helm, standby, safety. The light was coming now, a rose flush spreading up into the sky and tinting the sea far away to port, while on starboard the sky was still navy, with stars sharp as tacks.

I gave my watch an hour to wake up, filled by Petter and Mona doing knots with them under the banjer lights. The rose deepened to orange, veiled by mist, so that I was able to look straight at the sun: first a sliver of crimson, then half a disc rising slowly to become a great red ball like a hot-air balloon. The stars on the other side of the sky dimmed, the sea lightened to grey, and then the mist burnt off and the sun blazed out, turning the water to molten gold. The sky arched above us, summer blue; the horizon was fretted with wisps of cloud. It would be a glorious day at sea.

At five, we began the process of setting the extra sail on each mast. The sun brightened the red of jackets and gold of hair, gilded the yards and warmed the creamy canvas as each sail was shaken free from its gaskets. The deck crew hauled the sail down and fastened the sheets. The water along the ship's sides curled faster in a lace of white foam. The ship's bell rang four times, five, six. Seven o'clock.

It was my job to wake Rafael; we couldn't have a mere AB going into an officer's cabin. The shock of Alain being alive had dissipated during the night. I didn't know why he was being Rafael, a Spaniard from San Juan, but no doubt time would make it clear. For the moment I just had to play along and treat him as the stranger he was treating me.

I tapped on his door, then pushed it open. He was lying on his back with one arm flung over his forehead to shield his eyes from the light. He hadn't closed his curtains; he never did. I gave his toe a shake. 'Rafael?' I said. 'Seven o'clock.'

He nodded and muttered a thank you, then his eyes flew open and registered me. 'Thanks, Cass. Do we get prayers at breakfast too?'

'Every meal.' I closed the door and went back on duty. The last hour was always the longest, with the smell of breakfast wafting out from the banjer door. The first half of my watch could go down for it now, and the others once they returned. I nodded down to Petter. 'Breakfast.' He sent the eight nearest him downwards, with sympathetic grimaces to the others, and gave me a thumbs-up sign.

Captain Sigurd appeared on deck then. 'A fine morning, Ms Lynch.'

'Beautiful, sir, and forecast to be like this for the rest of the day.'

He squinted upwards. 'We'll fly all sails. Tell the next watch.'

'Sir.'

'What about sea-room? Any vessels around us?'

I'd checked less than ten minutes ago. 'No, sir. A couple of fishing boats in the night, two cruise ships crossing to Norway and one coming from there, all well away from us.'

'Good.' He gave me an approving nod. 'Well done, Ms Lynch.' He strolled over to check the plotter for himself. I gave the helm a last check – it was the teacher, Unni Pedersen, on duty, with Frederik Berg on standby – then nodded to Petter, who came up to take over from me while I went down to breakfast. 'Still on 281 degrees. No other vessels, but keep an eye open for cruise ships; the Lerwick Port Authority website gives three in this weekend. They'll be out there somewhere.'

Petter nodded, and bent over the plotter. As I turned away, Berg came up to look over his shoulder. Petter straightened and smiled at him. 'I'm looking for these ships using the AIS, here.'

My stomach was rumbling. I followed Captain Sigurd down for breakfast.

It was a good day at sea. Our ship flew with her white wings curved above her, ten knots, eleven, twelve and a half, once Alain's watch had climbed to the top of the masts to release the royals. The sky was blue above us, the sea filled with dancing curves of light, and *Sørlandet* moved with a stately dipping motion. I leant against the rail and looked out at the horizon, and heard the work of the ship go on behind me: the trainees assembling to pull on ropes, the bustle and chocolate smell of the galley girls bringing out a tray of mid-morning brownies, the soft voices of the officers conferring above me, the bell ringing.

Geir did his talk at eleven. He'd made himself a little sheaf of notes, but he barely glanced at them. Once he'd unrolled his cloth board, he was confident.

'This is the Fetlar tafl board. Eleven squares by eleven. Other places have different sizes, and that affects the length of game. The four corner squares are the king's refuge. The centre one's where he starts, surrounded by his warriors.' He began placing them: the taller king on the centre square and the round-helmeted warriors two on each side. 'There are thirteen king's men.' He put his hand into the box and brought more warriors out. 'These brown ones are the attackers, and there are twenty-four of them. They begin on the patterned edge squares.' He placed them, five along each edge and one in front, only a square away from the outermost of the king's defenders.

'It's a strategy game. The defender's aim is to get the king to safety in one of the four corners, with a warrior on each of the three squares around him.' He picked up the king and warriors to demonstrate, then returned them to the centre. 'The attacker's aim is to capture the king by completely surrounding him, horizontally and vertically.' He lifted the king and put him between four brown warriors. 'The diagonals don't matter, because none of the pieces move diagonally. You move one piece on each turn, as far as you like. You take a piece by sandwiching it, like this.' He placed a white warrior between two brown ones. 'And that's it. The attacker begins.'

He gestured to the person nearest him. 'Grethe. Have a go.'

She considered the board for a moment, then moved one of the brown warriors a step forward. Geir nodded, and gestured to Janne, who lifted one of the white warriors and looked at it, then moved it outwards. Grethe moved a brown towards it.

Janne moved another white. 'Simple as that,' Geir said. 'Finn, Ivar, want a go?'

The two older sailors came forwards and made half a dozen moves in rapid succession, ending with Finn taking one of Ivar's men. 'A game generally takes around half an hour, depending on the size of board,' Geir said. 'The king usually wins more quickly than the attackers, although statistics have the number of wins of king and attacker as about even.'

I'd got the gist of it now; one of those games that was simple to learn, hard to play. It was 11.45; time to take a sighting. I glanced upwards at Alain on the quarter-deck. I'd tried not to see him moving on his rounds, head high, the officer cap set at a jaunty angle, pausing to speak to everyone. He'd lingered particularly beside Laura, tall and golden and beautiful like the girls he used to chat up in Edinburgh. I looked at them laughing together, and felt that stirring of anger again. Now the shock of surprise was over, I wanted him to acknowledge me. I didn't want an emotional scene, but I couldn't take this indifference either.

Agnetha, coming up behind me, nudged me, smiling. 'Playing hard to get,' she said. 'Doesn't he make you even consider swapping your policeman for a fellow sailor?'

'No.'

'He's interested. Haven't you noticed the way he watches you?'

As well he might, if he was wondering when I'd blow the gaff on who he really was. I turned around on the rail so that I was facing inwards, towards where Alain was checking the chart plotter, and let my gaze wander indifferently over him. 'No.'

Agnetha shot me a sideways glance. 'You two haven't met before, have you?'

Your voice gives you away . . . I gave her my blankest look, and tried to sound mildly curious. 'What makes you say that?'

'Just a sense of . . . oh, sparks being struck off each other. Have you?'

I shook my head and tried to tell the truth. 'The name Rafael Martin rang no bells.'

She gave me an odd look at that, and I knew I hadn't fooled her. 'So long as it doesn't affect the ship.'

She was my senior officer, and anything that affected one of the crew might also affect the ship. I answered her honestly. 'I don't know what's going on,' I said. I turned my chin along my shoulder to look directly at her. 'I really don't.' I spread my hands. 'You know this world. People sometimes just change their names because they want to move on. Leave something behind. I did know him, but he wasn't Rafael then.'

'Ah.' She was silent for a moment. 'You knew him well?'

I nodded.

Her hand rested on my shoulder. 'If you need to talk, then I'm here.'

'Thanks.' It was her old voice again. We smiled at each other, but there was nothing I could say. The ship's routines saved me as the trainees began to move into their watch lines. 'I'd better get my sextant. Must be coming up to noon.'

I went down into my cabin for my sextant, the navigator's badge of office, a hand-held triangle of carefully calibrated lenses and mirrors nestled in green baize within a wooden case. You took a sight on the sun or a star, read off the angle between them, worked your way through the thick book of tables and then worked out where you were on the Earth's surface. Captain Sigurd and I were agreed on our total distrust of even the most foolproof of electronic systems, backed up, as *Sørlandet*'s was, with not one but two independent chart plotters. Using a sextant to take sightings was a skill I was determined to keep honed, and so I'd taken over the task of doing the noon sights for this voyage while Nils did the midnight one.

The sextant was the one thing I'd kept of *Marielle*. It was a black forties instrument in a battered case, and we'd learnt to use it in the Forth, practising until we were both able to pinpoint our position accurately. I'd see Alain recognise it. He'd know I'd kept it.

I headed to the very aft of the ship, where I'd get peace. I wedged the case into one corner of the captain's coffin, the big wooden box that covered the steering gears, unfolded the horizon mirror and turned the screw until the two horizons joined into one, then waited, checking my watch, until it was dead on noon. I put the filter over the mirror and turned the arm slowly until the noon sun sank to the horizon.

I sensed Alain coming up behind me, even before he spoke. 'Shooting the sun.' There was no need to answer that. 'Your own sextant?'

I nodded, feeling a pulse beating in my throat. He came up beside me, and held out his hand. 'May I?'

I made a note of the reading on the graduated arc, then passed it over, watching as he went through the routine of focusing the horizon, bringing down the sun and reading off the angle. The black metal fitted in the crook of his hand as it always had. 'Nice instrument. Where did you get it?'

'In a junk shop.' I'd spotted the wooden box and opened it, curious, then become breathless with excitement when I'd recognised what it was. 'In the Grassmarket, in Edinburgh, before it was gentrified.' He gave a nod that suggested he'd barely heard of Edinburgh, and didn't know any areas in it, gentrified or not. The memory kept unrolling in my mind. It had been one of those shops with bits of everything, overpriced junk and unexpected treasure. We'd been looking at sextants in chandleries, costing two hundred pounds upwards, way above what we could afford, and here was one for thirty-five pounds, lying casually on the table among a heap of binoculars and box cameras. If it worked, of course . . . I'd closed the box and strolled over to where Alain was immersed in old books, pausing on the way to lift this plaster figure, admire that piece of clothing. I'd touched his arm and breathed 'Sextant' at him. His bright glance showed me he'd heard, but he didn't react, just read a bit more of his book, looked at another one, then took my arm and strolled with me towards the entry. We spent a good ten minutes trying every pair of binoculars and speculating about the age of the cameras before he opened the box, took the sextant out, as if he'd never seen one before, then asked the shopkeeper what it was. It had come from a navy man, the shopkeeper told us, and was supposed to be in working order, though of course he couldn't guarantee that. We beat him down to twenty-nine pounds, and left triumphant, Alain carrying the box as if it held spun glass.

It was Alain's fingers that moved the arm round now. He finished taking the sightings, glanced at my scribbled figures, and checked them against the arc. 'Same.' He turned the sextant in his hands. 'A lucky find.'

'Yes,' I said, watching him. 'We thought so, at the time.'

His brows rose. 'Your policeman's a sailor, then?'

'No,' I said. 'This was ten years ago. Another boyfriend.' There was no sign of response. 'He was a sailor, but he died.'

His hand gestured, a fluid curve towards me. 'I'm sorry.' His eyes returned to the sextant. He bent down to replace it in its case. 'So you kept it, in his memory.'

I nodded. My throat was too choked for me to speak. Every time I'd used it since, I'd seen Alain's hands lifting it out of its case, taking the sight, stowing it away, just as they were doing now, careful as a lover, making sure each lens was nestling exactly in the place created for it. He closed the lid, lifted the box and gave it back to me. 'Thanks.' His grin flashed out, not the charming smile he'd used on Laura, but a companionable grin, as if we were Alain and Cass again, on *Marielle* together. 'Let's see who can work the tables fastest.'

'Slow and steady gets it right,' I said austerely, and followed him into the nav shack.

I was very conscious, as I went, of Agnetha's eyes on our backs.

I was back on duty for 16.00, and watched from the aft deck as my watch straggled out. I had the two older sailors on helm and standby. The Danish man had gone forward to lookout and Laura was standing by the nav shack, waiting for instructions. I gave her the safety round card. 'Just follow this list. Look for smoke, and smell for it too, and gas. Anything unusual.' I indicated the ship's bell. 'Your other job is to ring the bell, starting with eight bells to end the watch in—' I checked the clock. 'Four minutes. Then every half hour. Take your time from the clock in there. The first half hour is one bell, then a pair for the hour, then a pair and single for the hour and a half. Ding-ding for the hour, then ding for the half.'

'And I do four double dings now, for the four hours of the last watch.'

'Bang on.'

She nodded, and I left her to get on with it. My helm was settled on the right course, legs braced, gloved hands firm on the wheel, eyes fixed on a mark ahead instead of anxiously glued to the wavering compass needle; I could leave him too. I checked that there were no other ships around, poured myself a cup of coffee from the thermos, and took up my station on the aft deck, looking out over the deck, up at the tiers of sails.

'Lovely, isn't it?' Laura said, coming to stand beside me. She checked her card. 'Report back, it says.' She gave a mock salute. 'I've done my round, sir. All's well.'

'Good work,' I said.

She leant against the rail beside me, face turned to the sun. Suddenly, with the antique tracery of rigging behind her, I saw what she reminded me of, with that smooth hair and English rose complexion. I'd seen her face looking out from Renaissance portraits, hair hidden under a coif, hands demure: an oval face looking at you directly with a world of secrets behind the eyes. Then she smiled, and the secretive impression dissolved. She had a wide, friendly smile, not charming like her brother's, but honest and open. 'This is wonderful. All the world washed away, just the sea and the sky.'

Looking now I could see the strain Oliver had talked about, showing in fine lines around her eyes and a tired look to her skin. A car crash, he'd said; that would have been a shock. I didn't see anything to cause me extra concern.

'My parents would have loved this,' she said suddenly. Her eyes filled with tears. She swallowed. 'They died, on Hogmanay. I don't quite believe it yet. I keep thinking, "I must phone Mum" and then I remember I can't tell her anything any more.' She paused, blinking furiously, then continued, 'It was one of those stupid accidents. They don't know what happened. There was no other car involved. They just went off the road, as if the steering had gone, or locked, or the brakes. The car was too burnt out to be able to tell.' She brushed a hand across her eyes. 'Dad was such a careful driver, and he looked after that car like . . . like . . .' She stopped there, and turned abruptly away from me. 'Time I did another round.'

Oliver spoke from behind me. 'Keeping the ship safe, Laura?'

Laura jumped backwards, as if he'd tried to push her. Her face closed against us; she waved the card at him. 'Next round.'

Oliver turned to me, smiling easily, with his blue eyes watching for the effect he was making. If she was Elizabeth's demure maid-of-honour, he was the roistering courtier, with a pearl drop in one ear, his head high on a stiffened lace ruff, one hand on his sword swirling back his velvet cloak, one white-stockinged leg elegantly crossed; one of Drake's buccaneers, paying court to Gloriana. He shed his charm impartially, as if he couldn't help it, but his sister was given his best smiles.

I went down to do a deck round, and was just coming back again through the nav shack when I heard Petter say my name. He was leaning against the rail, with the big fireman, Berg, beside him, and they were tilted in towards each other, backs to me; it was only a freak of the wind that had blown my name to me. There was something so private, so conspiratorial, about the way they were standing that I stood in the shadow of the doorway for a moment, watching them. Petter was talking earnestly, hands gesturing, and Berg was alternately nodding and raising one large hand to slow him down. Then he asked a question, and his eyes went over to Alain. Petter shook his head, emphatically, and I saw his lips frame my name again. Berg shrugged and nodded. One hand came up to clap him on the shoulder, and then they both headed down to the main deck, ready for mustering, leaving me wondering what that had been about.

CHAPTER FIVE

Friday 30th July, Lerwick

Low water 03.00 BST (1.0m)
High water 08.41 (2.6m)
Low water 15.31 (0.9m)
High water 21.10 (2.7m)

Moonrise 01.41; sunrise 04.57; moonset 18.42; sunset 21.39
Crescent moon

I woke for my shift at half past three, dressed and headed up on deck, leaving Cat sleeping on my berth. The ship's nav lights were still on, but now we were up in the north it was light on the water, with the low crescent moon casting only a faint glimmer across the wrinkled sea and on the white tiers of sails. Behind us, the two Fair Isle lights gave four white flashes every thirty seconds to the south, two every thirty seconds to the north. The island itself was a grey bulk on the horizon, only just darker than the clouds it was floating on, a faerie island which could only be seen at dawn. Only the lighthouses anchored it to reality.

I took a long breath of salt air, then headed up to Nils. 'Anything happening?'

'There are a couple of oil vessels about.' He pointed to them on the plotter. 'Here and here – nothing we need to worry about. And a fishing vessel, headed for Peterhead. We'll cross it at 04.47. Our course is 44 degrees.'

The deck was quiet. The outgoing watch members were sitting drowsily by the banjer or leaning against the rail, gazing out, bodies swaying easily to the ship's motion. I looked for Daniel among them, and couldn't see him at first, then a movement past the main deckhouse caught my eye. He was standing behind it, out of sight, but he'd just ducked his head around the corner, as if he was looking for someone, then whisked it back and waited there: I could still see his navy and charcoal arm.

I hadn't forgotten my uneasy feeling about Daniel and Oliver. If they were going to meet on the quiet, now was their time. I stayed at the rail, head up, waiting.

The first comers of my watch were straggling up on deck, yawning and stretching their arms, then heading for the side to see if there was anything new in sight. Laura was among them; she disappeared forward to the heads, and as her footsteps padded along the side deck, Daniel's protruding arm slid behind the deckhouse. She paused and turned her head as she passed; I saw her lips move a 'Good morning' then she continued forwards.

I kept watching until the physicals came to change over. Nils settled my helm, while I instructed my safety watch – Erling, the older boy. Laura's voice rose gaily from below me: 'I told him he wouldn't wake up. Does he get keel-hauled in front of everyone?'

'I'll go,' Mona replied.

I glanced away from Erling, and saw Daniel slipping into his watch line. By the time I was able to look properly, he and Oliver were facing each other across the deck, Daniel meek as mice, Oliver still struggling his arms into his jacket. If they'd meant to meet, Oliver hadn't been as worried about it as Daniel had.

'All set?' Nils asked at exactly 04.00. 'I give you the ship.'

'I have the ship,' I replied formally, and he nodded, ran a hand round the back of his neck, took off his cap, and headed below.

I checked the helm was steady on course then went aft to look at Fair Isle, insubstantial on its layer of cloud. The idea of a vanishing island was ringing a bell in my head. An island that came and went . . . then I remembered. It was Eynhallow, Orkney's island of the Finns, a race of magician folk who could hide their island from mortals.

More recently, there'd been a queer thing happened on Eynhallow, and I knew about that from an Orkney man I'd met through our youth sailing. It had been back in 1990. The Orkney Heritage Society and RSPB had organised their annual joint trip over to the island, which was a bird reserve, so normally there was no access to it. He'd been one of the crew of the boat, and helped count the folk on board. 'Eighty-eight, we'd counted,' he assured me, 'but when we got them all back, there were only eighty-six of them. Well, we called the coastguard, and there was a massive land and sea search, but nobody was found, or any sign of them, and in the end we just had to agree that we'd miscounted in the first place.' He grimaced. 'Well, I suppose maybe we did. But we hadn't thought so at the time. We knew they'd scatter all over the place, which was why we'd counted at all, to make sure we left nobody. And there was this dark man.' He frowned, remembering, and went into yarn mode. 'He was there and he wasn't there, somehow. A seaman, he was, short and dark-avised, with a gold ring glinting in one ear. I could see him clearly out of the corner of my eye, but when I tried to look straight on at him, somehow I couldn't grasp his face. Well, I thought nothing of that at the time, I was busy steering to the shore, but afterwards, I wondered . . . When we were counting the passengers, on board ship, well, he wasn't there among them.' He shrugged the mood off. 'There're queerer things happen than we can explain. A Finn returning to his old home, likely.'

It was Fetlar, where we were going tomorrow, that was Shetland's island of the Finns.

It was a quiet shift. I did my three-point fixes, as per instructions, and noted them in the log. I let my watch have an hour to wake up, gently tying knots and practising splices as we jolted over the Fair Isle roost, then we trimmed the sails and set the t'gallants on each mast, which took us to 05.45. Battleship-grey clouds blew like smoke over the eastern horizon, blotting the sun to a grey disc, then parted at last to let it dazzle like fire on the water. Above it, the mares' tails were lit brilliant white, and mackerel stripes were spread across the high blue sky; wind coming.

Agnetha came up to join me just after six. 'I couldn't sleep.' She glanced up at the fretted sky. 'Wind coming.'

I nodded. 'We'll get the forecast at seven.'

'A clear run under sail up your channel, to see this island – Mousa, was it?'

'Where the broch is. It's incredibly impressive – you'll see.'

'Looking forward to it,' Agnetha agreed. Her lips tightened, and she took a long breath, looking determinedly out to sea. I knew that feeling; morning sickness. She'd kept her baby. A pang of envy shot through me.

She saw me noticing, and her mouth drew down, rueful. 'I haven't told anyone but you. I still . . .' She drew another long breath, gazing outwards at the shining sea. 'I can't bear to leave this, but I can't bear to get rid of all I have of Mike. I'm torn, but I know I have to decide soon.' She held up a hand. 'Don't say anything. I have to decide by myself.'

I put my hand over hers, and grasped it. Her fingers clung to mine. She flushed. 'I've even been envious of you, not having to make the choice any more . . . I'm sorry.'

That fall down the steps had lost me my baby, only a day after I'd known it was there, a tiny scrap of flesh and bones that had dissolved into blood. A part of me was still grieving. She had no need to be envious; if I could, I'd risk my life at sea to have it back, curled and growing inside me. I shook my head. 'I'll have to make the choice too, soon enough.'

She nodded at that. 'Your Gavin's conventional.' Her head straightened; she shot a quick glance around us. Her voice softened to a murmur. 'I ran a check on Rafael Martin.'

I didn't ask what she'd found; that was confidential.

'He's conventional too. Nautical college, a variety of ships after that. A clean record spanning back ten years.'

Ten years.

'If he sowed wild oats before then, he's left them behind him.' She turned her head to look at Fair Isle receding behind us. 'Like you said, people sometimes just want to move on. Forget the past.' She held up her hands in an *I'm not saying any more* gesture, and looked out towards the horizon.

Nautical college, a variety of ships. A clean record. But why had he left me worrying all these years? Didn't he know I thought I'd killed him? Or was it his punishment to me, for having tried? And why should he change his name, anyway? He wasn't linked to any criminal enterprise. He'd bought *Marielle* for a song because she'd needed so much doing to her, and we'd worked on her together, scraping together money for new rigging, re-cut sails, wood, varnish. Oh, sure, there might have been drugs worth a million on board, but if they had been, I couldn't think where, for I'd crawled into or baled out every locker, every bilge space on board. Even while I was snorting derisively at the idea, I remembered his gun. He couldn't have bought that in Scotland, nor brought it into the country legally; handguns had been banned here for over twenty years. He must have known someone . . .

I turned to look at Agnetha. I wasn't sure what to say. I spread my hands, and managed, 'It was more than ten years. When I knew him.'

Her hand came up on my shoulder. 'Your Gavin's a good bloke.'

I nodded. 'I don't want fireworks any more.'

'No.' Her hand gripped, then let go. 'But sometimes fireworks won't be told. Keep talking to me.' She turned and went below before I could think of an answer to that.

I sent Johan for morning coffee all round, and leant back against the rail, face turned to the sun. The gold light dazzled off the varnish of the ship's boat, dangling from its davits beside me, and glinted on the polished brass. I'd see Gavin this evening. The sails were tiered above me, our beautiful ship swayed on the waves, and the sun warmed my face. The world felt good.

There was a movement beside me. I knew it was Alain even before I turned my head. He leant against the rail beside me, facing backwards as I was, his arm almost touching mine. 'A beautiful morning.' He turned to give the ship a swift, comprehensive glance. 'You've added more sail. Only the royals still to go.'

I looked at him standing there, head tilted back, cap at a rakish angle, somehow more vividly alive than any of the rest of us, and felt that rush of gladness again. He was alive, and I wasn't a murderer. Then, with it, came anger. I was tired of trying to pretend everything was normal. Whatever he was doing under this alias of Rafael Martin, I wanted him to admit who he was. I wanted him to forgive me.

I knew it could be dangerous. *Sparks being struck*, Agnetha had said. *Fireworks*. We hadn't got bored of each other and drifted apart; we'd loved and fought and made up in Edinburgh, across the Atlantic, in Boston, and been torn apart halfway home. For years afterwards I'd still felt I was Alain's girlfriend. Now, at last, I'd broken free of his ghost, and begun a new life. I didn't want to go back to explosions. I just wanted closure.

I kept looking at him, and knew I still loved him. But that had been then, and this was now. We were both different people. Now I was thirty, and I'd done enough adventuring. I could look out at this wide sea horizon from *Sørlandet* and know that Gavin would be waiting for me in port, so long as a policeman's duties allowed. In a few years we could settle down and have children. I'd get my red-sailed *Osprey* down from Dad's garage roof and teach them to sail. I'd learn to bake scones and make jam. I wasn't going back.

Once I'd handed over the ship, I lay down for my post-breakfast nap, with Cat curled in the crook of my neck, but I couldn't sleep. Alain's presence was too sharply with me. I framed conversations in my head as I watched Shetland creep past in my porthole: the black rock of Sumburgh Head slashed slantwise, with pointed teeth below, and the seabirds wheeling. The thatched roof of the Crofthouse Museum was set in a sea of buttercups. That bright puce on the shore was a last clump of red campion.

My phone pinged. *Good morning. See you in Lerwick xxx*

Gavin was on his way. Once I was with him again, this unsettled feeling would ease. I'd know where I belonged.

Above my head, there was a tramp of feet on deck. The sails were being furled for anchoring off Mousa. I swung my legs down and headed into dazzling light. The sun shone on the scrubbed decks, drying the last corner pools of water, and on the creamy sails, bleaching them to cloud-white. On land, it was harvest time, with rectangles of lime-yellow standing out in the green sweep of hill, either combed with the dulled green of drying hay, or dotted with black plastic bales like a giant's chequer pieces waiting to be moved. The rumble of machinery drifted towards us: a shining green tractor trailing a whirl of gulls.

I joined a group of trainees who were leaning on the rail, looking forward. We were between Levenwick Ness and the island itself, with the broch coming into view around the headland, a fat stone chimney-pot, grey-green with lichen.

'That's Mousa Broch,' I said to the father of the family. Egil, that was his name. 'We're anchoring up in the bay just ahead, to go and explore it.'

Phones flashed as we came closer. The broch stood solitary on its headland, twenty metres from the water, with a jagged tumble of rocks below it. One part of the top of it was higher, as if stones had been lost from it, pushed down for later building, but the walling of the curved sides that spread towards the base was unbroken. Closer yet, we could see how carefully it had been made, of long, thin stones fitted together. The entrance came into view, a black square looking seawards.

We anchored just off the bay at the north end of the island and ferried the trainees over to the jetty by the pony pund, ten trainees and one crew member to each load. I was on the first one, to lead the way over the hill, along the shore and across the wooden walkway over the stone beach to the broch itself. If it had looked imposing from the sea, it was twice as impressive from the shore;

the sheer size of it, tall as a three-storey house, and the closely fitted stones covered over with grey-green lichen. We paused halfway along the walkway, and I did my tourist guide bit.

'Brochs like this are only found in Shetland, Orkney and the north of Scotland. This one's the best preserved anywhere – the rest have mostly been taken down to reuse the stones, though you can still see the foundations on Google Maps. There were around a hundred of them in Shetland, all built over a relatively short period, from 400 BC to 200 AD. It's 13.3 metres high, and the walls are five metres thick.'

'What's inside?' Laura asked.

'It's a passage into an open space,' I said. 'There's a double wall, and between the walls there are little cells. There are stairs too.' We'd been on a school trip, when Inga and I were nine. I remembered us climbing up the uneven steps and waving to the ones who'd stayed at the bottom. The teacher with them had looked horrified and told us to come back down *right now*; it was only looking from below that I realised how high we'd been, leaning precariously out. 'You can get right up to the top. The view's amazing.' I went back to my tourist spiel. 'There were two eloping couples took refuge in the broch, in separate incidents. One was a couple from Norway, Bjorn and Thora Lace-sleeve. They fell in love at a party, and Bjorn abducted her and took her to his house. His father was friendly with her brother, so he insisted they didn't live together, but he didn't send Thora home.'

'That's romantic,' Daniel said. He smiled at Laura, and put his arm around her shoulders. 'Running away to live in the sun together. Don't you think that's romantic?'

She gave him a squashing look and hunched her shoulder free. 'Then what?'

'Her mother helped them elope, and they headed for Iceland,

but got shipwrecked on Mousa. They married, spent the winter here, then set off for Iceland and lived at Borg.'

'A happy ending,' Daniel said, nodding. 'Escape and live together for ever.'

For ever, in the Viking past, was likely to be quite short, especially for a young man who'd stolen a chief's daughter. 'The other one involved Harald Maddadsson, one of the Orkney earls. This was in 1153. This Erlendur had asked for his mother Margaret's hand, and Harald refused him, so they ran away, and took refuge in the broch. Of course Harald couldn't get them in there, so they made an alliance, and Margaret and Erlendur were married.'

'Romantic,' Daniel said again, and tried another smile at Laura, but it was met with indifferent eyes and a polite lip-curve. He looked baffled for a moment, then gave a stiff smile, and turned away to talk to one of the sirens. I wondered suddenly if that was what he was doing aboard – if Oliver had set him up to chat up Laura. I suppressed a smile. The reality of quick showers on a moving vessel, watches at strange hours and three layers of protective clothing against the North Sea winds was very different from the rose-tinted vision of bronzed, T-shirt clad Beautiful People admiring sunsets over palm-tree islands.

'Can we get inside?' Geir asked, abandoning his cool teenager pose.

I nodded. 'Yes, on you go. I'll wait to tell the next group about it. Keep your heads well down as you go in. Watch the steps to the roof, they're really uneven, and obviously, don't lean over the top. The stones of the parapet may be loose.'

By the time the next group had joined me, the first heads were appearing at the top of the tower. Geir waved, and yelled, 'Hi, Cass!' I did my tourist guide spiel six more times, and went up to the broch with the last group.

The square entrance led to a low, flagged passage, which opened out into the wider circle. When it had been inhabited, there would have been mezzanine-floor scaffolding for the people, and animals stabled in the cells within the thick walls, and the warmth of a blazing hearth. Now, even filled with bright waterproof jackets and impressed chatter, it had a dank chill after the brightness of sea and sky outside, with the tall circle of stone wall pressing in on you, and the dark openings like lairs of wild beasts. The space swallowed sound and gave strange echoes. I saw Laura shiver and press closer to Fireman Berg, a solid, reassuring presence in his black jacket.

I moved over to them, and continued my tourist guide act. 'You'll be surprised to learn that archaeologists haven't yet decided what brochs were for.'

'Defence,' one of the Swedish men said promptly.

I shook my head. 'Seems obvious, doesn't it? OK. You've seen the enemy approaching, so you all run for cover, bringing the crucial things they would steal with you – your cows, horses and sheep.' I pointed at the narrow doorway. 'Through there.'

They turned, looked, thought about it. 'Were cows smaller then?' Laura asked.

'No,' Fireman Berg replied promptly, as if he had a farming background. 'Not as small as that. Maybe they chased the animals out onto the hill, and then ran for cover.' He frowned. 'Even so, if you could catch them to milk, so could the enemy.'

'Another theory is that they were communication towers. Each broch can see another broch from it. When you go out again, have a look across the sound, and you'll see the ruins of another one. However . . .' I gestured into the dark passage behind me, where the stairs began. 'Anyone been up those stairs?' I looked up at Geir and Erling, watching us from halfway up the ladder of lintel stones. 'What were they like?'

'Pretty dangerous,' Erling said enthusiastically. 'Angles all over. If you came running down, shouting, "The enemy's in sight!" you'd break your neck.'

'They weren't in regular use, either,' Geir said. 'They're not worn at all.'

'Who was the enemy anyway?' the teacher asked. 'Did the Romans get up here?'

I shook my head. 'They saw it, *Ultima Thule*, but didn't visit.'

'Us!' Geir shouted. 'Here come the Vikings!'

'Not at that period,' the teacher said. 'So were they just houses?'

'That's the current thinking,' I agreed. 'Iron Age status symbols: my broch's bigger than yours. *But—*'

They all laughed. 'I should have known it wouldn't be that simple,' Berg said.

'But,' I continued, 'several of them are built on tidal islands, or inaccessible cliffs, the last handy place for a house. So the jury's out. Anyway, go and explore.' I checked my watch. 'We'll move on round the island in half an hour, at 14.00.'

I stayed to answer questions as best I could. At the same time I kept a rough eye on where everyone was as they moved in and out of the cells and passages. Everyone peered up the stairs, and a good few went up, with the sound of manoeuvring on the narrow steps floating down as they returned. I checked my watch. Ten to two. Alain was still up there, with a couple of his watch, and Petter with Oliver and Berg. Laura had gone out into the sun again; I heard Oliver's voice calling downwards, then he came charging out of the dark hole, headed through the entrance and returned, shooing her before him, just as I was about to start rounding them all up to move on.

'You really need to come up, Lols, the view's fantastic.'

She sighed, laughed, and went before him into the dark entrance. I headed up after them. The stairs were a jagged, uneven path between the two broch walls, with an unnerving section in black darkness before the light from above penetrated down, and the walls were rough under my hands. I went cautiously, feeling each footstep, and found myself running into Oliver's back in the dark. I felt him start.

'Sorry,' I said. 'Cass, behind you.'

'Black, isn't it?' he said cheerfully. 'Only for a couple of steps, though, I can see the light now.'

I kept following, and gradually there was a greyness, then the square of light, and we were up on the parapet, a narrow, flagged walkway with a waist-high wall around it. Petter was taking a photo of Berg against the view of Sandwick, and Alain and his two trainees were squeezing round them, ready to come down. I could see from Laura's face that she wasn't happy about being so close to the edge.

'Great, isn't it?' Oliver said.

She glanced at me, behind him, as she nodded. Her face was white.

'Time to be coming down,' I said. 'We've got the seals to see.'

I flattened myself against the parapet to let them past me, and was just following when suddenly there was a clatter and a thump. Laura screamed, and Oliver shouted, 'Watch out!', and I heard the awful sound of shoes striking the sides of the stair, and a thump as someone went down. The clattering ended, and the echoes died.

Then there was silence.

Alain and I moved together. I was first onto the steps, hand on the wall. It was black dark after the brightness outside. I shouted a warning 'Hold still!' and stopped to let my eyes adjust. Alain came up against me. It felt a long ten seconds before the blackness became grey. A tangle of arms and legs was sprawled on the stone stair, both of them tumbled together, Oliver lying face upwards with Laura underneath him. I came swiftly down to them. 'Don't try to move, either of you.' Oliver raised his head. 'Hold still,' I repeated. The whites of Laura's eyes gleamed at me from the darkness beneath Oliver's outflung arm. She gave a stifled yelp, and tried to free herself. 'Take it easy, Laura,' I said. 'Let me help you disentangle yourselves, or you'll fall further.'

Laura lay still again. Berg was on the step below them, ready to stop them rolling downwards. I knelt beside them, the cold stone gritty under my knees, and looked. Oliver had ended up mostly on top of Laura, his legs stretching to the step below.

'Laura, can you breathe OK?' I asked.

'Ye-es.' Her voice was shaking. I heard her take a deep breath. 'Yes. I don't think I'm hurt, just a bit squished.'

'Just keep still.' *Reassure the casualty.* I laid my hand over hers, and felt it tremble like a trapped bird, then turn to grip mine. 'There's no blood. That's a good sign. Oliver, do you feel you've done yourself any damage? Anything hurting?'

'No damage,' he said. He managed a smile. 'Laura broke my fall.'

'Right then.' I reached out my right hand to his left. 'If you can manage to turn over downwards, putting your weight on your right hand, you should be able to balance and stand up on the step below.'

'Take my hand,' Berg said. He supported Oliver's weight, keeping it off Laura as Oliver fumbled his way over and got his right hand onto the step. His back arched, and Laura drew a deep breath. I held my hand out, and she grasped it. As she came free, she scrabbled herself upwards and slid out from underneath.

Oliver righted himself and stood to his full height, one hand reaching out to clutch the wall, then bent over to rub his knee. 'Phew, that was a nasty one. Are you OK, Lols?'

She managed a shaky laugh. 'Just squished. Nothing serious.'

'Here, take my hand.'

She shook her head. I stayed beside her as she edged her way down the stairs, leaning heavily on the rough wall. In the daylight outside, the others clustered round her, concerned. Her face was chalk-white, and there was the beginning of a blue bruise on one cheek, but she shook her head at all enquiries. 'I'm fine. But you're right, Cass, nobody would use those steps in a hurry. The lookout tower theory is definitely out.'

She was making a joke of it, but in this clear light, with the sun full on her cheek, there was something strained about her, a whiteness of the eyelid, a bruised shadow under the eyes. I was trying not to stare, yet at the same time trying to analyse what she reminded me of. The memory came back suddenly: Alain, just after the boom had swung over and hit him, with a queer, glazed look in his eyes, and his hands moving mechanically. A sudden, stunning blow – yes, that was it. Something in her eyes, her movements, was like someone who'd had a severe shock – not a physical injury, like Alain, but a mental shock. There was a blindness about the way she leant one hand on the lichened walls and looked around, as if she wasn't really seeing the blue of the water, or *Sørlandet*'s masts rising above the green hills. Her eyes were turned inwards, wrestling over and over with some problem she couldn't share.

I kept an eye on her as we began the walk across the island. She was limping slightly, and Oliver offered his arm, concerned. He gestured towards the way we'd come, but she shook her head. I went over. 'Can you manage the walk, Laura? You can easily go back to the ship, if you'd rather.'

'You might be better, Lols,' Oliver agreed.

She shook her head, blonde hair flying out round her face. 'I'm fine,' she snapped at him.

'Here,' Alain said, appearing at my elbow. 'You go and lead the way, Cass. I'll stick with Laura.'

She took his arm, and we moved on: past the old ruined Haa House to the West Pool, where we watched the dog-nosed grey seals sunbathing; alongside the beach, and back by the cliffs. She stuck close to Alain all the way, and he did his best charmer act. By the time we reached the jetty she was laughing.

CHAPTER SIX

We moored right in the centre of Lerwick, at the Victoria Pier. I wasn't off duty till eight, but I'd told my parents to come earlier, at seven, so that I could show them around the ship. Dad's black Range Rover bulldozed its way onto the pier on the dot of ten past, and I watched them get out: Dad in a dark suit over a white polo neck, Maman in her swirling white wool coat which she insisted on wearing outside in Shetland even through the summer months. I shook my head, smiling. It was a fine summer day; the crowd that had gathered to watch us come in were wearing T-shirts and licking ice creams. Her dark hair was swept up in its usual chignon, protected by a silk scarf. She saw me looking, and waved a gloved hand.

I hurried down the gangplank and gave them each a hug. 'Well, what do you think of her?'

'He's beautiful,' Maman said. She held me back from her. 'Let me look at you! I like the uniform.'

'Very smart,' Dad agreed. He put his arm round my shoulders. 'Sure, I never thought I'd have a ship's officer for a daughter.'

Maman gave the mast height an apprehensive glance. 'You don't climb all the way up there?'

'Not often.' I linked my arm through hers, and drew her forward. 'Come on board. I need you to dazzle Captain Sigurd so that he'll let me come to Glyndebourne. Don't forget that ships are *she* in English.'

He was on the aft deck. I led them up the officers' gangplank, stifling my apprehension with faith in Maman to have him eating out of her hand in five minutes. Actually, it took thirty seconds: one sweep of her dark lashes as she shook his hand, English-style, an admiring glance round the ship, and a prettily accented 'thank you' for turning her vagabond daughter into a ship's officer whose whereabouts she could follow on the Internet. He stared at her in disbelief, and said, 'But you're Eugénie Delafauve!' Maman smiled and admitted it, and our stately captain actually blushed. 'I have several of your recordings. This is a huge honour, madame.' He offered her his arm. 'Will you allow me to show you round your daughter's ship?'

They headed towards the ship's wheel, with Maman pausing to greet Cat, who was already up on his bench, watching the harbour with the benevolent gaze of the highest-ranking cat in town. 'A very well-behaved animal,' Captain Sigurd said, 'and an asset to the ship.'

I grinned at Dad behind their backs. 'I think it's safe to book those flights.'

They were an odd couple, my parents. Oh, not in looks: Dad's height and handsome Irish looks were a great foil for Maman's French elegance. It was just that you wouldn't have expected the son of a builder to fall for an opera singer. All through my childhood they'd struggled with making the marriage work, until the call of her music world had finally been too strong for Maman, and she'd taken flight back to France, to her old director, and a cameo part that had dazzled the critics. It had taken her fifteen years to swallow her pride and return to the marriage that they'd never quite ended; and so now here they were, with Dad proud as a cormorant on its rock to have his beautiful wife on his arm again. He joined her for her shows, and they'd spent most of last winter in France, with him running his business empire by computer and phone, while she, work permitting, had returned to Shetland for the theoretical warmth of the summer. They'd been back together for a whole year now, and I was daring to believe it would last. Dad was even trying to speak French . . .

By the end of the tour of the ship, Captain Sigurd was practically human. It turned out that he was a particular fan of Rameau, the composer Maman specialised in. Not only had I got my leave for Glyndebourne, but Captain Sigurd was pressing her to remain on board for the voyage to Fetlar, 'To see how well your daughter discharges her duties aboard.' As Maman was seasick on the flattest of crossings, there was no chance whatever of her taking him up on that, but she disclaimed convincingly and accepted an offer of a cup of coffee in the officers' mess. I glanced surreptitiously at my watch as we headed below. Quarter to eight. Gavin should have landed, if his flight had been on time. He'd be here soon. My heart gave a joyful leap. Ten minutes or so.

I'd noticed Alain watching us as we'd gone round, so I wasn't totally surprised to find him already in the officers' mess, cup in hand, standing by the shelf as if he was just consulting a reference book. He'd never met Maman; she'd been gone by the time I'd started going round regattas. He might remember Dad, but I didn't think Dad would remember him, one of the flock of life-jacketed teenagers rigging boats before the race and coming ashore after it, hair streaming with water.

Alain set his cup down and began to retreat in a wave of apologies, but of course Captain Sigurd introduced him: 'Rafael Martin, our third officer, who joined the ship at Kristiansand.'

'I follow Cass's watch,' Alain said, and made a continental bow over Maman's hand. Her dark eyes looked him over thoughtfully.

He moved on to Dad, and I saw straight away that I'd underestimated Dad's memory for faces, a business asset he'd cultivated until it was second nature. His brows drew together, his eyes sharpened to Siamese-cat blue. 'Rafael Martin,' he repeated, as he shook hands. I could see he knew it wasn't right; I hoped his computer brain wouldn't come up with the true answer.

I should have trusted his discretion. The conversation flowed normally: the weather, where we were headed after Shetland, our plans for the rest of the summer. It was only once I was discharged for the day, and we were safely in the middle of the car park, with Cat grumbling about being put on his lead when he'd been contemplating a foray ashore, that he turned to me. 'Cass, who was that young man?'

'In the officers' mess?' Maman asked. She returned to French. 'He's too charming, my Cassandre. Stay with your Gavin.'

'I intend to.'

'Rafael Martin,' Dad repeated. He turned from my genial Irish dad to the ruthless businessman. 'I recognised him straight away, though it took me a moment to place him. He's that French boy from Yell who used to go round the regattas. His father was a teacher there. I'll come up with his name in a moment. What's he up to pretending to be a Latino?'

Dad had been in the Gulf when Alain had died. Maybe he'd never linked the French boy from Yell with my dead lover. Maman, too, was looking puzzled. 'You're not going to let him draw you into trouble, are you, Cassandre?'

'No,' I said. I couldn't tell them everything. 'I told the chief officer I'd known him under another name, so she's keeping an eye on him.'

I wasn't sure how much longer I could stall, but just then a taxi pulled into the pier and Gavin got out of it.

He'd seen our ship, of course; you could hardly miss her, with her three masts rising up to the height of the town hall on its hill. His head turned towards her, admiring first, then looking for me on deck. I gave Cat's lead to Maman and started towards him, in that awkward crossing-the-space way, and he saw the movement and began walking towards me too. We maintained a measured pace, ending with a kiss on the cheek. As I put my face to his, the taxi air freshener (pine forest) overlaid his natural smell of Imperial Leather soap. He swung his bag into his other hand, and tucked my arm through his. His hand was warm as our fingers meshed together. 'I like the cap.'

'I don't.'

'Do you have to keep it on all the time?'

I made a face. 'There's a muster tomorrow at eight-thirty. Maman and Dad are taking us home for dinner.'

We clambered into Dad's black Range Rover, Gavin and I in the back, hands linked. Cat settled into that elbows-folded pose of a cat who wasn't going to like this, even for the sake of a skulk round the beach and some sparrow watching in the bushes. 'We're going home,' I told him.

I settled back into my seat and turned my head to look at Gavin. I loved his face. He wasn't handsome exactly, with his nose benkled from a rugby-playing youth and his long mouth set in a solemn Scots line, but there was an intelligence about it, his grey eyes giving the air of noticing everything. He'd had his hair cut since last I'd seen him; if he let it, it would cluster in curls round his head, the dark russet of a stag's ruff. Now it was police-style inch-long, neat around the ears, and just wrinkling at the ends. The hand which held mine was tanned, square, made for strength and use, not beauty.

He turned his head to smile at me; his fingers tightened. We didn't need words.

It was the height of summer around us. The verge was knee-high with cauliflower-topped cow parsley and the first puce spires of rosebay willowherb. A field of waving grass rippled like the sea, turning from rose to grey as the light caught the feathered heads. The sheep were the creamy white of *Sørlandet*'s sails, marked in stripes with the long sweep of clippers. A foal the colour of toffee lay stretched out dozing while his mother grazed beside him. The field was yellow with buttercups as high as her knees.

Looking at the horses reminded me. I turned back to Gavin. 'Did you ever hear from Rainbow, about a foal from her stallion?'

He nodded. 'She put him to the mares this year, and I've to get first pick of the foals next June.' His thumb tensed on the back of my hand, but his voice remained casual. 'Ideal children's ponies, if you'd consider it.'

I'd been considering it, these long two months since I'd lost the baby. The grief and shock I'd felt at the time had subsided, but there was still a sore place in my heart for the child that had never had the chance to grow. I turned my hand in his. 'Black, like the stallion, or chestnut, or broken coloured?'

He smiled. 'A good horse is never a bad colour.'

We'd been talking too quickly and softly for Maman to follow, but Dad had heard. I saw a quiet curve of satisfaction touch his lips, quickly suppressed. I had no doubt Maman had impressed on him that settling down, marriage and children were all taboo subjects. She didn't want Dad to turn me contrary; she and Gavin approved of each other.

We'd passed the blue sea of Laxfirth and Catfirth, the shining loch of Girlsta. Now we'd come to Sandwater, the otters' loch, and the moorland in the heart of Shetland's cross shape. The hills closed around us, their heather slopes mottled olive among the jigsaw outlines of peat banks and brighter green fissures of burns, then opened again as we reached Voe, and the blue glimmer of Olnafirth. These waters had filled my youth, from Brae, at the head of the voe, out to the Rona, the gateway to the wide Atlantic. Across the water, as we drove on, Busta House stood serene above its pier, white crowstepped gables picked out by a sudden glimmer of sun. Cat's nostrils twitched and he stretched his neck upwards, as if he was recognising home. 'Nearly there,' I told him. 'You're doing well.'

We came into Brae proper, and passed between the houses to the boating club straight. Now I was craning my neck for a glimpse of my *Khalida*. There was just time to pick out her mast from the others, then the car swung around onto the single track road leading above the west side of the voe to the bridge and island of Muckle Roe. I felt a pang at my heart, and leant back to catch my last glimpse before the hill hid her. Gavin's fingers tightened on mine. 'Just a couple of hours,' he murmured.

Our house was almost at the end of the road, with only Inga's further on. It was an eighties single-storey with picture windows looking over the voe. A smell of rabbit-and-olives casserole greeted us as we opened the door. I sniffed appreciatively. 'Maman, you're a star. Wait till you taste this, Gavin.'

'And neither of you are driving,' Dad said. 'Wine, Gavin, or whisky?'

We both opted for wine, which turned out to be a velvety Burgundy. Cat accepted a plate of rabbit trimmings, and smoothed down his ruffled fur and feelings on the Chinese rug in front of the peat fire, while we sat at the table and shared dry-cured sausage and plump white asparagus straight from France.

'The last of your cousin Thierry's,' Maman said. 'He gives his wishes, and you are to have the eggs the next time you visit, Gavin, to . . . to . . . *couver*, Cassandre?'

'To set.'

'Yes, to set under a hen. He has a new breed, I can't remember the name, but he thought you would like them.'

'Mother would,' Gavin said. 'She's the poultry woman.' He turned his head to smile at me. 'Unless Cass could be tempted to set up a cage along at the cottage?'

I gave him a horrified look. 'Me, hens?'

'And your mother is well?'

'Very well.' He spread his hands. 'I don't know if Cass mentioned how late a baby I was. She'll be eighty-four next birthday. We've cut down on the milk cows, to save her work, and one of the factor's boys helps with the garden, but she enjoys still being in charge of the dairy and bossing Angus about over where to plant things. Her brain's as sharp as ever, God be praised.'

'And your brother?' Dad said. 'Kenny, isn't it?'

Gavin nodded. 'Very busy, between the sheep and the cows. He's been doing some judging of Highland cattle for the shows, so that's got him out and about.' He smiled at me. 'No sign yet of him bringing home a wife to take over the farm.'

'He is your older brother?' Maman asked. 'No, do not rise yourself, Dermot. Have more *saucisse*.'

Gavin nodded. 'He's bred a bull calf which he says has star quality. Charlie, he's calling him. I'm no judge, but he looks good to me. It's not just looks, though – he's got a cheeky way with him. Eye-catching.'

'So he has his own . . .' Maman paused to find the word. 'His own place to star. He breeds these Scottish cows with the long fur.' She went into the kitchen and came back with the casserole and a ladle. 'He is not jealous of his clever little brother who is soaring in the police.'

Gavin shook his head. 'Soaring's far too generous – but no. Kenny's a happy man. The farm's all he's ever wanted. He's sorry for me, having to work in the city.'

'It could be hard though,' I said. 'Having a younger sibling who outshone you.' I was reminded of Oliver the golden. Was he older than Laura, or younger? It was hard to tell; she had a maturity that he lacked. I suddenly wondered how I'd have turned out if the baby brother Maman had miscarried all those years ago had lived. I'd have had to take second place to *the boy* . . .

'Wake up, Cassandre.' Maman tipped a ladleful of rabbit on my plate, the meat tenderly pink, garnished with green and black olives. I helped myself to tatties, and took a mouthful. It was meltingly soft.

'Mmmm. Wonderful, Maman.' I resolved to get the recipe before I went to stay with Gavin. It was the sort of dish that would cook well in a haybox.

'Ah,' Dad said, 'I fell in love with her beautiful face, and discovered I'd married a woman who could cook as well as she sang.'

Maman laughed. 'So what was distracting you from your food, my Cassandre?'

'I was just thinking,' I said. It would be unethical to ask Gavin to investigate the Eastleys, but Dad had business contacts everywhere.

'The ship?' Gavin said. He was quick. I nodded.

'People I'm not sure about. A charming brother with no staying power, whose sister looks worried about him all the time. Watches him.' I wondered about mentioning this morning's fall in the broch, but decided it was too sensation-seeking. 'The other thing . . . oh, I'm beginning to sound as if I'm paranoid.' I explained about Daniel, and the uneasy feeling both Agnetha and I had about him.

'Agnetha's on top of her job,' Gavin said. 'You too. If you say he's not the usual type, I'm happy to take your word for it.'

I looked across at Dad. 'I don't suppose you could tug your grapevine? I don't know what the firm's called, but it's accountants, and their surname's Eastley.'

Dad reflected, and shook his head. 'But I know someone who will know. You just want a few quiet questions?'

I nodded. 'Nothing that'll get back to them.'

'Just the general feel of them.' He glanced at his watch. 'Not too late yet . . . I'll give Richard a phone while you're having your coffee.'

Dessert was lemon souffle – 'The Co-op has nothing like the cakes from *Délices de St Michel*,' Maman sighed – and after it, Maman and I headed through into the kitchen to do the dishes while Dad made his phone call, Gavin deliberated over a shelf of malt whiskies, and Cat went out to check on the sparrows in the garden. Dad had installed the latest in dishwashers for Maman's return, but she wasn't going to trust a machine with the plates which had belonged to her great-aunt in Tours. I was given the dish mop and Marigolds, while she wielded the dishcloth.

I could see she wanted to talk to me. She gave a flick of her dark eyes towards the sitting room and went into soft, rapid French. 'My Cassandre, Dermot remembered the young man's name. It didn't mean anything to him, but I knew it.' She gave another quick check over her shoulder, in a way that would have had First Conspirator written on her brow in any opera house. Luckily Gavin was back-on to us, considering the respective merits of a 1995 Ardbeg and a thirty-five-year-old Old Pulteney. 'What's going on?'

'I don't know,' I said. I passed her one of the plates, dripping with soap suds, and was given it back.

'Rinse it, darling. But he is who Dermot thinks he is?'

'A dead man. Yes.' I turned to look at her. 'Except he's behaving as if he's never seen me before.'

'But he knows you?'

I shook my head. 'He must know me. But what can I do, Maman? It's no crime to use another name. Maybe he's still angry. From his point of view, I knocked him overboard and left him to drown.'

She glanced at my cheek. 'You had reason.' She stacked the last plate on the pile and lifted them into the cupboard. 'So what will you do?'

I began on the knives and forks, fishing each one dripping out of the soapy water, rinsing and laying them on the draining board. 'Wait. Watch.'

Maman made a face. Waiting and watching was her least favourite reaction to a difficult situation. 'He behaved as though . . .' She paused, and shot another glance sitting-room-wards. 'They will wonder what we are talking about so earnestly.'

'I'll say you were telling me to turn respectable.'

'That's what I do want to tell you.' She put an arm around me. 'My Cassandre, you and Gavin could be very happy. He could be your rock, the home you would sail back to. Don't let this charmer lead you astray.' She frowned. 'Or make misunderstandings. I tell you, he is mischievous.'

'I know.' I spread my hands. 'But I have old loyalties too.' I glanced towards Gavin, then back at her. 'How can I tell this one, if I don't know what the other one is up to?'

It gave her pause. 'Yes,' she said reluctantly. 'But don't leave it too long.' She hung the drying cloth over the cooker handle, and laughed. 'Don't be the lady in the ballad, who ran off with the gipsies.'

I turned to stare. 'Maman, where on earth have you been hearing ballads?'

'Oh, my mother was a great fan of an American singer, Joan Baez.' She sang a couple of lines: '*The gipsies came to the castle gate, And oh, but they sang merrily . . .*'

The song jingled on in my head, '*They sang so sweet and so complete, that they cast their glamourie ower her.*' Glamourie. It was a good word for Alain's brand of charm.

Gavin turned his head at Maman's singing. 'The Earl of Cassilis's lady, and the gipsy?' He stretched his hand out to me, smiling. 'Now if it had been a sailor . . .'

I hoped he wouldn't remember this conversation when he met Alain.

Dad came back in then. 'Did I hear you singing, Eugénie?' He sat down on the couch. 'Well, Gavin, what's it to be?'

'The Old Pulteney.' Dad handed him a glass, and he took a long breath of the smell. 'Ah, that's a treat.'

Dad poured himself a generous measure and settled back. 'Well, now, Cass, I got some interesting information on your firm. Ryder and Whittingham, it's called. Richard knew the mother well – her maiden name was Whittingham, and it was her great-grandfather's firm, founded back in the 1880s. The office is in Queen Street, the heart of the New Town.'

'Very respectable so far.'

'Oh, respectable entirely. The son was their golden boy, hope of the house, a fifth-generation Whittingham on the board – except that he wasn't a sticker. Exam results achieved by last-minute work, left school at sixteen, tried college and flunked out. "Very flash," Richard said, "all show, but no substance behind it." He's in his late twenties now, and still in the office.'

'A reason for him to resent his clever sister,' Maman agreed.

'The daughter was a couple of years younger. She tended to be overshadowed by the boy, but she's hard-working, with a good flair for money. She went to St Andrews, got a First.'

The old-established firm had obviously done well. St Andrews was one of the prestigious universities, and keeping up with the crowd there wouldn't have been cheap.

'The father wanted to promote her to a seat on the board, but I gather the mother wanted to hold it for Oliver, once he settled down.'

So much for equality. Their father wanted to promote his little sister above him. That was enough to breed resentment in someone used to having the world lie down for him to walk on . . .

Dad took a sip of his whisky. 'Good stuff, this.' He set the glass down again. 'After that, it gets interesting. The parents died together in a car crash, just before New Year, did you know that, now?'

I nodded. 'I got the impression that it was part of the reason they'd taken this holiday.'

'Sure. Well, the firm was slightly shaky at the parents' death – the recession, all that. Laura was given her mother's seat on the board, straight away. Voted in *nem con*. "Good judgement," Richard said. The last audits gave it a clean bill of health. There was talk that they might get rid of the brother, ease him out, like. There's been no action yet, but his days are numbered. Your Laura might be able to block that, of course, but it would put her in a difficult position.'

'Resentment on resentment,' Maman said. 'Humiliation, to have to depend on his little sister to be allowed to keep the job that should be his by right.'

Humiliation enough to drive the golden boy to attempted murder on a steep flight of stone stairs? Was that what had given Laura that shocked look?

'It gets even more humiliating. I knew Richard would know all about it.' Dad leant forward. 'This ought to be confidential, but it was the speak of Edinburgh,' he said. 'The will was read after the funeral, and a fair shock it caused. Everyone expected there would be an equal division between the two of them, but that wasn't the case.'

'Was there much to leave?' Gavin asked.

'Shares in the firm, of course, a quarter-holding each, worth a good bit, and their house in Heriot Row. A four-storey Edinburgh New Town house, with a garden behind it.'

Gavin nodded. 'Moving upwards towards a million.'

'The sister got pretty near the lot, in consideration of debts incurred by the son. That wasn't the wording of the will, but that's what the facts were. An equal amount to what they'd spent on him was to be given to the daughter, before the remainder was divided. Richard didn't know the exact sum, but it was substantial. They're both still living in the house, but the sister owns most of it.'

'Spent on him?' Gavin cut in. 'Spent on what, did he know?'

'I asked that too, but Richard had only a vague idea. He had some notion of college debts, and a couple of failed business attempts.'

Gavin was looking thoughtful. 'It's worth a watching brief.' His hand linked with mine. 'Your ship wants you back at eight-thirty tomorrow morning, did you say?'

I nodded. 'A huge concession. I'm being allowed to miss the formal raising of the ensign at 08.00 precisely.'

Gavin rose. 'Then shall we head for *Khalida*?'

CHAPTER SEVEN

Dad drove us back round to the marina. Cat was out as soon as I opened the door; he recognised home. I followed, looking eagerly at my *Khalida*. My friend Magnie had kept an eye on her for me, of course, but it wasn't the same as seeing her. I let us onto the pontoon and hurried forward, then remembered to hold back and wait for Gavin. He smiled. 'On you go. How long has it been, three weeks?'

Cat was already trotting down the pontoon ahead of us, tail held high, the evening sun lighting his pale underside. He leapt aboard, then turned to wait for us. I paused on the pontoon to look up at all the halyards leading to the top of the mast. I'd frapped them before I left, tying them outwards so that they wouldn't rattle, and they were still secure. The wind indicator turned on its pin. The jib was furled tight, the sail cover still neatly on, the plastic covers of the mooring ropes where they would stop chafing, and the fenders between her white sides and the metal pontoon. All was good.

I opened the hatch, and that familiar smell of old diesel came back at me. Cat swarmed in before me, sniffing all round to make sure no other cats had invaded his territory, then headed out again to sit on the cabin roof. Yes, she was as she should be inside too: the varnished wood gleaming, the faded navy cushions dry. That feeling of *home* swept over me. I looked down into the cabin and loved her, this little wooden space with its fish horse-brass above the sink, and the lantern swinging gently above the chart table, and the sun striking gold gleams from my bookshelf. My berth was made, waiting. For a moment, I wanted to put the kettle on, settle down with a book, and be Cass of *Khalida* again, but I had our joint bed to make up, in the forepeak. I looked up at Gavin. 'Shall I put the kettle on?'

He shook his head. 'I'll stay quietly in the cockpit while you talk to her.'

He seated himself peaceably on the slatted seat, fished a tin out of his pocket, and began looping invisible line around a tiny hook. I started the engine and left it to run while I checked everything else: no sign of water in the bilges, nothing dislodged in any gales they'd had in the last three weeks, and all the ropes properly secure. I gave the sink a quick rinse and ran a damp cloth over the work surfaces, took the duster and gave the fish a shine, plumped up the cushions, shook up my downie, and shuffled the books to make sure air was circulating between them, then shoved the sails out on deck to clear the forepeak, and made our bed.

Satisfied, I came up into the cockpit to sit beside Gavin. The wind had fallen now. It was still daylight, but the bright land colours had dimmed. The eastern sky was the creamy blue of a duck's egg, barred with dark lines of cloud; there was an amber flush to the west, with a pink light highlighting the edges of the clouds. Even as I watched, the amber brightened to a bar

93

of molten gold, then faded. The thick white clouds that rested on the highest hills spilt over, running down the river gullies like milk first, before the whole mass of cloud lippered over and blotted out the hill crests. The engine snuffled like a friendly seal at *Khalida*'s stern, and the white tirricks screeched above us as they swooped, dived, soared again. Cat was a pale blur scouting along the tideline at the slip.

'All's well.' I leant back against the white fibreglass and felt my bones relax. 'It's good to be home.'

His shoulder was warm against mine, his spread kilt-pleats touching my regulation cargo breeks. 'Kenny and I have been working on beefing up the mooring at the cottage.'

'Your grandparents' cottage?' I'd seen it in my visit to his loch: a square-built stone cottage with a white porch, skylight upper windows and a slate roof that glistened mauve in the rain. They'd left the tenancy of it to Gavin, but so far he'd lived mostly at the farm on his weekends off, rather than travel the extra three miles by boat each day.

His eyes were intent on the tiny fly in his hands, but his voice showed how much it mattered. 'I wondered if you might like to come and stay during your winter leave, while your Academy pupils are home for Christmas. You could moor *Khalida* there.' He turned to look at me. 'You'd have the sea road to the isles at your door. The Atlantic's only six miles away. If I was called away, you could just take off, and explore Skye, or Lewis, or head for St Kilda.'

I heard his meaning. I wouldn't be trapped on land while I had *Khalida* on a mooring, ready to take off as I liked. This lover wasn't going to hide his selkie wife's skin to stop her returning to the sea.

'I'd like that.'

'Good.' He smiled, and returned his attention to the fly. 'We were looking at rigging a pontoon too, using a bit of salmon walkway, from the rocks at the point – it's the only place it's deep enough. But the mooring will hold you for now. Six railway wagon wheels joined together with heavy galvanised chain, and the first ten metres of line is chain too, then twenty-millimetre rope.' He turned his head to kiss my cheek, then trailed his lips along to kiss me properly, and murmured into my cheek, 'I don't want to be the man responsible for letting your *Khalida* be dragged ashore.'

We kissed again. I was just about to suggest moving below when a car slid down the road and stopped at the pontoon in a scuffle of gravel. We exchanged a mouth-turned-down glance. 'Visitors, at this hour?' he said.

It was Inga. She fished round the marina gate for the key and headed down the pontoon towards us.

We'd been best friends all our schooldays, Inga and I. We'd been driven together to nursery, with Maman and her mother taking turns, then we'd jolted in the back seat of the minibus to primary school and secondary. We'd gone to discos and moaned about homework, and had a shared part in all the childhood pursuits of the area, from New Year guising through to the bairns' Christmas party. She was plumper now, after three children, and her long, dark hair had been cut to a practical bob, but she still had her enthusiasm for action.

'Now then,' she said, and clambered neatly over the guardrail to join us in the cockpit. She proffered the ice-cream tub she had in one hand to me. 'A fish from the freezer for Cat. I microwaved it for him.'

It would be good bribery for getting him back into the car tomorrow. 'Thanks. Cup of tea?'

Inga shook her head. 'I winna bide long. Dinna want to spoil your peace, this bonny evening. I just saw the pair of you down in the boat.' Inga's picture window had a commanding view over the voe which let her keep well abreast of any marina goings-on. 'I was wondering, Gavin, how you'd feel about being kidnapped on Monday?'

It was a good conversation-stopper. We gaped at her, open-mouthed. Inga unwound her scarf from her neck and leant back. Behind her, the street-lights flickered on, reflecting orange on the water. Squares of light had sprung up in the houses, darkening the land around them, but the sea was still silver. Cat moved from the slip to the pier and sat there, contemplating the water.

'It's part o' a week o' protests against increasing centralisation. Computers and technology, along wi' dis "austeritee", are hitting the country areas harder as the toon. You ken there's been aa the fuss about the junior high schools, Cass, them wanting to close them to save money. Oh, they say it's for the good o' the bairns, to gie them a better education, but aabody kens it's no. It's aboot costs. We're focusing on education on Tuesday, the good reports the junior highs have had from the inspectors, and the local jobs that'll be lost. But it's no joost here. It's spreading Scotland-wide.' She nodded at Gavin. 'You should ken aa aboot that, wi' Police Scotland instead o' the local forces.'

Gavin made a non-committal face.

'Yea, yea,' Inga said, 'I ken you canna comment. But there's a gradual sucking away o' jobs from the rural areas, and focusing them in the town. Then the big supermarkets move into that same town, and sell produce for half the price. Shetland used to be self-sufficient in milk afore Tesco came. Noo half our dairies have had to close. More country jobs lost. And they do online shopping, their own brand goods at half the price local shops can manage, delivered to your door. Well, it's no wonder the country shops're fighting for survival, and it's just as well local folk value them enough to keep using them. Once the shop is gone, the heart's out o' the community.'

'And the stupid things,' Gavin said. I could see Inga had touched the right nerve. 'Firms south'll no deliver to us, because everything's centralised with couriers. I went into a shop in Inverness to buy a bookcase, and the shop there had almost nothing, because half of the firms they used to deal with won't deliver north of the border.'

'Yea,' Inga said. 'They make it harder and dearer to bide in the country, so that nobody real, that was born in the place, can afford it.' Her dark eyes focused on Gavin's face. 'We were doon in the Highlands for a visit, Charlie and the bairns and me, an' you ken, compared to Shetland, I towt it was like a tourist theme park. Every hoose we passed was a B & B, or a tea shop, with the verges clipped round it, and an auld cart filled wi' flooers in front.' Her voice grew passionate. 'I dinna want Shetland to become like that. Tourists can come and welcome, an' park their motorhomes on a bit o' space, but I want real industries, things that keep our world running. I want to see the folk going in to clean the school and make the maet and serve in the shop. I want to see the peerie boats heading to the creels and the mussels. I want our roads with lang verges o' wildflooers, an' auld cars roosting by byres, an' tractors clanking aboot, an' sheep grazing on the hills, the way they're aye done.'

Gavin nodded. 'I don't want to live in a theme park either. Our loch's gradually getting busier with weekend walkers, and there's a car park for them, but so far there's no point in creating a caravan park.' He grinned. 'They couldn't get down our road.'

'So far, though,' Inga said, 'we're managed to protect our local infrastructure. We kept our coastguard—'

'After a fight,' I said. The government's first idea had been to control all shipping emergency services from Portsmouth, and only howls of protest from seafarers throughout the UK had persuaded them to leave services in Stornoway, in the heart of the cliff-fanged western isles, and in Lerwick, two hundred miles out in the North Sea.

Inga nodded. 'But they've centralised the emergency services, you ken, dialling 999, so that some peerie wife wi' a Yell accent has to try and explain to someone in Inverness.' She went into mimicry. 'Me man's collapsed. He's had budder wi' his puddins, and da doctor said if he went poorly I was to ring da ambulance straight away. I'm Ruby o' da Hoyt, an' I bide joost sooth o' Efstigarth. Na, I dinna ken the number o' the road . . . B 9-something. Weel, why sood I ken? There's only ae road tae the hoose . . .'

Gavin nodded. 'Tell me about that! You're better off than we are in that respect, with your smaller distances. There's an awful lot of the Highlands to be covered by ambulances from Inverness, or the emergency helicopter.'

'We hae ferries, though,' Inga said. 'Only forty miles from Lerwick to Unst, but there are two ferries on the way.'

'Didn't they send an ambulance to Yell, when it was needed at the south end of the island?' I asked.

Inga rolled her eyes. 'That's no' the worst – they had a sick baby in Orkney and someen in the Aberdeen hospital sent the air ambulance to Shetland. And if they can get it wrong just fae Aberdeen, think what they could do from further south. Dundee, they're talking about now, for the emergency services phone centre.' She paused to watch the dark head of the marina seal scull past, then resumed. 'Anyway, the next thing was, they came up with this airport plan. Well, the radar is controlled in Scotland already, Aberdeen, but they still hae a real person at

Sumburgh to do a visual check as the plane comes in. They want to get rid o' that, save a bit o' money. They'll have one person down in Portsmouth somewhere, watching the video screens for every small airport in Britain, and telling the pilot, "Yes, yes, on you go, the screens say it's clear."'

'The boat for me, if they do that,' I said. 'Do they ken where we are? Do they really think we'd trust a video link for something that important?'

Inga grinned. 'Wir MP telt them. "If it's that reliable," he said, "then build your central control tower up here in Shetland." So far there's no' been a comeback, but I doubt they're still plotting.'

'I bet they are,' Gavin said.

Inga leant forward. 'And now the latest scheme baffles all common sense. You're no' going to believe this. Wir power station in Lerwick is due for replacement. They're no' going to bother.'

I stared at her, mouth open.

'So how are you going to manage for power?' Gavin said. 'Dermot's wind farm?'

'Oh, na,' Inga said. 'That's for getting magabucks by sending electricity south. Na, they're going to run a cable. No' the cable that's taking the wind farm's energy south, another one, to bring energy north to us.'

Words failed me.

'A cable fae Caithness was the latest news, lying on the seabed right in the middle o' the fishing channel, to be dredged up twice a week. A fine, reliable source o' electrics, that. Oh, they're going to give us a backup emergency generator. That's awful good o' them.'

I found my voice. 'You are *joking*.'

Inga shook her head, and returned to the point in hand. 'So that's the first thing we're drawing attention to, on Monday. Closing the power station will lose twenty-five jobs, so we're doing twenty-five high-profile kidnaps. Both wir MPs are game, and the leader o' the cooncil, and one of the BBC Radio Shetland journalists. Charlie's friends wi' the husband o' a weel-kent Norwegian model, that'll add an international slant an' a bit o' glamour, and we hae a German artist working at the Sumburgh light, and she's willing too. Wha else?' She began ticking them off on her fingers. 'We want twenty-five o' them, to represent the lost jobs. The head warden at the Sumburgh bird reserve, and the boss o' Shetland Arts, and your minister, Cass. And I saw the pair of you there, and thought, well, it would be fine to have a high-up policeman too, if Gavin would play ball.'

'I'm not that high up,' Gavin said, 'but I don't see why not.' He looked at me. 'Monday. What's our schedule, Cass?'

'Sailing first thing from Fetlar, around the top of Unst, past the cliffs of Eshaness and into Hillswick for a Shetland meal and an evening's entertainment at the St Magnus Bay Hotel. More fiddles, and a local guide to tell us stories. Oh, and a visit to the wildlife sanctuary in the morning, to see their seals and otters.'

'When do you get into Hillswick?' Inga asked.

'18.00,' I said. 'We'll anchor up in the bay and ferry folk to the beach in the dinghies.'

Inga made a face. 'You won't be going ashore in Fetlar on the Monday morning?'

I shook my head.

'OK,' Inga said, 'then we'll make you our last kidnap, Gavin. If you get the first boat ashore, we'll take you from Hillswick. We're holding everyone at a secret location, then doing the big release for the TV cameras at eight, in time for the evening news. We'll definitely be on the Scottish news, and we're hoping for the BBC an' aa.' She got up. 'Thanks to you. Enjoy your weekend, and see you on Monday.'

Gavin made a *You're welcome* gesture, and rose as she did. 'See you then,' I agreed.

We watched her walk along the pontoon, get into her car, and drive off. The sky had cleared while we'd been talking, and the first faint star shone out above the hills. Gavin's arms slid around my waist and drew me back against his chest. 'Do you think we'll be allowed to go to bed now?'

'Definitely bedtime,' I agreed, and turned to kiss him.

PART THREE

Bluff and Counter-bluff

CHAPTER EIGHT

Saturday 31st July, Lerwick

Low water 03.45 BST (0.6 m)
High water 09.28 (2.0 m)
Low water 15.56 (0.7 m)
High water 22.13 (2.0 m)

Moonrise 02.58; sunrise 04.45; moonset 19.31; sunset 21.36
Crescent moon

Ah, it was good to wake in my own *Khalida*, even if it took me a moment to orientate myself to being in the forepeak berth. I lifted my head to look out through the open companionway. It had to be just before four; the last rags of darkness still clung to the land, but the sky and sea were both milk-white. Gavin was warm beside me; I curled up into his back and dozed again until six, when the alarm went off. We kissed, and stayed in bed for a bit longer, then he rose, wrapping his kilt round him, and went out into the cockpit to turn the gas on. 'Cup of tea?'

'Luxury.' I stretched lazily, then sat up to shove the foredeck hatch open. Cold air flowed in on me. It was clear daylight now, with the makings of a bonny day. The sky was streaked with parallel bands of cloud, dazzling white in the east; the grey sea was glass-calm within the marina, but fretted with a light wind in the voe. A tirrick dived with a splash just astern of us, and rose again with a fish glinting it its beak.

We showered in the clubhouse, then had breakfast facing each other across my little prop-leg table. Everything was blessedly familiar: the china bowls with the faint gold rim, the faded navy cushions, the locker smell on the cardboard cereal cartons. Gavin looked across at me and smiled. 'Home?'

'Home,' I agreed. 'But *Sørlandet* is home too, only in a different sort of way. Workplace-home, without the chance of going home-home every night.' I drew my finger along the gold-grained wood. 'It's good to be back.'

Gavin looked down at the tea in his mug, and swirled it round between his brown hands. 'If you could keep *Khalida*, could you bear to give up *Sørlandet*?'

I couldn't answer. Of course I could still sail the wide oceans in *Khalida*, but she was small and slow. If I took off on her, it would be a year, two years, three, before I came back. *Sørlandet* was a better key to adventure: Tierra del Fuego, the storms of the Roaring Forties, the Polynesian islands. I'd see tropical stars again, and feel that velvety warmth in the night. There would be flying fish on the decks . . . but in *Khalida*, they'd be on my own decks, and I'd have the immensity of the ocean all to myself.

The silence stretched between us. 'I don't know,' I said at last. 'It's not the boat, it's the sea. The ocean, out there, calling me.' I looked straight at him. 'But I'm thinking about it.' I spread my hands. 'I'm trying . . . will that do?'

He nodded. 'That'll do.' Suddenly, he leapt up. 'Creator Lord, is that the time? Your Dad'll be here any moment.'

Dad drove us in, with Gavin in the front beside him, talking about turbines. Cat sulked beside me in the back. His projected morning had included a lengthy foray along the shore – the point at which I'd grabbed him – and no doubt a casual pass by the sheltered housing in case any sympathetic pensioner had a bit of fish or saucer of milk to spare. Not even Inga's fish consoled him. He folded his front paws, greeted my attempts at reconciliation with a warning flick of his tail, and was out of the car and trotting up *Sørlandet*'s gangplank the second I opened the door.

Alain was on duty now, watching us arrive from the aft deck, a cup of coffee in his hand. It irked me to have him come to the gangplank to meet us. 'Hey, Cass.' He held out his hand to Gavin. 'Rafael Martin, third mate.'

They shook hands. Gavin gave him a long, thoughtful look, face closed into that police blank honed on provocative teenagers after pub closing time. I couldn't read what he was thinking. 'Gavin Macrae.'

I could see Alain not being sure what to make of him. He'd seen the kilt as a Scottish joke, but Gavin's air of being somebody to reckon with, an eagle surveying his own world, made him pause to reassess. He shot a quick glance at me, another back at Gavin. 'I wouldn't have taken you for a police officer.'

'We come in all sizes,' Gavin said equably.

'Glad to meet you,' Alain said. 'Cass has told me all about you.'

I wasn't going to give him the satisfaction of a reaction. Gavin's arm went round my waist. 'Chatting? That doesn't sound like you.'

His tone was light. I strived for an equal casualness. 'Oh, I didn't need to chat. Tall ships are a hotbed of gossip. They'd have had you a chief superintendent, at the very least.'

Round one to us. Alain stepped back from the gangway and launched into round two. 'You all set to give us this tour of Lerwick, then, Cass?'

'Oh,' I said, disconcerted. 'Aren't you on duty?'

'You're not the only one who can hand over to a watch leader,' he retorted.

Dash. As if I wasn't nervous enough, without having to worry about what mischief Alain would be stirring against Gavin behind my back. I went into officer mode. 'All well during the night?'

His eyes danced. 'The price of British drink was appreciated.'

By which he meant, I supposed, that everyone had hangovers; though naturally not Petter, who was waiting for me up on the aft deck. I reported in, thanked him for letting me have the night off, and promised to do the same for him sometime. Captain Sigurd did the official morning muster and headcount, then Gavin and I headed out onto the pier to gather my group together.

We were moored in the centre of Lerwick, looking straight across the Esplanade car park at the line of shops along what had once been the waterfront. A shiny red bus with snail horns protruding from its forehead was squatting on the pier, waiting to take trainees on a 'Historic Shetland' trip down to St Ninian's Isle and Jarlshof. For those who preferred, I'd offered to guide a walk around Lerwick. When we gathered on the pier I found I had most of my watch and a handful from the other watches, twenty-four in total, all looking at me as if I was an expert. It was paralysingly unnerving, and Alain's eye on me didn't help.

I began by explaining the buildings we could see. Facing us was the road going up into Commercial Street, known locally as Da Street, with the Market Cross in the middle, and the tourist office behind. Moving to the right, I showed them Don Leslie's, where we bought sweeties as children, then the white harbourmaster's house. The town ran upwards in a ladder of grey rooftops, up to the red Victorian baronial crenellations of the town hall.

I was just pointing out The Shetland Fudge Company for take-home presents when I saw Daniel coming out of the narrow lane beside it, walking quickly as if he was worried he'd be late. He saw our group and stopped dead, eyes scanning us all in an irresolute way, as if he hadn't expected so many of us. His gaze sharpened on Oliver, pointing out a bobbing guillemot to Laura, then he saw me looking, and turned his head away. It was as if he'd gone out to get some information and wanted to report back privately, before the tour began, only he'd left it too late. He might, of course, have been up photographing the town hall in the early sun, or admiring the flower park, but he'd shown no signs of being an enthusiastic photographer. He'd mentioned climbing, so I supposed a quick, illegal ascent of the fort wall before anyone was up was just possible, but he wasn't carrying any rope. He couldn't have been shopping so early. Nothing opened till nine o'clock, and if he'd been after a daily paper he was definitely out of luck; they didn't arrive till ten.

I was thinking this through while I was still describing the fudge known as Trow's Bogies, and Oliver turned at last to look. His gaze passed indifferently over Daniel – too indifferently? Then Daniel's head went up. He'd seen something on the pavement opposite us. Someone? I scanned the seafront: a group of people waiting at the bus stop, a woman in a red jacket using the TSB cash machine, several teenagers sitting on Don Leslie's windowsill, a mother with a pram going up towards the Market Cross, a yellow jacket coming down from the tourist office.

Daniel eased himself back into the shadows, but I could still make out the paler blur of his face, watching us.

I'd tell Gavin about this later.

We went left first, past the shop with the huge K-boot on its wall, past the peerie dock, filled now with yachts fluttering the flags of every nation, and up by the Queens Hotel to the flagged road that was bounded by Lerwick's oldest houses on one side and sandy beaches on the other. We paused at the Lodberrie so that I could point out the window slits in the store for drying hung fish, and the pulley and double doors just above high-tide level for loading goods into boats and getting cargoes ashore. We walked past the beach of clear, clear water washing over coloured stones, and saw the Foula mailboat doing duty as a shed roof, and the projecting rock known as the Duke's Neb, in doubtful compliment to His Grace of Wellington.

It was at that point I began to get a prickling feeling between my shoulder blades. I resisted the urge to turn and look. 'These big houses were built as merchants' town residences, but this one's a children's home now, and that's a hotel.'

While I spoke, I glanced backwards, and caught a flash of yellow out of the corner of my eye, that Formica yellow of an oilskin jacket, slipping out of sight around the corner. There had been someone in yellow coming down from the tourist office – the person Daniel had been watching out for?

'A children's home?' Oliver asked, in my ear.

I turned to face him, seeing out of the corner of my eye that Gavin's head was up, and he too was looking in the direction of the yellow flash, mouth closed in a thoughtful line.

I tried to remember what I knew about Leog. 'There's a respite centre for children with special needs, and there's one for . . .' I tried to think of a PC equivalent for 'bad bairns', and substituted, 'children who've been in trouble.' I turned my head to nod at the steel-encased drainpipes, and caught that yellow flash again. 'The boxing round the drainpipes is because one of the residents took to climbing up onto the roof.'

Gavin nodded, with the air of someone who'd been called out to rooftop children. Alain gave it a quick upwards glance. If he'd been sent there, he'd have climbed it too, and danced on the roof afterwards.

I kept going, leading them on at a gentle stroll, with a weather-eye cocked behind me. We went past the town's first bank, with the safe reputedly still in the basement, past the former sheriff's house to Battery Close, where there had been a gun emplacement in the World Wars, and back up by one of the town's steep lanes, to show them where the poor lived, ten to a room, with an open sewer running down between the houses. Finally, we reached the town hall, and I ushered them in between the dolphin lamp posts. I gave a last, casual look behind me as I reached the top step. Nothing; then there was a flash of yellow, as someone in a waterproof jacket turned their back to me and dived into Pitt Lane. I knew Gavin had seen it too; he gave me a bright glance, but said nothing.

Male, female? I couldn't be certain.

We followed my group through the imposing doorway. 'Downstairs is the council chamber.' They had a quick peek in, then we climbed the wide stone steps into a blaze of stained glass light. I gave them a moment to take in the beamed ceiling with its painted shields, and the intricate rose window, which cast a patterned carpet on the polished floor. 'These are Victorian images of some of the key figures in our Norse history.' I gestured towards the left-hand corner and hoped nobody would ask searching questions.

'He's got a raven on his head!' Laura said.

'He's Harald Fairhair, who first settled Shetland. They used ravens to navigate.' I knew this bit. 'They knew Shetland was two

111

days' journey from Norway, so they'd row or sail out to sea for a day and a half, then release a raven. It would fly in the direction of land, and they'd follow it.'

'Like Noah's ark,' the teacher commented.

'The next pair are bishops.' The mitres were a clue. 'That's Bishop William the Old of Orkney, who went on a crusade with Earl Rognvald. Earl Rognvald was a poet and adventurer, and he was the one who built St Magnus Cathedral, in Orkney, in honour of his murdered uncle.' I turned to point Earl Rognvald out: 'Over there, with the Arab headdress, and the chain-mail socks.'

They revolved obediently to look, which gave me the chance to skip the next couple of windows, a Norse husband and wife and a couple of warriors with shields, about whom I had no information whatever.

'The girl in the alcove window is the Maid of Norway, Margaret, who died in Orkney on her way to marry Edward of England.' I had a sudden blank as to which Edward. 'Then King Haakon, and Earl Rognvald, the crusader, and this last one is the marriage window, commemorating how Shetland went from being Norse to being Scottish.' I'd learnt this bit off, because people always wondered why the isles were so Norse. 'Princess Margaret of Denmark and Norway became engaged to King James III of Scotland in 1468, and her father had no money for her dowry, so he pawned the Northern Isles to Scotland.' Nearly done. 'Tradition has it the windows were set the wrong way round, which is why they're looking away from each other.'

I gave them a bit of time to admire and photograph, then ushered them all forwards in front of me, pausing at the door to wait for Alain, who was still admiring Earl Rognvald.

'Sounds an interesting bloke,' he commented. He turned to look at me. 'Have you read any of his poetry?'

I gave him a *for goodness' sake* look. 'Do I look like I read poetry?'

'You might have hidden depths.'

I shook my head. 'Norse poetry's not in them. As far as I can gather, the Vikings spent most of their time behaving like quarrelsome three-year-olds.'

'Shame on you, deriding our heritage like that.' *Our?* I turned quickly towards him, but he was already starting towards the door.

Our last stop was just two minutes away: past the Garrison Theatre, where our Brownie pack had shrieked with laughter at the panto every Christmas, and down to Fort Charlotte. I ushered them towards the arched stone gateway. 'This fort belongs to the Territorial Army now. It was first built for the Dutch wars, then rebuilt for the American ones. Now look at this for a view.'

We all paused to admire the sound, with Bressay green across the water, and *Sørlandet*'s masts soaring over the grey roofs of the town. The group took photos of the battlement wall, and the black cannons against the dancing sea, and I juggled cameras for one of all of us, with *Sørlandet* behind – and then, glory be, my stint was over.

'Just down there,' I said, pointing to Da Street, 'is Lerwick's main shopping street.' I led them through the arch, down the last ten metres of cobbles, pointed them forwards to souvenirs, knitwear and The Shetland Times Bookshop, and waved them off with a sigh of relief.

'Hey,' Laura said, beside me, 'why don't we go for a coffee somewhere?' She looked round and spotted Fine Peerie Cakes behind us. 'You've done a great job, you deserve a rest and a piece of cake.'

'I certainly do.' I flicked a glance at Gavin, and turned to Laura. 'Better still, a hot chocolate with cream on top.' Out of the corner of my eye, I saw Gavin nod.

'Great idea,' Oliver said heartily. 'On you go, Laura. We'll find you and Cass a nice cafe somewhere, and I'll inspect the shops, and take you along to the best knitwear.'

'There's a cafe right there,' she retorted, 'and I'm not taking fashion hints from any man who thinks cabbage green is a colour.'

Fine Peerie Cakes was a little friendly place with flowered oilcloth covering the tables, plump china teapots and an array of cupcakes with whirl-piled icing. We sat down at the window, and in three minutes the woman in charge came bustling over with two fat cups smelling deliciously of chocolate, and lippering over with swirled cream.

'My favourite cure-all,' I said. I took a sip of chocolate and cream mixed, and leant back with a sigh. 'Goodness, that was exhausting. Give me a race in a force 7 any day.'

Laura laughed. 'Yes, I'm beginning to feel my ankle again. I thought it was fine, but maybe not.'

'Your fall yesterday?'

She nodded, and smiled. 'I'm used to skiing falls. Stone staircases are much harder.' The smile changed to a frown. 'But I'm still not sure how I came such a cropper. Whether I tripped and fell, and brought Oliver down, or whether he fell on top of me. It all happened too fast.'

I kept silent, letting her think.

'He tripped, I think. Yes, I'm certain. I was going downwards, and then there was a scuffle behind me, and a clang, then I felt him push me, and then we were both rolling downwards.'

The white look was in her face again. I remembered how uneasy she'd been when they'd first climbed the mast, and wondered if she was trying to share suspicions she didn't dare articulate. I tried to start her talking. 'Is he your only brother?'

She nodded. 'There's just the two of us. Mum and Dad, well, Dad

114

was a doctor, and Mum was in a firm of accountants in Edinburgh. My great-great-grandfather was one of the original partners. That's where we both work now.' She smiled. 'Nothing like as exciting as a tall ship, but I enjoy it. Maths was my subject at uni. St Andrews, I loved it there. I got involved in everything – they had ceilidhs and sports clubs and an operatic society – all sorts of fun things. I even went on a glider once.'

'Did Oliver go there too?'

The blonde head shook. She made a face, mouth pulled down. 'Oliver, well, he's less settled. Not really academic. Oh, I don't mean he's not clever, school just wasn't his kind of place.'

Sometimes it was true. As a teenager in France, I'd been too homesick, too land-bound, to give the work my very best shot. Other times, it was what parents said about their children rather than the blunt 'bone idle and disruptive with it' that teachers would say in the privacy of the staffroom. Laura seemed to be an indulgent sister who accepted the family excuses line. Not that I was much good at people, but I'd learnt over the years to assess who could be trusted with what, and I wouldn't have put Oliver in charge of anything that required sustained concentration. He'd fall into chat with the first person who passed, and forget he was steering the ship.

'He had a shot at one of the Edinburgh colleges, but it just wasn't him. There was a row about that, of course.' She made a hands out gesture. 'Oh, I don't remember, I was busy swotting for exams and touring possible universities. But he wasn't going back to college, so Mum got him into the firm.'

She paused to sip her chocolate. I remembered Dad's friend's account of the family. Laura didn't outshine Oliver in looks or charm, but she'd been a stayer at school. Her graduation photo, but not his, would have adorned the family mantelpiece . . . Oliver wouldn't have liked that.

'He's good with figures, and she thought he'd be great on the selling side, but his heart just wasn't in it, you know? She was disappointed about that, she hoped he'd enjoy being practical. But there isn't anything else he really wants to do either, so he's just stayed with the firm, doing bits and pieces.'

'While you're flying upwards in it,' I suggested.

She nodded, mouth still turned down. 'I'm one of the directors now. There's always been a family seat on the board. Oliver was—' She came to a sudden stop, mouth twitching, eyes turned away from me, as if she was remembering something unpleasant. That went with the Oliver type too, I thought; not willing to work themselves, but resenting the promotion of others, especially his little sister.

'He thought it was unfair, since he was older, and the boy?' I suggested.

She laughed at that. 'Yes, how old-fashioned can you get? There was a row about it, just before the crash.' She broke off abruptly, mouth working. Tears filled her blue eyes. She took a deep breath and went on. 'Dad was adamant. I'd worked for it, he said. They were going to create an extra seat for me.' Her hands came back up to clutch the cup. 'Poor Oliver, it made it harder for him, that they'd been on bad terms before they died.'

That was a bit of gossip Dad's friend hadn't known.

Laura's eyes brimmed over. 'And then, after all, I got Mum's seat.'

There was nothing I could say. I waited in silence while she mopped her eyes with her hankie. 'Sorry,' she said.

'No, it's OK.' Seven months ago, Oliver had said. The worst of the shock should have worn off by now. That white look about her eyelids, and the blankness of her eyes should have been replaced by grieving; unless something else had brought it back – something like the fear that her adored, indulged big brother was trying to get rid of her.

I wondered whose idea this holiday had been, and felt that was something I could safely ask. 'I know it's hard, but don't think about it just now. Focus on your holiday. A tall ship must be the cleanest break from reality that you can get – a really good idea.'

She nodded. 'That's what Oliver said. We'd always meant to go to the northern isles as a family.'

Oliver's idea. I didn't like this: the sister a high-flyer, the brother in the family firm at the 'find him a job' level, the row over his position and hers – the row that had blown up just before a car crash that didn't seem to have any cause. *She hoped he'd enjoy being practical* . . . Then that fall down the stairs. *I felt him push me* . . . I was about to take the bull by the horns, lean over and say, 'What's wrong?' when there was a cheerful bustle at the door and Oliver came in, with Gavin behind him.

They headed straight for the counter and ordered coffee, then Oliver came over to us with a plate of assorted fancies: a chocolate brownie, a cupcake with a swirl of moon-frosted icing, slices of lemon meringue pie and pecan maple cake.

'I thought you'd want some forbidden carbohydrate,' Oliver said. He'd left Gavin to pay for it, I noticed.

'I never refuse fancies,' I said cheerfully. 'What d'you say, Laura?'

Her smile was steadier now. 'But there's no gym to work it off.'

'There's a whole sailing ship,' Oliver retorted, 'with three masts, and the voyage to Fetlar this afternoon. Plenty of exercise opportunity there.'

Gavin, coming over now, gave me a bright, intelligent glance and sat down beside me. He offered the cake plate to Laura, then to me. I took the lemon meringue pie. It was beautifully tangy; worth the calories.

The men seemed to have walked halfway along Da Street, up

one of the lanes and back down another before coming to join us. 'It's a quaint town,' Oliver said. 'All this grey stone, and the little alleys running seawards.'

'I must try to visit the museum this afternoon, before we go,' Gavin said. 'Do you know if there's a tradition of Inuit men visiting?'

I gave him a blank look. 'Not that I've ever heard. Do you mean on the whaling ships?'

Gavin shook his head. 'Blown here from Greenland. There were several sightings of them in Orkney, and one even made it to Aberdeen – his kayak's in a museum there.'

I suspected a programme on the History channel during quiet night shifts. 'We're a long way from Greenland.'

'There was a little Ice Age in early modern times that extended the size of Greenland almost to Iceland, and they came along the edge of it, then across the sea. Apparently, that's where the Orcadian idea of the Finn men came from, the sorcerers who could raise a magic cloak and disappear on water. The Inuit could raise a sail on their canoe, but because it was so low in the water, they could also hide among the waves the moment they dropped it.'

The Finns again . . . 'I thought the Finns were a Norse thing,' I said. I would need to ask Magnie more. 'In Shetland they were Laplanders. Shaman people.'

Gavin shook his head. 'In Orkney they were linked with the selkie people.' He turned his head to smile at me. 'There's an Orcadian woman after your own heart too, Cass. Isobel Gunn, from the early 1800s. She dressed as a man and signed up with the Hudson's Bay Company. One of the best loggers they had, and apparently fooled everyone until she became pregnant.'

'Not quite everyone then,' Oliver said.

'So what happened to her?' Laura asked.

'Well, naturally, she couldn't be allowed to continue as a logger.'

'Naturally not,' I agreed. 'Even though she was one of the best.'

'So she became a housemaid instead, until they could ship her home.'

'Much more suitable,' I said, drily, and Gavin smiled.

There was a sudden throat-clearing noise beside us, then the grandfather clock began its chimes. Eleven o'clock. We were hoping to make the 11.30 Mass, since there would be no chance to get to church tomorrow. I flashed Gavin a quick glance, and then smiled at Laura and Oliver. 'We need to leave you – I have stuff to do in town.' Why did it sound so show-off to say, *I'm going to church*? I picked my cap up from the table, and put it on, checking its straightness in the clock glass, and looked over at Laura. 'I hope you're OK now.'

She nodded and smiled. 'I'm fine. We'll explore carefully.'

'You do that. See you on board.'

We came out into the bustle of a Saturday morning street, with country folk in ganseys carrying shopping bags, and toonies in light summer frocks strolling and meeting their friends.

'If we have time,' Gavin said, 'I'd like to drop in on the police station and say hello to the folk I've met here.'

Sergeant Freya Peterson, no doubt. 'Course,' I said lightly. 'I'll just check on Cat, then head for the church – meet you there?'

'Twenty minutes?'

'Plenty of time.'

He set off at an unhurried walk up the lane by the town hall, kilt swinging, and I headed for the ship: down past the Clydesdale Bank and towards the sea, where she lay swan-white against the pier, her long masthead banners flying out in the breeze. It would be a good sail up to Fetlar. I wanted to run, but a good officer never gave the appearance of being hurried, according to Captain Sigurd, so I compromised on a brisk walk.

As I came around the bank corner, I stopped dead. Alain was standing at the foot of the road, two hundred yards from me. He was talking to someone, a woman, smaller than him, hands gesticulating. Even as I looked he glanced forward and gestured to the ship, and I shrank back into the shadows.

Her back was to me. She had straight, dark hair cut in a chin-length bob. I couldn't see any more than that, no details of her face or skin, though there was something foreign about that dark, glossy hair . . . French, like Alain, or Spanish?

She was wearing a bright yellow jacket.

CHAPTER NINE

I couldn't spy on one of my fellow-crew, and I couldn't ask either. I didn't want even to imagine Alain's amused look if I asked, like a jealous lover, 'Who was that woman?' I turned my shoulder on them both and headed for the ship at a measured officer walk. By the time I was at the gangplank, Alain was walking along to the toilets, and the yellow jacket was nowhere in sight.

The ship was open to visitors now, with Lars, Alain's watch leader, at the gangplank, issuing laminated visitor tickets and taking names. It was a new system which, in theory, should mean we would be able to name everyone on board if we needed to. The idea was that you doled out a ticket to each visitor, who then had to print his or her name beside the ticket's number on the register sheet. I suspected that there would be a flaw in practice, but at least it meant nobody could hide on board to hitch a ride to wherever. There were a good few folk aboard already, strolling round the decks and looking up at the masts.

I went below to check on Cat. He was settled comfortably on my berth, with the air of someone who'd eaten too well to need any more tinned stuff. There was a suspicious raw-fish smell about his paws. I had no doubt he'd remembered the fish shop opposite, and tried his luck. I left him to sleep it off, and headed towards the gangplank.

That flash of yellow caught my eye again, as someone folded up a jacket. It was Alain's woman, hair glinting in the sun. She was queueing up to come aboard. I gave her a swift glance as I came down the gangplank, but she turned her head away, as if she sensed me watching. I got only an impression of high cheekbones and a bronzed complexion.

Well, why shouldn't she want to come and see our ship? Perhaps she'd simply been asking him if we were open to visitors. I shoved the woman out of my mind, and strode swiftly along the seafront and up to our church. Mass would be in the little chapel, but I went to the church first, and felt its peace enfold me. It was beautiful, our church, with a green carpet sweeping between the wooden pews and a tall, carved altar like a miniature cathedral outlined against the gold paint behind it. I knelt in a patch of sunlight, chequered green and white from the panes of the tall windows, and prayed: for Maman and Dad, for Gavin and myself, for our lost child, for Laura and Oliver, and for Alain, whatever he was up to.

I was about to rise when the door I'd come in by snicked on its latch. There were footsteps, then someone settled into the pew behind me. Alain's voice came suddenly in my ear. 'You don't still believe in all this?'

I wasn't going to leap up, as if I was ashamed of praying. I turned my head to look over my shoulder at him, heart thumping. He was Alain, and he knew me, and he'd slipped up. 'Why did you say *still*?'

For a moment he was at a loss. His mouth fell half open, as if he didn't understand what I was talking about, then his eyes cleared. 'Oh. Well, it's the twenty-first century.' He gestured round at the candles, the altar table with its embroidered cloth, the flowers arranged beside the tabernacle. 'All this superstition. Angels and saints and the like. In this day and age?'

The French militant rationalist at his worst. He could say what he liked now; he was pretending to be Rafael, and he'd made a quick recovery, but no Spaniard, steeped in the traditions of a country that had never disowned its Catholic heritage, would have spoken like that. 'Time makes no difference to whether something's true or not,' I said. 'If you feel like that about it, then don't you think it's a bit of an insult to the feelings of the people who created it for you to be in here at all?'

His eyes danced. 'Can't I admire it as a work of art?'

'It isn't a work of art,' I retorted. 'It's a church. A building created for a purpose.'

He laughed and came round to sit beside me. 'That's better. That spark in your eyes suits you. Let me take you to lunch.'

I shook my head and looked him straight in the eye. 'I'm waiting for Gavin. We're going to Mass together.'

His brows rose. '*Kinder, Küche, Kirche.*'

I felt my temper rising. 'Now, if you don't mind, I'd like to be left in peace.'

He shrugged, and rose, then looked down for a parting shot. 'Who were you praying for so earnestly anyway?'

'You,' I said. It silenced him for a moment, leaving his face naked and young. Then he turned on his heel and left. The snick of the door echoed for a long moment after he'd gone.

There was something constrained about Gavin's manner when he joined me. I wasn't sure whether he'd seen Alain leaving the church, or whether meeting up with Freya Peterson had reminded him how much easier it would be to have a wife who didn't hanker for the ocean. We stood side by side for the readings and went up for communion, but I didn't feel that usual sense of togetherness, and we were silent as we walked back down to the ship.

Gavin glanced at the busy decks. 'Listen, I'll go and check out the museum.' He turned his head to look upwards at the town hall clock. 'Leaving at two, right?'

'Muster at one, though.'

'A very quick look.' He strode off in the direction of the museum, head up, kilt swinging, and I felt a pang at my heart as he became lost among the crowd on the Esplanade. *Goodness' sake, Cass* . . . I checked my cap was straight, and joined Jonas at the gangplank. 'How's the new system working?'

'A bit complicated.' He grimaced at the clipboard in his left hand, the wad of laminated tickets in his right. 'I'm having to explain it over every time.'

'You look very efficient,' Oliver said, appearing suddenly in front of me among the line of tourists. 'Do I need to sign back in?'

I shook my head. 'Just make sure your peg in the peg board is in the right place.' I looked past him. 'Is Laura OK?'

'Yeah, sure. She was just a bit stiff after her tumble yesterday.' He gave me that dazzling smile again, and I felt a trickle of unease down my spine. He thought he was clever enough to get away with anything, and cute enough to talk his way out of punishment if he was caught. *I felt him push me* . . . 'I can see why you need this system. I've been exploring the ship, and there are a hundred places stowaways could hide.'

'Oh?' I said, watching him. 'Where would you hide a stowaway, then?'

He waved a hand. 'Oh, there are the tunnels below the banjer, and the sail locker, and the kitchen area, and the cubby-hole where the anchor chain goes. Loads of places.' The hand rose in a *Wait up* gesture. 'But don't worry.' That untrustworthy smile again. 'I'm not planning to elope with a local girl, like your broch couples. Your captain looks like he'd crack down hard on any monkey business.' He paused to scan the busy pier. 'Laura's fine. She went off shopping.'

He sketched a cheerful wave at me and strolled onto the ship, then, five minutes later, came off again, being charmingly helpful to a family party with a double buggy, a toddler and a five-year-old. He helped carry the buggy down the gangplank, prised the tickets from the mother's hand and passed them to Jonas, then waved at me again and strolled off. I watched his upright back crossing the pier and wondered if Laura had felt safer shopping on her own.

The ship was filled with people: curious teenagers, older men in fishermen's jackets, women in jeans and vest tops, a family with half a dozen loose children swarming around them. Out of the corner of my eye, I saw Petter moving forward to intercept them and take them aft for shots at the wheel. I turned my head to give a *Good man* nod. There was chattering and laughter on deck, with people posing in the bows for selfies, or getting Nils, who was on duty there, to take a group shot. If you hadn't photographed yourself being there and shared it round your entire acquaintance, you hadn't been. Cat had obviously decided a bit of admiration would be acceptable, for he was holding court from his bench on the aft deck, his spectacular plumed tail curled round his white paws.

Oliver's comments about stowing away had unsettled me. Oliver, the king, the golden son. I tried to think of ways of circumventing the system. Getting on without being given a ticket . . . no, I didn't see how you could do that. Jonas was bang in front of the gangplank, handing them out, and although it was possible to climb aboard at other places, you couldn't do it without being noticed. You'd have to get aboard, plus ticket, then find a way of getting the ticket off without you. If you came on board with a group, you could get them to bring the ticket off, shoving them at the gangplank officer in a fistful – but of course that meant accomplices. To come on board alone, and stay there . . . You could drop the ticket on the ground just as a lot of people were coming off, then nip back up the gangplank. When it was picked up, the officer would assume it had come from the crowd. I started watching groups more carefully, but there were few groups of potential stowaways, just family groups. You could . . . you could . . . I ran out of ideas, shook my head, and returned to standing to attention. My back was beginning to feel as if it had gone solid. Not much longer.

The snail-horned bus returned at 12.30. The bus door opened and the trainees piled out, chattering enthusiastically to each other. Oliver's stowaway could have waited for this moment and slipped in among the crew members. I scanned the pier quickly, and saw nobody hanging about, ready to slip. My experiences on our Belfast voyage had made me paranoid; or I'd been thinking too much about that Eynhallow story, with the extra people who went missing . . .

12.40. The trainees who had stayed in Lerwick were straggling back aboard now, carrying bags blazoned with The Shetland Fudge Company, Jamieson's of Shetland or The Shetland Times Bookshop, and chatting to each other about what they'd seen in their morning. Listening in, the two older men had gone to see the boat hall in the museum, with Shetland model boats suspended from the ceiling so that you could admire the boat shape, and then headed for the Marlex to try the local beer. Fireman Berg had joined them there. The teacher had several bags of all-over jumpers and gloves for friends, which she was showing to the wife of the couple. The family had been to the Up Helly Aa exhibition. There was no sign yet of Laura – and then I saw her crossing the car park, striding as if she was worried she was late, with a bookshop carrier bag in one hand, and a knitwear one in the other.

Agnetha came over to us. 'Many still to come off?'

Jonas glanced at his list. 'Four. A family party – those ones up there, trying the wheel for size.'

'I'll clear them for you,' I said.

I went up and chatted to the family for a few minutes, then explained that we were preparing for sea, and if they weren't planning to sail to Fetlar today, they might want to go back ashore. The father, a burly fisherman in an all-over jumper with an anchor and cable pattern, laughed at that. 'Lass, dinna tempt me. A voyage aboard would be a rare treat.' He lifted up the younger boy. 'Come on, now, Robbie, boy, we need to leave. Thanks to you, lass.'

I watched them head off down the gangplank. At the far end of the pier, beside the old LHD building, Oliver was lounging towards the boat with long, unhurried strides that suggested he was permanently late and didn't care. Daniel was walking beside him, but as they came in view of the ship, he turned away with a wave of the hand and crossed the road to the Spinning Wheel, ducking his head away from the ship as if he didn't want them to be seen together. I saw Gavin give them a quick glance as he crossed the pier to come aboard.

'Good museum?' I asked.

'It was very interesting. I didn't see the half of it – I got stuck in the crofting life part, and never got upstairs at all.' His hand touched mine. 'Next time.'

I turned my hand to cling to his for a moment. 'Yes, a proper visit, together.'

He nodded. 'Muster?'

'Any moment,' I agreed.

Daniel had come aboard now, scurrying across the gangplank, and five minutes after him, on the dot of five to one, my friend Magnie came across the pier with his rolling seaman's stride. He knew all the stories about Fetlar and enjoyed nothing so much as a new audience, so I'd suggested to Agnetha, and she'd suggested to the captain, that he would be a good guide to have on board.

He'd dressed for the part. He had his best seaman's cap on his red-fair curls, and his ruddy cheeks were shining with a recent shave. He was wearing the last all-over gansey his late mother had knitted for him, horizontal stripes of stars and anchors in shades of blue with dazzlingly white bands between them, along with black cloth breeks instead of jeans, and his funeral shoes, polished to a mirror gloss. He greeted me with a raised hand and explained to Jonas, 'Magnie Williamson. Cass aksed me aboard to tell your trainees a bit aboot Shetland.'

Jonas waved him through, and went up to Agnetha. 'That's all the visitors off.' He checked the pegboard and stowed it away. 'Everyone on board now.'

'Call the trainees up on deck.'

Jonas disappeared down into the banjer. Gradually the trainees straggled upwards and formed into their lines, with Gavin at the end of my watch, sock ribbons and kilt fluttering in the breeze. The watch leaders checked the numbers, and Nils got Jonas to ring eight bells. Now we were back under ship discipline, and all on duty for making the ship ready for sea: securing loose items, hauling the hawsers back on board and retrieving the fenders as our ship moved away from her berth.

The pilot steered us out of the north mouth. We came past the old stone walls that kept water from town, past the glass block of Mareel and the brown sails of the museum, cradled behind Hay's Dock, where ships had left for the whaling each spring; past the cargo ferry and the new pier with the fishing boats moored up. The seals came out to swarm around us as we passed the fish factory, huge grey selkies with long snouts like pointer dogs. Once we'd passed the Skibby Baas we were into open sea, with the two skerries of the Brethren and Green Holm before us and the messy bulk of the Rova Head landfill site well astern.

Magnie was on duty already, leaning against the port rail, with Laura and the Danish couple beside him. 'That rock there, off the point, that's called the Unicorn Baa, after a ship that struck on it. She was chasing the Earl of Bothwell after the Battle of Carberry Hill, where Mary, Queen of Scots was defeated.'

Beside me, Gavin nodded. We'd stood back to let the trainees take the rail, shoulder against shoulder, with the mainmast ropes warm on our backs. 'He ended up a prisoner in Denmark,' he murmured. His manner was back to normal. 'The mummy they display almost certainly isn't his.'

'More late-night shifts watching the History channel?'

He shook his head. 'Not these days. That stuck in my mind from years ago.'

It would be a fine passage. It was still a bonny day, with only a rim of sun-whitened clouds on the horizon, and a southerly force 5 sweeping us upwards. Nils began setting the sails as soon as we passed the Green Holm. Fetlar was fifty miles from Lerwick, seven hours at seven knots. I'd have liked to go inside Whalsay, to give our trainees a look at the 'Bonny Isle', but the tides didn't fit, so we headed on a straight line outside it. The green land slipped past us, Catfirth, Linganess and Dury Voe, with the cloud shadows chasing each other over the hills.

By the start of my watch the clouds had thickened, and the glimpses of sun were gone, although the day was still bright. There was a white fret on the wave backs, and catspaws swept dark over the sea surface. Whalsay became clearer, with the former laird's house, now converted to the island's junior high school, prominent on the hill. The white superstructures of Shetland's pelagic fishing fleet towered above the breakwater. The marina was filled with smaller shellfish boats that kept the fishermen busy in the eleven months their big boats weren't at sea.

Magnie pointed across the harbour at the little stone house on a rock above it. 'That, now,' he said. 'Have a look through my spyglass. That's an interesting place. In medieval times Shetland was part of what they called the Hanseatic League, and that was one of the trading stations.'

I listened with half an ear as he explained the historic trading links between the Baltic, Norway, Shetland and Scotland, and compared them to the way the big fishing boats operated now, selling their catch electronically as soon as it was in the hold, and taking it to the buyer in Norway, Shetland or Ireland to be processed. The Whalsay folk had seen us coming, of course, and a number of little boats buzzed out from the marina and bounced across the water to circle us, cameras flashing. We forged steadily on between them, with Fetlar ahead. We were making good time; we'd have the anchor dropped by sunset. Beside me, three bells rang: 17.30.

Alain came up beside me then, dressed for duty, cap level on his unruly curls. 'The old boy's a great talker, though it took me a while to understand his accent.'

'He's westside,' I said, and thought, *You grew up with a far stronger, in Yell.*

'Anything here I should know about, once I take over?'

'That's Fetlar, the green island dead ahead. We're making for Houbie, in the Wick of Tresta.'

I was just smoothing out the Fetlar chart to show him when there was a ringing from below us. Laura's head went up, then she fished in her pocket for her mobile. She looked at the display, glanced around, then came aft to the cubbyhole between the engine deckhouse and the aft deck, and leant her shoulder against the white-painted wall there. We heard the snicks of the phone, then her voice floated up to us. 'Hey. It's Laura . . . yes, off Shetland . . . It's great, I'm really enjoying it.' Her voice changed from chatty to businesslike. 'So?'

There was a long silence. I imagined her nodding, below us. 'Yes . . . what kind of figure are we looking at? . . . I understand, of course, but sizeable? . . . OK, yes, when I get back will be fine. We'll need to take this to the board in any case, and they'll want full details.'

On deck, Oliver was looking around as if he was wondering where she'd gone. Alain gave me a quick, bright glance, raising his brows. I shook my head at him and bent back over the chart, trying not to listen.

'Yes . . .' Uncertainty snagged through her voice now. 'Could you tell – was there any indication of who's responsible?' There was silence again, then her voice, flattened with defeat. 'Yes. Yes. No, I won't talk to him yet. Let's save it all till we get back to Edinburgh . . . Thanks, Graham. If you want to have a look in your diary . . .' There was another pause. 'Yes, we get back on the 8th. The 10th would do fine. 09.30. I'll book that with my secretary once the office is open, all directors to attend, an urgent and confidential matter . . . yes, thanks.' She sighed. 'Well, thank you, Graham. See you on the 10th.'

I heard a snick as she put the phone away; just in time, for

Oliver came striding over. 'Lols, I was wondering where you'd got to.' His easy laugh floated up to us. 'You're not supposed to be thinking about business all this trip.'

'I wasn't,' she said. 'Just answering a text.'

'No phones while on duty,' he teased, and drew her back to the centre of the deck. I caught a glimpse of her face, tilting upward to us as he pulled her away. Not shocked, exactly, more the thoughtfulness of someone who'd had a suspicion confirmed. Someone who was setting the wheels in motion.

I gave Alain a sideways glance. He was watching them, frowning. 'I wonder what all that was about?'

'Business,' I said, 'and none of ours.'

'Sizeable, she said. Someone monkeying with the accounts.'

I won't talk to him yet . . . It was jumping to conclusions that she meant Oliver the golden. She could just mean she wouldn't phone the person. But the impression that it had been Oliver they'd been talking about stayed with me. *Was there any indication of who's responsible?* She'd asked that like someone who knew the answer.

'None of our business,' I repeated, and turned back to my chart.

18.30, twenty nautical miles to go. I looked across the ship: at the trainees relaxing on deck, leaning over the rail watching the green land to port, or the sea horizon to starboard. Laura had moved to beside Magnie. He was telling her one of his Finn stories, about an ancestor who'd been on board ship with a Finn man. The ancestor had been worried about his wife, who was expecting their first child, and the Finn man had offered to send his spirit out to see how she was. The end of the tale floated up to me.

'The Finn man went as cold and still as if he was dead, and they were faered to wake him. But by and by the colour came back to his face, and he sat up, and said that yes, all was well, she'd had a baby boy. And there in his hand, to prove he'd been in the house, was the very silver teaspoon me grandfather's grandfather had telt him was on the mantelpiece. And the baby was called John Cast Anderson, after the Finn man, that was his name, Cast, and there's been a baby in every generation o' wir family since with that middle name.'

Several hnefatafl games were in full swing amidships, on a variety of boards. There were two more like Geir's, with the little moulded warriors and cloth board; another was a chess board with twists of paper as pieces, and one was a board drawn in chalk on the deck, with white and grey beach pebbles moving towards each other.

'It looks fun, that,' Alain said, and swung down to Laura. His gestures showed he was suggesting a game; she demurred, then capitulated, and he headed for the officers' area and came back with a chess set and a piece of chalk. When Laura pointed out that there still weren't enough men, he fished in the box and added several draughts counters. They settled down to their game.

Beside them, Oliver had one of the new boards, and was playing Daniel with a frown of concentration over a jutted underlip. By the number of little brown warriors standing beside of the board, he was losing. Even as I watched, Daniel leant over, slid a piece across the board, and scooped another up.

I checked our course, then leant back over my rail. Gavin came up beside me, a mug in each hand. 'Officer Lynch's white chocolate.' I sipped it gratefully. The creamy sugar taste of it was far too sweet for normal use, but out at sea it hit the spot nicely. Gavin had tea; I caught the brown smell of it before the white chocolate drowned everything else. He nodded over his mug at Daniel, whose king was now safely in the corner, though not yet with his sheltering guards that would finish the game; he was amusing himself by picking off Oliver's last warriors. 'If your suspicions are right, that's the brains of the pair.' The game ended; Oliver gave a curt nod and went below. Laura leant over to Daniel. She lifted the little king up.

'He's an awfully bad loser,' she said, laughing.

She was doing well herself, I noticed, with a little line of Alain's black pieces by the chalked edge of their board. I remembered him playing at pool in the students' union. A win was an excuse to offer the girl a drink, but losing meant he could expect her to soothe his supposedly ruffled feelings. Sometimes he lost on purpose.

Alain wasn't my problem any more.

I was off duty and lounging at the rail beside Gavin as we came straight up towards the Wick of Tresta. We caught a glimpse of Brough Lodge on its headland, a long castle front with a jumble of walls behind, before we came into the bay, held in a curve of grey cliffs grown over with grass and sea daisies. A long sandy beach lay at the bay's head, with a loch behind it, and a big house in a clump of trees. We dropped anchor opposite the houses of Houbie, close enough to smell the land world: the mown grass, and the sweetness of the flowers that brightened the green parks.

Magnie let us have a look, then gathered us around him under the silvery glow of the anchor light, switched on, naturally, the second the anchor hit the seabed. 'Now, folk,' he began, 'you're arrived at Fetlar, the most easterly of the larger Shetland islands – only the Out Skerries are closer to Norroway. The historians tell wis that aa o' Shetland was settled by Picts come up fae Scotland afore the Vikings came around 800 AD, but the folk o' Fetlar ken different. This was the island o' the Finn folk, Laplanders, what we'd call Sami folk, and they were shamans. They could send their spirits out into a bird, or a fish, and they could see the future, and control the weather, and I'll tell you mair aboot them in a start.'

He swept his arm out eastwards. 'Now, along that direction is Funzie. It's what they caa' an ophiolite area, the remains of an ancient ocean crust that was thrust up when three continents collided some four hundred million years ago. There's a geowall up there, that'll tell you aa' aboot it, and that's a three-mile walk from the pier here. The Loch o' Funzie is where you'll see the red-necked phalaropes. You canna mistake them – the women hae a bright red patch at each side o' their heads, and they go oot enjoying themselves while the men bide hame on the eggs. You might see red-throated divers too. Mind, you mustna disturb the birds – joost watch fae a distance. Mind, too, no' to go too close to the cliffs. Some are solid, and others might just crumble under you. Keep ahint the wall.'

My gaze went around the trainees and paused on Oliver. His eyes moved up and flicked across at someone on the other side of the ship – Daniel? I snapped my head around and glimpsed a dark, glossy head, whisking out of sight behind the banjer. Then he turned and said something to Laura, and she nodded. A stray puff of wind carried her reply over. 'Yes, I'd like to see those birds. But there was an old house too, we saw it as we came in.'

Magnie heard her and nodded. His other arm went out. 'The other way is Brough Lodge, the big castle-like hoose that you saw as we cam' closer.' He looked at Laura. 'You canna get inside it noo, lass, but it's worth a look from the outside. Brough Lodge Trust are gradually doing it up into a knitting centre. It was the former home o' the Nicolson family. The Interpretative Centre has home movies o' them in the twenties and thirties, that show the house as it was then. The last Lady Nicolson died in Lerwick in the 1980s.'

I'd heard Magnie's mother speak of her. As she'd got older and more reclusive, the house had fallen to ruin around her, and her weekly order from the shop (so gossip said) had been a crate of cat food and several bottles of whisky.

'The knitting centre's a way o' making more jobs here on the isle. The current population is around sixty folk, mostly either retired or wi' young families. There's a primary school, but to go to the secondary, the bairns hae to bide in Lerwick all week, from the age of eleven, and you can understand the parents arena keen on that, so folk tend to move away when their bairns get to that age. For work on the isle here, well, it's good farming land, and there are small-scale enterprises, like the Blue Coo ice cream, and of course there's fishing – but it's no' easy for communities like this to survive. Buying things here helps the island economy, so do hae a look in the shop for postcards and souvenirs.'

I noticed the fireman, Berg, nodding in agreement, and wondered whereabouts in Norway he came from. There were marginal communities in the fjords too, as the cities sucked everything towards them.

Magnie paused for a breather, then pointed forwards towards the centre of the island. 'Now, if it's older archaeology that interests you, then there are a couple of very interesting places, and we're back to the Finn folk to talk about the first one. It's Finnigert, a great wall a metre thick, that divides the island from north to south. We ken noo that it's Neolithic, but tradition says it was built by the Finn folk. See, this guidman, Kolbenstaft, had a lock o' bother wi' sheep eating his corn. He said to his wife one night that he'd gie his best cow to ony een that would big him a dyke to keep them oot. Well, that very next morning, when he went out, he fun' a most splendid dyke, joost where he wanted it – and no' a trace o' his best cow. You can follow the wall right across the island.' He smiled. 'On your way, you'll find a stone circle. Haltadans, it's called, and the story is that it was trows who were

136

celebrating a wedding so hard that they forgot about sunrise and were turned to stone. It was a limping dance, and there's a tune for it, which is a trowie tune – one of the tunes a fiddler said he heard coming from inside a green hillock.

'Closer at home, if you're no' one for walking, then we have Houbie here, wi' the Fetlar Interpretative Centre, which'll tell you aa' aboot life here in centuries past. Gord, there, where the shop is, was excavated by the telly *Time Team* back in 2002, and they found a Viking hoose wi' a most beautiful blue stone floor. The blue roof on the headland there, that's the hall, where you can have your lunch. Just a peerie way oot past it, there's a mound known as the Giant's Grave, and that's a Viking ship burial. The *Time Team* excavated that and found a tortoise-back brooch.' He passed round a photograph, then bent to his bag and brought out a sheaf of coloured pages. 'And this is a leaflet that the bairns in the primary school did, to shaw visitors the walks in Fetlar, so you'll no' get lost when you explore tomorrow. The whole island's seven miles long, and four broad, so that gives you an idee o' distances.'

The heads bent over the maps, with murmurings of interest. Beside us, a gannet dived in a flash of snow-white wings. The sun had gone behind Lambhoga now, leaving only an amber glow in the still-blue sky. Over on Yell, the mist was starting to creep white tendril fingers over the hills, a sign of a fine day tomorrow. From the aft deck, a thread of guitar notes drifted down towards us.

Jenn stepped forward. 'Timings for tomorrow: breakfast at 07.00, we'll muster at 08.00, and then start ferrying you ashore after that. The villagers have organised a minibus to run people to either end of the island. It'll go back and forward as a shuttlebus, so you can wait for it where you are, or start walking and be picked up on the way. As Magnie said, there's lunch in the hall, from 13.00 to 14.00. The hnefatafl contest begins at 14.00. We'll have dinner on board at 18.00, then ferry people ashore for the dance. It starts at 19.30.'

Gavin's arm came around my waist. 'Dancing together . . . we haven't done that since the Scalloway Up Helly Aa.'

'Fun,' I agreed, and found myself giving a huge yawn on the word. His arm tightened.

'Early night?'

I nodded. 'I'll be on duty at four again, while we're at anchor like this. The trainees can sleep, but someone has to watch over the ship.'

Alain's eyes followed us to the aft companionway, and I felt myself awkward all over again. But he had chosen to be Rafael Martin, I reminded myself, and Rafael Martin had no claim on me.

We came into my cabin, and closed the door against the world.

CHAPTER TEN

Sunday 1st August, Lerwick

Low water 04.25 (0.5m)
High water 10.44 (1.9m)
Low water 16.43 (0.6m)
High water 23.01 (2.1m)

Moonrise 03.17; sunrise 04.46; moonset 20.22; sunset 21.34
Waning crescent moon

The water was already lightening when I awoke the next morning. We lay curled around each other, Gavin's arm over my waist, my hand on his shoulder. Cat had oozed himself into what was left of the pillow. I lifted my head to look at my watch. Quarter to four. Time I was on watch.

I slid out from Gavin's encircling arm and felt him stir, murmuring a sleepy query. 'Watch time,' I said. 'You go back to sleep.'

I dressed quickly: jeans, navy gansey, officer jacket, cap. I'd shower after my shift was over. I bundled my hair into a band, put my cap over it, and headed upwards.

It was a grey morning. The sky was covered with an even mist of cloud, darkening to thick stripes on the west and north horizon, with just a hint of brightness to the east, a glimpse of blue to the south, to suggest that it would clear as the day went on. The water lay mirror-still between curves of olive-rust seaweed. Dew darkened the decks and brightened the green of the grass.

The ship was quiet, with the trainees sleeping below; only the officers were on watch. Nils was sitting on the bench by the nav shack, nursing a cup of tea. He turned his head to greet me as I came up the steps and spoke softly into the morning hush. 'All is well. There is no movement on the anchor. The tide will turn at 04.35. Ten minutes after Lerwick.' He rose and stretched. 'I will sleep all morning, while the trainees explore. Well, I give you the ship.'

'I have the ship.' I left Petter making morning coffee, and padded off for a safety check, down the aft steps and through the banjer first, with its rows of hump-occupied hammocks swaying gently in the dim light. As I passed my slumbering watch, I heard the soft buzz of a mobile phone vibrating, and saw a light shine through the canvas. I smiled to myself. Somebody had forgotten to switch their alarm off. An arm fumbled with it, a head moved. I slipped down into the pantry and tunnels, sniffing for smoke, went up again by the forrard stair, gave a quick check into the paint locker, and continued onto the foredeck. I stood there for a while, one hand on the ropes, the other on the rail, and watched the hills flush with colour as the light strengthened. A Manx shearwater bobbed on the water beside the boat. It looked up, spotted me, and scurried away. There was a light on in one of the houses, with someone passing back and forwards in front of it. The sound of a baby wailing carried across the water. Gradually the wails died to whimpering. The light was switched off. I wished the mother good luck at getting back to sleep.

I was just about to return to the main deck when I caught movement out of the corner of my eye; someone coming quietly along the port side of the ship. It was a man, tall, with a cap pulled down to shadow his face. He went into the space between the two rows of toilets, and I heard voices whisper up from the boards under my feet, too soft for me to catch the words. My brain caught up with my ears. I'd taken over the ship before I'd gone below, so that phone had buzzed after four, too late for an alarm call for one of my watch. It had been a phone call. *Meet me, before anyone else is about. I need to talk to you.* The voices below me whispered, urgency rising from the stealthiness.

I let go of the ropes and slid one foot forward, then the other. No; the voices softened. I must have been directly above them. I slid back, and lowered myself to one knee, bending my head downwards in the hope of catching some actual words, but it didn't help. I couldn't even tell if the voices were male or female, just that the whispered dialogue was urgent, one voice urging something, the other countering. At last there was a sentence I did catch, hissed low and vehement: 'We've come too far to give up now.'

I bent my head lower until my nose was almost touching the deck, but I heard only quick, short breathing, as if someone was suppressing anger. Then footsteps clattered down the starboard aft stair. It was Petter, bringing me a coffee. There was silence below me, followed by the soft rush of feet. I raised my head to look, but saw only the back of the tall man, disappearing round behind the port side of the banjer house.

Petter had brought ginger nuts as well as coffee. 'Thanks,' I said. 'You didn't pass any of the trainees on your way along?'

He nodded. 'The one of Nils's watch who looks out of place. I can't remember his name.'

'Daniel,' I said. Then I realised that Petter had come along the opposite side of the ship from the way the tall man had gone, and anyway, Daniel wasn't on my watch, so it couldn't have been his phone ringing. He'd made the call, to meet someone from my watch . . . Oliver? 'What was he doing?'

Petter gave me a curious look. 'Coming back from the heads, I presume. Why?'

I persisted. 'You didn't see anyone on the other side of the ship, going into the banjer?'

He shook his head. 'There was someone, but I couldn't tell you who it was. One of the men.'

It could have been Oliver I'd seen, meeting Daniel in the middle of the night, while Laura was asleep. *We've come too far to give up now.*

Petter was staring at me.

'It's just,' I said, lamely, 'that he's so out of place. I can't help wondering if he's up to something, and I heard people whispering below me, just now. I wondered who it was.'

'What do you suspect?'

Murder . . . I spread my hands. 'I haven't any right to suspect anything. He maybe was given the trip for a birthday present, or because his mother thought he should be forced to socialise . . . what should I know? It's just that something doesn't feel right.'

'Your instincts are saying that.' Petter nodded. 'Mine too. If you like, I could go ashore this morning, and follow where he goes.'

I had an uneasy feeling about that. Then I had a better idea. 'Yes. Yes, do that . . . but don't follow him, trying not to let him see you. Go with him. Chat to him, be sociable, as if you just happen to be interested in the same places. If you're watching him, he can't get up to mischief. Whatever he's planning, he won't do it with a witness.'

Gavin and I could watch Oliver, and Laura would be safe for today.

By 06.30, a soft breeze had sprung up, blowing warm from the east, and a haze of sun turned the still damp road to a shining ribbon. I was just thinking about taking Gavin down a cup of tea when Alain came up behind me, and leant on the rail. 'All's well?'

'Anchor solid,' I agreed. 'The makings of a bonny day.'

He nodded, still staring out beyond me. Then at last he turned his head and smiled, and the familiarity of the movement caught at my throat. His voice was so soft that only I heard. 'Wish me happy birthday, Cass.'

I gave him a blank look. He'd been a spring baby. We'd celebrated his twenty-first with a bottle of real champagne aboard *Marielle* when Edinburgh was pink with cherry blossom. April 18th. I wasn't good at remembering birthdays, but I'd never forgotten his. I swallowed to clear my throat. 'Happy birthday.'

His voice was rough. 'It's not really my birthday.' He tilted his head to mine so that our eyes met. 'It was the day I woke up in hospital. San Juan, Puerto Rico. The first day that I remember.'

I felt as though a hand had clenched over my heart. I couldn't speak, just waited.

'I'd been picked up with a head injury mid-Atlantic by an Argentinian fishing boat. I was clinging to a horseshoe buoy, but there was no ship's name on it.'

I remembered that. We'd lost one on the way over, and bought a replacement in Boston. We'd never got round to writing *Marielle* on it.

'The ship's skipper did an emergency trepanning.' He pushed the curls away from his temple to show a neat, round scar. 'Then they took me to the first hospital on their way home, San Juan. I woke up on the first of August.' He turned round to face outwards again, and made a sweeping gesture with both hands. 'Nothing. *Nobody*. Whoever I was before, it was gone. Once I got better, they tried all the Spanish newspapers, local and in Spain, but there was no response.'

My heart ached. They would have spoken to him in Spanish, and when he'd replied, fluent as he was, dark-haired, high-cheekboned, tanned, they'd have taken him for a Spaniard. Why should they have tried French, or English?

'So I rechristened myself. Rafael Martin. The only thing I was sure of was that I'd been a seaman. The town paid for me to go back to school, get the qualifications I'd had before – I know I'd had them before.' He pushed the memory away with both hands, and turned to smile at me. 'I'm a vagabond, Cass. Would you take on a man with only a third of a history?'

'I'm a vagabond too,' I said. It was the wrong thing to say; his hand came over mine and squeezed, hard and brief. He'd always gone straight for what he wanted. I took a step backwards. 'I'm in a relationship.'

'So I see.' He'd never been fazed by setbacks either. 'Would you really prefer a landsman to adventuring with me?'

I'd forgotten, in the grieving I hadn't felt I deserved, how infuriating he could be. 'This ship and Gavin are all the adventure I need,' I said. 'I've grown up, even if you haven't.'

'What's the point of growing up, if it stops you having fun? Besides, if I sowed my wild oats, I don't remember it. I have to sow them over.'

'Well, you can sow them without my help,' I retorted, and pushed myself away from the rail. 'I'm busy running this ship.'

I swung away from him into the nav shack and began checking the Navtex, pressing the buttons with hands that weren't quite steady. The 05.00 forecast confirmed what I could see: winds E, light, swell slight, visibility good – a bonny day.

Nothing. Nobody still echoed in my head. *Would you take on a man with only a third of a history?* I'd achieved stability after all the wandering years, I had my parents back, I had Gavin. I didn't want to be charmed into throwing all that away.

The smell of freshly baked bread drifted out from the galley: breakfast time. It was only as I headed down the narrow nav shack stair, cap under my arm, that the full implications of what Alain had said struck me. If he really didn't know who he was, then I would have to tell him.

Not now, though, not here.

It was going to be a fun conversation. I tried it out in my head. *You know how you were found drifting from a ship, with your head injured? Well, I put you there . . .*

I shook my head, and contemplated not telling him for a moment, but I knew that wasn't an option. I'd think of some way to do it. There was no hurry; he'd lived with not knowing for eleven years. My heart rose suddenly at the thought of his parents. I'd been too miserable to contact them after his death, and I'd felt guilty about that ever since. Now there was good news for them: *My son was dead, and now he is alive . . . he was lost, and now he is found.* They'd left Shetland, but someone in Yell would know where they'd gone. Father Mikhail could find out for me; that would make the least fuss. He could ask the Yell minister. Maybe even the minister could write to them and tell them where Alain was. Perhaps seeing his mother again would jog his memory.

That gave me a sideways thought. It was odd that seeing me had meant nothing. In novels, someone who'd lost their memory had it brought back by familiar surroundings, or by meeting someone they'd known before. There hadn't been a flicker of recognition at our first meeting, not even a puzzled look, as if he couldn't place me. If he'd had the least inkling he might have seen me before, surely he'd have bombarded me with questions?

Either it was true, and his past was gone beyond recall . . . or, I suddenly thought, away from his presence, he was lying. He knew he'd slipped up in the church. I'd recognised him, I was suspicious, perhaps he knew that Agnetha had been checking up on him, and he wanted to divert me away. He'd been rescued as he'd said – that was the only way it could have happened – but the lost memory thing was a sprat to lure a whale. He'd always enjoyed making a tall story out of a minor incident, spinning a yarn in the pub afterwards.

I remembered that glimpse of a yellow oilskin in Lerwick, the glossy dark head of the woman he'd been speaking to. I wouldn't go for an explanation yet. I'd wait and watch.

Breakfast was an odd, constrained meal. I was too conscious of Alain beside me and Gavin opposite, his face closed against me. He'd been up and dressed when I went into the cabin. I wondered if he'd seen Alain and I talking so intimately; if he'd seen Alain take my hand. I was glad to get away on deck and do a last GPS check of our position before all the hustle of getting the trainees ashore began. I was off duty by that time, but I stationed myself beside the peg board, checking that everyone signed out properly, and helping the trainees over the side and into the inflatable. Daniel was in the third load, so I nodded to Petter to go in that one, and joined Jonas on the inflatable for the next two loads. We were using the Leagarth pier, a double stone slip running out from below the Interpretative Centre.

One last load. Laura was among the group waiting, with only six others. I glanced around for Oliver, and she caught my look.

'Oliver's not feeling great this morning. He's going to spend a couple of hours lazing about, then maybe he'll come over for a look around the village.'

'That's fine,' I said. 'There'll always be someone on the ship to run him over.' I felt a ridiculous sense of relief. He would be on the ship while she was ashore, and Petter had clambered into the shuttle bus with Daniel, headed for Brough Lodge. Laura climbed down and sat beside a tanned girl in a knitted cap. I turned the key in the ignition, nodded to Jonas to let us go, and buzzed over to the pier, where the shuttle bus was already waiting again.

'Eastwards first,' I heard the driver say, 'to Funzie, with the phalaropes and the geowall.'

'Eastwards sounds good,' Laura said. 'Which way are you going?'

'Oh, I want to see the birds,' the girl replied.

I pointed our prow shipwards again. Jenn had taken over at the boarding ladder. She nodded up at the group on the foredeck: Oliver, a couple from Nils's watch, one from Alain's. 'Five still on board, including your Gavin.'

'Fifty-seven ashore,' I said.

She lifted her head and frowned. 'Fifty-six?'

'Fifty-seven. Five tens and a seven.'

She shook her head. 'No, that can't be. Five on board, and sixty-one trainees.'

I looked at the pegs still in the holes. It was a simple system: trainees just had to remove the peg of their hammock number from its hole as they left the ship, and put it back in as they returned. For added clarity, there was a banner headline: ON BOARD = PIN IN, ASHORE = PIN OUT.

'Four pegs still in,' I said. 'Red 63 and 64, blue 7 and white 36. That's where it's gone wrong – white 36 is Gavin, and Oliver's stayed on board too.'

147

Jenn dug in her pocket for her list. 'He's white 34.' She lifted a peg from the box and stuck it in the hole. 'I wish they would take this seriously. He's never bothered to put himself back on board in Lerwick.'

'I suppose I miscounted,' I agreed reluctantly.

'Well, that's it sorted now.' Jenn put her list away, and headed off below, leaving me uneasy. The pegs had been right in Lerwick. I remembered Jonas checking them, and saying everyone was on board, just after Magnie had arrived. I went slowly aft and sat down on the bench, trying to think. I'd counted each load: five tens, and a final seven. Maybe I'd counted Jonas in the last load – but getting it right was second nature.

Gavin came to sit beside me. 'We're off guard duty over Oliver, then.'

'He's not feeling well, Laura said.'

'What are you puzzling about?'

'The numbers didn't tally, for people going ashore.' I tried to visualise the last load. Laura and the girl with the knitted hat. Two. A couple of men from Alain's watch, binoculars at the ready for bird-spotting. Four. On the starboard bow, Jonas, then the pair of teenagers from Nils's watch. Six. The teacher, Unni Pedersen, at my elbow. Seven. I shook my head. 'No, I definitely had seven in the last load. There must have been only nine in one of the earlier trips.' I sighed. 'Still, I'd better report it.'

Alain was standing at the aft rail, looking out over the green headland and sparkling water. His voice echoed still in my ears. *Nothing. Nobody. Whoever I was before, it was gone.* I headed up to him. 'There's a mismatch in the numbers ashore and on board.'

He lifted his head. 'So?'

'I counted fifty-seven off, and there are five aboard. Sixty-two instead of sixty-one.'

He frowned over it for a moment, then his face cleared. 'Your friend Magnie. Did he go ashore with the trainees, to direct them towards the things they wanted to see?'

I felt a ridiculous relief flood me. 'Of course. That solves it. Thanks.'

I was turning to go when he put his hand on my arm. His eyes were dancing. 'Cass, how's your baking?'

I heard his lips on the point of adding *these days*, and my suspicions flared up once more. I gave him a black glare. 'Better than it used to be.' It was only half a lie; it was hard to bake without an oven, but I'd become a dab hand at girdle bannocks and pancakes, and I'd even tried pizza base.

'Good,' he said. A wicked smile curved his mouth. 'Your man looks like he's used to his mother's home cooking.' He was watching for my reaction, and when I gave none, he prodded more. 'You'd need to learn to make jelly, too.'

I raised my brows at him. My voice was cool. 'For children's parties? A bit premature.'

For a moment he seemed disconcerted, then his face cleared. 'You Brits call it jam.'

Had it been a slip on purpose to remind me of his American persona? I watched him watching me, and wasn't sure. 'I already know how,' I retorted. I hadn't actually tried it on board, but I'd watched Inga do it, and the theory was simple: equal amounts of fruit and jam sugar, boil until a teaspoonful set on a saucer, put into jars, cool, eat. His grin warned me not to rise any further. I took a deep breath and pronounced my words with clear calm. 'That's fine, then. I won't write that anomaly in the log.'

I swung round on my heel and returned to Gavin. Although he smiled at me, his eyes were still withdrawn, wary. 'All well?'

I wanted to slide my hand into his, but that sense of distance between us stopped me. 'I forgot Magnie. He went ashore in the first load.'

'That's that, then.' He rose. 'Well, are we going to go and explore?'

PART FOUR

Beginning the Attack

CHAPTER ELEVEN

I'd decided to leave Cat aboard so that we could have a good walk. He could come ashore for the afternoon, while we were at the hnefatafl contest. I left him grooming his tail on his favourite bench, and got Jonas to put us to the pier before he went back to do the formal bringing-the-captain-ashore, with the senior officer being last on and first off, which always wasted a ridiculous amount of time. We headed east first, past the Interpretative Centre, where there were a cluster of trainees photographing each other against the rainbow wall mural or trying out the red phone box; past the fretworked elegance of Leagarth House and the modern village hall. The road was smooth under our feet, and the verges bright with orange hens and chickens flowers. It was fertile earth, with thick grass growing in parks each side of the road. Seawards, there were large sheep of breeds I didn't recognise; the rich pasture obviously made it worth experimenting. One was more like a goat – black, with a white stripe down its nose – and another had a square, blunt face and chunky legs like a pig.

'That could be a Badger Face,' Gavin said, pausing to look at the black one. 'It's a Welsh breed, very hardy, with fast-growing lambs. The broad-faced one's a Beltex. They're meaty, you get good gigot joints from them.'

He was making conversation as if we were strangers, instead of the lovers we'd been last night.

'Mint sauce,' I said.

He laughed and nodded downwards. In the field below us, there was a stone-covered mound, overgrown with longer grass. 'That'll be the Giant's Grave. Shall we go and look?'

'Yes, let's.'

We strolled down towards it and checked out the interpretation board.

'A woman,' I said. 'I didn't know they got boat burials.'

'A woman of some status too. Unless there was a man and wife buried there.'

'No, don't spoil it. I like the idea of Viking women getting some status.' The big Up Helly Aa in Lerwick still didn't let women be in the squads, although they joined in all the country ones, and the south mainland of Shetland had even had its first woman Jarl.

'It was a faeren,' Gavin said, still reading. 'The boat.'

It was a lovely spot to be buried in, this headland looking out towards Norway. The waves shooshed gentle on the broad pebble beach below. I gazed out over the bay, and wondered about the woman who'd been buried here. Perhaps she'd been one of the original pioneers, sailing across this burnished water to a new life; or maybe she'd been the ruler of this community, or of noble blood in Norway. I was sorry they'd disturbed her grave.

'You wonder when grave-robbing becomes archaeology,' Gavin

said, echoing my thoughts. 'Did you read about the woman they found in Siberia?'

I shook my head.

'She'd been laid in a cave, with horses around her. Never disturbed, until the archaeologists came.' He looked down at the boat-shaped hump in the green grass. 'When my time comes, I hope they'll leave me to rot. Dust to dust.' He smiled. 'And from which earth, and grave, and dust, My God shall raise me up, I trust.'

His voice made a poem of it. I looked a question.

'Sir Walter Raleigh, a man after your own heart.'

I thought about the words, and the man standing beside me who could recite them with such simple certainty, and loved him. 'I like that.' *My God shall raise me up, I trust.*

I slipped my hand into his, and this time he didn't move away. The wind was soft on our faces as we strolled on. Around the corner, the land each side of the road became moorland, with a line of square plantie-crubs marching along it. The first glimmer of the Loch of Funzie lay before us, a saucer-shaped reflection of the sky cradled in the green hills, with the land dipping beyond it, so that it looked as if it was suspended in the air. There was a gaggle of trainees there, and a couple of bright T-shirts straggled up the wide green hill, the silence swallowing them.

A couple of bright T-shirts . . . I jerked my head up towards the hill, but the people I'd seen had gone over its crest. They'd had their jackets tied around their waists. One set of dangling sleeves had been powder-blue, the colour of Laura's jacket. I glanced up at the hill, wondering if we should be following.

Gavin followed my gaze. 'You're concerned about those two?'

I nodded. 'Laura had a jacket that colour.'

'Keep it casual.' He fished a neat little monocular out of his sporran. 'See if you can see the phalaropes.'

There was a handy picnic table overlooking the loch. I scanned the trainees at it. No Laura. Past it was a chittering of terns on a rocky beach, a red-throated diver with a chick sculling along behind her, but no starling-sized bird with red cheeks bobbing about. 'Shall we try the hide?' I suggested.

It got us moving towards the hill where they'd disappeared. I kicked off my shoes to walk across the soft turf. The peat was springy under my feet, the grass bright with candy-pink ragged robin and drifts of feathery bog-cotton.

The hide was in a little plantation. We'd almost reached the wooden hut when there was a sharp crack in the distance. Gavin jerked his head up and whisked around in a swirl of kilt-pleats. 'That was a shot.'

We waited, breath stilled, but the sound didn't come again. Gavin was looking diagonally upwards to a valley in the land between this hill and the wall that guarded the cliffs. For a moment, I thought something flashed yellow. 'Did you see that?'

'An oilskin jacket.' He was already swinging his leg over the fence. 'That was a pistol shot. Let's get there.'

It wasn't far to the top of the hill, but Gavin took it at a fast pace, and it turned out to be one of those deceptive ones where you think the rise above you is the summit only to find another one further on. The ground under my feet changed from soft turf to the harsh bristle of sparse heather stems and cool, damp spagnum moss that oozed water between my toes. We came out at last at a square cement structure, a war lookout post. My chest was heaving, but Gavin was barely out of breath. He hauled out his spyglass and took a long look round.

The whole sweep of hill was in our view now, though not

the sloping tops of the cliffs behind their long stone wall. There was nobody in sight; no sound except the cry of the kittiwakes swooping around the headland.

'What's that flashing?' Gavin said, and pointed. Past the valley, almost at the wall between us and the cliffs, the sun caught something that winked in the grass. Slowly, we crossed towards it, losing it as it blinked out, finding it again. 'Stay here,' Gavin said, as we got to within twenty metres of it. He went slowly forward, eyes on the ground, and stopped at the spark of light. He fished out a plastic bag out of his sporran, put it over his hand, and bent forward to pick something up. Then he stood up, frowning. I could see him calculating. He went off to the left, and began walking forwards, slowly, eyes on the ground. I took a step forwards, and he held up his hand to still me. Two more steps, then he straightened and turned. He fished out another bag and his pen-knife, and bent down. I saw him cutting a root of heather and placing it in the bag. A dark drop fell from it as he lifted it. He went forwards to the wall, gave a long look in each direction. I heard him call, twice, and wait, listening. Then he shook his head, and returned to me, taking care to come exactly as he'd gone.

The bag with the heather root was smeared inside with blood and greyish-white tissue. The other bag held a gun cartridge.

I stood there, gawking, as Gavin placed the bags in his sporran. He gave me a wry smile. 'I'll feel stupid if it's rabbit remains.' He glanced down at the heather. 'A pity it's such springy stuff. There are no signs of footprints, but I didn't want to walk any more than I could help. If it turns out to be a forensics job, as I hope it won't, the less interference the better.'

He bent down to spear a white paper hankie to the place with a heather stem. 'There.'

We walked slowly back to the road fork and paused there. 'Well,' I asked, 'what do we do now?'

'Continue sightseeing.' He made a sympathetic face. 'Yes, I know, but I can't start a full-scale fuss over a shot in the countryside. We need to wait till your trainees are counted. Till someone goes missing.'

There was a bleak coldness in the pit of my stomach. 'We won't know till teatime. Some of them were going to stay out all day.'

'Then we have to wait till then.' He gestured his hand round the empty hill, and along the line of dyke. 'There's nobody here, nor behind the wall.' His glance returned to the white hankie fluttering against the green heather. 'I'm afraid that it won't make any difference. If someone is injured, it's not a flesh wound.'

We walked slowly back down the hill. My mind was refusing to grapple properly with it all. Oliver safe on board, Daniel watched; how could Laura have come to harm? Then I remembered that flash of yellow oilskin; the woman who'd followed us in Lerwick. I thought of Laura, with her blonde hair glowing against the tracery of the rigging, and felt sick inside. She might have been Gloriana in the family firm, but Oliver wasn't going to allow any crown but his.

The shuttle bus had just arrived at the loch, disgorging a dozen people including Daniel, with Petter still in attendance, and Frederik Berg at his side. Whatever skulduggery was going on, Daniel hadn't fired the shot we'd heard. Then I remembered Magnie and decided to double-check. 'Petter, you know you took Magnie in the first load, to the pier – did you squeeze him in as an extra, or did you take only nine trainees?'

'Magnie went over with ten trainees. I stayed behind to keep the load number right,' Petter said.

That was what had been knocking at my memory. I had seen

him leaning over to catch the ropes when the inflatable returned, then clamber aboard to steady it for the next load of trainees. My counting hadn't been wrong: fifty-seven. We'd had an extra trainee on board who'd gone ashore here. I had a sudden memory of Oliver being charmingly helpful with the family's tickets as they left the ship. That had been after the woman in the yellow jacket had come on board. Was that when he'd palmed her ticket back to Jonas? It couldn't be just coincidence that it was Oliver's peg which had been taken out; one of the few people who'd stayed aboard, so that there'd be no fuss about a missing peg when its owner tried to sign out. Oliver and the woman acting together. No wonder he was flourishing his alibi so triumphantly, dozing innocently on deck under the gaze of the on-duty crew . . . and we'd failed to keep Laura safe.

Gavin gave me a quick look. I saw that he'd caught the implications of that too.

Daniel glanced at the shimmering loch, then set off back towards Houbie. Petter gave me a worried look. 'The bus will go to the end of the road and then come back. If we keep walking behind him, and he gets on it, we will lose him. But if we get on, and he doesn't, it is the same.'

'You get on it,' I said. My legs gave a spasm of protest. 'If he joins you, well and good, and if he doesn't, well, you enjoy the rest of your day, and we'll keep with him.' But if that shot had meant what I feared it did, we were shutting the stable door after the horse had gone.

'I was right,' I said, once the minibus had trundled off. 'We did have one too many.'

Gavin nodded. 'We'll see who turns up at lunchtime.'

We walked back towards Houbie at a gentle pace, Daniel in front of us. We'd gone about a mile along the road, when Daniel stopped, looked around him, gave us a second glance, then fiddled in his bag for a camera and flourished it ostentatiously. He took a few shots from the road, then turned into a side track towards a crofthouse, and meandered down it with an elaborate air of 'just wanting to photograph this'. Gavin and I exchanged glances, and strolled on. As we got nearer, we saw the sign: CAMPING BÖD.

'Böd – is that a bothy?' Gavin said, not altering his stride. 'Basic accommodation?'

I nodded. It was a cheap way of seeing Shetland: a bed, a shower, and cooking facilities, usually in a gloriously scenic place. This one was gable-end on to the road, a substantial two up, two down with small-paned windows and a slate roof. There was yellow lichen growing up the chimney stack and a blackwood porch jutting out in front. I glanced at the cottage with what I hoped was an air of casual curiosity, and was just in time to see the porch door closing. Another glance showed me a dark silhouette moving in one window, then a twitch of the curtains as the person dodged behind them. I didn't see what Daniel would be doing in a camping böd, and if his motive was simple curiosity, he had no need to be so furtive about it.

'Let's inspect the Giant's Grave again,' Gavin said, 'and see what he does.' He checked his watch. 'It's still an hour to lunchtime.'

We strolled across to the green mound with its boat-shape surround of stones and reread the interpretative board, then sat down on the soft turf by it, looking out over the shining water, faces sideways on to where the camping böd sat above its beach. I was glad of the rest; this soft life on board a tall ship had made me less fit, and my legs were aching. The grass in this field had been cropped short by sheep, and it was sprinkled now with curly dodies, the lovely spotted orchids, pyramids of pink with puce-trimmed petals.

We sat in silence for ten minutes. Now, I told myself, now was the time to break this barrier between us. I wanted to tell him everything. Rafael was Alain, who was dead and had come back to life . . . but if Alain didn't know it himself, surely he had the right to know first. I owed him that much loyalty.

There was still no sign of movement from below us. Gavin's head was turned away from me. 'Cass?'

His voice was rough. I waited, suddenly cold in the green summer warmth.

His hand closed over mine. 'Cass, on the way to Belfast, when you had that fall . . . you had heavy bleeding after it.'

It was the last thing I expected. My breath caught in my throat.

He still wasn't looking at me. 'And you didn't eat any breakfast that morning.' His fingers slid between mine, warm. 'That's not like you.'

My tongue felt heavy. 'Yes.'

There was another long silence. A skylark soared up above us, twittering. At our feet, the clover smelt of honey.

'I only just knew myself,' I said at last. 'At least, I thought . . . I hadn't done a test or anything . . . I was just feeling sick in the mornings, and I felt bloated, and not right.'

He'd thought it through. 'The week we were together in the fjords?'

I nodded. 'Seven weeks.' Dammit, I'd cried when I'd lost the baby. I wasn't going to cry again. His arm came round my shoulders, tilting my head against his cheek. 'I wanted it to live,' I said, into his chest. 'I didn't know how we'd manage, but I wanted it to live.'

'I'd have wanted it to live too.' His words breathed warm in my hair. He held me for a few minutes longer, then set me away from him and took my hand again. 'Weren't you going to tell me?'

I shook my head. 'It was too bad to share.'

His fingers tightened on mine. 'Nothing's too bad to share.'

Silence fell again, but a gentler silence, with his shoulder warm against mine. We sat there, hand-fast, and watched the sunlight play over the sea, and listened to the waves mouthing the pebbles. The grief that filled the empty space within me was comforted. Some day, please God, I would meet my child. *And from that earth, and grave, and dust, My God shall raise me up, I trust.*

My thought was broken by the snick of a latch across the bay. At last, the böd door opened. At its first movement, Gavin turned his head towards Houbie, rose, gave a leisurely stretch, and said, 'Well, shall we get along?'

'I suppose,' I said, and made an equally slow pantomime of getting up and dusting myself down. 'Lunch is calling.'

'In the hall, isn't it?'

I nodded. 'But I want to fetch Cat first, d'you mind? Half a mile further, and back.'

'No problem.'

We sauntered along the road, the wind gentle on our faces, blowing our voices back to the tall figure on the road behind us. He walked with a reluctant air, as if he'd wanted to linger longer at the böd but didn't want to have to explain his absence. I chose an innocuous topic. 'Did you put in for the hnefatafl contest?'

'I did. I saw your name too.'

'I'm not chess-minded. I expect to get knocked out in the first round.'

'It's the best of three.'

'Three chances to get slaughtered,' I said cheerfully.

We chatted on, keeping a wary eye behind us. Daniel kept

following, and much as I wanted to discuss what he'd been up to, I bit my lip and speculated instead. He could have been hiding something to be retrieved later, or picking up something that someone else had left . . . no, why would he have needed to stay so long for that? He could have been expecting to meet someone – Oliver, who'd established his presence on board, but who could then have got on a shuttle boat any time after all the other trainees had left.

Oliver, or the woman in the yellow oilskin jacket. If she'd been the extra passenger, she'd had time to go along the road, ambush Laura on the headland. She could have gone back to the böd to wait there until it was time to make her own way to the mainland by ferry, rather than risk coming back aboard our ship. I was wondering when the ferries were – that is, if there were any on a Sunday – when my brain caught the implications. *Ambush Laura on the headland.* I thought of the blood-smeared heather, and my stomach lurched. I'd had enough of violence.

We left Daniel behind at the hall. He met a group of trainees going up from Houbie just as he arrived at the turn-off, and went in with them. I felt like someone who'd just manoeuvred a net around a hooked fish. 'Got him.'

'Don't be too quick to impute sinister motives,' my policeman warned. 'He could just not have wanted to gooseberry with us, but didn't know how to avoid us without looking rude. Or perhaps he needed the toilet. There's an awful lack of handy bushes round here.'

I hadn't thought of that. I hesitated over a reply, and his fingers caught mine. He was laughing.

We'd just reached the pier when a boat curved out from the ship with several passengers on board. I went down the slip to catch her prow, and found it was the stay-aboards coming ashore for lunch. Oliver was among them; he greeted me cheerfully as he headed for the shuttle bus. The driver leant out to us. 'I can come back for you, if you're just going across to the ship and back.'

I considered how Cat would feel about being bundled into a minibus and suspected he wouldn't like it. 'No, we're fine,' I called back. 'Thanks.'

We chugged the inflatable over. Gavin held it against the ship while I fetched Cat, muttering darkly about being disturbed from his sleep, even if I said it would be fun once he got ashore. I let him off his lead at the pier and we strolled slowly along. Cat bounded ahead of us, grumpiness forgotten, pausing to chase waving grasses, then turning to check we were still behind him. I hauled a piece of string from my pocket and trailed it when he showed signs of boredom. Even with Gavin stopping to murmur blandishments at the grey Highland pony in the field next door, we still made it to the hall on the stroke of one.

It was like most Shetland public halls, a new extension built around the original hall, with a wind turbine below it to provide year-round background heating. The entrance was on the short side of the building, at the car park. Gavin motioned me in ahead of him, I called Cat to heel, and we walked together into a most delicious smell of soup.

The Fetlar folk had done us proud. There was a hand-painted banner with WELCOME TO THE CREW OF *SØRLANDET* above the stage. A Shetland flag hung on one side of it, and a Norwegian flag on the other. They'd set out tables for us, laid with mugs, spoons, and central dishes of bannocks. The hall was already half full of trainees, all rosy-cheeked from the sun and wind, with Daniel among the ones he'd joined. I couldn't see anything in his expression to tell me what he was feeling; he was joking with the girl beside him. Then, as she turned away from him, his face clouded over into a brooding frown, as if he was puzzling over something. He glanced out of the window towards the bay, then, as the girl turned back to him, he pinned the smile on again.

I looked round for Oliver. He'd joined the two older sailors from my watch, but he glanced up at the door as we came in, then looked away when he saw it was only us. I gave a slow look round the hall, checking every face.

Laura wasn't here.

CHAPTER TWELVE

Captain Sigurd was presiding over the top table, on the stage, with Agnetha on one side and Henrik down at the table foot. There was no sign of Magnie; I had no doubt he had a crony in the village that he was visiting. 'I think we're above the salt,' I murmured to Gavin, and led him towards the officers.

Captain Sigurd indicated Gavin and me to the seats beside Agnetha, giving Gavin Nils's place. Cat slid under the table as we sat down. He was used to being persona non grata at eateries, and had learnt to keep out of sight until someone took an interest in him, at which he'd rise, swish his tail, let himself be admired, and show readiness to accept anything interesting which came his way.

One of the local women bustled over in a hall-issue pinny, blue and white check with *Fetlar Hall* sewn on the bib, and offered us choices.

'Now, then, welcome to Fetlar. We hae reestit mutton soup or lentil, that's suitable for vegetarians, all made wi' home-grown vegetables, and o' coorse the mutton's from the sheep on the hills here. Reestit mutton, that's a leg o' lamb that's been soaked in salt water, then hung up over the Rayburn to dry in the air and get a peaty flavour from the smoke.'

Two other women, equally be-pinnied, followed her, trundling a trolley bearing two doublehanded black cauldrons with a ladle handle sticking out of each. They were serving up the soup with speedy expertise honed over years of dances, weddings and funerals. I opted for the reestit mutton, then dug the tin of tuna out of my pocket, peeled the lid back, and put it down for Cat. The woman peered under to see what I was doing.

'Now, there's a beauty. And wi' a harness, an aa'. I'm never seen that on a cat afore. He's no' really allowed in here, but he looks as if he'll behave. I'll hae a look for a saucer o' meat scraps, after we're finished serving. Or maybe he'd like some cream?'

I thought he maybe would. She bustled on to the next table and explained reestit mutton all over again. Captain Sigurd said grace for our table, and we launched in.

The reestit mutton soup tasted as good as it smelt. It was thick with lumps of tatties, carrots, and chunks of the smoke-dried meat. The triangular bannocks that accompanied it were home-baked, with a slice of saat flesh in them – salted roast beef. I was just launching into one when my eye was caught by a movement on the road up above the hall: a flash of yellow. I nudged Gavin and gave a tiny tilt of my head towards it. He looked up sharply. Someone in a dark jumper was walking swiftly along the road, with that momentary flash of yellow again from a jacket bundled under an arm. We saw the figure for just a moment before it rounded the bend that led down into Houbie. I wanted to rush outside to see where it went, but you didn't leap up from Captain Sigurd's table.

I finished my soup, brooding, and reached for another bannock just as the woman returned with a plateful of beef trimmings. She slid it under the table. Cat did his courteous back-arch, sniffed at it, and tucked in. I could see I'd be carrying a half-eaten tin of tuna back to the boat.

While I ate, I kept an eye on Daniel and Oliver. Daniel was eating away and chatting to the people on each side of him; Oliver was increasingly uneasy, with constant glances at the door. I nudged Gavin and glanced at Oliver. Gavin looked, nodded, and returned to his second helping of soup, but I knew he'd been watching too. Alain, alerted by my movement, raised his head and gave Oliver a steady stare, then turned to me. His tone was carefully judged as two of the ship's officers talking to each other, excluding Gavin as an outsider. 'That's the one on your watch who stayed aboard?'

He knew perfectly well it was; he'd been officer in charge all morning. I nodded.

'Doesn't he have a sister, blonde?'

He knew that too, and her name. I remembered all the times I'd come home, knackered from a day of waitressing, and collapsed into an early night while he went off to the students' union with tall, golden girls like Laura. He gave a long look round the hall. 'I don't see her.'

'She isn't here.'

'That seems to worry him.'

'She's an adult,' I retorted, 'and capable of deciding she prefers a picnic on the open hill to lunch with her brother.'

Alain rolled his eyes and included Gavin in the conversation. 'I won't argue with my superior officer.'

I thought of saying, 'That'll be a first,' and bit the words back. Whatever Alain was playing at in this alpha male contest with Gavin, hovering on the edge of provocation, I would make it clear I wasn't being part of it.

The women came back to take our orders for the sweet: sherry trifle, sticky toffee pudding or rhubarb crumble, served with Fetlar Blue Coo ice cream or custard. While the rest of the table was deciding, I slipped in a quick question. 'We passed the camping böd along the road. Do you have many people staying just now?'

'Yea, yea, we get a few in over the summer. Young folk, mostly. The TV *Shetland* series, you ken, it's brought a lock o' visitors. There's a couple now, and a lass expected today – did she come wi' you, now?'

I shook my head, heart thumping.

'Oh, well, she'll likely have been on the half eleven, or coming on the four o'clock.'

I wished I had a copy of the timetable. 'I didn't think there'd be any ferries on a Sunday.' Under the table, Gavin's knee pressed against mine. I took it as a warning.

'Oh, yea,' she said, 'there are five, though you have to book the first and last, or it doesn't run. Seven thirty-five, eleven-thirty and four, like I said, and then seven thirty-five and nine-forty at night, so if you want to jump ship you've got several chances.' I laughed, disclaimed and didn't ask any more. She smiled, then looked round the table. 'Now, what are you all decided?'

Gavin went for the crumble; I ordered sticky toffee. When she moved on to the next table, I took the opportunity to excuse myself. I hurried to the porch and looked out, but the road running down into Houbie was empty. The person could have gone into the Interpretative Centre, or into any of the houses, or continued along towards the ferry. Four o'clock; time to catch them if Gavin thought we should.

When I returned to the table, Alain leant across me to Gavin. 'Are you taking part in the big competition?' He glanced at me. 'I'm not bothering to ask Cass if she is. Anyone less chess-minded . . .'

Another giveaway; he couldn't know that if we'd really only met three days ago. I didn't react, though I suspected the times I'd beaten him at Scrabble were written clearly on my brow.

'I thought I'd try it,' Gavin said. 'I've never played before.'

'It's very simple,' Alain said. He didn't quite make the words an insult, but 'even for you' was hovering in the background.

Gavin gave no sign of having heard the provocation. 'Good,' he replied. He turned his head to look Alain squarely in the eye. 'Are you playing too?'

'Sure. May the best man win.'

He wasn't rattling Gavin, but I could feel my own temper rising. I slipped my arm through Gavin's and smiled up at him. 'Watch out. Lucky in love . . .'

Alain scowled. 'There's no luck involved in hnefatafl. It's just out-thinking your opponent.'

Mercifully, the plates of pudding arrived at that moment. The sticky toffee pudding was a square of ginger sponge with a glazed fudge top, a generous dollop of caramel sauce, and an extra pour of cream. There was a saucer of cream for Cat, who polished it off in two seconds flat, then set to washing his whiskers with the air of a cat who sent his compliments to the chef. The sponge was most beautifully sticky, and when I'd finished it, Cat and I were at one in approving. Then came tea or coffee, and the morning's walk had made me thirsty enough to drink two mugfuls of best Shetland tea, mahogany dark from having been stood on a hot ring to brew.

Behind me, there was clattering of chair-legs on floor, and that preparatory chattering as people rose and headed out into the bright day again.

Gavin set his mug down. 'Half past two it starts, doesn't it? Do you fancy a quick walk down to Gord? That was the other dig the *Time Team* did, just by the shop.'

'The Viking house?' Alain said. 'I'd like a look at that too.'

I turned the blackest of glares on him. 'I'll tell you where it is, when we get back.'

He raised both hands in a fending-off gesture and leant back against his chair, laughing. I wanted to shake him. He was giving Gavin a totally unwarranted impression of intimacy between us. I didn't know how I could explain it without explaining who he was, and I didn't see how I could do that until I knew what he was up to. New loyalties, old loyalties, they were tugging different ways.

The captain rose, making our table free to go. Cat had found himself a windowsill to sit on; I gave his lead to Agnetha, in case he got restless, and Gavin and I strolled back down the road towards the pier.

'So,' Gavin said, once we were safely clear of the hall, and I braced myself for questions about Alain – but they didn't come. He looked as if he'd dismissed the whole thing from his mind. 'A ten-minute stroll to Gord, a look, ten minutes back. That should clear our heads for intense mental competition.'

'Have you ever played?'

'One game with one of your trainees on the way here. I get the gist, though I can see keen players would evolve complicated strategies.' His arm came up around my shoulders in a brief hug. 'It'll be fine.'

I understood what he wasn't saying. He knew there was something going on, but he trusted me. I hooked my hand up to take his and leant my head against his shoulder, then we separated again and walked on.

The original shop would have been near the pier, of course,

171

because goods came by sea. There was a new shop now, five minutes' walk up the road. It was low and wide, with a roof like an agricultural shed. The house next door was labelled GORD B & B. Someone was watching us from a downstairs window; the owner, no doubt, checking that we stayed on the paths and didn't damage her flowerbeds. I sympathised. It must be annoying having a TV-famous archaeological site in your garden. There was a curtain-twitcher upstairs too, a dark woman who was busy washing her hair in a sink at the bathroom window; I saw the wet drip of it as she raised her head, wrapped a towel round, then spotted us and drew the curtains against us. *Dark* . . . the woman I'd seen talking to Alain had had dark, glossy hair, and the person with the yellow jacket under one arm had come this way. But Daniel had been looking for someone at the camping böd. I shook the thought away.

There was no sign whatever of a Viking house. The lawn ran smooth from one side of the garden to the other, with the clothes pole in the middle. We were just standing looking over the wall at it when the woman downstairs came out. I recognised her as the one who'd taken our soup orders up at the hall, and smiled. 'That was a most splendid lunch up at the hall.'

'Yea, yea. I'm blyde you enjoyed it.'

'I'd a thought you'd still be washing up.'

'Oh, these modern dishwashers, the clearing up's no the chore it used to be.' She leant on the fence in a prepared-to-chat way. 'Dishes in, twa minutes, dishes out, and dried in twa minutes more. All you hae to do is put them away. Besides, I hae me visitors to look after.' She nodded backwards at the house. 'We're been busy all this summer. I had a family staying, from Belgium, and a German man, and a woman from Scotland for two days, and now I've an Italian lady. It's been non-stop. What thought you to the desserts, now?'

172

'Delicious,' I assured her. 'I had the sticky toffee pudding, but I wanted to try them all.'

'And what's come o' your cat?'

'I left him up at the hall, while we walked down to look at—' I gestured to her smooth lawn. 'Nothing to see now.'

'Yea, they filled it all in,' she said. 'The *Time Team* dig.'

'A Viking house,' I said.

'A lock o' folk come to see it. The end of it was under our clothes line, then the foundations run under the house. It's a pity they hid it all, but apparently that's what they aye do. They didna hae time to stabilise it, or whatever they call it. They did do a board though, there.'

She led us over to have a look. The interpretative board had photos of a covered drain, a wall, a floor lined with dark blue schist, and a polished platter, big enough to serve a whole family, made of dark green soapstone.

'The big plate, that's in the museum now, in Lerwick.' Archaeology finished, she changed tack. 'Whereabouts are you from?'

'Muckle Roe,' I said. 'But I've spent the time since I left school on board ships.'

'Aye, aye. I ken you now. Your father's involved wi' the wind farms.'

I nodded, and hoped the conversation wasn't going to get controversial, but it seemed she just wanted to place me on her mental map of the residents of Shetland. 'If you're interested in archaeology,' she said, 'you might want to take a look at the muckle wall. Finnigurt.'

The Finns again. *There was a massive land and sea search, but nobody was found, or any sign of them, and in the end we just had to agree that we'd miscounted . . .*

She pointed. 'It's just ower there.'

'I don't think we have time,' I said. 'We're signed up for the hnefatafl contest.'

'Ah, you'll enjoy that. Well, have a fine afternoon.'

We chorused our thanks and headed back up the hill.

The hall had been transformed again. Now the stage had 'World Hnefatafl Championship' blazoned along it, and the marshals for the event were dressed in full Viking rig. The tables had been laid with new white cloths, glasses and water jugs. The hnefatafl boards and bags of players were set out. There was a water urn in the corner, with cups beside it and several trays of fancies, covered with snowy-crisp dishcloths. Each table had a number, and there was a list on the door of where each player was to sit.

Geir had done a good job of publicising on board, so there were sixty-four on the list, divided into eight groups of eight. They'd put the ship's crew against each other, I noticed, with the serious players in a separate league. I did the arithmetic: game one would give four winners at each table, game two, two double winners, game three, one group champion, and then the champions of each group would play each other, putting the best of us sailors against the real enthusiasts. Five games, allowing forty-five minutes for each, took us till 18.15. I expected to be knocked out early on, giving me time to relax before I was due back on duty at 16.00.

Cat was still on his sunny windowsill. He recognised me coming up to the door, and gave his silent miaow in greeting, but didn't bother to move. I went over and stroked him, then looked for my place. The Danish husband, Carl, was my first opponent. Gavin was at the table next door, against Mona. I wished him good luck, then sat down at my number, smiled at Carl, and repeated my thought. 'Beginners together.'

'A good thing.' He looked across at Geir, on the serious tables, setting out his pieces with a determined air. 'Geir has inspired almost all of our watch.'

There was an odd emphasis on *almost*. I looked at Carl with more interest. So far I'd only really noticed him as the non-sailing spouse. His wife, Signe, was keen and reliable, first to volunteer even for galley duty, and when she was on watch, she stayed there, no matter how cold it was on the foredeck. Carl had taken part in an unenthusiastic way, giving the impression of quite enjoying himself, but not bowled over by the tall ship experience as Signe's shining eyes showed she was. His eyes were sharp enough, set close together over his thin-bridged nose, and constantly shifting, like a herring gull eyeing up a chip packet. He might not have thrown himself into the sailing, but he'd have kept a keen eye on the emotional ins and outs aboard the ship.

He justified that opinion by a glance at Alain, over on another table, then one back at Gavin. 'Your partner?'

'Gavin,' I said. Experience of Inga's mother-in-law, the gossipiest woman on the west side, prompted me to add voluntarily, 'He's a police officer here in Scotland.' To give information not only saved you the third degree but meant that the right story might get round the first three circles of people it spread to.

His sand-brown brows rose. 'Police?' I'd expected him to glance at Oliver, or Daniel, but oddly his gaze went straight to Frederik Berg, the fireman. 'Oy, oy.'

'Off duty.' I reached for the bag with the little resin figures in it and tipped them out. 'Attack or defence?'

'We have to toss a coin. The person who gets the face side is the king.'

I fished a coin from my pocket, tossed it, and found myself looking at the Queen's profile. 'I'm defence.'

We reached for our figures and began placing them in position. The warriors wore round helmets and clasped long swords in front of them, while my king, twice the size of his minions, had a patterned shield below his forked beard, a short blade, a flowing cloak, and a helmet with the nosepiece moulded over the crown.

The games I'd watched had shown me the importance of keeping your opponent guessing. It didn't matter if you had to sacrifice a warrior or two; kings were ruthless. My strategy would be to keep my warriors moving outwards, into a different corner each time, until my king had a protected near-corner space to move into. After that, it would be a matter of fine-tuning until he was safely in his 'den'.

It worked a treat. As Carl moved his tan warriors to counter each of my moves, I whizzed another warrior into a different corner, keeping an eye all the time on where I could move my king. It didn't help Carl that he was chatting instead of concentrating, that 'not really trying' pose that saved his pride should a woman beat him.

'Odd that Laura didn't want to come and play,' he said. He shot a glance at me out of his narrow eyes. 'Maybe she just wanted to get away for a while.' He took a warrior I'd placed casually in his reach. 'You've got a ship's doctor on board, haven't you?'

I made another casual-seeming move into a different corner. 'Should we be worried about her?' I was worrying already, but as a member of her watch, he might have seen a side of her that was hidden to us officers.

'Well . . . I think she's fragile. Her brother keeps a close eye on her, have you noticed?' He made a move that seemed random.

I studied it for repercussions while he kept talking. 'A touch of paranoia . . . have you ever mentioned cars to her?'

I gave him a blank look. 'Cars?'

'Well, I did . . . oh, just in passing, yesterday. I asked her what kind of car she drove, and it seemed to trigger off something.' He leant towards me and lowered his voice. 'She said she used to drive, but she'd got rid of her car now. It was too easy to tamper with. Those were her very words. What do you think of that?'

I moved my warrior to confront his on a safe diagonal. *Too easy to tamper with.* The parents had died in an unexplained car crash. 'What a strange thing to say.'

'That's what I thought.' He moved another warrior up to the one I'd placed so temptingly, freeing the space I needed. 'She said she took taxis in town, and trains for longer journeys. She only hired a car if she really needed one, from a different car firm each time, on the day she wanted it, just turning up and taking what they had.'

It sounded paranoid, the way he was putting it, but I was accustomed to Inga's mother making a full suit of clothes from a scrap of cloth. I tried to think of a way in which it could be reasonable. I'd heard people say it was cheaper to take taxis than keep a car in town. The car hire thing could be made up for extra excitement; I couldn't see why Laura would tell these details to a stranger, even allowing for the intimacy of a quiet dawn hour on foredeck watch together, with just you and the sea all around you. I kept my eyes on his, and nodded. 'But what was she afraid of?' On the board, my hand moved the king smoothly to his new position, one move off the corner.

He shook his head, and took the warrior I'd left exposed. 'That was all she said. Too easy to tamper with. Maybe she's one of these people who's got obsessed with terrorists.'

Terrorist threats these days were a stranger driving a car into a crowd, not a booby-trapped car. No. Laura feared someone closer to home. I needed to repeat all this, germ of truth and embroidery, to Gavin. 'Well,' I said, 'maybe you're right, she just needs time to herself. I'm sure she'll turn up soon.'

He looked across my shoulder. 'Her brother's not saying anything, but you can see he's worried, the way he keeps looking at the door.'

I turned. Yes, Oliver's laugh was forced, and even in the half minute I looked at him, he glanced over at the door twice. I turned my head back to my own table, moved my king into the corner I'd set up for him, and surveyed the board with satisfaction. I had a nice group of little warriors ready to move in around him, and even if Carl did his best to take them, I reckoned I'd still won the game.

He saw now what I'd done, and pored over the board. While he thought, I flicked a glance over at Daniel. He had that same air of uneasiness, although he was hiding it better than Oliver, but every snick as the door opened had him forcing himself not to glance up.

Carl nodded to himself and brought his first tan warrior over, but it was too late. It took another dozen moves of slaughter on both sides, but I kept moving my protective warriors in, and managed at last to place the three I needed around my cornered king. Game over; twenty-five minutes.

Carl took losing well. 'Good game,' he said. 'The speed's the thing, isn't it? Moving swiftly.'

'Luck,' I said. I stood up and stretched. Around us, a good number of players had also finished their games, or were fighting that last battle. Gavin was leaning forward, chatting to his opponent; I could see the king had won there also, but I didn't know which side Gavin had been playing.

A bell rang and one of the Vikings stood up. 'I see you're all finished that game, so we'll move on to the next round. Winners play winners at your table; losers, you can play each other, or sit a game out and get a cup of tea or coffee. Don't forget to fetch one to the players. Or, of course, you can head off to explore our beautiful island, whichever you fancy. The shuttle bus is still at the door, and it's a fine day outside. Round two.'

He struck his bell again, and I looked around me. I'd been too clever for my own good; now I was up against Frederik Berg, and this time I found myself with the tan warriors, attacking. He was following the strategy I'd used, but I could see he was thinking several moves ahead, so that every accidental-seeming placing meant I couldn't take his warrior without having my own swiped from behind. His king was in its corner with three ivory warriors guarding him, and most of my pieces left standing forlornly outside the board edge, in sixteen minutes.

'Neat,' I said. 'Will I bring you a cup of tea?'

He made a face and fished in his rucksack for a can of Diet Coke.

I checked my watch. Nearly half past three. It was time I headed for the ship. I went over to Gavin first, to see how he was doing. His opponent was a red watch trainee, and from the numbers of warriors taken, the game looked pretty even. Gavin was attacking, and his pieces were gathered around the centre, so that the king was trapped within his men. It looked like a war of attrition was brewing, with each picking off the other's men one by one. It didn't look as if the king could make it to a corner now, but he could still be surrounded in the centre. An intense game; I was vaguely surprised Gavin hadn't brought out his fly-tying kit, as he did with suspects whose attention he wanted to distract, but perhaps it wasn't counted honourable under these circumstances.

179

I laid a hand on Gavin's shoulder. 'I'm heading for the ship.'

He nodded. 'If I win this game, I'll need to stay put. Otherwise, I'll call from shore for you to fetch me.'

I nodded and left him to it.

CHAPTER THIRTEEN

Cat had slipped out during the change-over. I had no doubt I'd find him in the hall grounds, watching birds. I paused at the tea trolley to pick up an angel cake and a piece of millionaire's shortbread for an on-duty snack. I was just folding them into a napkin when Oliver came forward with that air of someone who doesn't want to make a fuss, but has decided something needs done. He went straight up to Captain Sigurd, surveying us all benevolently from the organisers' table on the stage, and spoke softly to him. The captain listened, asked a question, and Oliver replied with a headshake and a vehement gesture of his hands. The captain lifted his head and looked around until his gaze rested on me. He nodded, and I walked over.

'Ms Lynch, Mr Eastley is concerned that his sister hasn't come back yet. You were on the island all morning. Did you see Miss Eastley in your walk?'

'No, sir,' I said. I'd leave it to Gavin to talk about blood.

'Please ask your watch if they saw her.'

Petter and Mona were playing each other at Gavin's table. I went over to them and said softly, 'I don't suppose any of you saw Laura in your travels?' Gavin didn't turn his head, but I knew he was listening. 'She's not back, and her brother's worried.'

Petter shook his head, but Mona nodded. 'She walked from here towards the bird loch.'

'On her own?'

'No, with a woman from one of the other watches.' That jogged my memory. I'd seen her going off too. 'They said they'd walk first, to stretch their legs, and get the bus back if they felt tired.'

'What woman?' I asked. 'Is she here?'

Mona glanced round the tables, took a second long, slow look, then shook her head. 'I don't think so. I didn't notice her particularly. She was smaller than Laura, and wore a knitted cap. Not one of our watch. That's all I remember.'

I went back to the captain. 'She went east, sir, on foot, with another woman, from the blue or red watch. She's not here either.'

'Laura often skips lunch,' Oliver said, 'so I'm not worried, exactly.' His face showed that he was. 'Maybe she and this other woman were having fun watching birds or something, rather than coming back here. But I'd have thought she'd want to see the tournament.'

Captain Sigurd's gaze returned to me, then moved to Alain. I could see he thought it was a fuss over nothing, but he had to do the right thing. 'Ms Lynch, can you ask Mr Martin to come over. Then convey my compliments to Ms Solheim and say I would be obliged if she would join me here.' I rolled my eyes mentally at this careful grading of officers, and went off to Alain. His warriors had just surrounded Johan's king, and they were shaking hands over the scattered bodies. 'The captain wants you,' I said, and headed for Agnetha, to convey Captain Sigurd's compliments.

'I would like you, Ms Solheim, to take over the ship,' he said, once we were gathered around him. 'Ms Lynch is more familiar with this terrain. Ms Lynch, Mr Martin, take your watch leaders and ABs and split into four pairs. Take the bus to the east and west of the island, have a walk about, and see if there's any sign of Miss Eastley.' He turned to the organiser beside him. 'A preliminary look – they should be away only the duration of one game. If there is no sign of her in the obvious places, then we will need to take our search further.'

The organiser nodded. 'I'll look at how we can reorganise once you've taken the people you need.'

'Should I go too?' Oliver said.

I had a knee-jerk reaction against that, and spoke out of turn. 'We'll have plenty. Four pairs.'

The captain silenced me with a look. 'I think, Mr Eastley, you would be better here. Be assured my crew will do everything they can to make sure your sister isn't on the hill with a twisted ankle.'

If that was all . . . I needed to give Gavin the chance to mention the shot we'd heard, the blood he'd found. On top of that, I needed to tell the captain about the extra person who'd come off the ship. While they were just roaming around, it did no harm; I'd already determined that I'd personally count everyone back on board. But now, with Laura missing . . . I waited until he acknowledged me. 'Sir, I think we may have two people unaccounted for.'

His brows rose. 'Ms Lynch?'

I explained. 'I counted fifty-seven off the ship, and five left aboard. Somehow we had an extra trainee.'

'Did you report this to the officer of the watch?' His gaze moved to Alain, who nodded.

'I reminded Ms Lynch that her friend Magnie had also gone ashore, and he was the extra one.'

'Except that he wasn't,' I said. 'I checked with Petter later. He stayed aboard while Magnie went over. Ten trainees in each load, then seven.'

Captain Sigurd's brows drew together, and his lips pursed. I sympathised. He'd get done for calling out the coastguard too soon, making a fuss about nothing and sullying the good name of the ship, but equally, if Laura turned out really to be missing, he'd be pilloried for calling it out too late. 'So we may be missing two people. Well, we will conduct a preliminary search before taking further steps.' He turned to Johanna. 'Ms Rasmussen, can you go and ask the shuttlebus to wait for a moment.' His gaze returned to Alain and me. 'Do you both have mobile phone coverage?'

We hauled out our phones and checked them. Three bars.

'Very well. Keep me informed of your progress.'

'Sir,' we said in unison, and went off to gather up our crew. I paused at Gavin's shoulder on the way past. 'We're doing a quick look for Laura. Oliver's worried about her not being back.'

He rose. 'I'll come with you. Can you make sure you and I do the area where we heard the shot?'

I nodded. 'Should you mention it to the captain?'

'I'll talk to him.' He headed to the captain, bending over his shoulder on the other side from Oliver. Gavin made a gesture indicating moving apart; the captain rose and followed him to the window, where they had a low-voiced conversation, then Gavin took out his mobile and turned his back on the room, shoulder hunched against all-comers like a journalist reporting a scoop.

Two people. I had a hollow feeling in the pit of my stomach.

Two people missing, and this was Shetland's isle of the Finns. Was it going to be Eynhallow all over again? The land and sea search that found nothing . . .

Alain and I headed out to the carpark, where the dark blue shuttle bus was waiting for us. Our watch leaders and ABs were already aboard, along with Fireman Berg. 'I may be of use,' he said, 'if you're searching.'

'You will,' I agreed. I'd put him in a pair with Petter, leaving Gavin and I together.

We spent a moment sorting out who'd do where. Alain would do the western end of the island, and my team would take the east. I took out my OS map. 'OK. This is just a preliminary search, over the hill. This jagged coastline, it would take a bigger team than us to search every geo, and a climbing team or the chopper to get her up if she's fallen down.' I didn't add that the chances of her having survived such a fall were low; they knew that too. I looked at the two headlands, the Snap to the south, Strandibrough to the north, and turned the map to show my ABs. 'Gavin and I will walk up this bit here, looking over the south headland.' My calves gave a twinge of protest. 'Johan and Mona, you get off at the Haa o' Funzie with us and walk north, and Petter and Mr Berg, you get out at Everland and go up the hill from there.' I turned to the driver. 'Does that sound sense?'

She nodded. 'Yea, lass. It's no' like searching a forest. If she's there, you'll soon spot her, especially if she was wearing a bright-coloured jacket.'

'She wore blue,' Mona said. 'Powder blue. That should show up.'

The terrain was flat enough, sloping up to only 85 metres at the highest point, Baa Neap. I spread my map between my team. 'If you two walk along to Baa Neap,' I said, 'and climb the hill, you

185

should get a good view over the headland. Petter, Mr Berg, you go to Strand and walk along, then go up the further hill here, Kegga. You should see each other. Meet up in the middle, then cut back across to Everland to be picked up – watch this marshy bit. OK?'

They nodded.

I handed Petter the map. 'Don't try anything dangerous. No climbing down cliffs or anything like that, and keep well back from the edge.'

I'd just got my seat belt on when Gavin swung himself aboard and sat down beside me. 'I've put Freya on a watching brief.'

With Alain's eyes on me, I didn't pull my usual face at the mention of Sergeant Freya Peterson, Gavin's super-efficient sidekick. She was taller than me, which was a starter reason for disliking her, blonde, made-up with corporate glossiness and obviously heading for Chief Constable. 'Is she here in Shetland?'

'Between Police Scotland cases.'

'Say hello from me when next you speak.'

'I will.'

We sat in silence as the minibus jolted us along eastwards, past the phalaropes' loch and on to the end of the road. The Haa o' Funzie turned out to be a roofless building with a substantial shed in front of it and a new-build house next door. A traditional Shetland collection of cars, trailers, tractors and boats surrounded the buildings. The shuttle bus driver turned in their yard, and dropped us at the beach, a ridged bank of flat stones which shelved steeply down to the sea. There was a serious undertow, with the swell sucking and exploding over a rock in the middle of the bay, even on this calm day. The Out Skerries floated at the edge of the sea, with the tall light of Bound Skerry a grey pillar against the horizon. The cliffs we were about to go round jutted vertically from the sea; their green tops curved downwards, then the olive grass plummeted in a fifty-foot drop.

On the plus side, you could spot individual seagulls on the smooth grass. There was no powder-blue jacket. The smooth water of the bay showed no sign of anything floating, just a couple of buoys that marked lobster pots.

We waved Johan and Mona off, and walked back to the cattle grid. The green fields beside it were filled with peaceably grazing sheep, black and white cows on one side of the road, brown on the other, and a small herd of ponies. When we paused, they began to wander towards us, no doubt associating tourists with spare sandwiches or apple cores. Gavin watched them with interest. 'That skewbald's an odd throwback,' he said, pointing out a red and white one at the side of the herd. 'I was reading up about Fetlar, and apparently the landowner ran an Arab stallion on the island to improve the breed.'

'I'm more concerned about their hooves and teeth,' I said, watching warily as they approached.

His arm came up around me. 'I'll protect you. Look at her pretty dished face, and her slim legs. That's pure Arab. I bet she'd fly her tail if we saw her trot.'

I noted the slim legs. 'The fat belly's pure Shetland.'

They came to within a couple of metres of us, then veered away again when they saw we weren't offering anything edible. We walked up the landward side of the fence above the beach and cut upwards to where the wall began, pausing halfway to look across the geos at the cliff foot. There was nothing suspicious on the beaches, nor anything floating.

As we walked, I told Gavin what Carl had said about Laura not having a car. 'Too easy to tamper with,' he repeated, as I had. He thought a moment, then pulled out his phone. 'Good signal . . . Freya? Yes. Can you call up the report on the Eastley parents' death? . . . Round about New Year. Thanks. Speak to you later.'

We walked on in silence, feet soft on the grass.

'If there was anything in the shot we heard,' Gavin said, 'this would be where the body was disposed of. What's the tide up to?'

'High water was half past eleven.' I visualised the tidal atlas I'd been looking at only yesterday. 'The tide swept downwards then. Two or three hours later it turns and comes back towards us.'

'We heard the shot at 10.47.'

'Slack tide.' I checked my watch. 'It's had three hours of heading seawards. The coastguard have computer programs to calculate the speed of drift from a given point.'

'Your captain doesn't feel justified in calling them yet.'

We continued along the line of the cliffs, looking over. The lie of the land let us see most of the hill on this side, but the cliffs curved round in a series of steep geos, V-shaped clefts of rock. We did our best to look into every one, leaning up against the wall and craning our necks over. The vertical rock showed how deep the water was here. 'If she's dead,' I said, and felt a shudder down my spine at the word, 'there's nothing we can do. The chopper would be better.'

Gavin nodded, and glanced at his watch. 'Quarter past three.'

It felt as though we'd been walking for hours. 'I'll check in with the others.' I rang Petter first, then Mona, and lastly Alain. There was no sign of Laura. Wearily, I prepared to keep walking. Gavin, I noticed, was more used to this than I, after a childhood crawling through the heather in search of stags.

We'd come at last to Gavin's marker, closer to the point of the headland than I'd realised, when his phone rang. He put up a hand to stop me walking, and listened. 'Yes . . . really? Interesting . . . I'll explain when I see you.'

He pocketed the phone and looked at me. 'The parents died in a car crash on a country road outside Edinburgh. It was a single-vehicle incident, and the eventual conclusion was mechanical failure. There was no sign of anything else, and the father hadn't been drinking. No dead seagull who'd flown into the windscreen. The car went off the road, hit a stone wall, and went on fire. The mechanics couldn't tell what the cause had been.'

'But Laura gave up her car after it.'

'Yes.' He glanced at me. 'I only had that one meeting with her, in the cafe. What was she like?'

I gave him a blank look. He amended the question. 'Where would you put her, on board ship?'

I wrinkled my nose. 'It's hard to say, because she was obviously still suffering from the shock of her parents' death, so I wouldn't be giving her a lot of responsibility.'

'Officer?'

'Oh, yes. She had the air of an organiser. It would have been her rather than Oliver who did all the bookings.' I kept thinking. 'Jenn's job. All the paperwork for the trainees, and forms for each port.'

'Not the sailing side?'

I shook my head, trying to tease out my feelings. 'No. She felt too much of a loner. She was friendly, of course, and I think she'd work well in an office team, but I wouldn't see her going out for a pint afterwards. Maybe it was because she was the director's daughter. She got set apart from the start.'

Clever. Inner toughness. An organising brain. Someone who could see both detail and the wider picture; who could work out the implications. Someone who would know how carefully her parents drove, how well-serviced their car was.

'She was doing pretty well at hnefatafl.' Unless, of course, Alain

189

had been letting her win. I remembered her anxious glance at Oliver. 'I bet she was Oliver's big sister, even though she was younger. When he got into trouble in his teens, she'd have fished him out.' Loved him, looked after him, known his weaknesses . . . known, too, if he was any good at mechanics. If he'd know, for example, how to weaken a steering column or tamper with brakes.

'Your dad's friend said that in the will she'd been given money equivalent to his debts.' Gavin paused for a moment, eyes on the blue sky. 'Where would you put him on board?'

I had no difficulty with that one. 'On a series of short, challenging tasks that let him think he was in charge, but under strict supervision that pretended it wasn't looking. Bosun's mate – no, nothing with a title that gave him a superior.'

He laughed and slipped his arm through mine. 'There's always a superior on board ship. What about me?'

I'd never thought about that, but the answer came straight to my lips. 'Captain.' It startled the breath out of me. 'Once you'd learnt to sail,' I managed to add, and focused on my feet for a bit. When I dared to look sideways at him, he was smiling. I brought the conversation back to reality. 'This is a perfect place for throwing a body over. But wouldn't you see marks, if someone had been dragged over the hill to the cliffs?'

'Probably.' He looked from his marker to its nearest piece of wall, twenty metres away. 'They'd have to get her over the wall too. Are those missing stones?'

I turned my head to where he was pointing and saw a ragged place in the neat lines of stones that topped the wall. He got his spyglass out, peered intently and nodded to himself, then passed it to me. I swept along the upright stones until I came to it; several leaning against each other. I gave him the spyglass back. 'What now?'

I could see he was dying to go and examine it properly, but holding himself in check. 'If this is a crime scene, we mustn't contaminate it.'

He caught my glance over the wall at the next section of cliffs and understood what I was thinking. 'If she was shot and thrown over, then she's not alive. This is as close a look as we can allow ourselves.' His arms came around my waist. 'Go limp.'

I obliged, and felt him heft me into the air until my waist was level with the top of the wall. Obligingly, I dangled my arms over the other side. 'If you were to shove me right over now, I think I'd just roll into the water.'

Gavin nodded and set me on my feet again.

There was nothing floating in the glimmering water, or swirling in the undertow.

We came away from the edge then and went landwards, pausing at the loch of Funzie Ness to drink the peaty water from clasped hands, and taking a rest on the clifftop looking out over the Snap, a sea-worn hole in the cliff shaped like the eye of a needle, outlined with a seam of whiter rock. The curved bottom of the opening was filled with sea-rubble, too darkly shadowed by the bright water behind for me to make out details of what was lying there. Behind it, the cliffs were shallower, slanting down to the sea in grey diagonals.

'There was a cave marked hereabouts,' Gavin said, 'but I don't see any sign of something accessible. Come on. We're past the worst now.'

He held out his hand to ease me up, and we walked onwards. Looking ahead, I could see that he was right; after we'd come past these last two geos, the dramatic clefted cliffs gave way to a smoother outline where we could just follow the curve of the land until we reached the camping böd.

We were trudging along in silence when Gavin's phone rang. He fished it out of his pocket, glanced at it and answered. 'Freya?'

I made a face at the burnished water.

'OK. Yes, we're just doing a preliminary walk around. There's no sign.'

I thought *preliminary* was a bit dismissive of our efforts. It was an amateur search by professional standards, but I reckoned we hadn't missed anything.

'Oh? Interesting . . . yes . . . OK. Yes, worth asking. OK, speak to you later.'

He put the phone away. 'The person who booked into the camping böd was an Anna Reynolds, from Edinburgh. She paid in advance, using PayPal.'

'Edinburgh – like Oliver and Laura.'

'The voters' roll has her as the same age group, so she could well know them. Freya's following that up, in so far as she can when we've no evidence of a crime having been committed. She didn't cross over to Fetlar on the 11.30 ferry.' He paused, gave a long look around the empty, glimmering sea, then slipped his hand into mine.

'Nearly there. A good negative result: no injured person, no body, and best of all, only this last stretch of road before another cup of tea.'

We came along the fifty metres of hill towards the beach and the camping böd. We'd intended to go straight past it, when I saw the curtains in the window move – no, it wasn't the curtain that had moved. A shadow had passed behind it. I let my knee sag and went down, ending up on the ground, then sat for a moment, holding my hands each side of my ankle, and making an *It really hurts* face. Gavin was down beside me instantly. 'Turned it?'

'We're being watched from the cottage Daniel went into,' I gasped, through gritted teeth. 'Can you help me there?'

Gavin gave me an amused glance. 'Sometimes you're very like your mother.'

'Absolutely no resemblance.' I used his arm to heave myself back to my feet and limped forward.

'Just keep remembering which ankle you sprained.'

'Right.' I made it clear to the shadowy watcher that I couldn't possibly put any weight on it.

'You're overdoing it a little,' Gavin said.

'How do you know how much it hurts?' I retorted, and hirpled through the gate, pausing to support myself artistically against the picnic table. A red hen passed me, fluffing its feathers out. Beside me, the window glinted my own reflection back, a small window with a dozen panes in rows of three and a scatter of shells on the sill. I felt the prickle of someone watching me from behind it. I straightened and limped the final two metres to the cottage door. I knocked first, then pushed the door open, Shetland-fashion, calling, 'Is there anybody home?'

It was a spacious porch, lined with new wood, and with several bags of peats sitting in one corner. The door into the house was closed.

Nobody answered, but I had that feeling that someone was there, keeping quiet and hoping I'd go away. I limped further in and called again. There was a scurrying noise on the stairs, as if someone was running down them quickly, trying to pretend they'd been downstairs all the time, then the inner door opened.

It was Daniel. His surprise wasn't convincing. 'Cass! What's happened to you?'

'I turned my ankle.' The wooden stairs ran straight up ahead of me, with a room on each side. The shadow I'd seen had been

193

on the left, the sitting room. I limped in and plumped myself down on the wooden settee. 'I thought this looked just the place to have a roll of bandage, to strap it up for the last bit of walk to the hall.'

'Yeah.' He turned round in the middle of the room in a helpless way. It was a bonny room, lined with the same bright wood as the porch, with basic chairs around the outside, and a black iron stove jutting out into the hearth.

I was in the wrong place for a first aid box. Gavin went into the kitchen, on the other side of the stair, and came back with a bandage. Daniel watched as I pulled my sock down and began winding a figure-of-eight round my foot.

'I just thought,' he began, 'that, well, Oliver was saying Laura was missing, and I remembered this place and thought I should check it out. I'd passed it earlier. And I was out of the tournament, so I was at a bit of a loose end.' His eyes followed my hands. 'And I thought, well, she could have been hurrying to get back, in case he was worrying, and turned an ankle or something. That's why I was looking upstairs.'

He plummeted right to the bottom of my list of people to be in a conspiracy with. Gavin was looking uneasy at this voluble giveaway, and as soon as I'd finished my bandage and got my shoe back on, he gave me his arm. 'How's that?'

I put my foot down with artistic care, then stood on it. 'Fine. That'll get me home.' I turned to Daniel. 'Thanks. See you back at the hall.'

'Yeah, yeah, I'll come with you. You might need an arm or something.'

'No, I'll be fine,' I said. I could feel Gavin's unhappiness. 'Could you maybe go on ahead and say that we're on our way? Then I can take it easy.'

He didn't ask why I couldn't phone in, just scuttled off like a guillemot chick suddenly confronted by a sailing boat.

'Thanks,' Gavin said, once he was safely out of earshot. 'I was dreading he was going to come out with something I'd have to take official notice of, with only you as a witness. You've no idea of the hassle that would cause in a trial. We'll interview him properly later.'

'He was waiting for someone here. Anna Reynolds?'

'Don't think about her any more either. I've already asked you more questions than I should have. Freya'll come as soon as your captain phones the coastguard, so she can do the official stuff.'

'Google Anna Reynolds, images, and see if I recognise anyone?'

He shook his head. 'Identikit first, then photos.'

I foresaw a long evening ahead.

When we got to the hall, the shuttle bus was just drawing up with Alain and his team aboard. Petter, Mona and Johan were already at the hall, standing beside Captain Sigurd, with Oliver hovering in the background. I went up to Captain Sigurd. 'No sign, sir.'

'Very well.' His gaze dropped down to his watch. 'If she was not in trouble she would have returned by now. I think we must contact the coastguard.'

PART FIVE

Warriors Taken

CHAPTER FOURTEEN

The coastguard would take time to arrive, of course. Captain Sigurd gathered the crew into the first room as you came into the hall – the playgroup rendezvous, judging by the plastic cars parked in one corner. A buzz of excited chat came from the main hall. It sounded like the break between the all-comers' jamboree and the serious play-offs. I hoped Geir would do well.

Captain Sigurd looked around us all.

'I have given the coastguard what information we have. Laura Eastley was last seen heading eastward with another woman, who does not seem to have been a bona fide trainee, although she came off the ship. That was at 09.15, so it would be reasonable to expect them to have returned by now. Her phone is switched off. There are coastguard volunteers at Baltasound and Mid Yell, who are being assembled for a search. They will come across on the next ferry, at 19.35, and take control, along with local volunteers.'

He paused for emphasis. 'In the meantime, there is nothing

further that we can do. I count on you all to support me in making sure our other trainees continue to enjoy the voyage. Our programme of events will continue as planned with the final rounds of hnefatafl, a meal on board ship and the dance in the hall this evening.'

He looked across at me. 'Ms Lynch, you and your watch may now go and take up your duties, relieving Ms Solheim. The trainees will be coming soon.'

I collected Cat and headed out. Gavin was waiting for me by the door. 'He's made it official?'

I nodded. 'I'm back on duty.'

We walked down the hill to the pier with Cat trotting ahead, tail high. Now the beach was a smooth curve of rock above glistening olive-brown kelp. At the far side of the bay, an otter was hunting in the shallows, chestnut back darkened with water, the cat head bobbing up then ducking under again. We chugged over to the ship, handed the dinghy to Agnetha, and Gavin went below to boil the kettle while I checked the anchor was holding then did a walk round the ship. All well.

After that I went to the clipboards in the nav shack. The one with the names from yesterday should be there. I found it and ran my finger down the list. Williamson, Williamson, Tait, Georgeson, Jamieson, Nowacki, Kowalski, Reynolds. My finger went past it, then returned. *Anna Reynolds.* She had been on board, and Oliver had used the family to smuggle her ticket off.

I took the register to Gavin. 'She was here. Look.'

We sat down and looked out over the hills, cup of tea in hand, Cat washing his whiskers at our feet.

'And I never told you about what I overheard this morning.' The flurry of disembarking had driven it clean out of my head. 'Someone I think was Oliver was talking to her.' I explained how I'd heard a phone ring, in the banjer, and how I'd heard the whispering, forrard, between the heads. 'I only caught one phrase. *We've come too far to give up now.*'

'You're certain it was Oliver and Reynolds?'

I shook my head. 'The phone rang in the hammocks of my watch, round about where Oliver and Laura were, and the person I saw going up there was tall and male. But . . .' I frowned. 'Petter saw Daniel coming back, on the other side from the way the tall man had gone. So it could have been Daniel speaking to Reynolds . . . but he couldn't have been the person getting the phone call. Could she have been in cahoots with both Oliver and Daniel?'

Gavin's mouth turned down. 'I don't like that idea of a threesome, when it comes to murder. Two, possibly.'

'But Daniel seemed to be looking out for someone at the camping böd.'

'And Oliver stayed aboard until he could come off with a group of other people and head straight for the hall, under everyone's eyes, until he started worrying about Laura being missing.'

'Giving himself an alibi, while the woman did the actual murder?'

'You're reading my nasty suspicious police mind.' His phone rang. He fished it out of his pocket. 'Freya? . . . OK, good. Right . . . Yes, I'll get her to do that. We'll see you then.' He pocketed the phone again. 'They're sending the chopper and lifeboat for a sea search, so Freya's coming up with them. About an hour, she reckons. Who else might have seen the woman that Laura went off with? We need to get a decent description while people's memories are fresh.' He fished in his sporran for a notebook and pencil, found a new page, and waited, looking at me.

'Me,' I said. 'Mona was the one who noticed her going off with Laura – Mona Jakobson. Jonas was the other one on the boat, he might have noticed. Then the people on the boat.' I wrinkled my nose, trying to remember.

'Stop there,' Gavin said. 'I don't want you inducing false memories. Freya can get a list of them as she talks to you. Anyone else?'

'Jenn might have spotted her as someone who wasn't a trainee – the rest of us would just assume she belonged to one of the other watches.' Suddenly, I remembered the pier in Lerwick, Rafael's head bent over the glossy dark one.

'Yes?' Gavin said.

'I don't know if it's the same woman . . . but in Lerwick, as we were going round, I had this feeling of being followed.'

Gavin nodded. 'I had it too.'

'Did you see anyone?'

He nodded again. 'The yellow jacket. A woman, you thought?'

'I saw her again, at the corner of the pier.' I had a heavy feeling in my stomach, but if we were talking murder, then my allegiance was to Gavin. 'Her hood was down, so I could see her hair. She was talking to Rafael.' I paused, then added, 'But she could just have been asking him if the ship was open for visitors.'

He gave me a long look out of those grey eyes that were so like Alain's, but with a kindliness that Alain had never achieved. I could see that now. Brilliance, charm, life, all those danced out of Alain's eyes, but never this understanding tolerance. I stretched out my hand to Gavin's and was grateful I had come to so secure a haven.

We sat there in silence. The sun was warm on our faces; a tirrick flew past, forked tail white against the blue sky. A tissue-paper sliver of moon hung above the pink-tinged hill. The water lapped against the ship's sides. Cat moved on to his paws, slurping noisily between each toe.

Our peace was broken by the roar of the outboard starting up. The first boat headed out from the pier, and I went to the guardrail to catch her rope and help the trainees on board. Geir was in the second load, clutching his trophy: second place. Once we'd got all the loads on board, the watches lined up for a muster. I looked slowly round. There was no yellow oilskin jacket, no dark, glossy head. But then, why should there have been? She'd done what she came for . . .

I was just about to hand over to Petter and head below for dinner when I heard the roar of the lifeboat engines in the distance. A look with the spyglasses found it, the orange superstructure above a great wash of water, heading straight towards us. I assembled a team for the gangplank and got my ABs ready with fenders. The trainees held their phones and tablets up as it came closer, closer, then curved to a halt five metres from us. The propellers churned as she edged up to us; on the shore, the white wash raced up the pebble beach and broke into lacy foam.

The sunlight glistened between the two boats, rippling on the lifeboat's navy hull, then blacked out as we caught their lines and pulled the two together. Sergeant Freya Peterson was standing on the deck, blonde hair pulled back too tightly to be ruffled by the wind. She was wearing her usual smart black trouser suit, teamed with a POLICE waterproof jacket as a concession to the maritime life. A laptop bag was slung over one shoulder. She came easily across the gangplank, shook hands with Captain Sigurd and Agnetha, and turned to Gavin. 'Hi. So, what've you done so far?'

Up on the aft deck, Alain's arm came around my shoulders. 'There you are,' he murmured. 'A perfect match. Cop and cop. It would save you having to learn to bake.'

I shook his arm off and didn't answer.

'I've commandeered Jenn's office for interviews,' Gavin

replied. 'Cass ferried the woman last seen with Laura Eastley over to the shore, and there are several other people who might have noticed her.'

'Good.' She raised a hand to the lifeboat. It cast off and left the bay in a swirl of water, then began feeling its way eastwards, with several crew members on the high deck, spyglasses in hand. Faintly, over their engine throb, I could hear the higher whine of the coastguard helicopter, and soon it swept over us, displaying the red and white chevrons on its belly. It would have heat-seeking infra-red cameras, in case Laura was still alive somewhere in that wilderness of rocks and sea.

Sergeant Peterson and I shook hands briskly. 'Then I'll start with you, Cass.'

I followed her into Jenn's office. Naturally it was also her cabin, with a bunk bed and a porthole window, but her desk was pulled across the room to leave a square workspace behind it, with shelves of files and paperwork. Sergeant Peterson went for the chair behind the desk. Gavin sat on the padded seat in front of the bed and prepared to take notes. Sergeant Peterson cleared Jenn's computer to the side, took out her laptop, and faced me over the desk.

'Well, Cass, tell me about the woman that Laura was last seen with.'

'I don't know that of my own knowledge,' I said. 'I just put them on the pier and brought the boat back. It was Mona who said she'd seen her going off with another woman, heading towards the bird loch.'

'Noted. But it was you who ran Laura's group over to the pier, wasn't it?'

'Yes.'

'Right, let's see what you remember about that boatload.

Close your eyes and take us round who was sitting where. Start beside you.'

I closed my eyes. 'Unni Pedersen, from my watch, was right beside me. I had to avoid bumping her with my elbow as I steered. Then two teenage boys from Nils's watch. There was a bit of shoving going on, Jonas had to calm them down. Then two men from blue watch on the other side. Then the girl up in the bows, and Laura.' I felt a sudden surge of excitement. 'That was her, the stranger. I remember thinking I didn't know whose watch she was on.'

'Fix your memory on her. Say everything you can.'

'Dark. Dark-browed, and with dark skin – that ruddy tan you get among' – I groped for a comparison, and remembered people I'd seen in the north of Norway – 'Sami folk, maybe, or Inuit.' *Finn people.* I shook the thought away. 'That kind of look. High cheekbones, a broader face. Her hair was bundled up under her hat – she had one of those knitted caps with the ear flaps, red-patterned, and fleece-lined.'

'Eyes?'

I tried to remember, and got a flash of the sea's colour in her face. 'Oh, blue! I was surprised at that. Blue, with dark lashes. I'd have expected them to be brown.'

'Was she wearing make-up?'

I shook my head.

'Age?'

'Maybe thirty.'

I was remembering what the Orkney man had told me about his Finn man: *He was there, and he wasn't there somehow . . . when I tried to look straight on at him, I couldn't quite grasp his face . . .* I felt like that now. The more I tried to remember her face, the more it slipped from me, just the blue eyes with a slight slant to them, and something tight about the lips as she'd smiled at Laura, that curled-in smile like a Greek statue.

'How did she look on the boat?' Gavin asked.

That was the sort of thing I did notice. 'At home. She came down onto the boat as if she was used to it.' Memory surfaced. 'She was wearing boots, some kind of soft leather, and jeans, and a navy jumper, and she had a little rucksack on her back, grey.'

'OK, let's go back to them coming on board the rubber boat. Can you remember what order they came in?'

I thought. 'She must have been one of the first, because I directed them to sit forward. She and Laura, and the two men from the blue watch. They were first on, then Laura, then the stranger.'

'Was there any interaction between Laura and the strange woman?'

It was coming back as I visualised them. As I'd looked round to check they all had a secure hold, she'd spoken to Laura. 'She said something about the scenery, from the way she looked around. Laura looked at her and nodded.'

'How about once you got to shore? Think about the seaweed smell of the pier, and the boat bumping against it. Did you see them go into the minibus?'

I shook my head, then memory suddenly returned. 'Oh, yes. They didn't get on the minibus. But they did speak to each other then. The driver said she was going east first, and Laura said, "Eastwards sounds good." Then she asked the other woman which way she was going, and she said . . .' I closed my eyes, trying to remember, feeling the concrete pier gritty under my hand as I fended the boat off. 'She said, "Oh, I want to see the birds."'

'Try and imitate her voice.'

I tried. '*Oh, I want to see the birds.* It had a sing-song feel about it. No obvious accent, normal Scots.'

'High register, low?'

'The low side of medium. Friendly sounding.'

'OK. Can you guess at her height, compared to Laura?'

'Smaller, I think, but not by loads.'

'That's a good start,' Gavin said. He flipped back a couple of pages of his spiky writing. 'About thirty, dark-browed, blue-eyed, average height, tanned with high cheekbones. A red-patterned ear-flap hat, navy jumper, jeans, soft leather boots. Do you mean walking boots, or town boots?'

'Town ones. Pixie-style short ones.'

Gavin nodded and scribbled. 'A small grey rucksack. Was she pretty?'

'I just can't see her face clearly. I don't think so. Striking.'

'Do you think it was the same woman as you saw on the pier, in the yellow oilskin?'

Sergeant Peterson looked up sharply at that, and Gavin made a *Tell you later* gesture.

I shrugged. 'I'm sorry. It was all too brief and far away. I just can't tell.'

'Well, let's see how you do with the computer imaging.' Sergeant Peterson opened up her laptop and tapped away. 'Tanned, high cheekbones, blue eyes, dark brows.' A pause, then she turned the laptop around. There was a face on the screen. 'Rounder chin, I think,' I said, 'but the breadth of the face looks right. A slight slant to the eyes.'

Sergeant Peterson tapped a few keys, dragged the mouse. 'Yes?'

I shook my head. 'It looks roughly right, but at the same time it's nothing like her.'

'Keep trying.'

We tried for a bit longer, but I just couldn't fix the face in my memory long enough, and I was relieved when Sergeant Peterson saved my best effort, turned the laptop away from me again, and tapped away. Then she turned it back. 'Have a look at these.'

She'd called up Anna Reynolds on Google, and swiped me through photo after photo of women: old, young, dark, fair, curly-haired, sleek, laughing, posed. No . . . no . . . no . . . and then, there she was, in a party shot, leaning against a kitchen worktop. I lifted my hand to stop the flicking of photos. 'I think that might be her. The girl with the drink.'

She was striking rather than pretty, as I remembered, with broad cheekbones and slightly slanted eyes, spiked with dark lashes. Her hair was glossily dark, straight, hanging below her shoulders. She wore a scarlet top, laced across the chest. I stared at her, trying to get an impression of character. She looked competent, determined, someone who would work for a plan she'd decided on. Someone who would commit a murder?

Sergeant Peterson turned the laptop back and began tapping again. 'It's a photo from someone else's Facebook page. Edinburgh, April of this year.' She scribbled down the names, and took her phone out. 'Andy – Freya here. I'm trying to find out more about an Anna Reynolds, who's in a Facebook party shot. I'm sending you the link, and the address from the voters' roll. I need to know where she works, friends, particularly if she's a friend of Oliver Eastley . . . Yes, see what you can find out, and call me.'

She put the phone away, and turned back to me. 'So, she was booked to stay in the camping böd, but she came up on the ship with you. As a trainee?'

I shook my head. 'I think she came on board in Lerwick. A stowaway.' I spread my hands. 'We had one peg too few.'

Sergeant Peterson raised her fair brows. 'Explain.'

I did my best, and she nodded. 'So this woman didn't have a pin to take, and took someone else's, to avoid drawing attention to herself.'

'She didn't have to have help on board to know about that,' Gavin said. 'She could just have watched the other trainees going off, and copied them. With you standing there, she'd know it would have looked odd if she hadn't taken one.'

'But it would have caused just as much fuss if she'd taken someone else's, and then they came along and theirs was missing,' I said. 'I don't think it was coincidence that the peg she took was Oliver's.'

'But she was one of the last off the ship,' Gavin said. 'There would only have been a handful of trainee pegs to choose from. I think we should keep that as a possible coincidence, rather than proof that they were working together.'

'But his peg being missing drew attention to him,' Sergeant Peterson said.

'Yeah,' I agreed, 'but it's not like the peg gave him an alibi – his alibi was that he was here, on the ship, in the full view of the officers on board, all morning.'

'Tell Freya about the conversation you heard this morning,' Gavin said.

I did my best.

'*We've come too far to give up now,*' she repeated. 'Who said that?'

'I can't tell,' I said. 'I only caught that because it was hissed, slightly louder. I don't know if it was a man's voice or a woman's.'

'But someone was having second thoughts,' Sergeant Peterson said. She nodded to herself, lowered her laptop screen, and looked over at Gavin. 'So, what have we so far?'

'A brother and sister,' Gavin said. 'The parents recently dead, in a car crash which so shocked the sister that she gave up her car. The parents' will left the bulk of their estate to that sister, who's the golden girl of the family, taking her place as a director of the firm, while her brother is still an office boy.'

'And if she were to die, presumably the brother would inherit everything.'

'Not to mention getting rid of the little sister who outshone you,' I added. 'Oliver would like to be king.'

Sergeant Peterson gave me a look which reminded me I was the interviewee. I ignored it. 'I don't suppose Oliver has any mechanical skills?'

'The car accident?' Gavin asked.

Too easy to tamper with. 'If Laura suspected him of having caused the parents' death and was worried he was going to make her have an accident too, that could be why she gave her car up.' I'd had a car myself only briefly and illegally, in the longship time, but I knew how loath people were to give up driving.

'I can find that out,' Sergeant Peterson said, making a note. 'It wouldn't be unusual. Most young men can tinker a bit.'

'Then there was the incident in the broch,' Gavin said. He nodded an *Over to you* to me.

'On Mousa?' Sergeant Peterson said.

'We stopped off there, yesterday,' I said. I gave as clear an account as I could of what had happened, finishing with Laura's words: '*He tripped, I think. Yes, I'm certain . . . there was a scuffle and a clang behind me, then I felt him push me, and then we were both rolling downwards.*'

'What did you think happened?'

I shook my head. 'I didn't see it. I was coming down above them. But I don't see why he'd try to kill her there. The stairs are too narrow to fall far; she came off with a few bruises and a warning that he was a danger to her.' Gavin began a nod, then suppressed it. I envisaged Oliver. 'But Oliver's an opportunist type. He might just have looked at this stone stair and decided it was worth a try.'

'But the real plan was for here,' Sergeant Peterson said. 'Eastley got Reynolds on board surreptitiously and established an alibi, while Reynolds did the actual murder.' She wrinkled her ruler-straight nose. 'A girlfriend, a wife. Andy will pick that up, if there's a legal connection between them.'

'If there was a known connection,' Gavin pointed out, 'then his alibi would do him no good. It would be an obvious conspiracy.'

'OK, I think we're done. Gavin?'

He read me back what he'd written in a deadpan voice, and I signed it. Sergeant Peterson raised her head. 'Well, thank you, Cass. Can you send in Mona now?'

I nodded and left them to it.

CHAPTER FIFTEEN

I'd vaguely noticed the bustle of people tramping about on deck – the trainees being ferried over to the hall for the evening dance. The last inflatable-full was loading as I came out on deck. I glanced at my watch and was surprised to see that it was only 19.45. Handover time. I went up to relieve Petter, and found Alain by the nav shack too, long legs stretched out towards the sea rail, a cup of coffee in hand. He looked up and smiled as I came up the stairs. 'Third degree over?'

I shrugged.

'Must be awkward, being interviewed by your boyfriend,' Petter said.

'He wasn't allowed to ask any questions,' I said. 'What was the forecast?'

'Calm now, rising to a 3 gusting 4 later, visibility poor through the night.' He nodded southwards. 'Mist rolling in.'

I looked and saw a grey cloud blotting out the sea. It

was the Shetland east coast *haar*, caused by warm air from Spain. It blew up the Channel, gathering moisture on the way, which it released as fog when it came to our colder waters. Unfortunately, the airport was on the east coast, so you could have several days of no newspapers or mail from the south, to say nothing of a lot of people waiting at Sumburgh or taking the boat instead. The mist stopped at the central spine of Shetland; the west side could be basking in sunshine while the east was steekit.

'That's not going to help their search,' Alain said. He tilted his chin up towards the helicopter, distant in the sky, rotor blades whirling.

'Here come the land force,' Petter said.

A navy coastguard pick-up was moving on the road, followed by the shuttle bus we'd used earlier. We watched as the two vehicles came to a halt by the Interpretative Centre, and a dozen people in blue boiler suits clambered out. 'The search team?' Alain said.

I nodded. 'I'll tell Captain Sigurd.'

He'd come out while we were speaking, and was on deck, watching. He turned to me as I moved towards him. 'Ms Lynch. I think there should be representatives of the ship with the search party. I will send you, Mr Andersen and Mr Martin. My compliments, please, to Ms Solheim, and I would be obliged if she would take over the ship from Mr Martin.'

'Sir,' I said. I headed below, found Agnetha and gave her the message, nodded into Jenn's office to tell Gavin I was going with the search party, grabbed my black jacket from my cabin, sprayed myself liberally with anti-midge stuff, shoved the canister in my pocket to share with those who hadn't yet met a Shetland midgie, and reappeared in time to clamber into the inflatable.

213

The last drift of wind had died. A gull creaked as it flew over, then settled on its own reflection, beady eyes watching us. When we arrived at the pier, we were instantly attacked by midges, clouds of them, zooming in like fighter pilots. Alain swore in Spanish, and I passed him the spray. 'Don't miss your ears.'

The search party had got their gear on now: black overall trousers with a high-vis strip around the mid-calf, neon-yellow jackets and blue helmets with head torches strapped to the front. One was getting a yellow duffel bag marked 'Stretcher' out of the pick-up, another two were comparing OS maps, and a third was pulling on a chunky first aid rucksack. Another was giving out hand-held torches. No time was being wasted; they knew exactly what they were doing, and what they would need for the task.

One, still dressed in his blue boiler suit, was directing operations. Nils explained who we were, and he introduced himself: Jon, the senior coastal operations officer. He was splitting his team into three groups to cover more of the island quickly, with local help. A dozen locals were standing in a bunch, waiting. We watched as he divided them, allotting the jobs of communications, first aid and navigation within each group.

'Right,' he said, once that was done. 'Everyone ready? Radio check first – channel 99.'

There was a minute of crackling and buzzing as each communications person checked in on a neon hand-held.

'Good. We have two missing women, last seen together. They're both in their mid to late twenties.' The communications person in each group was scribbling this in a notebook. 'They were last seen heading along the road towards the east end of the island. One, Laura Eastley, was half expected back at the hall for lunch, but didn't turn up; we don't know any plans for the other one, possibly called Anna Reynolds. Laura was definitely expected back at five, so she's three hours overdue, maybe longer. Laura was wearing a powder-blue jacket, Anna a navy jumper, and perhaps a yellow oilskin jacket.'

He gave a look around to check they'd got that, and his team nodded. 'The chopper did an infra-red sweep but found nothing. We have some possible sightings, but there have been trainees all round the island this morning, and it seems several of them have light blue jackets. We've got three teams of ten, so that'll help us cover the ground. We'll begin the search at the ends of the road, with teams sweeping northwards and southwards, and a team in the central area.' He looked at the locals. 'Are there any of you who live at the east end? We can put five of you with each team.'

Several of the crofters in boiler suits and boots stepped forward. Jon nodded to Alain and Nils to join them.

'Take the ropes and investigate the cliffs. Keep in contact.' He gave a glance out at the sea, where the mist was moving steadily closer, but didn't comment. The parties clambered into the shuttle bus and local cars, and set off in procession along the road. He turned to my team. 'You search the central section of the island.' He looked around at the locals. 'Five of you, and Cass.'

'I'll go with that team too,' a voice said from the shadow by the phone box. Oliver stepped out into the light. His face was drawn, his mouth pulled down at the corners and his eyes reddened, as if he'd been crying.

I could see from Jon's face that he wasn't sure that was a good idea. They hoped, of course, that they would find Laura tucked under a peat bank with a turned ankle and mild hypothermia, and Anna staying to look after her, but they had also to be realistic. If it had only been a broken ankle, if Anna was an innocent tourist, she'd have phoned or come for help by now. Finding his sister's body might be the shock that pushed Oliver over the edge. 'I think, sir, that you should remain here, so that you can get any news as soon as it comes in. This will be the command centre.'

Oliver shook his head. 'I want to come with you. I want to make sure we look everywhere.'

'We'll do that, sir.' Jon put a hand on his arm and nodded to one of the women hovering in the hall doorway, the woman with the Viking house under her lawn, on duty again for the evening dance. 'You have a cup of tea, and wait for news.'

Oliver's shoulders sagged. He allowed the woman to lead him into the hall, talking soothingly. 'They ken fine what they're doing. Now you just come in and think of what you'll say to your sister when she arrives, giving you a fright like this . . .'

Once he was safely away, Jon took his radio out. 'Shetland Coastguard, this is Baltasound Base.'

'Shetland Coastguard, receiving you. Go to channel 67, over.'

Jon changed channels. 'Shetland Coastguard, we're heading out to search. The team personnel are—' His eyes went over them and he reeled off a list of numbers, followed by the number of locals. 'Over.'

The radio crackled. 'Shetland Coastguard. Roger. Message received. Attempt contact every thirty minutes.'

'Will do. Baltasound Base out.'

Jon went back to our briefing. 'Your group, take the bus up to the airstrip, go straight north past the Fiddler's Crus, up to the chambered cairn on Vord Hill, then down to Funzie Girt, the Neolithic wall. Check both sides of it, then once you reach the sea sweep back over, heading due south to the school road.'

We bumped up the road and along the airstrip in the minibus,

216

then clambered out at the end of it and assembled into a line, the four coastguard men spread out with two locals between each pair. The visibility was still reasonable, though the white cloud lay heavy along the tops of the hills.

'We'll close up if we need to,' our leader said, 'but to search thoroughly we need to keep no more than twenty metres apart anyway.'

We spread out, and suddenly the hill seemed much wider. What could this thin strip of people manage against this broad moor, riddled with burn-gullies and heathery knowes, where even the lowest crumbled peat bank could hide someone lying beside it? I'd never measured before how small a human body was, compared to this rough wilderness. We tramped steadily on in our line, eyes flicking from the figure at each side back to the ground at our feet: the knee-high tussocks of pink-tinted heather, the trickles of burn, the spread of marshy ground, lime-yellow with moss, the grey stones jutting up, the black wedges of exposed peat. There was no time to pick a long way around the marshy places. If I could jump from one tussock of grass to another, I did; if not, I waded through. Soon I felt the first cold water oozing through my socks.

Tramp on, on, looking and looking. From time to time the radio crackled, reporting the position of the other parties. The air was cold on my cheek. We came to the Fiddler's Crus, where criminals used to be sentenced. The white stone was the judge's seat. The circles were clear enough, three low walls overgrown with turf, with the stones jutting through like teeth. We went around each one, but there was nobody there, so we climbed on, up to the ruined chambered cairn on Vord Hill, then down to Funzie Girt, the Finns' magical wall, a great dyke with the top foot made of fells. Three of the locals went to the other side of it; the rest of us remained on this side and walked along it. We paused for a breather when we reached the sea, then worked east again, along a jagged section of steep banks, until we met up with the first group. I glanced at my watch and was surprised to find we'd only been walking for an hour.

As we set out homewards, the mist closed in, rolling across the sea and filling the bay with cobweb grey, so that Sørlandet's masts were blotted out, then her hull, and then it spread to the pebble shore. The summer noises of soft wind and terns chittering were blotted out; the green of the hills around us faded to white, and the temperature dropped abruptly from a summer evening to autumn chill, with moisture clinging to our cheeks and lashes.

'Gather round,' our leader said. We clustered around him. 'Keep within sight of each other, and close in if the mist thickens. For now, not more than ten metres apart. We won't cover as broad a sweep of ground, but we won't lose each other either.' He fished in his pocket and brought out a bag of plastic pea-whistles. 'Have one of these each. Blow it if you lose touch with either of the people on each side of you.'

He fished in his pocket again and brought out three hand-held compasses. He gave one to me. 'Cass, you take the right-hand end of the line, and Brian, you take the left hand. I'll go in the middle. Keep us heading south-south east – 157 degrees.' He raised his head to speak generally. 'We'll come down the side of Busta Hill, cross the burn – the left-hand end, you'll be crossing two burns – and come up the Muckle Scord. We'll pause and gather at the top of it, then spread again to come down the side of it to Skutes Water, and the school road.'

We spread out into our line and set off. I was having to force my tired legs to keep moving. We came briskly down the hill. I had one eye on the compass needle, the other on the neon figures to my left. The mist cleared as we reached the cleft of the valley and the burn running down to the loch, a grey pool in the distance. I scooped up some of the peaty burn water to drink as we passed, rubbed my wet hand over my face, and trudged on. Uphill now, feet thudding down in the heather or speeding up slightly as they found a sheep track. As we climbed the steep slope, the mist thickened. It was disorientating; you couldn't tell what size things were as they loomed up in the distance. What I took to be a pony grazing became smaller as we got closer, and shrank to the end of a stone wall, less than my hip height. Now I could see only my nearest three searchers, then two. All along, the line was tightening up. I moved in closer, five metres, to keep in touch with my left-hand neighbour, and trudged on.

We paused at the ridge of the hill. I leant over, bracing my hands on my thighs, and tried to steady my breathing. The grass was too chilled to sit down on, and I feared that if I sat, I'd never rise. Our leader counted us. 'Sixteen. Good.' He fished in his pocket and passed round a handful of bite-sized fruit bars. 'Last stretch, folk, just one mile more, and downhill too, to make it easy for us. Keep south-south east till we reach the Haltadans and Skutes Water, Cass and Brian, then we follow the burn east to the school.' He gave an anxious look into the whiteness. 'If anyone gets separated, keep going downhill, blowing your whistle. We'll gather again at the burn.' He let us all look at the map again to fix this last piece in our heads, then we spread out and set off. My compass hand was growing numb in the mist-chilled wind; I tucked it as far into my sleeve as it would go and stumbled downhill, keeping the compass needle steady.

Suddenly the wind intensified, the mist swirled and blotted everything out. The neon vest beside me disappeared. I heard a whistle from my left and pulled my own out to answer, a good, sharp blast, then paused to think. It was no good me trying to walk towards the sound; in mist, sound played tricks on you. I stood still and listened. I could hear footsteps, but they seemed to be behind me – no, to my right. I turned my head to stare in that direction, but there was nothing, and unless I'd turned – and I was sure that I hadn't – then my next person was to my left. I raised the compass. South-south east. I faced that way and turned my head over my left shoulder. Nothing; and the noise of the whistle had faded into the whiteness too. I was on my own.

Sailors hate mist. It plays with distance; it hides the sea, the shore, the deadly rock you wanted to avoid. Lost in the mist was the last place I wanted to be. At sea, you'd make for open water, or drop anchor until it had gone, or creep along the ten fathom line on the chart to your destination. I swung my arms to warm myself up, stuck my whistle between my teeth, then tugged my jacket around me. I had a compass, and I'd been walking for ten minutes. If I kept going for another five, I'd get to the loch.

I gave the whistle a blast. There was a scrabble and a scurry almost under my feet, making me jump back, heart pounding. A shape moved in the mist, swelling upwards, then I saw grey wool as a sheep leapt up and bounded off, and heard the patter of hooves as others joined it. Thanks, ladies. I took a deep breath, gave another blast, walked twenty paces and blasted again. Between blasts I listened, but there was nothing. The hairs on the back of my neck prickled, as if someone was watching me from the whiteness.

I walked on. The mist thinned for a moment, and I saw something ahead of me, a pony lying down maybe, some twenty metres ahead. I blasted again, but it didn't move, and it was too small for a pony, flatter to the ground. I felt my breathing tight as I came towards it. There were two legs straggling towards me, a body hunched under a dark jacket. My foot caught on a stone and I stumbled forward and fell, hands flat on the mossy ground, knees soaked through. I pulled myself back onto my hunkers, and felt a stone under each hand, smoothed, sizeable boulders buried in the earth. I knew where I was now. This was Haltadans, the stone circle where the trows had been turned to stone as the sun came up. I pushed myself to my feet and walked forward to the centre.

It wasn't Laura, but a man. He was lying between the two centre stones with his legs stretched long and his arms tight round his body. One hand clutched his shoulder, white against the navy and grey Musto jacket. His hood was pulled up, shading his face.

I went forward in as few steps as I could to crouch down beside him and feel for a pulse. The cold weight of his hand told me straight away that he was dead, but I tried, all the same, then put my ear to his mouth in the shadow of the hood to listen for the sound of breath, or feel the warmth of it. Nothing.

Carefully, handling it with my fingertips, I slid the hood back.

It was Daniel who lay there, mouth twisted open. I noticed his eyes first, staring sightlessly up into the mist. Then I saw the neat red hole, crusted with a blacker rim of blood, in the centre of his forehead.

My heart thudded as if it wanted to leap from my chest. It was the suddenness of it, finding him like that, and him being the wrong body, and that horrid red hole, so neatly in the centre of his forehead, as if someone he trusted had walked up to him and pressed the trigger before he could even react. If his face had any expression, it was disbelief.

I tried to think what Gavin would have done. Time, first. I checked my watch: twenty to ten. I crouched down, keeping my feet still, and touched his hand again. The outer side of it was cold and damp, but underneath, where it had lain against his jacket, my fingers felt a faint warmth lingering. The pathologist would know what that meant. The blood round that hole had dried.

There was nothing I could do but fetch help. I called the map to memory. Straight south would bring me to the top of the loch, but slanting slightly to the east would either get me help sooner or have me miss the loch completely. Safe, not sorry. I said a prayer for Daniel, standing over his crumpled body, then set off due southwards, going always to the left when I had to deviate, then picking up my straight path again. I could see only ten metres before me, tussocks of hill grass, the dulled colours of the flowers, sheep tracks leading into the blankness. My footsteps were silent on the turf; I could hear only my own breathing, the rustle of my jacket, and the silence was more menacing than sound would have been. There was a killer with a gun out there, perhaps not far away, hiding in this mist. He, she, could be following me, and I'd never know it.

I stumbled on. No time to keep looking at my watch. Southwards – and then, with a snick of stones under my feet, I'd found the loch, fringed by a pebble beach. I turned left and made my way along, feet crunching the stones until I couldn't bear the noise in this silence, feeling it was signalling my presence too easily to someone waiting in the mist, and moved back to the grassy rim. At last I heard a faint whistle blast ahead of me. I grabbed my own from my neck and gave a good answering blow that split the mist around me. From somewhere on my hill side there was a scrabble, a noise of thudding feet. Startled sheep, I told myself, and found the energy to break into a jog.

The search team burst into view twenty strides later, a group of shapes in the mist, gradually becoming neon vests, dark trousers, hooded faces. I skidded to a stop beside them and leant over, catching my breath.

'Cass,' our leader said. 'Good. That's everyone. OK, homewards, keeping together.'

I put out a hand to stop him and tried to control my breathing. 'Wait,' I managed. I took another couple of breaths. 'There's a dead man up there. Up at the Haltadans. He's been shot.'

CHAPTER SIXTEEN

The fiddle and accordion music, the thump of dancing feet, echoed through the wall. I sat in a corner of the playgroup room, warming my hands with a mug of tea, and still shivering with a combination of cold and shock. Someone had flung a knitted-squares blanket over my shoulders, and someone else had pressed this mug of well-sugared tea into my hands. I sat and watched while our group leader explained to Gavin. Sergeant Peterson began mustering her troops, and Gavin came over to me. 'You found him, Cass?'

His hand was warm on my shoulder. I nodded. 'In the middle of the Haltadans,' I managed, through chattering teeth. 'At 21.40. It was Daniel, and he'd been shot.' I took a deep breath and clutched my mug in both hands. 'The skin that was exposed to the air was cold, but where it was against his jacket it was still warm.'

He made a note of that. 'Any sign of anyone else around?'

I shook my head. 'It was too misty. I felt like I was being watched, but I was on edge. Probably imagination.'

'OK. Stick here with other people until you go aboard again.' His hand tightened on my shoulder, then lifted. 'I'll see you back on board.'

I nodded and watched through the window as they piled onto the shuttle bus. It had just brought the third rescue team back: Alain's. He gave the mustering officers a quick, intelligent glance, and came into the committee room. He sat down beside me. 'You found her?'

I shook my head. I wasn't sure what I was allowed to say, but my group of the rescue team knew it wasn't her. 'A body. Not hers. A man.'

He jerked back from me, staring. 'A man? What had happened to him?'

I shouldn't answer that, I knew, and surely 'Who?' would have been a more natural question. I shook my head again and drank more of the over-sweet tea. It was surprisingly comforting.

He gave me a curious look. 'Where did you find the dead man?' My search team knew that too. 'In the stone circle.'

'A local man?'

I took refuge in evasion. 'I'm not supposed to talk about it.'

Alain made a face and was silent for a moment, then he glanced over at the door. 'If they're looking at a body they'll be hours. Drink that up, and let's get you back on board.'

Stick here with other people. I shook my head and stood up, letting the blanket slip from my shoulders. 'I'm fine now. We're on duty, remember.' I jerked my head towards the music. 'The dance. Any word from Nils's team?'

'They're not back yet, but there was nothing the last time we spoke.'

I glanced out of the window. 'It'll be dark soon.'

'Nothing,' Alain repeated. 'Two women disappeared.'

There was a massive land and sea search, but nobody was found, nor any sign of them . . .

'I need to report to Captain Sigurd,' I said, and headed for the door into the main hall.

The blast of sound hit me: the fiddles and accordions giving it laldy in a Foula Reel. I looked around, but there was no sign of the captain. He'd likely stayed on board, where the VHF radio would help him keep in touch with the lifeboat, chopper and coastguard operations. The coastguard SCOO would have reported back.

I went back to the committee room, and over to the window. Gavin and his team would walk up to the Haltadans more quickly than I'd come down, going straight across from the end of the airstrip. I imagined them gathering around Daniel's body and putting some sort of protection over it until scene-of-crime could arrive from Inverness or Aberdeen.

The shuttle bus passed the hall, heading for the east of the island, to get the team Nils had gone with. I waited for five minutes, ten, until the lights reappeared in the distance. When the minibus pulled up on the tarmac, I could see by the faces that they'd found nothing.

I left the window and returned to the main hall. It looked like everyone was having a good time. There was the entire population of the island as well as our trainees: children running round, teenagers in vest tops and jeans, women in flowered dresses, men who'd shed their search jackets and changed into cloth breeks and shirts. Seats were set out all around the hall, but they were mostly empty; the Foula Reel I'd heard had just ended, and the floor was packed with people clapping the band

and laughing with their partners. They'd got some Shetland Folk Dance members to lead the dancing, women in ankle-length striped skirts and scallop-edged shawls over white blouses, and men in dark breeks and waistcoats, with kerchiefs knotted round their necks. One woman stepped forward to the microphone. 'Don't sit down, here's a nice gentle dance to let you catch your breath and let you get romantic with your partner. It's called the Valetta Waltz, and it's one of our easiest waltzes.'

Four of the group came to the cleared centre of the floor. 'We'll just demonstrate it,' the leader said, and they walked through a simple dance, swinging out and in, two steps, repeat, walk a square, waltz for four. 'Take your partners, please, and we'll walk through it a couple of times.'

Alain had gone straight for what had to be the Gord B & B woman's Italian tourist. Her hair was glossily dark and curly, held back with a scarf tied Alice-band style over her head. Her dark eyes had been made enormous with mascara and eyeliner, and the scarlet of her lips exactly matched her shiny stilettos. She was wearing a floral sundress, patterned in pink and black, with its flared skirt stiffened out with petticoats. Her arms were smooth and evenly tanned, that tan of a world where the sun shines all the year round. She stood out from the casually dressed trainees and Sunday-best locals like a hummingbird in a flock of sparrows.

Nils came up behind me and spoke in my ear. 'Will we set a good example, Cass, the officers dancing with the trainees?' He nodded towards the seats where a handful of people were still sitting. It was the last thing I felt like, but I nodded, and we went forward to ask them to dance. Nils had one of the women from his watch, and I persuaded one of my two Swedes, Valter, to give it a go. We managed not badly, though with none of the grace of Alain and his partner, twirling merrily around the middle of the floor. Even as she danced, she was talking animatedly in broken English, freeing her hand to gesture, and he was laughing. I shouldn't have felt jealous, I had Gavin, yet there was a pang at my heart that she could be so carefree with him where I was tongue-tied, unable even to say, 'Do you remember . . . ?' I turned my head so as not to look at them, and focused on Valter. By the third section of music, we'd mastered the steps enough to try some conversation. 'Your search did not find the missing sister,' he said.

'No,' I agreed. We did the walk in a square, the four waltz turns, then went back to swinging.

'These cliffs are very steep. She could have fallen. It is sad, a girl so young.' He looked around. 'Her brother, will he stay with the ship, or wait here for news?'

'I don't know.' We began the square again. If Laura had gone over the cliffs, her body might never be found. I tried to think what would look natural for Oliver to do. To continue his holiday would seem heartless. To go home straight away would look uncaring. No, he'd stay in Lerwick, waiting for news for two days, at least, and then go home.

'Is there a shuttle to the ship all evening?'

I was sure Jenn would have told them that. 'Yes, there's a boat on duty.'

'Ah, then he will have gone back, the man who looks out of place.'

My heart missed a beat. 'Who?'

'He is in the red watch. Daniel.' The square again, the waltz. I waited for the swing and steps, and Valter continued. 'I was watching him earlier. He did not dance, he was too busy playing with his phone – you know, the way younger ones do nowadays, always sliding and tapping. Restless. I thought perhaps he did not

228

like the fiddle music. It is not to the taste of young ones. Then he went out, and he has not come back, so I thought he must have gone back to the ship.'

Playing with his phone. 'Was he phoning someone?'

Valter shook his head. 'Texting, or checking his emails, or updating his Facebook profile, how should I know? But I don't think he was talking. Anyway, he went out, and he has not come back, so I suppose he got fed up and returned to the ship.'

It began clicking together in my head. Daniel had made a lousy Second Murderer, giving himself away all over the place. He'd gone to the böd to meet up with Anna Reynolds, but she hadn't been there, and he'd been like a cat on hot bricks, wondering what had happened, if something had gone wrong. He'd gone back there to look again, drawing even more attention to the place. Maybe she'd been upstairs, waiting, while Gavin had bandaged my ankle. She'd have seen how hopeless a conspirator he was. To make herself safe, she'd need to get rid of him before he gave them both away . . . so she'd texted him. *Meet me at the stone circle.* They'd met, and she'd killed him.

But if that was how it had been, where did Oliver fit in?

The dance ended with a flourish. Valter made me a formal bow, and I did a curtsey-bob as best I could in jeans. The big fireman, Berg, swooped on the pretty Italian and Alain's arm came around my waist. I shrugged it off, and he caught my hand. 'No, don't sit down. I'm getting the hang of this.'

'We'll liven you up again,' the leader said, 'with a Gay Gordons, the one we did earlier.'

'I didn't,' I said perversely, although a youth of hall and regatta dances meant my feet could do a Gay Gordons in their sleep. 'And I've walked miles today.'

'We just need to watch the others,' Alain said.

Before I could protest his arm was around my shoulders, his other hand reaching for mine, and we were marching round in the circle. Four steps, turn, keep going backwards; four steps forward, turn, continue backwards. Time fell away. I was back at the regatta dances we'd attended as teenagers, back at student ceilidhs, whirling around in the four steps of polka before we turned side by side for the march again, our bodies fitting together as if they'd never been apart. His arm was firm around my waist, his hand tight on mine, and our steps matched just as they had always done. The memory of the fun we'd had, and the sadness of these eleven years I'd been mourning him, swept over me. I felt tears well up in my eyes. They'd play three tunes for each dance, but I disengaged myself as soon as the first tune stopped. 'Thanks,' I said, in as casual a tone as I could manage.

He didn't let go of me. 'They do each dance three times.' His eyes were mocking now. 'Only two to go. I can't steal you from your detective in just two dances.'

'You can't steal me from him at all,' I retorted, and did my best to keep a distance between us, stiff in his hold.

'I shouldn't have reminded you,' he murmured. 'You're spoiling it now. It's just a dance.'

It might have been just a dance to him, but it was a million memories to me. I gritted my teeth and tried to relax, and was glad when it ended at last. I tried to pull away, but he had hold of my hand still. 'Come on, you could do with a drink. The bar's here.'

A struggle would have everyone looking at us. I let him tow me over to the bar hatch, to where a local of our own age was serving.

'Noo dan,' he said. 'What'll you hae?'

Then the moment I'd never thought of came. There was a man draped across the bar, our age too, medium height, with fair hair that was already receding. He turned to look as we came over, and the look turned to an incredulous stare. He leant forward with the wavering abandon of the very drunk, pushed himself off the bar, and slapped Alain on the back. 'Alan! I'm no seen dee since the Anderson. What's du been up tae?' He turned to me. 'Cass, lass! I kent dee straight away. Still together then, and still as mad aboot boats as you ever were. Good work. There's ower many divorces this days.' He reached behind him to his hip pocket, and brought out a quarter bottle of Grouse, and flourished it into my hand. 'Hae a dram.'

The universe seemed to stand still. Suddenly there was a deathly silence around us, and the air felt as if it was pressing in on my chest, sucking the breath from my lungs. The bottle was smooth against my palm. If ever I needed a dram, that time was now. I took a large swig and felt it burn down my throat.

Alain hadn't looked at me. He tilted the bottle to his lips and drank, five long, steady mouthfuls, his throat moving each time, then gave it back. The drunk clapped him on the back, leant forward to give me a whisky-reeking kiss. 'Fine tae see dee,' he said, and ambled towards the dance floor.

The band flared out into the Pride of Erin. My feet felt the music, long step, long, short, short, short, but around us there was still that silence. Alain's fingers were tight on my wrist. He gave a yank towards the door, and I followed him into the car park without protesting. There would have to be an explanation, and easier here, now, than on board ship. He glanced at the too-close open door, then towed me to the far edge of the car park.

There was another long pause. The night air was chill on my cheek, the sea still clouded with mist. Venus hung in the east. The music throbbed from the hall.

He pulled me round to face him. His grey eyes were coal-black with fury in the summer dimness. 'You knew. All these days.' He made a gesture with one hand. He was so angry he could hardly speak. 'You *knew* me. And you didn't say anything.'

Suddenly, with his eyes blazing at me, time dropped away. The guilt I'd felt over his death was swept away by the anger I hadn't known I'd suppressed all these years. He was alive now, and I could let it out. I flared back at him in French. 'What the devil did you want me to say?' My hand went up to my cheek. 'Hey, Alain, remember this? Trying to kill me in the middle of the Atlantic?'

He grabbed me by the shoulders and shook me, and I shoved him away from me. 'Don't you touch me!'

He caught me up again, and this time he kissed me. The familiarity of it swept over me, the old spark of passion flared up again, and for a moment I responded. I'd never thought I would kiss him again, and our mouths clung together as they always had, our bodies . . . Then I remembered Gavin, those eleven years with all the changes they'd made, and pulled myself free, holding my hand against his chest to keep him back. 'No, Alain. No.'

'Alain.' He tasted the name, and replied in French. 'I'm French?'

I nodded. There was a low wall surrounding the car park. I sat down on it, the rough stones reassuringly solid. 'Alain Mouettier. Your mother was from Yell, and your father was French. He taught at the Mid Yell school.' I nodded across at the south end of Yell, dissolving into the darkness. 'You grew up in West Sandwick, over there.'

'French.' He shook his head. 'I never thought of being French. I knew I could speak it, of course, but they spoke to me in Spanish, and I was fluent.'

'You did Spanish at university. Edinburgh. You did your language year in a school near Seville and came back speaking like a native.'

'I looked in Spain. They said my accent was southern Spain, so

I spent a year travelling round, trying to find somewhere familiar. And all the time—' He looked across at the dim hills. 'Are my parents still here?'

I shook my head. 'They moved, after . . .'

'After that.' He sat down beside me, leaving a hand's width between us. The anger had drained out of him. His hand came up, very gently, to touch my cheek. 'I tried to kill you?' His voice was incredulous.

My anger had spilt away. I gave a long sigh. 'It was me who left you there, in the middle of the Atlantic.' At first, when I couldn't believe that he was gone, I'd explained to him in my head, over and over again. Now, with him alive beside me, it was hard to find the words. 'You weren't trying to kill *me*. You got hit on the head with the boom. You were concussed, seeing double. You thought I was pirates, and ordered me off. When I wouldn't go, you shot at me. I tacked her, and the jib knocked you overboard.' My voice was steady, but I could feel tears running warm down my cheeks. 'I searched, and searched, but there was a good sea running. I couldn't find you. I thought you'd gone straight down. In the end I just had to keep going.' It had taken two weeks to reach Scotland, with his ghost haunting me every mile of the way.

'The trawler that picked me up, they said there was no name on the lifebuoy.'

'We lost one on the way over. That was our replacement. We bought it in Boston, in a little chandlery in a back street. We never got round to putting her name on it.'

'What was she called?' His voice was very soft. 'Our ship.'

'*Marielle*.' My throat was husky. I paused and swallowed. 'She was a Liz 30.' Now I was crying in earnest. 'She was sold, after.'

His arm came up around me, and this time I didn't shrug him away. 'How long were we lovers?'

233

'A year.' I leant my head on his shoulder. 'Do you really not remember, not even now I've told you?'

'Nothing.' I heard the smile in his voice. 'Oh, I know, that's not how it works in the movies. I'm supposed to have a blinding flash of enlightenment when it all comes back. No. It won't work like that. I was lucky that skipper saved my life, but that part of my memory is gone. The doctors said I'll never recover it.' Now he was teasing me. 'You'll just have to tell me all about it.'

'We were young,' I said. 'Mad teenagers. Well, I was nineteen, and you were twenty-one. We were going to take *Marielle* round the world after you'd done your final year. Crossing the Atlantic was our shake-down cruise.'

He was silent for a moment, shaking his head. 'Suddenly, I have a past again. All these years, it's been so strange. I'd given up hoping that I'd ever find out. Now I have so many questions I don't know where to begin.'

He paused, and I let the silence lie between us. Below, in the bay, the round head of an otter drew a V of ripples behind it; a curlew gave its bubbling call on the hill behind us. He gave a long sigh. 'I grew up here, with this. This honey smell in the air, and that bird calling. Wouldn't you think I'd remember?'

'The honey's the heather,' I said, 'and the bird's a whaup.'

'When did we meet? You and I?'

'At the regattas. Sailing. We were both in Mirrors at first, then you moved up to crewing in an Albacore for one of the Yell men.'

'Childhood sweethearts?'

'No. I was still only fourteen when you were seventeen, and ready to go to university. You went to Edinburgh.' It was so hard to sum up a life in a few sentences. 'Arts. You did Spanish, philosophy and politics in your first two years, then specialised in Spanish. You had a flat off Dalry Road, and we met again when

I was waitressing in a cafe there. I was eighteen, and you'd just done your year in Spain. I stayed at your flat for a bit, then you bought *Marielle*. We lived on board, so that we could afford to do the Ocean Yachtmaster course at college in the evenings.' I was smiling now. 'It was cheaper than the flat, but a lot colder, and absolute chaos. Rewiring, pulling the joinery apart, fitting a second-hand engine. Half the time we barely managed to find space for our mattress. But she was beautiful once we'd finished. We were so proud of her.'

'But you sold her.'

I slid my hand into his and felt his fingers close warm around mine. I knew he understood the wrench it had been. 'I thought I'd killed you. I couldn't keep your boat. Your parents sold her.'

'But you kept her sextant.'

I pulled away from him, suddenly suspicious again. 'How did you know?'

'Your face as I took a sighting with it. I didn't understand what had upset you.'

Dammit, I was going to start crying again. I gave my eyes a savage rub with the back of one hand. 'I'm sorry. It was such a shock to see you, and a worse one that you didn't know me, and such a relief now that you know.'

'When were you going to tell me?'

'I didn't know you'd lost your memory, did I? I didn't know what you were up to. Then, when you told me, I couldn't think of how to say it. I wondered about getting the minister to tell your parents . . .' I turned to face him. 'Besides, I didn't quite believe the lost memory stuff.'

He smiled at that. 'Convinced now?'

I nodded.

He sat for a moment longer, eyes on the horizon, then rose. 'Well, my little one, you'd better give your eyes some cold water before you come and dance the last dance with me. Did we dance together at the regattas too?'

'Sometimes.' I added, waspishly, 'When there weren't enough pretty older girls to go round.'

That had given away far too much. His head turned quickly towards me. 'You make it sound as if I led you a merry dance.'

I remembered his tall, beautiful fellow students, golden girls like Laura. 'Yes.'

'Well, I'm a reformed character now, and we're both eleven years wiser.' He held out both hands to pull me down from the wall. 'And now we know who we are.'

I shook my head, and jumped down by myself. 'No. That's who we were. Eleven years ago.'

'Oho. So you've turned respectable, and are sticking with your policeman.'

'Yes.'

He didn't reply for a moment, but I heard him whistle softly under his breath. I started to walk towards the hall. I felt drained. I just wanted to go back to the ship and curl up in my berth, with Cat in the crook of my neck and the water rippling at my ear.

Alain hadn't followed me. I nipped into the ladies' and splashed my face with cold water then stood for a moment, looking at myself in the mirror. There was no sign of the last half hour in my face; I just looked dog-tired, with a frown between my brows, and my mouth drawn down. The band had launched into 'The Lion and the Unicorn' – the start of the last dance. I just needed to help herd the trainees down to the pier and ferry them over. Then I could sleep.

I went through to the main hall and stood quietly, leaning

against a door-jamb. The tune changed to 'It's a Long Way to Tipperary', the dancing speeded up and ended with a flourish. A pause, a chord, and the band struck up in 'Auld Lang Syne'. I forced my heavy feet forward into the circle, smiled at the trainees on each side of me and joined hands. Alain was opposite me, his eyes on mine. *Should auld acquaintance be forgot, and never brought to mind, should auld acquaintance be forgot, and auld lang syne.* As we sung the chorus the circle stampeded forward, and Alain and I came chest to chest in the crowd, then pulled back from each other as the wave receded. *Then here's a hand, my trusty friend . . .* I swapped hands around so that my arms were crossed in front of me, and when the chorus came, we rushed forward like that, and ended back on the circumference, laughing, as the song finished.

'Goodnight, everyone,' the band leader said. 'Safe journey back to your ship tonight, and enjoy the rest of your time in Shetland.'

Gradually we filed through the doors, greeting and thanking the locals as we went. Alain found his pretty Italian again and ushered her out. I searched as far down in my heart as I could, and found I didn't care. That he was alive was enough.

The dance had kept them from thinking. Now, as we came out, we saw searchlights moving on the hill, and dark figures crossing the static pool of light that marked the Haltadans. I saw the heads around me turning and heard a buzz of speculation: 'They've found her.' The Danish wife turned to me. 'Is it true? Have they found Laura?'

I shook my head. 'Not yet. They'll keep searching.'

The eight loads that it took to get everyone back aboard seemed to take for ever. I was just embarking the last one when Gavin came walking down the road. He slid his arm round my waist, and I leant against him.

'There's nothing more we can do now. I'll come and get some sleep.'

I nodded into his shoulder. We got aboard and headed for the safety of my cabin. The porthole framed the searchlights on the hill; the water glinted coal-black in the moonless sky. Gavin's cheek was cold against my forehead, smelling of fresh heathery air. We curled up to each other, and slept.

Part Six

The King on the Move

CHAPTER SEVENTEEN

Monday 2nd August

Low water, Lerwick 05.11 (0.4m)
High water 11.35 (2.0m)
Low water 17.27 (0.6m)
High water 23.47 (2.2m)

Moonrise 04.28; sunrise 04.49; moonset 20.55; sunset 21.32
New moon

I slept like a log, and only woke when Nils touched my toe at 03.40. Breakfast had been put back an hour to allow everyone to recover from the evening, but the ship still needed watched. I rose without waking Gavin and went up on deck. The morning was glass-still, with the green of field and white of house mirrored below the doubled shore, and the sun shining through hazy wisps of cloud on the horizon. The last white rags of mist clung to the hills.

After I'd done all the usual checks, I leant over the aft rail, listening to the soft movement of the water against the ship's hull, and trying to make sense of yesterday.

Topmost in my thoughts was Alain. Now we knew. He knew who I was, and I knew what had happened to him, and that was that. He'd have a lot of adjusting to do, but I wasn't going to be part of it. Those eleven years had passed, and changed us both. I thought of Gavin's arms warm around me last night, and chose this life with all my strength. I didn't know where it would end up, but I wanted the potential it held for stability, for children, for the end of a wandering life. I wasn't going to succumb to glamourie, like the Earl of Cassilis's lady, who ended up alone on a moor.

I shoved the thought of Alain away, and focused on our situation here. We had two missing women, one dead man, and one living one, with no clear idea of the links between them. What did we actually know, for sure?

Anna Reynolds had been on board, as part of an elaborate plan that had involved her coming up to Shetland and stowing away from Lerwick to Fetlar. Why?

OK. Let's suppose that Oliver was the brains of the pair, and Anna the gun-woman. Oliver had established himself an alibi on board, but he could have done that as easily in Edinburgh. So what stopped Anna just shooting Laura in Edinburgh?

I tried to imagine how you might go about it. Walking up to her and shooting point-blank was out; too many people and windows. Assuming Laura didn't know Anna – and I thought that was a safe assumption, because she'd have reacted to suddenly finding Oliver's girlfriend on board – then it would have been hard for Anna to strike up an acquaintance and lure Laura to a lonely place in Edinburgh. Could she have started chatting in a pub, two women together, offered to share a taxi or walk home together for safety? I just couldn't visualise it, and every scenario I tried left a trail of witnesses as well as CCTV footage from every shop and pub on the way.

There were no CCTV cameras on Fetlar, and on board ship, trainees expected to talk to each other. It would be easy enough to detach her from the others if they'd walked along the road together: 'Fancy going to see what's over that headland?', 'Where do you suppose this path leads?', 'I've got a flask. How about a cup of coffee looking out to sea?' Then, once they were safely out of sight, a shot, Laura's body flung over the banks, and Anna would proceed with the escape plan: a night in the camping böd, off on the ferry to the mainland the next day, and back to Edinburgh the day after.

She could have got away with being a stowaway on *Sørlandet* for a day. It had been Oliver who'd asked about the system – Oliver who'd handed Jonas that fistful of tickets from the family – except it was Daniel who'd been up and about early in Lerwick, as if he was meeting the ferry, Daniel who'd been looking for her at the böd.

Someone had helped her stay on board. She'd been there to get off in Fetlar the next morning, which meant she'd been in Lerwick on Saturday morning. That was something Gavin could chase up, if he or Sergeant Peterson hadn't already: her travel to Shetland. If she'd had a pistol, she couldn't have come up by plane; the X-ray machine would have spotted it in her luggage. She must have come by ferry from Aberdeen, and for that you had to book a passage. She'd have left a trail, and since she'd booked the camping böd in her own name, there was no reason why she shouldn't have booked the ferry as Anna Reynolds too. The police would find out how long this conspiracy had been planned for.

I frowned. If you were plotting murder, then surely you should be covering your tracks a bit. A fake ID, fake bank account and credit card . . . but where on earth would you begin to get these? You'd have to know someone, pay someone, and that would lay you open to blackmail once Laura's death was announced. But then, Anna Reynolds wasn't supposed to appear in this at all. If we hadn't seen Daniel like a cat on hot bricks at the camping böd, we'd never have known her name, so just booking as herself was likely safest.

Daniel and Anna . . . but then where did Oliver fit in? *I don't like that idea of a threesome, when it comes to murder*, Gavin had said. If Oliver was the person planning the murder, and Anna was carrying it out for him, then I didn't see how Daniel came into that. Or was Oliver really innocent, a concerned brother, who genuinely hadn't felt well yesterday morning? It occurred to me at last to wonder where he'd spent the evening. The motherly woman had taken him into the hall, but naturally he hadn't been at the dance. I'd assumed he'd have been waiting for news in the kitchen, or down at the coastguard pick-up which was the command centre . . . but if the people in each of those places thought he was at the other, then he could have been on the hill, with a pistol, meeting Daniel. Except that that gave us two murderers, for if there was one thing certain, it was that Oliver couldn't have fired that pistol we'd heard in the morning.

There were soft footsteps behind me. Gavin's arm tightened around me; he kissed the nape of my neck. 'I can hear your brain ticking over. Anything useful?'

'No. I'm just trying to sort the facts out, and making no sense of them. If it was Oliver and Daniel, we don't need Anna; if it was Daniel and Anna, then Oliver is extra, yet he's the one with the motive.'

'There was information coming through all evening. We'll sort it out this morning. When do you leave for Fetlar?'

244

I turned to face him, my heart sinking in dismay. 'You?'

He nodded. 'Finding Daniel's changed everything. I'm going to have to stay on Fetlar . . . but listen, I'll get someone to drive me to Hillswick, and meet you there this evening.'

'All this won't change the ship's schedule?'

'That depends on how quickly we can eliminate the rest of the trainees from the enquiry. Probably not.' He made an apologetic face. 'Sorry I can't tell you more.'

'S'OK,' I said. 'What about your being kidnapped?'

He brought his hand up to his brow. 'I'd forgotten all about that. There's no way that'll be possible, I'll need to be here all day. Can you let Inga know? Tell her I'm really sorry.'

I glanced at my watch. Ten to seven. Inga would be awake by now, especially if she was masterminding twenty-five kidnappings. I called her.

'Inga? Cass here.'

'Aye, aye. I heard Radio Shetland last night, the coastguard search and the woman being missing. What's happening?'

'There was a death last night.' I glanced at Gavin. 'Is that secret?'

Inga snorted. 'Secret, Cass, in Shetland? Yea, yea, I'd heard about that too. Is Gavin too tied up to be kidnapped, then?'

'Yea. He said to say he's really sorry.'

'OK.' There was a pause as Inga sorted out several possibilities in her head. 'Right, it'll hae to be dee, then.'

'Me?' I nearly dropped the phone. 'I'm no' famous.'

'Oh, you're getting pretty weel kent,' Inga said. 'All this interfering in murders. Anyway, I've no time to get someen else, so if you widna mind – we'll just pick you up off the beach the sam as we were going to do with Gavin.'

There was no point in resisting Inga's organisation. 'Well . . . OK,' I said. 'Then what?'

245

'Off to a secret destination, then released at eight o'clock to face the world's press. Well, Radio Shetland and the Millgaet TV cameras. Don't worry about that, they'll be far too busy talking to wir MPs to interview you.'

'Good.'

'Right, see you at Hillswick then. Gie me a call when you're anchoring up, and I'll send Charlie over to get you.'

'I'll do that. See you later.' I snicked the call off and turned to grimace at Gavin. 'Secret destination. Radio. TV.'

'Ach, get well behind the MPs and celebrities, and you'll never get a look in.'

'Well,' I said, 'so long as they feed us. Inga's millionaire shortbread, for preference.'

Gavin laughed.

Breakfast was an awkward meal. I was too conscious of Alain beside me. His high spirits of last night had gone; now he wore his brooding look. I'd need to talk to him later, tell him all that he'd not been able to take in last night. I shot a doubtful look at him, then caught Gavin's eye on me, and was vexed to find myself colouring up. I needed to explain, and at least I could do that, now Alain knew who he was, but goodness only knew when we'd get time together. Tonight, perhaps, aboard in Hillswick.

Captain Sigurd gathered the trainees together on deck immediately after breakfast, with Gavin and Sergeant Peterson at his elbow. Four uniformed officers were set up at the table in front of the banjer door, with a pile of paper in front of them. Sergeant Peterson had what looked like the same sheets. I tilted my neck sideways and read it: a table of last night's dances, with times, and a space for writing in. Alibis, of course.

Gavin stepped forward. He was in his own world now, not

mine; *captain*, I'd called him. His stance, his eyes, his voice, made it clear this investigation was under control. 'Ladies and gentlemen, for those of you who haven't met me, I'm DI Macrae of Police Scotland, in charge of this case. I wish to update you on the situation here.' He turned to Agnetha, standing quietly at the head of our ranked line. 'Ms Solheim, can I ask you to translate into Norwegian, to make sure everyone understands?'

She nodded and stepped forward.

'Our search has so far found no trace of the missing woman, Laura Eastley. Her brother, Oliver, will remain on Fetlar for the time being.' He paused to let Agnetha echo him. 'However, I think you have now all heard the news that there was also a fatality on the island last night, during the dance. Daniel Christie, of the red watch, was found dead.'

He paused again as Agnetha translated, scanning the faces. Yes, the news had gone round. 'We would be grateful for your help first in narrowing down the time at which Daniel was last seen. Did anyone notice him at the dance?'

Several heads nodded, Valter's among them.

'Good. If you can pinpoint a rough time, that would help us. If you can remember which dance you were doing, say. We're particularly interested in when he left the hall. In a minute I'll get you to come and tell Sergeant Peterson about it.'

He paused for a moment, looking around them. 'In Scotland, the police gather information and put it to the procurator fiscal, who decides whether a crime has been committed. I would emphasise that we really are just at the gathering information stage, so please don't be anxious if we try to establish alibis for as many people as possible. This team of police officers will ask you about the dance. What I'd like you to try to remember is who you danced each dance with, or sat out with, and as I imagine most of you spent most of the evening with the same group of friends, there will be no difficulty with that. You can talk to the officers as a group, if you wish. Thank you.'

He smiled at them, suddenly charming. My jaw dropped. I'd never seen Gavin wooing witnesses before. 'And for an extra bit of help, his mobile phone hasn't been found, so if anyone ever chatted to him about coverage, or networks, and found out who his phone provider is, that would save us a lot of phone calls.'

He turned to look at our neat line. 'I would be grateful if the ship's crew would also try to recall their movements. Thank you.'

I sensed Alain's quick glance at me. But that had been after Daniel's death . . . or did I need to explain it all to Gavin before a dozen witnesses reported us returning after a half-hour absence?

Now wasn't the time. He wasn't my Gavin, but DI Macrae of Police Scotland, in charge of this investigation. He gestured towards Sergeant Peterson. 'Now, if those of you who saw Daniel would like to tell Sergeant Peterson about him, and everyone else, have a short think – without consulting others, please – then go over to the other officers, on your own or as a group, and describe your night. If you would prefer, Sergeant Spence, on the left there' – one officer raised his hand – 'speaks Norwegian.'

He stepped back to Captain Sigurd. 'We'll try to let you go as soon as possible, sir. Once we've got the preliminary statements, then it will take time to sift through them, but I think we'll be able to eliminate most of the crew and trainees. It would have taken not less than half an hour to go and return from the hall to where Christie was found – long enough for someone's absence to be noticed from a group. We can then focus on those people, and interview them in Hillswick or Scalloway.'

'I would like to leave a crew member with you to represent the ship,' Captain Sigurd said. 'There may be details you need to know during your investigation, and I would like to be updated.' He turned to me. 'Ms Lynch, I will ask Ms Solheim to take over your watch for this afternoon, and leave you with the police.'

Gavin frowned.

'Ms Lynch is my only officer who is also a native English speaker,' Captain Sigurd said. 'I understand that it is a confidential investigation, but I hope that you have faith in her discretion.'

I could see from the set of his jaw that this was an order. 'I understand you would wish the ship to be represented,' Gavin said, 'but I will have to clear this with my superior officers, if you'll give me a moment.'

Captain Sigurd inclined his head and Gavin stepped aside, lifting his phone. A short conversation, then he nodded, dropped the phone into his pocket and returned to us. 'That will be fine, on the understanding that Ms Lynch clears any information she gives you with me first.'

I nodded.

'That information is, of course, confidential to you unless you judge it necessary for the safety of the ship to share it with your officers.'

'Understood,' Captain Sigurd said, and he and Gavin shook hands.

All very well, I thought, them disposing of me as if I was a parcel, and no doubt it would be fun to sit in on a police investigation instead of being sent out of the room just as things got interesting, but what next? Would I stick with Gavin and rejoin the ship at Hillswick? What about Cat? And I was supposed to be being kidnapped for Inga. I let Captain Sigurd proceed off, then turned to Gavin. 'How long will we be in Fetlar?'

Gavin checked his notebook. 'There are two Gutcher ferries, 19.40 and 21.40. I'm hoping we'll have wound up the investigations here by the 19.40, but I've made a booking for the later one just in case. Once we've done the house-to-house and compared your crew and trainee statements, we can move to Lerwick. We'll run you to Hillswick on our way.' He gave me a doubtful look. 'You could be in for a boring day spent hanging around.'

'I'll bring a book. But what about Inga's kidnapping?'

'I'd forgotten that.' He was silent for a moment, thinking. 'Well, listen, the captain wants you here, but I don't see that you'll be allowed to do anything, and I don't think there will be anything I'll need to know. How about you stick with us for the morning and early afternoon, then get on a teatime ferry?' He checked his notebook again. 'There's a 16.40 that goes direct to Yell. D'you want to try and see if she could collect you from that?'

I fished my mobile out of my pocket again. Yea, yea, Inga reckoned she could get someone to get me from Yell, 'and hae a good day being police.'

That settled the question of Cat. He would probably have enjoyed another day ashore, but he wouldn't take to being in a basket for . . . I did a quick calculation, twenty-five minutes to Yell, twenty-five to cross Yell, twenty for the Yell ferry, then to our secret destination . . . at least an hour and a half of ferries and cars. He'd have to stay on board.

I went up to the bridge, where Agnetha was checking my navigation to Hillswick, neatly written out on two sheets of A4 in correct RYA style, starting with distance and hazards. 'It's pretty straightforward,' I assured her. 'Just the tides in Yell Sound, and then the only thing you can't see is the Uyea Baas. The scenery's good, too, black lava cliffs.'

She scanned my pages quickly and nodded.

'I'm going to have to leave Cat on board. Can you maybe feed him for me at tea time?'

'Sure. Maybe as well to keep you and Rafael separate for a day.'

For a moment I didn't know who she meant, and gave her a blank look, which she met with a *Come off it* expression. 'After last night's row?'

Of course. I felt myself going scarlet. Naturally, you couldn't keep anything private on board a ship, but I hadn't thought of that quarrel in the hall car park being overheard, with the band thumping out dance tunes. I should have known my Shetland better. 'I suppose the whole hall heard us.'

She shook her head. 'No, I just went out for a breath of fresh air.'

I pulled a face.

'I didn't understand a word. I don't speak Spanish. But there are a dozen garbled versions doing the rounds.' There was a chill in her blue eyes, a hint of contempt in her voice, which stung like a lashing rope. 'You'll have to make up your mind which of them you want. Gavin won't stand for being messed about.'

I was going to try and explain when Alain himself came in. He was still subdued, his eyes sliding past mine.

'I'll go and get ready for a day ashore,' I said. He looked up at that, startled, and opened his mouth to speak, but I dodged out quickly, with a 'See you later' flung over my shoulder. *A dozen garbled versions doing the rounds* . . . I had to explain to Gavin, the first chance I got.

For now, though, I shoved a book, a jumper, sandshoes, midge spray and my purse into my haversack, and went to add my tuppence-worth to the police officers at the banjer table. I had to be out of it, as I'd been with the search party – unless, of course, he'd been shot so soon before I found him that I was chief suspect. Again. That would entertain Sergeant Peterson, no doubt, but I was getting fed up of Fate dealing me this particular leading role. They didn't ask about what I'd done once I'd got back to the hall, and I didn't volunteer the information. *A dozen garbled versions* . . . I was writhing with humiliation inside, but there was nothing to be done about it. I gritted my teeth and remembered the Shetland mantra, 'If they're speaking about you, they're leaving someone else alone.'

Mona put me over to the pier, chatting slightly too cheerily about how it was a shame I was missing the sail, but how interesting it would be watching a police investigation. I felt her relief as I stepped out of the dinghy and shoved her off.

A soft breeze had sprung up now, just enough to fret the water and dag the edges of the hill reflections. The midges, mercifully, were gone; the sun was warm on my head and bare arms. I strode briskly up the road to the hall, and went in.

CHAPTER EIGHTEEN

The main room was filled with police. They must have gathered every officer in Shetland. There were several whiteboards, in the best TV cop style, with photographs of Laura, Anna, Daniel and Oliver. There was a screen rolled down one wall. Several computers had been set up on hall tables.

I'd come into a briefing. Gavin was standing in front of the pinboards, with an array of uniforms in front of him. He was leaning forward, listening to one of them, the gangly object who'd tried to keep me off my own ship in the longship case. Constable Buchanan. 'I followed up Anna Reynolds on Facebook, sir, and looked through her tweets. She works as the receptionist in an Edinburgh garage called Quality Wheels. It specialises in high-end cars, Porsche, Lamborghini, that kind of thing.'

'A possible link with Eastley,' another officer said. 'He drives an Aston Martin coupé.'

'She's got a core group of five friends who meet up regularly – meals, a night at the pub, clubbing on Saturdays, that kind of thing. Edinburgh's interviewed the one who appears most frequently on her Facebook page, and she didn't know either Eastley or Christie. However, there was someone that Anna was secretive about. The friend never heard a name, but Anna said he was someone who was used to girls being easy, so she was playing hard to get.'

Used to girls being easy sounded more like Oliver than Daniel.

'There's no mention of either man on her page. Eastley posts more than her; she prefers tweeting. Christie's a Snapchat man. They have several mutual friends, but they look to be at acquaintance level rather than actual friends, and there's nobody common to all three.' He yawned and passed a hand over his bristly chin. 'I worked through their photos. One of Eastley's friends posted this one.' He projected it onto a screen. 'Taken in April in a club called Satin Bows, in the New Town, very trendy among young professionals from the public schools.' The photo appeared on the screen. The focus was on a group of men holding scarlet and white scarves in the air. His pointer wavered into the corner. A couple of clicks and the corner of the photo expanded, expanded again. Behind the men were Oliver and the girl I'd seen in the boat: dark brows, blue eyes, strong cheekbones. There was something flirtatious about the way she was holding her glass up at him, something teasing about her stance, but you could see they were friends, not just-met acquaintances. 'The club owner didn't know their names, but he recognised them as a couple he'd seen there occasionally.' He paused to stress what was coming. 'He remembered them because each time they'd arrived separately, and drifted together, as if they didn't know each other. He thought one of them might be married, but that was none of his business.'

The photo stayed there on the screen, a moment caught by a casual camera.

'Playing hard to get,' Sergeant Peterson said, 'or being careful?'

'Otherwise,' PC Buchanan said, 'there's nothing between Eastley and Reynolds. No mention of him on her page, no mention of her on his. Her friends have a number of photographs of her, but none of him, and his friends don't have any of her. Edinburgh is doing a door-to-door of their friends, but so far nobody knows of a link between them.' He paused to take a breath. 'However . . .'

The heads which had gone down to their tablets came up again.

PC Buchanan brought two new photos on the screen: Nelson's Column and St Paul's Cathedral. 'These are from Eastley's Facebook page. They were taken in the first weekend of February.' The screen changed again: an Anna selfie in front of St Paul's, and an Oliver selfie in front of a red bus. 'And these were posted in the second weekend of March.'

'A double visit to London, a month apart,' Sergeant Peterson said. She tapped into her computer. 'The English qualification for marriage is a month's residence.'

'Good work,' Gavin said. 'That's all very interesting. Anything at the English Register Office?'

'They weren't open when I tried them, sir.'

'Get on to that as soon as this briefing is over. Eastley's office too – find out what he was doing in February.'

'Yes, sir.'

Sergeant Peterson gave that mermaid smile of hers, as if she'd spotted a ship in difficulties. 'Ammunition for when we interview him.'

Gavin glanced at his notes. 'Eastley still lives at home, the parental home, with his sister. He said there was a cleaning lady,

Elisabeta, but he didn't know her address – his sister deals with all that. Who was investigating Reynolds's flat?'

Another officer raised her hand. 'Constable Sinclair, sir. I talked to Reynolds's landlord. A small student flat. She's supposed to live there on her own, and as far as he knows, she does, but he doesn't care so long as he gets the rent. She's been there ten years, she pays on time through her bank, end of. His only personal impression of her is that she's smart and efficient, very businesslike but decorative with it.'

'As you'd expect from her job. Good. Her employers?'

The whiteboards were gradually being covered with scribbles.

'They think very highly of her. Good-looking, a good manner with the customers, efficient, an excellent organiser. "I can't find anything without her," was the way her boss put it. Nothing known about her private life, but he didn't think she had a boyfriend. She's the only woman in the firm, so there wouldn't be girly confidences.'

She checked her notes. 'This weekend. She was quiet all Friday morning, and a bit pale, then she said she was starting a migraine, and went home early. She was expected back this morning, but she hadn't turned up when I spoke to them, and she hadn't phoned in either. That was at 09.05. He seemed surprised – said it wasn't like her. I told them to ask her to phone us when she came in.'

'When did she go home on Friday?'

'Three o'clock, sir. The ferry left at seven. It's only two and a half hours from Edinburgh to Aberdeen, and plenty of trains. She was a foot passenger, without a cabin. She didn't have a return journey booked, and she wasn't on last night's ferry, or at least not under her own name.'

'She's used her name pretty openly so far,' Sergeant Peterson said. 'If she'd had an alias she'd have used it throughout.'

'She was expected back,' Gavin said. 'Let's think about what might have been planned. She was to isolate Ms Eastley and kill her while Oliver established his alibi on board. If she was to be back at work on Monday, then she expected to be on Sunday's boat, leaving at . . . ?'

'19.00, sir.'

'She could have got off Fetlar on the 11.30, if she'd been quick, or the 16.00. Struck up a conversation with someone on board and hitched a lift across Yell, even on to Lerwick.' He looked across the room at another officer. 'Ewan, you talked to the ferry crew.'

The officer he was asking shook his head. 'They were confident they knew about everyone on all of yesterday's crossings, sir. I've got a list. There were visitors for the tournament, a couple of local cars and some teenagers returning from a wild night out in Baltasound. I showed them her picture, and they were definite they hadn't seen her. They'll look out for her today.'

'So there's a good chance she's still on the island,' Sergeant Peterson said.

'Why would she book the böd, if she was planning to leave yesterday?' one officer asked.

'Good question,' Gavin said. He nodded to the officer who was writing on the whiteboard. She scrawled WHY next to the photo of the böd. 'In case whatever she was doing to Laura took longer that they'd expected, and missed her the ferry?'

'In which case,' Sergeant Peterson added, 'no doubt she'll phone in this morning to say her migraine hadn't quite gone, but she'd be in tomorrow.'

'OK,' Gavin said, 'that all hangs together as a potential scheme. Let's look at Eastley. Twenty-nine, charming, single, still living with his sister, failed attempts at college, working in a fairly basic capacity in the family firm, and apparently contented with that, saving his excitement for . . . something that put him so much in debt that his sister got both shares of the family home.'

'Horses and online poker,' another officer said. 'Visits to a casino. He's not exactly known to the Edinburgh police, but they weren't totally surprised I was asking about him.'

'So,' Gavin said, drawing a line on the whiteboard, 'we have Eastley needing money. We have a link between Eastley and Reynolds, which is either a casual attraction that they enjoy when they meet, but which doesn't go any further, or something that's being so carefully covered up that not even their friends know they're an item. Yes, the Register House is a priority. A hidden legal connection between them would be interesting.' He paused to look through his notes. 'Let's move on to the death of Daniel Christie. Freya?'

'Initial feedback from the ship says he was seen leaving the hall by a Valter Bengtsson, who put the time around 21.20. That checks with the band's timing of the dances. Several people noticed that he was fiddling with his phone, "texting", one of the teenagers said, and then he put the phone away and went out. The implication being that he received a text that told him to come to the Haltadans. So his phone would have told us something, if it had been left with him.' She looked at another officer. 'How are you getting on with the providers?'

'Vodafone, ma'am.' The officer looked pleased with himself. 'Good news, sir. There are a number of phone calls to Oliver and Laura's house.'

'Good work,' Gavin said. He nodded down at Sergeant Peterson. 'Another thing to ask Mr Eastley about. And the last call he received?'

'He received a text at 21.13, from an unregistered pay-as-you-go. It was the first communication he'd received from that number, but he'd tried to call it four times through the afternoon.'

'A single-use phone.' Gavin brooded for a moment. 'But he knew the number, had it stored in his phone . . . which would have given us the name. That's why his phone had to go. We might be incredibly lucky and get fingerprints from his jacket pocket.' He indicated a blown-up print of Daniel's face. I turned my head away, but couldn't shut out his voice. 'Obviously we have to wait for forensics, but it seems clear he was shot, and I'd have said he died where he was found. Someone he knew came up to him and shot him at point-blank range. It was a small-calibre weapon, and given we heard a pistol shot earlier, it seems reasonable to posit for the moment that he was shot with a pistol. Ms Lynch.' I jumped, and turned my head back to him. 'Would it be fair to say that it would be possible for a trainee to bring a gun on board the *Sørlandet*?'

'Yes,' I said. 'We don't search trainees' baggage. However if it was a trainee from outwith Norway, they'd have had to smuggle it into Norway, unless they bought it there.'

Sergeant Peterson began tapping into her laptop and scanned the page quickly. 'Gun ownership is strictly regulated in Norway, sir. A course is required for a permit, usually for hunting. A non-resident wouldn't be able to obtain a gun legally there.'

Gavin looked down at her. 'How about on the Shetland ferry, NorthLink? Is the baggage scanned?'

She shook her head. 'We meet the ferry with the drugs dogs, but there's no X-ray machine.'

Gavin was thinking as I had. If Oliver couldn't have brought the pistol, then Anna must have.

Gavin wound up his summary there, and I was just about to make myself a cup of tea when there was a stir among the officers, and one hurried forward. 'A call from Edinburgh, sir. An accountant who says he's also a family friend of Ms Eastley has come into their station. They've got him connected and ready to talk to you.'

There was a flurry of clicking, then one of the computer-gazing officers stood up, gesturing Gavin towards his chair. 'Put him on,' Gavin said. He leant forward so that his head was visible in the box in one corner of the screen. 'Let's hear what he has to say.'

I oozed into the back row of bystanders. Nobody was bothering about me; they were all staring at the screen.

There was a clunk or two, and then the screen opened in a Skype mode, and a suited man in his fifties looked out at us. He was visibly corporate: suit, tie, haircut, a distinguished member of a reliable firm. 'Graham Lynwood, chief accountant with the Edinburgh firm Stuart and Riccard.'

Gavin responded in kind. 'DI Gavin Macrae, of Police Scotland. I believe, sir, you have information for us.'

Mr Lynwood nodded and leant forward, his face filling the screen. There were anxious lines under his eyes, and a drawn look to his mouth. 'Is there any news of Laura?'

'Nothing yet, sir.'

'I've known her all her life.' His eyes shifted from the screen for a moment, then returned to us. 'Her mother and I went through university together.'

'Then you're just the person we want, sir,' Gavin said. 'Someone to fill in the family background.'

Mr Lynwood had an outsider's view of the family: father a hard-working GP, mother busy in the firm, children thrown together under the care of a series of au pairs, plenty of money, not much time. Oliver had been his mother's pride and joy, Laura her father's girl. She'd been the scholar, the prize-winner; Oliver had been the lightweight who'd flitted from course to course, trouble to trouble, until they'd got him a job in the firm. 'In spite of that, Laura was always devoted to her brother.' He smiled. 'I have this vivid memory of her as a schoolgirl with plaits, on her first day at school, barely up to his shoulder, leading him to the bus stop, as if she was the older one. She always looked after him. I'm sure he got in more trouble than Dave and Alison knew about, and she got him out of it.'

'What was her relationship with her parents as an adult?'

'Good.' He nodded to himself. 'She and her father stayed close, especially as there was no boyfriend in the picture. He was very proud of her. She took their death hard – not just the shock, but the sudden responsibility too.'

'I believe, sir, the firm was in difficulties due to the recession?'

'Yes, she had that to deal with. Luckily she has Alison's head for finance. By the end of the financial year they were in a steady position.' He paused, waved his hand across his face as if waving something away, then took a deep breath. 'Three weeks back, she phoned me with concerns about the firm's accounts.'

A collective shudder ran through the ranked officers in front of me. Gavin didn't move. 'Yes, sir?'

'She—' He paused and cleared his throat. 'Laura was worried that someone had been tinkering with the books. So she asked me to take a private look at them.'

'Without involving the other directors?' Gavin asked.

Lynwood shook his head. 'Irregular, I know, and if it hadn't been Laura, I wouldn't have considered it. But you see, I thought – I could see she thought – that Oliver was at the bottom of it.' He pulled out an immaculately ironed handkerchief and mopped his brow.

'And was there any suggestion in your investigation that her suspicion was correct?'

He nodded and mopped his brow again. 'She wanted to know the worst before deciding what action she should take.'

'And what was the worst, sir?'

Lynwood's eyes flicked from left to right, and he spread his hands in a *Hold off* gesture. 'I hadn't told her the full figure yet. I didn't want to spoil her holiday.'

'But you had told her that there was money missing?'

He nodded. 'I phoned her two days ago.'

My instinct was right, then. I remembered Laura's face as she'd put her phone away, a resigned, unsurprised grief.

'I said that there had been defalcations, starting immediately the audit was over. I said I didn't have the full amount, but that I feared it might be more than she could afford to repay herself – I knew she'd want to do that, if she could.'

'And her reaction, sir?'

'Well, she was in a public place. We agreed that we'd go into the full amount when she came home.'

He stopped there, looking as if he hoped nobody would ask any more.

'And do you know the full amount, sir?'

He took another deep breath and came out with it, eyes screwed up as if it hurt. 'It came to around two million missing, spread across a large number of accounts.'

There were indrawn breaths from the officers in front of me, and a low whistle.

'Two million, sir,' Gavin repeated, his voice matter-of-fact.

'Then I heard, on this morning's news – they named her as missing – I thought this information might be relevant to your enquiry.'

262

'Did your investigations lead you to any suggestion of who might be responsible?'

Lynwood spread his hands, as if to ward off too much precision. 'The fraud had been cleverly done, but not cleverly enough. There were indications that it would be possible to track some of the transactions back to a particular person.'

'The particular person she suspected?'

He gave a gloomy nod. 'We agreed that neither of us would say anything to anyone.' His brows drew together. 'I didn't want Oliver to get round her, to persuade her to agree to a cover-up. I wanted to be there when we confronted him.'

'What will your next step be, sir, if Ms Eastley doesn't turn up?'

His head came up again, and his face cleared; this was laid-down procedure. 'I'll take what I've found to the board of directors. There will need to be a full examination of the books by an outside firm. The directors will then decide what action to take, but I think prosecution will be inevitable.'

Sergeant Peterson leant forward to the screen. 'Sergeant Peterson, Mr Lynwood. Can you tell us anything about Laura's will? Who would benefit in the event of her death?'

He looked uneasy for a moment. 'I can, as it happens, because she discussed it with me.' He paused for a moment, thinking it over. 'This is, of course, confidential to your investigation.'

'Of course,' Gavin agreed.

'Her personal assets were left to Oliver. That is, their house – Oliver was still living there, although she owned it – and whatever private savings she had. Her shares in Ryder and Whittingham, well, we had a long talk about that. The firm had been started by her Whittingham great-great-grandfather, and built up by her family, particularly her mother. She didn't want . . .' He paused, sighed, and rephrased. 'She wanted to ensure its prosperity. She left her shares to be divided equally between the other directors, leaving Oliver with only his current small stake.'

Sergeant Peterson was scribbling in her notebook. 'Do you have any idea, sir, if Mr Eastley was aware of the contents of his sister's will?'

Lynwood spread his hands. 'As far as the shares were concerned, probably not. I think he would assume he would inherit from her.'

Gavin nodded, and bent his head to flip through his notes. 'Have you ever come across a man called Daniel Christie? Around the same age as Eastley and Ms Eastley.'

The smooth face frowned. 'Christie . . . Christie . . . it's a common enough name. Does he work in accounting?'

'Banking, at RBS HQ in Edinburgh.'

Lynwood's brow cleared. 'Daniel Christie. Yes. I've come across him. He's quite a whiz-kid in finance.'

'Do you know if he knew either Laura or Oliver?'

Lynwood took a moment to think about it. 'I don't remember either of them ever mentioning him. But it's pretty likely, if he went out of a Friday night, the way they all do nowadays, that he and Oliver would have met. Laura's not a party girl, more likely to go up to Aviemore for skiing, or go and climb a Munro.'

I tried to imagine Daniel on skis, or halfway up a mountain, and failed. But he could have known Oliver.

'Drives a flashy car,' Lynwood added. 'Oliver's a car enthusiast too – another possible link.' He paused, frowning, then lifted his head. 'Party. Yes. Back last Christmas, before Dave and Alison's death. There was one of those corporate gatherings, and Laura and Oliver were both present. It was given by RBS so it's highly likely that Daniel was there too.'

'What was the venue, sir?'

'St Andrew Square.'

'I don't suppose you remember the date?'

Lynwood swiped at his phone. 'The 5th of December.' His head went up. 'Yes, they did meet. I saw him chatting with Oliver, and then with Laura. She was at her golden girl best then.' His mouth twisted. 'It was the last time I saw her happy.'

Gavin noted that too. 'Thank you for your help, sir. We'll follow that up. Now' – he looked straight at Lynwood – 'in your judgement, sir, would Mr Eastley be capable of technically carrying out the fraud you found?'

Lynwood hesitated. 'It has been carried out, so I must suppose so.' He paused again, frowning and shaking his head. 'But I wouldn't have thought he had the financial brain.'

'How about Mr Christie?'

Lynwood spread his hands again. 'Given that I know nothing about his character or experience, I can't say, but I would concede that someone in his position at RBS would be technically capable.' He frowned again. 'You think he carried out the fraud on Oliver's computer – on Oliver's behalf?'

'I thought I'd run the idea past you,' Gavin said.

Lynwood shook his head. 'I can't comment.'

The conversation seemed to be winding up. I backed away quietly before anyone noticed me, and lay down on one of the hall benches in a corner, flinging my jumper over my legs and using my knapsack as a pillow. I'd been up before four, and my eyelids were closing. Words echoed in my head. *An Edinburgh four-storey New Town house, with a garden behind it . . . moving upwards towards a million.* If Oliver had had enough of the golden sister who outshone him – if he was short of money – then it was a goodly inheritance. A motive for murder. 'You need a break, Laura. Let's get away from it all.' Then he arranged to bring Anna, his secret girlfriend, up to Fetlar to do the killing, while he stayed on board, in full sight. If it hadn't been for Daniel fretting, we'd never have known about Anna – which brought me back to where Daniel came in, and who'd killed him. The elusive Anna, with her bright eyes, and broad cheekbones, like a Finn woman . . .

CHAPTER NINETEEN

I woke refreshed an exact twenty minutes later. It was just after eleven, and there was a busy hum of officers working on their computers or moving from table to table to compare notes, but nothing that I could be involved in.

My brain had woken up too. *A whiz-kid in finance.* Suppose the actual couple in the case was Daniel and Anna. Forget Oliver; the stumble on the broch stairs could just have been an accident. Imagine instead that Daniel and Anna were the murderous couple with designs on Laura's wealth. *That's the brains of the pair*, Gavin had said, watching Daniel beat Oliver at hnefatafl. He could have homed in on Oliver as someone to exploit: 'It's an unusual investment, Oliver, but it'll bring back rich dividends for someone with the nerve to think outside the box.' I could see Oliver falling for that line – except that he didn't have the money to invest. It was all concentrated on Laura, who was nobody's fool.

Oliver had access to it, though. If he'd let Daniel into the system, then Daniel could have got the money away, and left just enough of a trail to make Laura suspicious – a trail that led to Oliver. I thought of the hnefatafl king, mustering his troops, sacrificing them to get himself to safety. The fraud gave Oliver a double motive for murder: either for his inheritance from Laura, or because she'd discovered the fraud, and threatened to expose him. If Laura was to die, Oliver would be right in the frame for both the murder and the fraud. Meanwhile, Daniel had stashed the missing two million in some offshore bank account, and bought plane tickets for himself and Anna.

Then Laura had got suspicious. 'Go ahead with your trip,' Daniel had said. 'I'll come aboard too, and pretend to chat her up, keep her occupied. Behave as if everything's totally normal, but be ready to do a moonlight flit.'

Only what Oliver didn't know was that Daniel was planning to smuggle Anna aboard, to dispose of Laura. She'd been on the ship from Lerwick and she'd booked the camping böd in case she didn't kill Laura in time to get the ferry off the island. But then . . . then Daniel turned into the weak link. Financial skulduggery was one thing, but waiting while someone he knew was being murdered was quite another. He'd been like a cat on hot bricks, and the police questioning wouldn't have let up until he'd spilt the whole story. Any sensible accomplice would have got rid of him.

That sounded even better. Anna hadn't turned up where he'd expected her to, and she wasn't answering her phone, but she'd texted him. *Meet me at the Haltadans, that stone ring, once it's dusk. Ten o'clock.* She'd walked up to him and shot him. Now she'd slip off the island, like a normal tourist, and get the ferry home. She didn't know that we'd got her name. If it hadn't been for Daniel, we'd have known nothing about the böd. She'd go home and say she'd had the flu, and then she'd get on that flight to the tax haven wherever, with two million to live on, and Oliver left holding the baby.

I rose, stretched, and headed to the door for several long breaths of air. My beautiful ship was still moored in the bay, graceful as a swan above her glimmering reflection on the rippled water, but there was smoke coming from her exhaust now, and I could see people moving around the capstan. The anchor light was switched off at the same moment as the nav lights came on: someone was on the ball. The sun had broken through the clouds, and the water danced blue; the Out Skerries were clear on the horizon. I sat down on the wall where I'd sat with Alain last night, and watched her: the anchor coming up, the first black figures going up the ratlines, the sails unfolding into festoons, then pulling downwards to their white curve. My ship was leaving without me. I felt my heart was clenched in my breast. The air that had been warm was cold on my face. One figure on the aft deck looked up – I knew that tilted-back head – and lifted a hand to me, here on land. There was a lump in my throat.

I shook the feeling away. I'd be joining her in Hillswick tonight. I wasn't any use to the investigation, so I could go and explore a bit more of Fetlar. I hadn't visited the Interpretative Centre, or seen Brough Lodge, which had looked an interestingly ruinous pile. It was too bonny a day to waste watching the sails diminish into the blue distance.

I supposed I'd better tell Gavin where I was going. I'd just gone back into the hall when there was a crackle from the VHF, and a Shetland voice. 'Shetland Coastguard, this is the Lerwick lifeboat. Channel 67.'

The tone of his voice said it was important, and not good news. The officer by the hand-held turned it to 67 and waited. The soft bustle died down around him.

'Shetland Coastguard.'

'A local fisherman's found a body. Female, powder-blue jacket.'

I remembered Laura walking up the slip with Anna beside her, the light jacket bright against the grey tarmac.

Gavin picked up the radio. 'Shetland Coastguard, Lerwick lifeboat, this is DI Gavin Macrae, on Fetlar. The brother of the missing woman is still with us, on the island. Should we try for an ID now?'

The lifeboatman's voice was deliberately matter-of-fact. 'We took the body on board. He won't be able to identify the face.'

The body would have sunk, once the clothing was wet enough to drag it down. There were crabs down there, and lobsters, and shoals of little nibbling fish. I felt bile rising in my throat and swallowed it down.

'Request you bring the body to the pier here,' Gavin said. 'We'll get a preliminary ID based on the clothing, then I'd be grateful if you could take the body to Lerwick. I'll have you met there.'

A body that had lain on the sea bed all night wouldn't look like Laura. The mortuary folk would do their best before they asked Oliver to look at her. Then it came cold over me that a representative of the ship would need to be with him. I rose and braced myself.

The lifeboatman came on again. 'Yes, DI Macrae, we can do that. We're just off Nousta Ness now. We'll be with you in fifteen minutes.'

'Good. Thank you. Over and out.'

I'd half expected him to ask more questions, like where the

body had been found, until I remembered that every boat in Shetland had tuned instantly to 67 when the coastguard call came through, and every crew was gathered round the wireless, lugs pinned back and mobile in hand, ready to phone the news to their wives at home. It would be round Shetland in minutes that Laura's body had been found.

Now the whole hall was galvanised into activity. Gavin looked around and picked on Sergeant Peterson. 'Freya, you and Andrew interview the fisherman. We need to know exactly where the body was found. I'll break the news to Eastley and take him down to the pier.' He looked over at me. 'Cass, I think you should be present, and – Shona, is it?'

A WPO moved over. 'Sir.'

'Once we've got an ID, bring him back up here for tea, and stick with him. Ivor, see if Lerwick can arrange accommodation for him there. It's unlikely he'll want to go on with the voyage.'

WPO Shona caught up her jacket. I followed the pair of them meekly to a modern-build house with a red door, tucked neatly behind the willow-and-white showiness of Leagarth House. Gavin knocked at the door, then opened it and stepped in, Shetland-style. A little, bustling lady in a pinny was already in the passage. Her eyes took in Gavin, Shona in uniform beside him, and she nodded. She'd obviously heard already. 'Shall I call him down, or do you want to go up? You can have the sitting room to yourselves.' She gestured at an open door, with a squashy brown velvet couch beyond.

There was no need to call him. Already, a door was opening up above us and Oliver's voice called, 'Is that the police?'

He appeared at the top of the stairs. He'd aged ten years overnight, with deep lines creasing each side of his nose and running down to the corners of his mouth, and his skin drained to a lifeless brown. His hair was shoved back any old how from his face, and his jeans were crumpled, as if he'd slept in them. 'Is there news?' he said, then he saw we'd come mob-handed, and put out a hand to the bannister to steady himself. Shona went quickly up the stairs to support him.

'Come downstairs, sir.' She ushered him into the sitting room and lowered him into an armchair. 'Have a seat.'

'I'll make tea,' the landlady said, and hustled off towards the light at the end of the passage.

I let Gavin and Shona sit down first, then slid to the empty end of the couch.

'I'm afraid it's bad news, sir,' Gavin said. 'A body has been found.'

'Laura?' Oliver said. There was a queer eagerness in his voice, as if he'd been expecting this. I felt my suspicions of him rising again.

'We'll have to ask you to tell us that, sir,' Gavin said. 'She's on board the lifeboat, and they're bringing her into the pier.'

'Mrs Georgeson's bringing you a cup of tea,' Shona said. 'Drink that, and then we'll take you down.'

He gestured the idea away with his hand. 'I'm not thirsty. Laura . . . can't they tell from the clothes?'

'The lifeboat said she was wearing a powder-blue jacket,' Gavin said. Although he was taking care not to stare at Oliver, I knew he was alert to every move, every gesture.

Oliver dropped his tousled head into one hand. 'Laura.' He gave a couple of dry sobs, and I couldn't tell whether they seemed stagey because they were put on, or whether real grief was theatrical. Shona laid one hand on his arm, and the landlady scurried in with a tray of mugs and distracted us with enquiries about milk and sugar. She gave Oliver three spoonfuls without asking, and a tot of whisky from the cupboard, and pressed the mug into his hand. 'There, Oliver, you get that down you.'

She'd brought a plate of biscuits as well, but it felt heartless to take one. We sat and waited while Oliver drank his tea, and a touch of colour returned to his face. At last he set the mug down and lifted his head to look seawards out of the picture window over the bay. The lifeboat was manoeuvring into the pier. I could see the orange coffin-shape of the stretcher on the foredeck.

Oliver rose, and there was that same strange eagerness, as if he wanted to get it over with – as if he wanted his future decided, I thought suddenly. He had to have been part of the fraud, to let Daniel into the firm's computer systems. Maybe beneath the tears he was already dreaming of the Costa del Sol, or the Caribbean.

We walked the hundred metres to the pier in silence, in a procession: Gavin first, Shona and Oliver, then me. Shona was trained to do the professional comfort thing, I reminded myself, to make the right gestures. I lagged behind in silence.

The lifeboat men waited on the pier. They were dressed in their formal navy jerseys, like a guard of honour behind the stretcher as Oliver walked down the concrete. A red ensign was draped over the still shape cocooned within it.

Oliver went up to it, and hesitated. Shona was there before him, bending down to lift the lower half of the flag and expose the sea-sodden trainers, a diagonal of jacket, one dangling hand. The skin was already cold grey, with the ragged edges of flesh showing white. There was an odd bulge in the hip pocket.

Oliver swallowed and nodded. 'Those are Laura's clothes.' He looked down at the jacket. 'That's the jacket she was wearing. She must have gone too close to the edge. What's that in her pocket?'

He made as if to lean forward, brows drawn together, and Gavin put out a hand to hold him back.

'Don't touch, sir. There may be prints.'

I was making sense of the shape now. It was a stone, to help sink the body. There was one in each of the jacket pockets. Anna hadn't meant Laura to be found; she hadn't reckoned on how close inshore the creelmen came.

'Did your sister wear jewellery, sir?' Shona asked.

Oliver nodded. 'She had our great-grandmother's wedding ring.' He looked down at the crinkled skin. 'On her other hand. She always wore it.'

Gavin bent forward to lift the flag slightly higher. The other hand was mangled too, as if it had hit the cliff face as it had flailed in space. The gold ring gleamed against the grey skin.

Oliver's face was white, his mouth twisted, looking in horror at the contorted fingers. 'That's Laura's ring.' Then he leant forward and snatched the flag from her face.

I had only a second to look, before Shona on one side and two burly lifeboatmen on the other pulled him back, and another crewman covered her again. Oliver made a choking sound. By now Gavin was beside him: 'Now, sir, we wanted to spare you that. Come and sit down.'

He and Shona took Oliver over to a seat by the pier. I turned away and faced seawards, struggling against nausea.

That one-second glance had been enough. There had been no face left on the poor body in the stretcher, just a mass of brown tissue with splinters of shattered bone sticking out from among it. I tried to will the image away, but it was as clear in my mind as if I was still looking at it. One eye socket had been intact, with a slimy mass hanging from it down the bones of the cheek. I gritted my teeth against the bile rising in my throat. The other socket had been ragged, and nose and mouth were lost in a jumble of torn flesh.

I lost the battle with my stomach and went swiftly over to sick up my breakfast into the sea. *Damn.* Swearing to myself, I washed my mouth out with salt water and drank a cupped handful to take the taste away. I splashed my face, then took a moment to steady myself before going back up.

When I headed back up to the pier, Shona was persuading Oliver to move with her up the hill, and Gavin, after a sharp glance at their retreating backs, had moved forward to the body again. Her hair, darkened with water, clung to his hand as he lifted her head. I gritted my teeth and looked seawards, but I couldn't help still watching from the corner of my eye. The back of her head seemed undamaged, but the coxswain was indicating something to Gavin, and he was nodding.

We'd heard a pistol shot. Exit wounds were larger than entry . . . and the damage to her face seemed worse than even a direct blow against a cliff would make. She'd been shot from behind.

'Where was she found?' Gavin asked.

'She came up with his creel twenty metres out from the south cliffs of Funzie Bay. Below the steepest part of the banks.'

It was where Gavin's marker was. Laura had already been down on the seabed when we'd looked over yesterday afternoon, with the ripples of brown tang twisting over her.

Gavin pulled the map we'd been given from his pocket and unfolded it. 'Can you show me?'

The coxswain obliged, and Gavin nodded, and put the map away again. 'Well, you can take the poor lady to Lerwick now. Thank you, all of you.'

'No sign of the other lady?' the coxswain asked.

Gavin shook his head.

'She'll be long gone,' another lifeboat man opined gloomily. 'Even if she was here to shoot that man last night, she coulda been on this morning's ferry.'

Gavin shook his head. 'It was watched, and Lerwick's checking the passengers on tonight's south boat too.'

Unless we had two murderers instead of one. Anna to kill Laura, Oliver to get rid of Daniel, who'd done the financial skulduggery. Anna could have been gone on a midday ferry, as soon as she'd killed Laura, down on a bus to Lerwick and on the evening ferry south, leaving Oliver to shoot Daniel.

Gavin's hand came on my shoulder, making me jump. 'Back to the hall.'

I was grateful that he didn't ask how I was. It was bad enough that the whole lifeboat crew had seen tough Cass Lynch spewing into the ebb at the sight of a dead body. I forced my voice to sound steady. 'Do you want me to stick with Oliver?'

He shook his head. 'We'll have people with him all morning. Your captain will have heard that we found the body, but you could report it officially, and say that she's been identified as Ms Eastley.' He gave my face a shrewd look. 'Why don't you go and tourist for a bit? Have a picnic in the sun, then I'll get someone to run you to the ferry.'

'Sounds a good idea.' I didn't sound convincing. I paused in the road, looking at him. 'Well . . . I'll see you later, then.' I tried for a matter-of-fact tone, the policeman's girlfriend who was used to this sort of thing. 'Now this is a full-blown murder enquiry, will you be joining the ship again?' *Will you be able to sleep on board?* was what I wanted to say, but I couldn't get my tongue around it.

He shrugged. His voice was as casual as mine. 'If I can.'

I knew I'd got it wrong. I leant forward to kiss him, but he moved

276

his head at the last moment so that my lips only touched his cheek, then stepped back from me. 'Have fun being kidnapped. Text me.'

There was a lump in my throat. I nodded, and forced my voice to be cheerful. 'See you in Hillswick.'

CHAPTER TWENTY

I turned away quickly before he could see the tears prickling in my eyes, and strode off down the road. I needed to talk to him. I needed to explain about Alain, before we went irretrievably wrong. Tonight, if he was on board . . . and then I had a sudden cold panic that he might use the excuse of the investigation to spend the night in Lerwick. I hauled my phone from my pocket and sent a text before my courage failed: *Hope we'll spend tonight together xxx*

I saw him get it. He paused, looked back, and raised his hand. I waved back and set off again, cheered. I was almost at the Interpretative Centre when his answer came through: *Hope so too. If not, not my fault xxx*

The cold feeling retreated. I paused to admire the Interpretative Centre's mural, and sat down at the bench to make my official report to Captain Sigurd. I used as few words as possible, clean mechanical language: a body had been found, which Oliver had identified as Laura. I could hear the ship's rigging creaking in the background, the waves against the hull, and that pang gripped me again, my ship sailing without me.

I would be back on board this evening. I checked my watch. Half twelve. I had until the 16.40 ferry to mooch about. It was only a four-mile walk, three and a bit to Brough Lodge – forty-five minutes, say – then another fifteen to the ferry. I could look at the Centre, see the old Brough Lodge movies Magnie had recommended, get some sandwiches at the shop, picnic at Brough Lodge, then explore the place itself before walking the last mile to the ferry.

The Centre was a Tardis inside, crammed full of Shetland spades, tuskers for casting peat, flat irons in every size, kettles, bottles, scrimshaw pictures carved on walrus tusks by long-dead seamen ancestors, a hand-operated sewing machine. There was a big board on Sir William Watson Cheyne, the owner of Leagarth House, and photos of the *Time Team* in action, watched by a ring of local folk.

The films were played on a screen set into the wall, and I found them unexpectedly moving. The Nicolsons hadn't expected them to be shown to tourists eighty years later; they were family home movies for now, practising golf shots on the lawn, watching their car being winched off the ferry, dancing down the steps in a foursome, arms around each other's waists. I remembered what I'd been told about the golden-haired girl smiling at the camera, and wondered what she would have said then if someone had told her she'd end her days an eccentric old woman among decaying grandeur. She, one of Britain's elite, with money, breeding and style? She'd have laughed at the idea.

As I came out, I ran straight into Alain's Italian dance partner, one hand up to struggle with her elegant but impractical sunhat, the other smoothing down her flowered skirts. Neapolitan promenade wear wasn't quite practical in Shetland, glamorous as it made her look, like a fifties starlet at Cannes, with her sweetheart neckline, bare shoulders and white-rimmed shades. The scarlet lips curved in acknowledgement as I held the door open for her, and she gave a murmured 'Zank you.'

'You're welcome,' I said, and went back to musing. Perhaps Lady Nicolson had been happy with her bottle of whisky and tribe of cats – who was I to judge? It just showed, I moralised to myself as I walked briskly along the road to the shop, that money wasn't as important as I'd thought in those struggling days when I was working as a waitress just to pay the marina bills. She'd had everything, and had still died in a squalor as bad as any half-pension council high-rise tenant could suffer. Yet perhaps she'd been happier than you'd think, judging from outside; she'd remained in her own home, with her cats as company, doing what she wanted, and not caring that she didn't wash as often as the social services thought she should, or that her food didn't pass the NHS nutrition guidelines. I thought of some of the meals I'd eaten on board long-passage yachts, where a tin was only condemned when the rust had actually eaten through into the food, and decided I was living in a glass house as far as that was concerned.

The shop had one room for the goods and another set out as a cafe, with home-made fancies under plastic cake containers on the counter. For a turnover of sixty people and summer tourists, the stock was impressive. There were tins and dry foods, and a cold-cabinet of milk, yoghurt, butter, cheese and fresh meat. The shelf next to it had loaves and fancies from Da Kitchen Bakery in Yell. The fruit and veg included cauliflowers, grapes and a pineapple. By the door was a display of locally made souvenirs, jewellery, cards and the inevitable puffin pictures, and shelves of passer-by food, Lindt chocolate, packets of crisps and chocolate digestives, and red-and-gold-foiled Tunnock's Caramel Wafers.

I went for a bag of rolls and cheese slices to fill them. I got a banana and a bag of toffees for pudding, and decided against a bottle of water to wash them down. There would be plenty of burns along the road, with velvety-peat water straight from the hill. I paid for my faerdie maet and strode out again, still thinking about the last Lady Nicolson.

I didn't want to end up a wild-haired live-aboard who talked to her cat. I'd learnt in these months aboard *Sørlandet* that only part of me was a natural solitary. I'd grown up in a community. I'd played on the beach with Inga and Martin, and gone round the regattas in a group of teenagers. I'd mixed with Alain's friends in Edinburgh. It was only since then that I'd been one of a group of people who met and parted again: deck-hands in the Med, sports instructors doing a season in a holiday hotspot, transient waiters in busy cafes. The only home I'd revisited had been the *Sørlandet*, as an AB each season; and then, three years ago, my own *Khalida* had become my fixed world.

Now I'd got to feel at home on board *Sørlandet* again. It had taken a while to adjust from the free and easy ways of an AB to the formality of the captain's cabin, but I'd got to know Agnetha. Petter, Mona, Johan and I had shaken down into a good sailing team. I was beginning to work well with Nils, and I respected Captain Sigurd's ability as a captain even while his fussy ways drove me round the bend. I belonged again.

I breasted the hill and turned to look back. A flutter of a light-flowered dress was going along the road towards the Gord B & B. Alain's Italian woman hadn't stayed long in the Centre. A quick look, to show willing, before she headed for a lounger on the beach . . . not that Shetland was an obvious beach-holiday destination.

I stopped at that thought, open-mouthed, then began to walk on again, thinking hard. Suppose . . . just suppose I'd decided to commit a murder on a far-away island, with no CCTV cameras to track me. I'd got my victim alone and shot her from behind while she was unsuspectingly watching puffins by their rabbit burrows, or gannets diving. I'd filled her pockets with stones from the wall to sink her body. So far, so good.

But here I was, on this island. I knew my victim would be reported missing fairly quickly – before the end of the day, certainly. There'd be a big search. They'd be looking for me, and they'd question the boys on the ferries to find out if I'd been seen leaving.

So . . . I thought, so, being clever, I wouldn't leave. Nobody would expect that. I'd stick around until the hue and cry was off. I wouldn't skulk in a B & B either; that would make my landlady suspicious. I'd draw attention to myself. I'd wear flamboyant dresses and so much make-up that my face couldn't be seen behind it, and piled up hair, and outrageous earrings, and dark glasses, and a hat which had to be held on to in a Shetland breeze, giving me a handy excuse to put my forearm in front of my face when I bumped into someone who might just recognise me. I'd say I was Italian, and didn't speak much English, so that my voice would sound completely different. I'd behave like a tourist, even to the extent of going to the dance; it would have looked odd for a tourist to miss that.

I tried to square the woman I'd just bumped into with Anna Reynolds, and found I couldn't tell anything. Height – no idea, for the woman in the boat had been sitting down, and the Italian had been wearing the stiletto heels she'd danced in yesterday evening. The woman I'd seen with Alain had been half a head shorter than him, the Italian woman almost as tall. Four inches of heels would do that. Skin colour: could have been anything under that bronzed tan; cheekbones: invisible, ditto. Eyes lost behind the mirror glasses, mouth scarlet. Her hair was glossily blue-black, darker than I remembered Anna Reynold's having been, and curly where Anna's had been straight.

Memory came back. That figure we'd seen from the filled-in longhouse, bending over the sink and bringing her dripping hair up . . . who washed their hair in a sink nowadays? I still did when I was moored up away from a shower, but the rest of the world had moved on. No. She'd been dyeing it, getting rid of that last tinge of dark brown for Italian charcoal.

Another piece of the puzzle fell into place. She'd booked the böd to change her look. She could get away with arriving in jeans, but she needed somewhere other than a windy hillside to do her full make-up before she met her landlady. Landladies had the sharpest eyes on the planet. Make-up, sunglasses, a stylish blouse. The practical but non-glam yellow jacket had been folded away before she reached the door. One of those elegance-plus silk scarves to hide her hair colour. As brief a hello as she could get away with, and up to her room to complete the transformation.

I needed to tell Gavin this idea. I fished my mobile out from my pocket and sent a text: *Had you thought of Italian woman being AR in disguise?*

I was only a hundred yards further along the road when my mobile pinged. His reply felt like a hug. *Keep up at the back! xxx Enquiries ongoing with Ital police. She's under surveillance. My ship xxx*

Don't go nosing around, he meant. Keep out of her way. I could do that, especially as she'd gone off in the other direction.

I looked down the hill and saw the last flutter of coloured skirt disappearing into the B & B.

It was a beautiful day for a striding walk. The hill was grey-green with feathered grass that flowed like water in the wind, and crossed with lines of butter-yellow mimulus where the burns ran to the loch. The cream and rose clover spilt over the edges of the verge onto the white lines of the road, and a curlew gave its bubbling call from the golden curve of sandy beach. I shoved the thought of the Italian woman away and concentrated on enjoying the feel of my legs marching steadily, my arms swinging in rhythm, the wind in my face.

The road dipped down to the place where the ring road to Houbie rejoined, then rose up again for half a mile. I stopped at the highest point to take a drink from a handy burn, cupping the clear water and splashing my face, then stood for a moment to look around. The east end of the island was spread out in front of me now, with the ferry terminal of Hamars Ness hidden behind a low rise of hill. *Sørlandet* was well into Yell Sound, her white sails tall against the green shore. The grey bulk of Brough Lodge was in view down to my left, a jumble of buildings stretching along, and an artificial-looking hill with a tower rising from it.

All downhill now. I strode onwards, gradually sorting out the buildings. There was a square keep in the centre, buttressed by two lean-to houses and crenellated within an inch of its life. It had a little round archery post sticking out on each corner and a sloping roof on top; the side nearest to me had two sets of arched windows, one above the other, the Great Hall, no doubt, complete with fans of weapons above the fireplace. The roofs were of grey slate and the windows boarded up with wood that shone pale gold against the brown stone. Behind the main house was a trail of farm buildings and a line of stone wall, tumbled in places, with two walls leading up to the oval folly and its lookout turret, perched on the seawards side of the hill. It looked just the spot for a lonely governess and a mad wife in the attic.

The real approach was by sea, of course. The road ran on a further hundred metres and ended at the jetty. I leant on the last fence post and contemplated the house. The family home of the film clip was long gone. This was a building in decay, with the steps they'd danced down choked by long grass. On my right was the lean-to and square keep; the rest of the long frontage looked like facade, with a wall the height of the house running for another hundred yards. First was a carriage-sized arched doorway with a pediment on top and a niche on each side – the courtyard entrance, I supposed – and there seemed to be a building beside it which might be the grooms' quarters or the factor's cottage. The wall continued to another arch with portcullis decorations about it, and then a red brick tower, double the height, with a Moorish arch at ground level and a square bell tower above, like an Italian church.

A board beside the road gave some of the history of the place. Central government's determination to get people out of inconvenient, expensive peripheries was just the latest in a long line of moves to shift people away from places that didn't suit the authorities. From the 1820s, Sir Arthur Nicolson had evicted his tenants across the island to make way for grazing his cross-bred sheep, and many had been forced to emigrate. I sensed satisfaction in the board's description of the 'Round House', a second folly built from the stones of evicted houses, which was so horribly haunted that Sir Arthur spent only one night there.

I'd been going to eat my lunch here, but it was too melancholy, the contrast between the wealth that had built this mansion and the people forced to leave their homes, between that light-hearted family in the film and these crumbling pretensions. An interesting old pile, no doubt, and it would make a wonderfully atmospheric place to hold conventions once it was restored, but just for once I thought I'd pay attention to the DANGEROUS BUILDING: KEEP OUT sign on the gate. Building work was in full swing: the road in front of what had once been the garden was well used, with a wider track up to the portcullis, a white Portakabin parked at the end of it and another beside the chapel wall. The keep bristled with scaffolding, the roofs were new and the guttering shone black with paint. Good luck to them. It would be another way of bringing folk to the island: money for B & B owners, caterers, cleaners, drivers, the local shop, employment for the craftspeople who ran the courses; a small stand for staying where you wanted to live.

Even as I thought about it, there was clanging and a thump or two from inside the courtyard, and the slam of a vehicle door. A pause, then a white builder's van skidded out through the portcullis, curved round the garden wall, spinning gravel from under its wheels, and headed along the main road towards the hot pies the shop would no doubt have ready for them. *Dennertime* the world over.

I turned my back on the turrets of the Gothic mansion, the splayed ribs of the flit-boat still tied to its rusted winch, and plumped myself down on the jetty, legs swinging over the clear water. Across the sound, the sun picked out the white superstructure of the ferry lying at Gutcher. The breeze ruffled my hair and the waves lapped at the shore. I hauled my lunch out of my backpack, tore the rolls apart, added the cheese, and munched. A seal sculled along the bay, giving me a good look in passing, then shuffled himself up onto the seaweedy point for an afternoon's sunbathing. Gradually his coat turned from gleaming black to sandy yellow.

I ate my banana and stowed the skin in my rucksack. Time I was moving. A quick scoit at this haunted ruin, maybe a climb up to the folly, and then on to the terminal.

I was just about to stand up when someone came around the bend in the road, three hundred metres away. I caught a flutter of patterned silk scarf above dark jeans and a flowered shirt.

It was the Italian woman, and she was coming straight towards me.

My ship, Gavin had said. Don't meddle with her. If she was Anna, she was involved in the deaths of two people, and she had a gun. I'd survived seeing her at close quarters once, in the safe doorway of the Interpretative Centre. I didn't give much for my chances if we had another encounter out here, with nobody watching.

It could be bad luck that she'd turned up here, part of pretending to be a tourist. But I remembered how quickly she'd gone through the museum, and the swift fluttering of her dress towards the B & B. Maybe she feared that the one glance I'd given her had been enough. Maybe she'd followed me here.

At sea, you thought through any move beforehand, because you'd make things worse if you jumped in and got it wrong. The cropped grass of the shore wasn't a place to play hide and seek with a murderer, especially when I didn't know how good a shot she was. She might be able to pick me off at a hundred paces. My only cover was the house. If I could get back up to it, then I could dodge her until the builders came back.

I'd be obvious against the pale pebbles and sun-glinting water the moment I stood up, but I could get as far as the shore end of the slip unseen. The water was only a metre below me, and a couple of feet deep. Keeping hunched over, I rolled my breeks up. I eased my legs over the side of the slip, toes reaching downwards.

The water oozed into my sandshoes, ice-cold after the warmed concrete. I let myself slide until I touched bottom, then crouched down below the level of the slip and began working my way forwards. The seal raised his head to watch what I was doing, and I froze, willing him to stay put. A seal panicking towards the water would be a dead giveaway.

He kept his nose turned warily towards me and wobbled his upper body round a little, but didn't do the seawards dash I'd feared. I got to the end of the slip and raised my head in the cover of the rocks. She was halfway between the hill and Brough Lodge now, walking with an easy stride, and somehow I had to get from here to the garden wall unseen.

I couldn't do it. There were no walls, no ditches, nothing, just the strip of tarmac between the verges of clover. Very well, then. As she had, I'd hide in plain sight. My officer togs could pass for a boiler suit at this distance. I pulled my breek legs down, stood up, came around the rocks onto the road, and then, with my most masculine walk, swinging my knapsack in one hand, I strode back towards the house. I was an apprentice joiner. I hadn't fancied the hot pies at the shop. I was a keen footballer who kept himself fit on healthy bread and cheese. Now I was going to boil up a cup of tea in our caravan before the others came back.

It was the longest hundred metres I'd ever walked. I didn't look at her, but I could feel her upright figure coming closer, closer. The garden walls seemed to be retreating even as I walked towards them. I swung over the fence, cut across the grass, and was climbing up the gap-toothed steps at last, heart racing. A glance along the road showed me she was almost at the gate. I scurried through the arch and into the main courtyard.

It had once been a flagged yard. Weeds thrust up between the paving slabs, and old stones and timbers were piled up along one wall with a fringe of nettles straggling in front of them. The house entrance was on my right, a weathered wooden door, surprisingly plain after the imposing facade. There was a boarded window beside it, behind a bristle of scaffolding. For a moment I was tempted to go straight upwards, onto the roof, but I'd be in plain sight, and if she could shoot I'd be a sitting duck.

The side door into what I presumed was the stable yard proper was blocked by metal builder fences, but straight across from me was a stone doorway with enough light to suggest there might be a way through. I darted for it, and was met by a flurry of starlings rising up suddenly from the floor in a giveaway whirr of wings and chak-chak of alarm. I flung my arm up against them, suppressing my own squawk of alarm, and whirled round to look at the main door of the house.

The shabby door was ajar. I leapt over the wooden step and reached out for it, heart thudding. It swung open silently, and I slipped through and stood in the entrance hall, looking round for cover.

I was in a wide vestibule, with a curved bannister leading up to the landing above. The handrail and fret-turned bannisters were swathed in plastic, and the floor was covered with ply sheets. There were cables and tools everywhere. The bright working light had been left on, and a radio burbled to itself in one corner.

It was tempting to run up that wide stair and hide myself in the furthest reaches of the house, but I could see the raggedness of some of the ceiling timbers. Besides, that was the classic girl in danger scenario. Go upwards and end up trapped. No. Let my pursuer search for me upstairs, if she liked. I'd hide downstairs, near the door. There must be a toilet, with a bolt or key to let me lock myself in. I turned on my heels, scanning the shadowy rooms, getting glimpses of a plastic-swathed tallboy, a wall of cream vee-lining, a still-intact window with the panes reflecting the light back at me. No obvious cloakroom, and most of the doors were either missing or wedged open.

She would be on me at any moment.

There were sheets of plyboard stacked against the wall opposite the stair, with just enough space for me to wriggle in behind them. Keeping one hand on the boards, I snicked off the too-bright light, flung myself on the floor and squirmed silently into the triangular tunnel. There was grit under my hands, and dust prickled in my nose and dried my mouth. The boards stank of the chemical they'd been treated with; I just hoped it wasn't as poisonous to humans as it was to beetles. I hauled myself forwards on my elbows until my head was just within the shadow of the far end. I was not going to sneeze – I pinched the bridge of my nose and tried to breathe evenly.

I'd been just in time. There was a rattle from the door handle, then the light broadened on the floor to reach the front of my hiding place. A shadow blotted it out. I closed my eyes and softened my breathing even further. *Father in heaven, help me.*

The radio drowned out her steps, but they vibrated through the plywood floor covering. I felt each move she made: a cautious step into the wide hall, a slow turn, looking all around her. The light narrowed and cut out as she pulled the door to behind her, then broadened again as she changed her mind and swung it open. My mind began doing crazy calculations. Eight feet long, and I was five foot two; that gave me just under three foot, a foot and a half over at each end. No, longer than that; the boards were stacked along the wall, overlapping. Say two and a half foot at each end. Was that long enough to hide the tan soles of my shoes? She took two more steps forward. A tiny, metallic click. I knew as clearly as if I could see her that the gun was in her hand, the gun that had killed Laura and Daniel, cocked and ready to use. I was dead if she looked behind my plyboard shield.

It felt like an hour that she stood there. I desperately needed a proper breath, but I didn't dare take one. My left calf was threatening a spasm of cramp. I eased my toe upwards, willing it to go away. She had to move soon. At long last, I felt the vibration in the floor again. She was checking out each room as I'd done, but without the builders' light she couldn't see properly inside. I could have been behind any item of swathed furniture, or crouched under a fallen roof beam.

If she was searching every room, she wouldn't miss the triangular gap behind the plyboard.

I'd burnt my boats, hiding like this. It told her straight away that I knew, left me no chance of bluffing it out. If she found me here, she'd shoot to kill, and the builders would get a nasty surprise when they moved their plyboard. My only hope was to get out and run if she went upstairs – if I could get out quietly enough. I didn't think I could, and wriggling out would be too slow. The door was only two steps away. I'd burst out, knocking the sheets flat, knocking them towards her if I could, and run like a deer. Even an expert shot would be lucky to hit a moving target.

She'd looked in all the rooms now. She was coming back. I felt her pause by the plyboard, but the brightness of the light outside was dazzling her against the darkness inside my tunnel. I lay still as an old roll of carpet shoved against the wall, and felt her pass by.

Then, glory be, the cavalry came. There was a skidding of wheels on gravel outside, and feet clumping towards us. Cheerful male voices were arguing the merits of Voe mince pies vs. Sandwick macaroni-cheese.

She was trapped too, but it was easy for her to talk her way out. She'd found the door open, it was such an interesting house, she just wanted a quick look . . . I lay and listened to her saying exactly that, still with her Italian accent and no doubt a fluttering of expressive hands. In a flurry of apologies, she let them lead her out of the house. I listened to the boots stomping across the flagstones, and considered my options. If I was lucky, they'd have a cup of tea to wash down their pies; in their caravan, if I was extra lucky. That would give me time to get out of here and high-tail it for the ferry – going across the hill, maybe, or along the coastline. I tried to visualise the map of Fetlar. Round the headland would be a couple of miles, compared to the mile of road, but it would be less visible. She'd known I was here; she might be watching.

My luck had run out for the day. The workmen's boots came clumping back in, the light was switched on again, and the drill began to buzz. There was nothing to do but brazen it out.

I wriggled backwards, not worrying about noise now, and got to my knees as soon as my shoulders were clear, then to my feet. My entire front was smeared with grey.

They'd stopped what they were doing, and were standing in a circle, staring at me, mouths open. They were all younger than me, and I didn't recognise any of them.

'You'd need to dust under there,' I said briskly, and was out of the door before they could think of a comeback.

Part Seven

The King Surrounded

CHAPTER TWENTY-ONE

The brief glimpse I'd had of the back doorway before the birds had flown up at me had shown a passage clear to the folly. I gritted my teeth and prepared to run the gauntlet of those beating wings again, but it seemed I'd startled them all away the first time, for none flew up now. I came into a small courtyard, with an enclosure in one corner that might have held the copper boiler with its fire below. A half-barrel beside it was filled with scummy water.

Behind me, I heard startled laughter, then the clanks of tools being set to work again. At the other side of the courtyard was a ragged end of the substantial wall which enclosed the green hill rising up to the folly. I dived between the buildings and pressed myself against it, looking to left and right. There was no sign of anyone on what I could see of the road. Anna Reynolds couldn't be far away. If I was her, I'd wait on the road for me coming out again. The builders might hear a shot, but they wouldn't see anything through the boarded windows. I needed the real cavalry, five minutes' drive away in Houbie: Gavin, to read her her rights, and a couple of uniforms to clap the handcuffs on.

My phone was in my knapsack. I hauled it out and switched it on, but instead of the irritating Nokia tune, I got a 'no battery' message. *Damn.* I'd forgotten, last night, to plug the wretched thing in to recharge. I was on my own.

Worse still, I was on my own with nobody to raise the alarm if I didn't appear for a couple of hours. Gavin thought I was on my way to Yell; Inga thought I was still on Fetlar. Neither of them knew about the murderer on my tracks.

For a moment, I wondered about going back to the builders and asking for a lift to Houbie. But Anna might not have recognised me; there was no sense in panicking. First, I had to find out where she was. The folly would give me a good view, if I could get to it safely. I looked ahead, assessing my chances. The wall I was pressed behind would take me up to it under cover, though the going was thick with nettles. Tough. If she'd had the same idea, but was coming to the folly from the road, she'd have further to go and several walls to climb, though I couldn't vouch for the state they'd be in. Even allowing for my later escape from the builders, I didn't think she'd had time to get there before me.

I hared it along the side of the wall, collecting several stings on the ankles. I grabbed a docken leaf at the end of the high wall, then paused for a cautious recce before scuttling across the last part. I passed the lookout turret, bent low to the cover of a crenellated wall, scrambled over the last piece and tumbled, breathless, into the shelter of the square gatehouse. I leant one shoulder against the wall for balance and began to rub one itching ankle with the docken while I caught my breath.

It was an odd place, an eighteenth-century notion of a medieval keep outpost. The entrance I was sheltering in was square, with an arched doorway outlined by white keystones. The seaward side of it had fallen away completely, and the sea danced blue in the frame of tumbled stone. Behind me, the oval tower was two storeys high, with a central arched window on the first storey, flanked by arrow-slits, and apparently no door at ground level. Perhaps the gatehouse had had some sort of suspended bridge to the high arch. A portcullis too, no doubt. I glanced back and up, and saw the remains of six-inch masonry nails sticking out.

There was a square window in the landward side of the gatehouse. I stood well back from it and took a long, slow look out. Brough Lodge was spread below me like a map: the courtyards I'd come through, the jumble of builder caravans running behind the facade of portcullis arch and chapel, the square tower of the house with its blank windows. There was no sign of movement, no flutter of the gay yellow and blue silk scarf. The lookout turret blocked my view; I leant out further, and saw the road stretching empty towards the north, until it disappeared behind the hill. I turned. It was equally empty eastwards, and she hadn't had time to reach the rise between here and Houbie.

I edged slowly into the sunlight.

Suddenly, startlingly close, there was a snick of stone on stone. Footsteps. She'd neither gone back to Houbie nor forward to the ferry; she'd come straight up here, to watch for me coming out. I felt as if I had an extra sense, quiveringly alive to her every movement. Silent as a shadow, I slipped to the other side of the folly. If she was as close as she sounded, I was too late to run. The swift footsteps rang out her confidence that I hadn't got there before her. I pressed against the warm brown stone, and listened.

She came up to the gatehouse, and waited there for so long that I thought I'd missed her moving. I was about to edge away when I heard her at last, clambering over the rummelled stones and moving with soft footsteps to the turret end of the wall. There was no radio chatter here to drown her, nothing but the soft whisper of the wind in the grasses and the occasional *beeeeh* of a ewe calling her lamb. As she waited there, looking out, I edged further behind the folly, taking care to keep off the crunching remnants of a gravel path round it. There was a door on this side – no, a window, set knee-height above the ground, with a broad sill. Inside, the earth floor was jumbled with fallen stones, pieces of wood and the remnants of someone's fire. I waited, ready to move either way.

She kept coming. I slid around the folly, back almost to the gatehouse. I heard her take a step up onto the window sill and drop gently down inside. A pause, then there were several soft footsteps. I froze against the other side of the wall. She'd come round inside, stepping over the fallen timbers; she was right beside me. I could hear her breathing. I was terrified that some kind of sixth sense would make her as aware of me as I was of her; her quarry, just on the other side of this wall. Then she moved away, back towards the doorway, and I tensed my legs, ready to slide round once more. I hoped she'd continue clockwise, and so she did; as I edged round the folly to the seawards side, she came around to landwards, and back to the curtain wall.

There was a long, long silence. I didn't dare risk a look around the edge of the tower; I just waited, my side an inch from the stones, legs stiff from standing, the ankle I hadn't had time to rub stinging like fury, breathing controlled to silence over my racing heart. I turned my wrist to check my watch: ten past two. Two and a half hours to play hide and seek with a murderess.

Fifty metres away, a sheep grazed, her lamb jumping around her. The land smell of green grass and flowers swirled about me. A lark was twittering high up in the blue sky, and there was chirping from among the stones of the keep, a nest of starlings. I closed my eyes, listened with all my strength, and prayed.

She moved at last. I heard her rise and stride off downhill. When she'd gone far enough for me not to hear her footsteps any more, I oozed my head around the corner of the folly to watch her go. Already she was halfway to the road. I kept watching. When she reached it, she took a long look both ways, then began to stride back towards Houbie.

My legs were trembling with reaction. I slid down to the grass and slumped there, my back against the solid wall, feeling like I was made of spaghetti. I fished in my knapsack for a couple of toffees and chewed them slowly, letting my heart rate subside to normal again as I watched her stride along the road and up the incline. Only when she'd disappeared on the other side of it did I rise again.

I came out around the seaward side of the folly and walked straight into Oliver.

He'd come up the way I'd planned to go down, on the straight line to the road that came past the back of the folly. I could see his footprints trailing behind him in the long grass.

He was as surprised as I was. We both jumped back, silent for a moment, then I took a deep breath, and managed, 'Goodness, you startled me!'

He gave me that charming smile. 'You gave me a shock too. Weird place, this.'

All my misgivings about him rushed back to me. He'd just identified his sister's body. He was supposed to be talking to the police, not playing tourist. I imagined the text Reynolds might have sent him: *Cass recognised me. She's here at Brough Lodge.* The road seemed very far away. I stared at him for what felt like half an hour before inspiration came to me. I gave a start, and glanced down at my pocket, then fished out my mobile. 'Sorry, I'll need to take this.' I turned half away from him but made sure my voice was clear. 'Gavin, hi . . . no, not yet – I'm at Brough Lodge, with Oliver, up at the folly . . . Yes . . . yes, I'll phone as soon as I get there. See you later.'

I switched off and turned to Oliver with a smile. 'That was Gavin wondering if I'd got to the ferry terminal yet.'

He pulled out his own smartphone and shook his head. 'I can't get a signal here.' His blue eyes and half-smile said clearly that he didn't believe my bluff.

He was standing right in my way, and I wasn't sure if he'd just ended up there or if it was deliberate. I turned towards the house and made a seawards gesture. 'Great view, isn't it?'

He nodded, but as if he'd hardly heard me. There was a puzzled, intent look to his eyes as he looked outwards, as if he was blind to the view, and trying to calculate something – then he glanced towards the road. 'I thought I saw someone else up here. Wasn't it that Italian woman, who was at the dance?'

But he hadn't been at the dance. He'd wanted to come searching with us, and the woman with the B & B had drawn him away into the hall kitchen. He could have come out into the hall later, I supposed, and seen the Italian woman dancing with Alain. Reluctantly, I nodded, trying to think what I could convincingly say next.

He didn't give me the chance. 'She seems an odd type to be wandering round old ruins. Did you speak to her?'

'No,' I said, and saw relief scurry across his face, like a cats-paw of wind on still water. 'She seemed in a hurry.'

'Too windy for her hairdo,' Oliver said. The tension had gone out of him. He gave me the benefit of that smile again and relaxed into charmer mode. 'So, tell me about this building. Is it a temple?' He gave it a critical look. 'It doesn't seem old enough.'

'A folly,' I said. 'The hill is the remains of a broch.'

He went back to questions. 'How come you're not with your ship?'

'Captain Sigurd wanted someone to stay with the investigation.' He gave me a quizzical look at that; I visibly wasn't doing anything of the sort. I improvised. 'Only the police didn't want me staying with it, so I'm heading for the ferry, to meet up with the ship again this evening.'

His face didn't change, but I felt him stiffen again. 'You're going to the main island?'

'I'll be meeting the ship at Hillswick, in the north of Mainland.'

He didn't like it, I could see that. He looked down, and away. I realised suddenly that Reynolds must be going on the ferry too. I'd be spending twenty-five minutes with her, in a twenty-seater cabin, in daylight, probably with only another couple of people. She'd been in my boatload; I was their only danger. It was time I got out of here.

I moved quickly past him. 'I'd better get going, if I'm not to miss that ferry.'

His mouth half opened, and I could see in his face that he knew when it was, which made it even more likely that she was going to be on it. I'd keep on deck, in full view of the crew, and Inga would get me at Gutcher. I sketched a wave, gave a casual 'Goodbye' and headed off down the hill towards the road at a speed that just stopped short of being a full-scale retreat.

He was still there, fiddling with his phone, when I reached the road. I set off at a brisk pace, the wind cool on my face, lifting the scent of clover from the verges and blowing the honey smell of heather from the hills.

It felt like the longest mile and a half I'd ever walked. I didn't want to keep looking back to check he wasn't following me. I felt too exposed; I longed for a stretch of open water, where I could tack in any direction I wanted, instead of having to follow this ribbon of tarmac, visible as a neon-pink sail on a still, grey sea.

I reached the ferry terminal at last. It was one of the newest ones, with a long breakwater stretching out to shelter the stubby arm for the ferry, and a smaller pier with a couple of fishing boats tied up at it. There was a generous car park, with the waiting room at one corner, and a wooden hut with a vending machine and a toilet. The two lanes, booked and unbooked, stretched their white lines towards the jetty. There was nobody in the waiting room. I headed up the hill above the car park and wriggled myself into a dry, heathery hollow. I had the rest of my toffees to eat, and Ellen MacArthur's *Taking on the World* to read.

The time passed slowly, even with Dame Ellen for company. The sea drowsed in the afternoon heat; the sun glinted off the windows of Uyeasound, on Unst, and spotlit the grey bulk of a ruined Haa House. I kept an eye on the ferry and saw its white superstructure pass from Gutcher to Belmont, then back to Gutcher, and finally, from there, to turn its nose towards us and chug steadily closer. A car came to the car park and took up pole position in the 'booked' lane. I waited until a couple more arrived, and the ferry bow had swung upwards, then I dodged among them and slipped aboard, heart pounding.

I hadn't seen Anna Reynolds come aboard, but I wasn't going to risk being caught below. I went to the aft end and leant my chin on the metal rail, the complete tourist with my knapsack, in full view of each of the seven cars on board. I kept my back to the foot passengers, but I thought I caught the flutter of a bright scarf descending into the cabin. The ferry motored serenely across the calm sea. I looked out at the green hills, and thought. I'd made sure I hadn't seen Reynolds get on, but that didn't mean she wasn't here. Oliver thought she should be; which threw us back to the original scenario of Oliver and Anna working together to kill Laura. My stomach contracted at the thought of the poor body they'd pulled out of the water. But then, what about Daniel? Had he simply recognised Anna aboard ship and spoiled their elaborate planning?

The ferry pulled into Gutcher, jaws opening as it turned the corner and pressed itself to the rubber-hung jetty. Before us was the Portakabin cafe, and the ex-post office with the WW2 bullet holes in the walls. There was a payphone there. While I waited for Inga, I'd phone Gavin. He could send a squad to pick Reynolds up at Toft, coming off the Yell ferry.

I was first off, striding towards the cafe. I'd only vaguely registered the black car with one rear door open when suddenly a blanket was flung over my head. A strong arm clamped round my shoulders and shoved me inside, pushing me across the seat. The door slammed. The car was moving before I'd even had time

303

to shout. I grabbed at the door handle, but it was locked. Cursing myself for stupidity, I sat myself up in my seat, clawed the blanket off and turned to face my captor.

It was Fireman Berg.

CHAPTER TWENTY-TWO

I stared blankly at him for a moment, then realised that Inga's husband Charlie was driving, with Berg in the front seat beside him. The hard edge beside me was Peerie Charlie's car seat. He was in it, grinning broadly, kicking his legs and clapping his hands.

I was being kidnapped. No doubt a dozen photos were already winging their way to the *Shetland News* website and Radio Shetland's homepage, so that the whole world would see me being hauled off under a blanket, like a criminal . . . yes, in the front seat, Berg was already working away on his phone.

Peerie Charlie pulled my sleeve. 'Aye, aye, Cass.'

'Aye, aye to you too,' I said. I pulled the rest of the blanket off myself and shoved it to the floor. 'I wasn't expecting the blanket.'

'Sorry,' Berg said. 'I hope I didn't hurt you?'

Peerie Charlie laughed. 'Funny Cass! Blanket over your head.'

'Yes,' I agreed through gritted teeth, feeling like Cat with his dignity ruffled. I tried for a friendlier tone. 'Funny blanket.' I leant forward to Big Charlie. 'Where are we heading for now?'

'Inga's secret destination,' he said.

'Secret to me as well?'

'You'll like it,' he assured me.

I was always dubious about things I was assured I'd like. The secret destination, wherever it was, would hold twenty-four strangers, two of them politicians, with a barrage of cameras waiting to greet us all when we were 'released'.

'Where's the secret?' Peerie Charlie demanded.

'If I telt you,' his father said, 'it wouldna be secret, would it?'

Peerie Charlie brooded over that for a moment, lower lip jutting out and one foot tossing towards the back of his father's seat, but he knew he'd get short shrift if he tried for a tantrum. Then his face brightened. He turned to me instead. 'Cass, I went swimming. Yesterday.'

'Good for you,' I said.

'I swimmed all the way across.'

'Even better.'

'So I come in the Picos now.'

I could see Big Charlie's reflection grinning in the mirror. The thought of taking a livewire like Peerie Charlie out in a Pico made me pause. Peerie Charlie's lower lip jutted again. 'You promised. When I could swim, you said.'

I had, too. 'So I did,' I agreed.

He brightened up immediately. 'Today?'

'I don't think there'll be time today,' I said. I managed a real note of regret. Given the choice between Inga's paparazzi and Peerie Charlie in a Pico, I'd plump for the roller-coaster ride of a dinghy steered by a three-year-old any day.

'Oh, I don't know,' Big Charlie said encouragingly from

the front seat. 'We could maybe find you time for a peerie skoosh around the marina. You'll no' be dat far fae the boating club, an' you're the last een I needed tae kidnap. I can be guard boat.'

He, of course, had spent his day kidnapping people and looking after Peerie Charlie, with the occasional touching base with the two older lasses, who were no doubt stravaiging round Brae with their friends. I could read his mind easily. An hour in peace on the water with me looking after Peerie Charlie would be a welcome break before he had to take Peerie Charlie home to bed, late, and bouncing from having spent a fair bit of the day in the car. A turn on the water with me could wear him out quite nicely. He might even be asleep before the football started.

'I can gie you a loan o' me drysuit,' Charlie added. 'We can pick up the boy's wetsuit fae the hoose.'

Peerie Charlie and I eyed each other from the corners of our eyes.

'Captain Cass,' I said to him. I'd trained him to obey aboard *Khalida*. 'If I tell you to do something, you do it.'

His face lit up in a huge smile. 'Sailing in a Pico now?'

'When we get to Brae. Just inside the marina.' I added to Big Charlie, 'I've a wetsuit aboard *Khalida*.'

Peerie Charlie bounced up and down in his seat. 'I steer.'

In for a penny . . . 'You steer,' I agreed. He could manage a reasonably straight course in *Khalida*. I tried to remember what the forecast had been. Outside the car, the sky had cleared to blue again, with just an airy, half-formed rim of cumulus round the horizon, like a child's scribbles. The sun was hot through the glass, the sea gently rippled. It was a pleasant August evening, with the water as warm as it would go. He'd take no harm from half an hour afloat.

I knew there was a good signal at the Ulsta ferry terminal, so I plugged my phone into the car socket to charge as we sped down Yell. As soon as it connected, I saw I'd had a call from Gavin and three from Alain. I left it to charge and borrowed Charlie's to phone Gavin, getting out of the car and walking over to the lee of the reservations hut, where I could speak in peace. His phone went straight to voicemail.

'Hi, it's me,' I said. 'Listen, I think Anna Reynolds was on my ferry from Fetlar. She could be on the bus, heading for the mainland. I'm at Ulsta, getting the next ferry to Toft.' I checked my watch. 'It's twenty to six now. We're heading for Brae, be there about quarter past.' It seemed too abrupt an end. I paused, then added, in what I hoped wasn't too offhand a tone, 'Hope I see you later. Bye!'

I got my cup of tea on the ferry between Yell and the mainland. 'So,' I said to Fireman Berg, while Charlie dealt with convincing Peerie Charlie he'd prefer crisps to a bar of chocolate, 'how come you're mixed up in all this?'

'Because of Petter,' he said. A tinge of red crept up under his tan, but his dark eyes met mine frankly. 'He does not talk about his private life when he is on *Sørlandet*, I know. We were married last summer.'

I still didn't get it. 'Well . . . congratulations. But are you being kidnapped too?'

He shook his head. 'Petter is.' He sighed. 'Petter feared you would laugh at him, you with all your sea experience, who have done every sort of odd job just to keep on the water.'

I gave him a blank look. Then I remembered Inga, sitting in *Khalida*'s cockpit: *Charlie's friends wi' a friend o' a weel-kent Norwegian model* . . . It all came together: Petter's good looks, his air of being posed. 'He's a model?'

'Not so much now,' Berg said quickly. 'The sea was always his dream. But you need money to sail, yes?'

'Yes,' I agreed.

'So, when he was in his last year at school, someone offered him money to do an advert, and then he was taken up by an agency. Men's clothing, T-shirts, that sort of thing. His face is known all over Norway.' He gave me a dry look. 'Not by you.'

'I don't read magazines,' I agreed. I tried to think of the right thing to say. 'I bet the pay beats odd jobs, any day. Wish I'd had the looks.'

He laughed at that. 'He does not badly.' I staggered as he clapped me on the back. 'I'll tell him his guilty secret is out.'

Big Charlie won the argument over the crisps, and we sat at a table with our paper cups, watching the dimpled waters of Yell Sound slip by us, almost calm, but with the swirls of whirlpool to show the way the tide would race through when it turned again. Yes, it was a fine evening for a sail, with the hills soft green in the sun and the water glinting pale gold.

I turned my mind to the 'secret place'. If we were going to be near the marina, there was no need to rack my brain to think of a venue for holding a fair number of important folk. If the boating club was too homely, then it had to be Busta House, just along the road. I looked across at Charlie. 'Is it Busta we're going to?'

He nodded. 'The hotel folk were well up for it, and it meant the kidnapped folk would be comfortable while they hung around. Scenic for the press photos too.'

Indeed it would be, with its white crowstepped gables and long steps down past the terraced garden. I cheered up slightly. If the press conference wasn't till eight, Inga would surely have organised some kind of meal there, and Busta's cooking was deservedly eart-kyent.

It was only ten minutes by car from the Yell ferry to Brae. By the time we'd got to the marina, Peerie Charlie was too excited to sit still in his seat. 'Captain Cass,' I reminded him, and sent him into the clubhouse with Charlie to get into his wetsuit while I rigged a Pico and trundled it down the slip to the water's edge. We launched the boat together, with me resigned to going in to the thighs, and Peerie Charlie squealing as the cold hit his toes. By the time we'd done that, Big Charlie had brought his motorboat curving round into the water between the pontoon and the marina opening. I lifted Peerie Charlie into the Pico, and he sat while I got the rudder and daggerboard down, then I scrambled in with him. 'For now, you just sit there comfortably. I'll steer first.'

I hauled the sail in, and within a few seconds we were moving. The wind was light enough to keep the boat on an even keel, so that all Peerie Charlie had to do was enjoy the feel of the boat surging forwards, the closeness of the water rippling past. He reached out to trail one plump hand in the water. We went up to the far end of the marina, then I warned him that I was going to tack, which meant I was going to turn the boat. I'd say 'Ready about' and if he was ready, he'd say 'Ready', loud and clear, just like on *Khalida*. The metal thing above his head would go over, I explained, reaching out and rapping it, and when I said 'lee-oh' he had to lean forward so it didn't hit his head. We practised that a couple of times, with him yelling 'Ready' loud enough to startle the marina seal, who was keeping a wary eye on us from behind the keelboats, then tacked in earnest. The boom went safely over his head, and we came back down to the pontoon and tacked round again. Charlie and Berg rocked peaceably in the mouth of the marina, between us and the open sea. Peerie Charlie waved at them, and shouted, 'I sailing!'

310

Charlie's phone flashed several times. Paparazzi everywhere.

'Do you want to steer now?' I asked.

He thought about it for a moment, considering the water so close, then nodded.

'OK, keep your head down while I stop the boat.'

I turned her nose to the wind, and we swapped places in a series of wobbles. I got him comfortably seated with his hand on the tiller. 'The tiller goes the same as on *Khalida*. Pull it towards you, and the boat's nose goes in the other direction.'

He tried it, and we went round in a circle, sails flapping.

'It's fine,' I said, and dealt with the mainsheet as the boat spun. 'Try again, gently. Pull it just a little way, until the boat's pointing at your dad.'

I kept hold of the mainsheet, controlling the sail, and put my other hand on the end of the tiller, keeping us on course. We headed towards the motorboat, with Big Charlie photographing us all the way.

'Now we need to turn,' I said. 'You say "Ready about" and I say "Ready".' We yelled the words at each other, and then I said 'Lee oh', and eased the boat around. 'Now you steer straight at my *Khalida*, see her in her berth there?'

He had the makings, Peerie Charlie, and so he should have, with every male ancestor on both sides a seaman. He sat up straight and concentrated ahead, like I told him, looking at a point above the boat's nose instead of at the water, and by the time we'd crossed the marina half a dozen times he was steering a pretty straight course, helped by me messing about with the mainsail. When I saw his concentration starting to go, I put him back on crewing, and we skooshed at top speed up and down once more, then turned the boat into the pontoon. I held her while he scrambled onto the jetty.

'Now you go upside-down swimming, like Dawn did?' Peerie Charlie asked from the safety of the wooden walkway. I'd forgotten that he'd watched us doing capsize practice.

'Next time. Now we get the boat ashore.'

He puffed up the slip beside me, putting his small weight on one side of the trolley, and we put the boat back in its place. We'd just stowed the mast when Big Charlie and Berg arrived. Charlie glanced at his watch with a harassed expression. 'Can you shower quickly, Cass? I had a text from Inga saying we'd need to be along there.'

'Well, you go,' I said. 'Perriebreeks and I'll shower, then we can walk along the shore to Busta. Can't we, boy?'

His teeth were beginning to chatter and his face was a bit white, but he nodded gamely. I took him into the clubhouse, got him warm and dressed, then sat him with a Mars Bar from upstairs while I showered. While we crunched along the beach together, he boasted about how straight he'd steered, and I said I'd take him out again. By the time we came round the point below Busta House, he was clinging heavily on my hand and stumbling on the stones, so that I was wondering if I should try carrying him. I'd be glad to get to Busta . . . then I saw the serried ranks of vans up in in the car park above us. Several had dark figures leaning against them, and I could see at least three tripods with lenses the length of a Pico's tiller. Suddenly a beach with a tired toddler seemed a good place to be.

'Lots of people,' Peerie Charlie said, looking up. He gave the car park a good look. 'Mammy there an' aa.'

Yes, there was a red car that looked like Inga's runabout.

'Mammy there,' I agreed. 'Daddy too.' I'd hand him over and hide in a corner until I could escape.

We scrambled over the sea wall between the beach and the

lower road, which ran between the shore and the long garden leading up to Busta House. I took Peerie Charlie's hand again, and we dragged along together, through the lower gates and onto the long sweep of grass.

Not everyone was up in the carpark, or corralled in Busta's impressive Long Room, with the portraits of the first owners looking down from the wall. We were halfway up the grass to the house when a woman strolled out of the terrace door and began walking down towards us. I froze, my heart beginning to race. It was Anna.

Her gaze went over us, a woman with toddler, then her head stiffened. She'd recognised me. A long pause, then she took a purposeful step towards us.

We couldn't turn and run away. Safety was behind her, up there in the house. Safety was the twenty-four other hostages looking out of the window. It was only her and me. If we went forward, I could tackle her, while Peerie Charlie ran on to Inga.

I bent down to him, my voice firm. 'Captain Cass speaking. We're going to keep walking. When I say "Go!" I want you to run past that wife to the house, shouting for Mammy as loud as you can. Run your fastest and shout your very loudest. OK?'

'Yes, Captain Cass.' He looked up at the house. 'What about the man?'

My gaze shot upwards. A man was hurrying out of the house, following Anna. Oliver . . . and then I saw the dark hair. Not Oliver; Alain.

For a stifling second I didn't know what to think, whether he was in with Reynolds too, or whether he was the cavalry somehow come to help us. I couldn't risk Peerie Charlie's life on guesswork.

'Dodge round him. If he grabs you, kick him.' His eyes went round and horrified. The nursery had strong views on kicking.

'Like Spidey fighting Iceman,' I said firmly. 'Keep shouting for Mammy all the time.'

Anna was only fifty metres from us now, standing, waiting, at the top of the flight of stone steps. I marched Peerie Charlie towards her. She hadn't found me hiding from her, hadn't seen me at the folly. I could still be an innocent bystander who hadn't recognised her. Twenty metres – ten . . . and then, when we were two metres from the foot of the steps, she tilted her head down, and I recognised the movement. I knew her. She wasn't the Anna Reynolds I'd glimpsed so briefly in the inflatable; I knew her better than that.

The Italian woman was Laura.

It seemed like an endless moment that we stood there, staring at each other. She saw in my face that I'd recognised her, not as the Italian woman, but as herself, as Laura, whose body had been fished out of the sea off Fetlar.

Her right hand went to her pocket. 'Go, Charlie!' I yelled, and launched myself upwards at her in a rush that swept the feet from her and left us rolling on the ground together, coming down the steps again in a flurry of hard stone angles. I felt the vibration in the ground as Charlie ran past us, short legs pounding like pistons. His scream filled the air. 'Mammy! Mammy, Mammy!'

I didn't have time to listen for Inga responding, for a door opening from above me. This was horrible. It felt all wrong, attacking another woman. Being attacked by her. I'd ended up on the underneath, with Laura's weight pinning me to the damp ground and her face distorted with fury above me, and it was the hatred blazing in her eyes that frightened me most. She'd thought she'd got away with it, and now here I was, making her whole plan come unravelled. Her hand had come out of her pocket as we'd fallen; now she reached for my throat and gripped, and although I was jerking upwards as much as I could, I couldn't get any purchase with my feet. She was bigger than me, but, I told myself, she wasn't stronger. I relaxed for a second, then dug my heels into the soft turf and thrust my body upwards, arching my back. Her body lurched sideways, but she kept that vice-grip on my windpipe. My head was beginning to spin with it. I flailed my hands up and shoved them against her face as hard as I could, feeling for her eye sockets with my thumbs. I found one and pressed, and felt her grip tighten. A red mist wavered in front of me, and I couldn't hold my arms up any more, then suddenly there were pounding feet all around me, shouts, radio crackles, and I felt her being pulled back, her hand leaving my throat. I lay there for a moment, gasping.

Gradually the mist cleared. Alain's face swung above me. His hands reached down and yanked me upwards. He burst into furious French. 'Cass, what the devil are you playing at? Why won't you answer your phone? I've been trying to reach you all day.'

I shook my arms free of his grasp. 'I had no battery,' I spat at him, in English, and turned my back. Up at the house, Inga had Peerie Charlie swung into her arms, with Big Charlie beside her, and a gaggle of spectators gawking from behind them.

Opposite me, Laura was held between two police officers, with Gavin standing by. She had gone into voluble Italian which, I gathered from her gestures, was accusing me of having attacked her. She ended with some gutter insults, and a disdainful spit at my feet, which I thought was a nice touch.

'She's Laura,' I said. My voice came out a croak. I swallowed and tried again. 'She's Laura. Hiding in plain sight.'

Laura gave a contemptuous hiss and went into heavily accented

315

English. 'I do not know her. I do not know who she is. She attack me.' An arm swept towards the spectators, taking an officer with it. 'You ask. They watch. They see her. She attack me.'

I wasn't going to let her shake me. Yes, the straight, blonde hair was now a mass of blue-black curls, and her eyes brown, her skin tanned, as you'd expect of an Italian brunette, but I knew the line of jaw, the set of her shoulders below the haughtily held chin. Gloriana. She was Laura, and there were a dozen ways Gavin could prove it: fingerprints, DNA, a confrontation with the accountant who'd talked to him this morning. A confrontation with her brother. I understood now why he'd had that puzzled look, up at the folly. I'd been right about him and Anna Reynolds pairing up in a murder plot; except that Laura had turned the tables on them. It was all fitting together now. Instead of Reynolds killing her, up on the hill in Fetlar, she'd killed Reynolds. The shot from behind had shattered her jaw, so that there were no teeth to ID the body, should it ever be found; she'd put her own ring on one finger, then smashed the hands with stones to spoil the fingerprints. She'd dressed the dead woman in her own jacket, and sent her rolling over the banks. I remembered Oliver looking at the hands of the body, and then snatching a look at the face. Had he recognised the shape of Anna's hands? Hands were as individual as faces . . .

'She's Laura,' I said again. 'Laura Eastley.'

'We must ask you to come with us,' Gavin said to her. He turned to me, voice neutral. 'You too, madam. We just need to sort out what happened here.' He nodded to Sergeant Peterson, and she fell in beside me. We marched in line up the steps, up the grass and up the next set of steps to the terrace. Peerie Charlie came running over to me, face flushed with excitement. 'I runned, Cass, and I shouted.'

'Well done,' I said.

He gave a quick look at Inga and lowered his voice. 'And the bad man tried to stop me, and I kicked him, and he had to let go of me.'

I looked over my shoulder at Alain, tousled and fuming in our wake, and suppressed a smile. 'Good,' I said.

CHAPTER TWENTY-THREE

Naturally, it was Gavin who took Laura away, still flanked by officers. I was handed over to Sergeant Peterson and taken upstairs to one of the bedrooms. She waved me to an armchair and sat down opposite me. 'This isn't an official interrogation,' she said. 'I'm just getting your version of events.'

I did my best to explain the day: seeing the Italian woman on the road, the game of hide and seek at Brough Lodge, and then Oliver suddenly appearing.

'And then, coming up to the house, I saw her, here,' I said. 'I didn't know whether I could pretend I thought she was just a normal tourist, or if she knew I'd deliberately hidden from her. In which case she knew I suspected her. But what really mattered was getting Peerie Charlie past her to safety.'

'How did you plan to do that?'

I was incriminating myself here, but there was no help for

it. 'I told Peerie Charlie that when I said "Go" he was to run to the house. I'd detain her somehow.'

Sergeant Peterson made a face and jotted something down in her notebook.

'Well, what would you have done?' I snapped. I'd had enough of today. I wanted a cup of tea. I wanted to go to *Khalida* and curl up in my own berth, and sleep. 'Peerie Charlie was knackered. The only way to get help was to pass her.'

Sergeant Peterson nodded. 'A difficult decision,' she said neutrally.

'Then the woman turned her head, and I recognised the movement. She wasn't Anna Reynolds, she was Laura. And she saw in my face that I knew her. She put her hand in her pocket. I knew she'd had a gun, and she could be reaching for it, so I launched myself at her. Under those circumstances, you could call it self-defence.'

'Your lawyer could certainly argue that,' she agreed. She closed her book and went suddenly human. 'But I hope she'll have more important things to worry about, once we've proved who she is.'

'Fingerprints,' I agreed. 'DNA. Or just waiting till the black hair dye grows out.' I looked her in the eye. 'Did you know she was Laura?'

'Information received,' she said, in best police fashion. I glared at her, and she condescended to add more. 'The Italian police were on the ball. The woman whose name was on the passport died in a car accident when she was seven. They're still investigating the house bought in her name back in May.'

May. Money had started going missing from April. I'd got the king of the game wrong: not Oliver, but Laura, who was planning her retreat to the sun. It was all clicking together in my mind. Someone had monkeyed with the office accounts, leaving a trail going back to Oliver. *Two million*, the accountant had said . . . that would buy a very nice house in Italy, with spare change to live off. Prison for Oliver, as revenge for her parents' death, and the *dolce vita* for Laura. I had no doubt of her ability to have plotted it all out.

Sergeant Peterson rose. 'Well, are you ready to face the paparazzi?'

I wasn't. I felt bruised all over from that rolling fall down the steps, from the horridness of it all. My throat hurt. There was Inga to face too; I'd seen the blazing fury in her eyes as she'd clutched Peerie Charlie to her. I just hoped she'd be too busy dealing with her hostages to blame me until the first fright was over.

I saw the flashing camera lights reflecting from the Long Room as soon as we set foot in the corridor, and heard our MSP giving it laldy about the loss of jobs and danger to people through centralisation. Delaying tactics needed. I glanced down at my breeks, saw the mud-stained knees and realised what a mess I must look. *Everything you do reflects on your ship* . . . 'I'll just wash my face and brush my hair.'

I went into the powder room and splashed cold water at my face. I had the beginnings of a bruise on one cheekbone and a scrape on my chin. I'd left my hair to dry naturally as we walked along the shore, and it was a mass of wild curls. Naturally I didn't have a hairbrush on me, but I combed it out with my fingers and re-plaited it. I brushed the grass and mud off as best I could, and was grateful I wasn't in my white dress uniform.

I came out looking more like an officer of *Sørlandet*, and went into the Long Room feeling like I was facing a firing squad. The minute I came through the doorway, all the cameras swivelled towards me, a crowd of black lenses topped by winking red lights. My name echoed round the room.

'Cass, is it true you just tackled a double murderer?', 'Cass, did you know what you were doing?', 'Do you know who she is?', 'Give us your version of events, Cass!' were all hurled at me, one on top of the other, like a foreboding of ravens caarking. The important thing was to keep cool. I ignored the flashes in my face and took a deep breath. Spin it. 'I knew she might be dangerous. I was just worried about getting the boy to safety.'

They liked that. 'Can we get a photo of the two of you together?' Within a breath, they were bringing Inga forward and organising Peerie Charlie between us. 'What's your name, boy? Can you give Cass a big smile? Now look this way. Cass, look down at him. Lovely.'

It was better publicity for an officer of the *Sørlandet* than being involved with a double murderer. Peerie Charlie squirmed in mock-shy mode, and I grimaced, and thank goodness Inga broke it up with, 'Now, folk, it's time we released you all. Thank you for coming to support us this day in our fight for keeping things local . . . and tune in to Radio Shetland or check out wir Facebook page to see what we have planned. This was Powersource Monday, and tomorrow's Education Tuesday, then we hae Shopping Wednesday, Emergency Thursday and Rural Jobs Friday. It's aa' interconnected, and it's aa' important to wir way o' life, so let's keep fighting together.'

Blessed word, *release*. I turned round to Sergeant Peterson. 'I need to get back to my ship.'

'I think your friend's organised something.' Her voice was neutral, but there was a spark of malice in her green eyes. I stared at her, suspicious, and she waved a hand towards the bar. 'The Frenchman who lifted you up from the grass. He's waiting in there.'

I wasn't going to wash dirty linen in front of her, and I definitely wasn't going to ask her if I could talk to Gavin before I went. I made my voice casual. 'Oh, Alain. OK. I'll see what he's planned.'

It was only as I was turning away that I realised I'd called him by the wrong name; but I didn't suppose it mattered. She'd called him *the Frenchman*, and it might have been because he'd spoken to me in French, but maybe he'd given his right name when she'd interviewed him, this morning. I stopped dead. Maybe they knew who he was. I should have thought of that. Like my Dad, Gavin had a razor-sharp memory for faces, a natural ability trained into a professional asset. Back in the longship case, he'd looked up the file on Alain's death. It would have had a photo in it . . . he'd have known Rafael's face was familiar, and put his memory to work.

This was getting worse and worse. If Gavin had known who Alain was, he must have been wondering why I didn't tell him. No wonder he'd drawn back from me. He wasn't going to force my confidence, but he would have expected me to explain . . . he wouldn't have thought of anything so bizarre as a lost memory, and Alain's belief he was Spanish. I had to talk to him.

Even as I turned back towards the stairs, I realised it was hopeless. Gavin would be tied up all evening, processing Laura. I didn't know how quickly they could get her identified, but he'd have to be there, in charge of it all. I'd be lucky if I saw him tonight in Hillswick. No doubt Sergeant Peterson would tell him I'd gone off with Alain . . .

I turned back towards the bar, shoulders slumping. I just had to go back to *Sørlandet*, and wait for him to contact me when he could. He'd had faith not to ask. He wouldn't dump me, not just like that. We were adults, and we had a relationship. He'd give me the chance to talk about it. I forced a smile on my face, and pushed the bar door open.

Fireman Berg was there, nursing a bottle of local brew. Alain, beside him, had a half of Bellhaven ready for me. 'Thanks,' I said. 'Thanks for waiting.' I took a long swig and felt it hit my empty stomach. 'I don't suppose there's any food going?'

'Next door,' Berg said, with a nod of his chin towards the restaurant.

I went to look. Two youngsters were busy clearing away the remains of what looked to have been an excellent buffet. I went straight in. 'I arrived too late for it,' I said apologetically, 'but I'm starving. Can I . . . ?'

The girl laughed, and gestured towards the plates. 'Help yourself.'

'You're a star,' I said. I loaded the plate with a chunk of fresh salmon, surrounded it with pasta salad, thanked them again, carried it to the bar and launched in. Over my plate, I looked across at Berg. 'Has Inga organised transport for us, back to the ship?'

He nodded. 'A taxi.' He tilted his chin upwards. 'It's in the car park. As soon as Petter comes.'

Good; and I'd be saved riding alone with Alain too.

'What happened out there? Wasn't that the Italian lady who was at the dance last night?'

I took another mouthful of salmon to give me time to think.

'She was Laura Eastley,' Alain said. 'I recognised her when I danced with her. I didn't know what she was up to, but it was none of my business if she chose to jump ship.' He added, in French, 'Then there was your bombshell, and that filled my head.'

I could understand that.

'We need to talk more about that.' He paused and gave me a sideways glance which turned into a teasing half-smile. 'Don't we?'

I hunched my shoulder against him and concentrated on forking slithery pasta into my mouth. Alain went back into English. 'It was only when I heard about the body, just after lunch, that I

323

realised her Italian disguise was to cover up murder. I reported to the captain, and he passed it on to the police.'

After lunch. After I'd left the police team and headed off to Brough Lodge. No wonder both he and Gavin had been trying to contact me.

'I was worried that you might recognise her too. I thought you'd be safe enough in Fetlar, with the police team.' He paused, biting his lip. 'What I couldn't remember was where she was going next. She'd told me, but all the names up here sound foreign. Then I heard the radio, as we were coming into Hillswick. There was an interview with a woman who said that they'd just got their last hostage, and named you. She said they were holding everyone at Busta House, in Brae. It was the name I'd forgotten. That was when I realised that you were heading straight for trouble. I phoned a taxi and headed here as soon as we'd docked.'

He'd insisted, Agnetha told me later. The ship was at anchor, the trainees all set for a musical evening in the St Magnus Bay Hotel, so they could manage very well without him, and if Agnetha wouldn't give permission, he was going anyway.

At that point, Petter sidled into the bar, not meeting my eyes. Berg hugged him. 'Relax, your secret is out. Cass was more envious than scornful.'

'Yes, I wish I'd had the looks,' I agreed. 'Beats waitressing any day.' I finished my last mouthful of salmon, drained my half-pint and stood back from the bar.

'Inga said our taxi's waiting,' Petter said.

Glory be. I followed the three of them up the long flight of steps to the car park. Halfway up, Alain turned and smiled at me again. 'So . . .'

I stiffened. I was too tired for any more scenes right now. When he reached his hand towards me, I drew back.

324

He raised one eyebrow. 'The prince usually gets a kiss after he's rescued the princess.'

'I rescued myself,' I pointed out tartly.

'With help from the police.'

I conceded the police, and admitted I was being ungrateful. If the police hadn't been on the spot I'd have been glad of him. 'Thanks,' I managed.

A satisfied smile curved the corners of his mouth. They bundled me into the front seat of the taxi and I sat back, willing myself not to look at *Khalida* as we passed the marina. *Sørlandet* would be anchored off Hillswick, with Cat waiting for me aboard. The thought was a comfort, even though I couldn't curl up and will the world away just yet. I'd need to join the rest of the crew and the trainees at the St Magnus Bay Hotel.

Hillswick had once been one of Shetland's fishing and whaling stations, developed back in 1700 by Thomas Gifford of Busta. Like most Shetland places, it was a cluster of houses spread along the line of the pebbled shore, with the church, manse and Haa House prominent. We came to the school first, at the head of the voe, passed the turn-off to the lava cliffs of Eshaness and came into Hillswick proper, with the scattering of houses below the road, including the historic böd, now a cafe, down by the shore, and the wildlife sanctuary, which we'd visit tomorrow. Above the road was the hotel, an imposing white wooden building. I had a vague memory of it being all wood inside too, varnished, like an old-fashioned fishing lodge.

The taxi dropped Petter and Berg at the hotel, then took Alain and me down to the beach. I was so tired I was stumbling. Jonas was on duty at the inflatable. He made no comment at seeing Alain and me together. No doubt the story of his dramatic dash to the rescue had gone round the whole ship. I gritted my teeth and greeted him cheerfully. '*Hei*. Are they all up at the hotel?'

'The whole crew, enjoying themselves.'

I glanced down at my mud-stained breeks. 'I just need to change, then I'll go and join them for a bit.' I'd be on anchor duty at 04.00, which sounded like a good excuse to be in bed by ten.

Alain flicked a glance at his watch. 'I should release Agnetha. I was due on duty an hour ago.'

All the more reason for me to head for the hotel. The last thing I wanted was to be alone with Alain. We left Jonas ashore and buzzed over to the ship. Cat raised his head from the bed as I came into my cabin. I picked him up and hugged him for a moment, enjoying the warm softness of his fur, then put him down as he growled warningly.

'Sorry, Cat,' I said. 'I've had a hard day.' I refilled his bowl, and changed into clean togs while he ate, then I sat for a moment with him purring in my lap. 'It's not easy being human, boy,' I told him. 'You have to talk to people. You can't just brush out your tail or bristle your whiskers and be understood.' I hauled my mobile out and contemplated it. The car had got it to half-charge, and there were two bars of signal, enough to send a text. I opened up 'new message' and looked at the blank screen. *Hi*, I typed. It was a start. It was a good five minutes and several starts and deletions before I achieved: *Still hoping you'll make it up here xxx* I hoped he'd understand all I was trying to say: *I love you, I want you, I don't want us to be over . . .*

I shoved it in my pocket, put Cat's harness on him, and headed out on deck. Agnetha was waiting by the rail.

'So, the handsome prince to the rescue act worked out?'

I gave her a withering look. She shook her head. 'You can't expect to keep anything secret on board.'

'He was just in time to see me rescue myself,' I said. It was barely worth asking, but I asked all the same. 'No word for me from Gavin?'

She shook her head. 'Has Laura Eastley been caught?'

I nodded, and explained as much as I'd worked out as we putted the inflatable back shorewards, beached her and walked up to the hotel, with Cat pausing to investigate promising clumps of grass or wall crannies, then bounding on rocking-horse legs to catch us up.

'Clever,' Agnetha agreed. 'Revenge for her parents, and a new life for her and Daniel . . . until he became a liability.'

I stopped dead in the middle of the hotel car park. I'd forgotten about Daniel. 'A liability?'

'He was going to pieces,' Agnetha said. 'Remember how worked up he was, in the afternoon.' She smiled. 'I was at the same table as him, for the tafl game. He was sitting on needles and constantly checking his phone.'

Laura and Daniel. Not an odd threesome of Oliver, Daniel and Anna, but two pairs: Oliver and Anna, and Laura and Daniel. Suddenly I remembered that first morning, in Kristiansand. Not Oliver: the man I'd seen had had his face masked by Laura's head. Daniel. I put new words to her urgent gesture: 'Go, before anyone sees us together.' And his hesitation when I'd asked them if he and Oliver knew each other; he'd been waiting to see if Oliver recognised him. I needed to think this out. I waved Agnetha forwards. 'I'll be in in a minute.'

She gave me a speculative look. 'Don't get run over.'

I moved to the low wall overlooking the dancing sea and sat down. Cat took that as permission to explore the next-door garden, and headed off into the bushes, tail flattened into hunting stealth. A flock of sparrows flew upwards, cheeping indignantly, and sat in a row on the roof gutter, heads turned sideways to watch him.

Laura and Daniel. They were the same age, far more likely to make friends at a teen disco than Daniel and Oliver. I remembered how rehearsed I'd thought his greeting to her had been. Laura would have rehearsed anything she could; she was a planner, not a chance-taker, like Oliver, who'd pushed her down the broch stairs . . . but now that memory was turned on its head too. Oliver had said Laura had stumbled and brought him down; it was she who said she'd been pushed. Another make-weight of evidence against Oliver for when she went missing. Laura had said that coming on board *Sørlandet* had been Oliver's idea; Oliver, I remembered now, had said it had been Laura's . . . Take that further. Supposing the whole thing had been Laura's plan, all along . . . trailing herself as bait, to see if her brother, having got rid of their parents, would really try to get rid of her too? The brother she'd looked after, got out of trouble, for all those years?

I remembered how her face had lit up as she'd recalled her university days. She'd enjoyed the freedom, away from parental expectations, away from Oliver's trouble. She'd got involved in outside activities: *ceilidhs, and sports clubs, and an operatic society* . . . I wondered if she'd been able to do that before, or if she'd been the mothering sister at home too, making her brother a snack and watching TV with him, while all her friends were doing after-school clubs. I wondered if she'd resented him as much as she loved him, escaped to university, then returned home to find him like an albatross around her neck. She'd have gritted her teeth and prepared to bear it, until his betrayal, the death of their parents. After that, she'd decided – and she must have decided almost straight away – he'd be thrown to the wolves, while she made a new life for herself. No, herself and Daniel, if he was in on it too. I tried to visualise his face. Yes, I thought, he might have been tempted by a share of two million pounds and a life in the sun.

Another block fell in place with a click. Laura and Oliver shared a house . . . which meant she had access to his computer. His emails. His phone. As soon as she'd been suspicious about their parents, she could have read everything he'd plotted with Anna: arriving separately on Shetland, travelling with *Sørlandet* to Fetlar, the booking at the camping böd, where Daniel had been waiting. He'd been waiting for Laura to return and tell him she'd dealt with Anna. Now, with a cold chill, I wondered if he'd known about her next move, the hiding in plain sight, or if he'd always been expendable. I looked out over the shimmering sea and felt the wind cold on my cheek. Maybe she'd have let him make it to Italy, if he hadn't been so on edge.

There was a sick feeling in my stomach. I'd liked Laura. I'd felt sorry for her.

The phone in my pocket bleeped. I grabbed for it and saw I'd a message from Gavin. I stood for a moment, heart thudding, almost afraid to open it. Slowly, I pressed the buttons, and found the words: *On my way now. See you soon. xxx*

The wind was warm after all, and the parks spread around the houses were the bright green of a summer day. Our swan-white ship reflected the dancing ripples on her hull. He was coming; it was going to be all right.

On my way now from Lerwick meant he'd be here in fifty minutes. I went in to join the crew and trainees, and chatted away about the beauty of Shetland, and parried questions about the police investigation with 'I believe there's been an arrest', and watched the grey space of car park for his car. There were two false alarms before he came at last, sitting by the driver, his head silhouetted against the dancing water behind. I excused myself and went out, trying to make it casual, when all I wanted was to fling myself into his arms and feel them close about me.

He came out into the sunshine. We looked at each other uncertainly for a moment, then I slipped my hand into his. 'How are you doing?' he said.

'I'm fine. You?'

He smiled at that, rather bleakly. 'Fine too.' He rubbed his hand up his face and over his hair, making it stand up. 'I've had enough of Police Scotland.'

I jerked my head round in surprise. 'I thought you loved it.'

He drew me towards the wall and we sat on it together, backs to the windows of watching eyes, faces towards the shining sea. 'I did, at first. It was exciting. I felt I was really at the cutting edge, making a difference, you know? Helping catch the big villains.'

'You were,' I said hotly, as if I was defending him against someone else's criticism. 'That people-trafficking ring you broke up, how many folk did you save there?'

He shrugged. 'Yes, but other villains have already oozed into the holes we left.' His fingers tightened on mine, and he began speaking as if he wanted to pour his soul out before he could think better of it. 'And now this. We'll never prove that Oliver killed his parents, whatever Laura believes, though she says she has all his emails to Anna to prove that he intended to kill her . . . but it's still her we'll be charging with murder and fraud.' The wind lifted a corner of his kilt, and he smoothed it down again. 'I'm not a city person, Cass. I don't do mean streets. I don't want to spend my days where each person I meet is worse than the next, and even the most respectable of Edinburgh accountants has another face. I'm used to the country, where the bad's mingled with the good in all of us. I want to go back to Inverness, where one day I'm dealing with a pub brawl and the next I'm looking for a missing collie. I want to see life whole again, instead of being a stranger in hostile city police stations.' He stopped as suddenly as if he'd run out of breath, and I was left not knowing what to say. I curled my hand around his, feeling our shared warmth. I understood how he felt. His hills were calling him, his ordered world where he knew everyone, just as the sea called me.

'Then you need to get out.'

'And be a DI in Inverness all my days?'

I understood that too. You only got one chance at promotion, and if you decided to go backwards, the powers that be would write you off. 'If you'll be happy there. That's what really matters.' I took a deep breath. 'You're not doing big good, like you are when you take villains off the streets, but isn't it as important to look after your own patch? Our own place, that's what we've got. If you can keep the folk of Inverness walking safe at night, that matters too. They deserve that.' I spread the hand that wasn't holding his and tried to explain what I felt when people said that the low crime rate of Shetland wasn't 'real life'. 'It's their lives. It's all they've got. They deserve you looking after their world for them.'

He was silent for a moment, thinking about that. Then he sighed and rose. 'When do you need to be back aboard? Do we have time for a dram first?'

We made love as if we were clinging to each other for protection against the outside world, then slept, curled around each other. When I woke again it was ten to four, and time I was on watch. I scrambled into my clothes, trying not to wake him, but I'd only been on deck for twenty minutes when he came out with two mugs of tea and stood beside me, watching the sun make a golden pathway from the head of the voe seawards.

I was the first to break the silence. 'Are you going to have to go down with Laura? To the mainland, I mean?'

He shook his head. 'I'm on leave. Sergeant Peterson can deal with it all now. She'll remain in custody, of course.'

'Poor Laura,' I said. 'She nearly made it to freedom.'

'With other people's money.'

'I s'pose so.' I sighed. 'I just don't think she had much fun in her life.' I remembered my teens: junketing round the regattas, then on tall ships, and waitressing, and doing up *Marielle* with Alain, the achievement and the dreams. 'She looked after her brother, then went straight from university into Mum's firm.'

'I felt sorry for her too,' he said. He paused, watching, as a kittiwake flew overhead, drifted down in a circle, then settled on the water, turning its head to look at us with bead-black eyes. 'When were you going to tell me about Alain?' he said at last.

'When I could,' I said. 'At first I just didn't understand why he pretended not to recognise me. Why he was going under another name. But then he told me he'd lost his memory. I wasn't sure I believed him. Then I didn't know what to do, how to tell him.' I turned my face to his. 'I couldn't tell you when he didn't know. It would have been like' – I spread my hands, trying to explain – 'like we were conspiring against him.' I looked Gavin straight in the eyes. 'I owed him that much loyalty, at least. I thought maybe I could write to his parents and tell them to come. Then, on Saturday night, at the dance, someone who'd known us both recognised us – congratulated us on still being together.' I made a face. 'The fat hit the fire.'

'The blazing row in the car park,' Gavin said. 'I heard at least six versions of it.'

I opened my mouth and he lifted his hand to lay a finger on my lips. 'No need to explain.' His grey eyes were steady on mine;

he used the words I'd used to myself. 'So long as you're sure that he's in the past.'

I nodded and threaded my fingers through his. 'I'm sure.'

We leant shoulder to shoulder, and watched the sun come up.

A NOTE ON SHETLAN

Shetland has its own very distinctive language, *Shetlan* or *Shetlandic*, which derives from old Norse and old Scots. In *Death on a Longship*, Magnie's first words to Cass are, 'Cass, well, for the love of mercy. Norroway, at this season? Yea, yea, we'll find you a berth. Where are you?'

Written in west-side Shetlan (each district is slightly different), it would have looked like this:

'Cass, weel, fir da love o' mercy. Norroway, at dis saeson? Yea, yea, we'll fin dee a bert. Quaur is du?'

Th becomes a *d* sound in *dis* (this), *da* (the), *dee* and *du* (originally thee and thou, now you), *wh* becomes *qu* (*quaur*, where), the vowel sounds are altered (well to *weel*, season to *saeson*, find to *fin*), the verbs are slightly different (*quaur* is *du*) and the whole looks unintelligible to most folk from outwith Shetland, and *twartree* (a few) within it too.

So, rather than writing in the way my characters would

speak, I've tried to catch the rhythm and some of the distinctive usages of Shetlan while keeping it intelligible to *soothmoothers*, or people who've come in by boat through the South Mouth of Bressay Sound into Lerwick, and by extension, anyone living south of Fair Isle.

There are also many Shetlan words that my characters would naturally use, and here, to help you, are *some o' dem*. No Shetland person would ever use the Scots *wee*; to them, something small would be *peerie*, or, if it was very small, *peerie mootie*. They'd *caa* sheep in a *park*, that is, herd them up in a field – *moorit* sheep, coloured black, brown, fawn. They'd take a *skiff* (a small rowing boat) out along the *banks* (cliffs) or on the *voe* (sea inlet), with the *tirricks* (Arctic terns) crying above them, and the *selkies* (seals) watching. Hungry folk are *black fanted* (because they've forgotten their *faerdie maet*, the snack that would have kept them going) and upset folk *greet* (cry). An older housewife would have her *makkin* (knitting) *belt* buckled around her waist, and her *reestit* (smoke-dried) *mutton* hanging above the Rayburn. And finally . . . my favourite Shetland verb, which I didn't manage to work into this novel, but which is too good not to share: *to kettle*. As in: *Wir cat's just kettled. Four ketlings, twa strippet and twa black and quite*. I'll leave you to work that one out on your own . . . or, of course, you could consult Joanie Graham's *Shetland Dictionary*, if your local bookshop hasn't *joost selt* their last copy *dastreen*.

The diminutives Magnie (Magnus), Gibbie (Gilbert) and Charlie may also seem strange to non-Shetland ears. In a traditional country family (I can't speak for *toonie* Lerwick habits) the oldest son would often be called after his father or grandfather, and be distinguished from that father and grandfather, and probably a cousin or two as well, by his own version of their shared name.

Or, of course, by a *Peerie* in front of it, which would stick for life, like the *eart-kyent* (well-known) guitarist Peerie Willie Johnson, who reached his eightieth birthday. There was also a patronymic system, which meant that a Peter's four sons, Peter, Andrew, John and Matthew, would all have the surname Peterson, and so would his son Peter's children. Andrew's children, however, would have the surname Anderson, John's would be Johnson, and Matthew's would be Matthewson. The Scots ministers stamped this out in the nineteenth century, but in one district you can have a lot of *folk* with the same surname, and so they're distinguished by their house name: *Magnie o' Strom, Peter o' da Knowe.*

GLOSSARY

For those who like to look up unfamiliar words as they go, here's a glossary of Scots and Shetlandic words.

aa: all

an aa: as well

aabody: everybody

aawye: everywhere

ahint: behind

ain: own

amang: among

anyroad: anyway

ashet: large serving dish

auld: old

aye: always

bairn: child

ball (verb): throw out

banks: sea cliffs, or peat banks, the slice of moor where peats are cast

bannock: flat triangular scone

birl, birling: paired spinning round in a dance

blinkie: torch

blootered: very drunk

blyde: pleased

boanie: pretty, good-looking

breeks: trousers

brigstanes: flagged stones at the door of a croft house

bruck: rubbish

caa: round up

canna: can't

clarted: thickly covered

cludgie: toilet

cowp: capsize

cratur: creature

croft house: the long, low traditional house set in its own land

croog: to cling to, or of a group of people, to huddle together

daander: to travel uncertainly or in a leisurely fashion

darrow: a hand fishing line

dastreen: yesterday evening

de-crofted: land that has been taken out of agricultural use, e.g.
          for a house site

dee: you (*du* is also you, depending on the grammar of the sentence
     – they're equivalent to 'thee' and 'thou'. Like French, you would
     only use *dee* or *du* to one friend; several people, or an adult
     if you're a younger person, would be 'you')

denner: midday meal

didna: didn't

dinna: don't

dip dee doon: sit yourself down

dis: this

doesna: doesn't

doon: down

downie: an eiderdown quilt, a duvet

drewie lines: a type of seaweed made of long strands

duke: duck

dukey-hole: pond for ducks

du kens: you know

dyck, dyke: a wall, generally drystone, i.e. built without cement

eart: direction, *the eart o wind*

eart-kyent: well known

ee now: right now

eela: fishing, generally these days a competition

everywye: everywhere

from, frae: from

faersome: frightening

faither, usually *faider*: father

fanted: hungry, often *black fanted*, absolutely starving

folk: people

gansey: a knitted jumper

gant: to yawn

geen: gone

gluff: fright

greff: the area in front of a peat bank

gret: cried

guid: good

guid kens: God knows

hae: have

hadna: hadn't

harled: exterior plaster using small stones

heid: head

hoosie: little house, usually for bairns

howk: to search among: I *howked* ida box o auld claes.

isna: isn't

ken, kent: know, knew

keek: peep at

kirk: church

kirkyard: graveyard

kishie: wicker basket carried on the back, supported by a *kishie baand* around the forehead

kleber: soapstone

knowe: hillock

Lerook: Lerwick

lem: china

likit: liked

lintie: skylark

lipper: a cheeky or harum-scarum child, generally affectionate

mad: annoyed

mair: more

makkin belt: a knitting belt with a padded oval, perforated for holding the 'wires' or knitting needles.

mam: mum

mareel: sea phosphorescence, caused by plankton, which makes every wave break in a curl of gold sparks

meids: shore features to line up against each other to pinpoint a spot on the water

midder: mother

mind: remember

moorit: coloured brown or black, usually used of sheep

mooritoog: earwig

muckle: big – as in Muckle Roe, the big red island. Vikings were very literal in their names, and almost all Shetland names come from the Norse

muckle biscuit: large water biscuit, for putting cheese on

myrd: a good number and variety – a *myrd* o peerie things

na: no, or more emphatically, *nall*

needna: needn't

Norroway: the old Shetland pronunciation of Norway

o: of

oot: out

ower: over

park: fenced field

peat: brick-like lump of dried peat earth, used as fuel

peelie-wally: pale-faced, looking unwell

peerie: small

peerie biscuit: small sweet biscuit

Peeriebreeks: affectionate name for a small thing, person or animal

piltick: a sea fish common in Shetland waters

pinnie: apron

postie: postman

quen: when

redding up: tidying

redd up kin: get in touch with family – for example, a five-generations
New Zealander might come to meet Shetland cousins
still staying in the house his or her forebears had left

reestit mutton: wind-dried shanks of mutton

riggit: dressed, sometimes with the sense dressed up

roadymen: men working on the roads

roog: a pile of peats

rummle: untidy scattering

Santy: Santa Claus

scaddy man's heids: sea urchins

scattald: common grazing land

343

scuppered: put paid to, done for

selkie: seal, or seal person who came ashore at night, cast his/her
skin and became human

Setturday: Saturday

shalder: oystercatcher

sheeksing: chatting

sho: she

shoulda: should have

shouldna: shouldn't have

SIBC: Shetland Islands Broadcasting Company, the independent
radio station

skafe: squint

skerry: a rock in the sea

smoorikins: kisses

snicked: move a switch that makes a clicking noise

snyirked: made a squeaking or rattling noise

solan: gannet

somewye: somewhere

sooking up: sucking up

soothified: behaving like someone from outwith Shetland

spew: be sick

spewings: piles of sick

splatched: walked in a splashy way with wet feet, or in water

steekit mist: thick mist

sun-gaits: with the sun – it's bad luck to go against the sun, particularly
walking around a church

swack: smart, fine

swee: to sting (of injury)

tak: take

tatties: potatoes

tay: tea, or meal eaten in the evening

tink: think

tirricks: Arctic terns

toorie, toorie-cap: a round, knitted hat

trows: trolls

tushker: L-shaped spade for cutting peat

twa: two

twartree: a small number, several

tulley: pocket knife

unken: unknown

vexed: sorry or sympathetic: 'I was that *vexed* to hear that'

vee-lined: lined with wood planking

voe: sea inlet

voehead: the landwards end of a sea inlet

waander: wander

waar: seaweed

whatna: what

wasna: wasn't

wha's: who is

whit: what

whitteret: weasel

wi: with

wir: we've – in Shetlan grammar, 'we are' is sometimes 'we have'

wir: our

wife: woman, not necessarily married

wouldna: would not

wupple: to twist or turn a bit of rope around something, to tangle

yaird: enclosed area around or near the croft house

yoal: a traditional clinker-built six-oared rowing boat

ACKNOWLEDGEMENTS

Thank you to all the people who helped me with research for this book: the journalist from *The Orcadian* who told me about the Eynhallow incident; Jonathon and the Walls Coastguard Team for letting me join in a search; Robert Thomson of Fetlar Developments Ltd for information on Fetlar and the game of hnefatafl; Maxie for playing several games against me, and showing me how quickly a young chess enthusiast could wipe out an ageing writer; Commander Roy on the finicky ways of captains; and Philip for our day out on Fetlar.

On the writing side, thank you to my wonderful agent, Teresa Chris, for all her support and encouragement, and to Susie and the editors and designers at Allison & Busby. Cass's adventures wouldn't happen without you!

MARSALI TAYLOR grew up near Edinburgh, and moved to Shetland as a newly qualified teacher. She is a former tourist guide who is fascinated by history, as well as a keen sailor who enjoys exploring in her own yacht. She lives on Shetland's scenic west side.

marsalitaylor.co.uk
@MarsaliTaylor